Born in Paris in 1947, Christian Jacq first visited Egypt when he was seventeen, went on to study Egyptology and archaeology at the Sorbonne, and is now one of the world's leading Egyptologists. He is the author of the internationally bestselling RAMSES series, THE JUDGE OF EGYPT and THE QUEEN OF FREEDOM trilogies, and several other novels on Ancient Egypt. Christian Jacq lives in Switzerland.

Also by Christian Jacq:

The Ramses Series
Volume 1: The Son of the Light
Volume 2: The Temple of a Million Years
Volume 3: The Battle of Kadesh
Volume 4: The Lady of Abu Simbel
Volume 5: Under the Western Acacia

The Stone of Light Series
Volume 1: Nefer the Silent
Volume 2: The Wise Woman
Volume 3: Paneb the Ardent
Volume 4: The Place of Truth

The Queen of Freedom Trilogy
Volume 1: The Empire of Darkness
Volume 2: The War of the Crowns
Volume 3: The Flaming Sword

The Judge of Egypt Trilogy
Volume 1: Beneath the Pyramid
Volume 2: Secrets of the Desert
Volume 3: Shadow of the Sphinx

The Mysteries of Osiris Series
Volume 1: The Tree of Life
Volume 2: The Conspiracy of Evil
Volume 3: The Way of Fire
Volume 4: The Great Secret

The Black Pharaoh
The Tutankhamun Affair
For the Love of Philae
Champollian the Egyptian
Master Hiram & King Solomon
The Living Wisdom of Ancient Egypt

About the translator

Sue Dyson is a prolific author of both fiction and non-fiction, including
over thirty novels, both contemporary and historical. She has also translated
a wide variety of French fiction.

The Mysteries of Osiris

The Great Secret

Christian Jacq

Translated by Sue Dyson

SIMON &
SCHUSTER

LONDON • SYDNEY • NEW YORK • TORONTO

First published in France by XO Editions under the title
Le Grand Secret, 2004
First published in Great Britain by Simon & Schuster UK Ltd, 2005
A Viacom company

1 3 5 7 9 10 8 6 4 2

Simon & Schuster UK Ltd
Africa House
64–78 Kingsway
London WC2B 6AH

Simon & Schuster Australia
Sydney

A CIP catalogue record for this book is available
from the British Library

ISBN HB 0-743-25954-8
ISBN TPB 0-743-25955-6

Typeset in Times by SX Composing DTP, Rayleigh, Essex
Printed and bound in Great Britain by Mackays of Chatham plc, Chatham, Kent

I enter and I re-emerge, after seeing what lies beneath . . .
I live again and I am saved after the sleep of death.

Book of the Dead, Chapter 41

Great is the Rule, and its effectiveness endures.
It has not been disturbed since the time of Osiris.
When the end comes, the Rule remains.

Ptah-Hotep, Maxim 5.

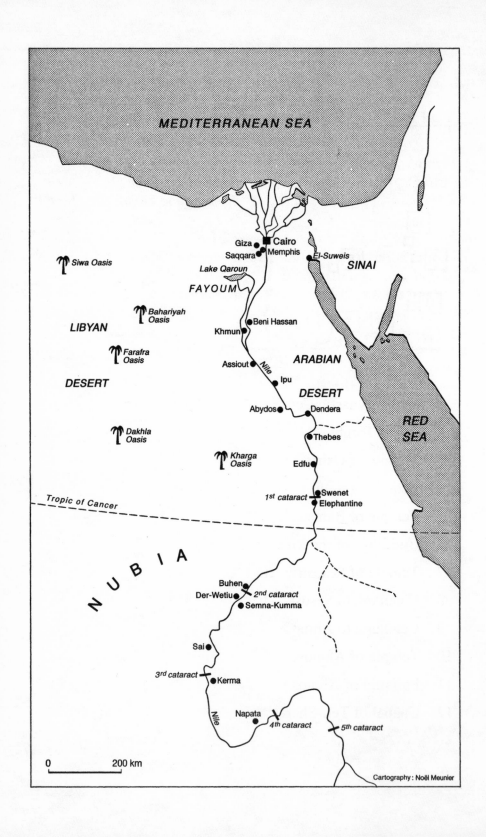

MEDITERRANEAN SEA

SINAI

Giza • Cairo
Saqqara • Memphis
El-Suweis

Lake Qaroun

FAYOUM

Siwa Oasis

Bahariyah
Oasis

LIBYAN

Farafra
Oasis

Beni Hassan
Khmun •

DESERT

Assiout •

Nile

ARABIAN

Ipu •

DESERT

Dakhla
Oasis

Abydos •

Dendera •

RED
SEA

Kharga
Oasis

Thebes •

Edfu •

1st cataract

Swenet
Elephantine

Tropic of Cancer

N U B I A

Buhen •
Der-Wetiu •
2nd cataract
Semna-Kumma •

Sai •

3rd cataract
Kerma •

Nile

Napata •
4th cataract
5th cataract

0   200 km

Cartography : Noël Meunier

ABYDOS

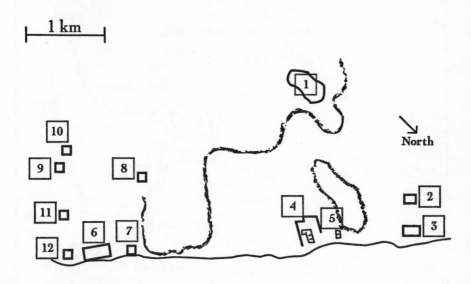

1   Early Dynastic Cemetery

2   Royal Tombs

3   Temple of Osiris

4   Temple of Sethi Ist and Osiris

5   Temple of Ramses II

6   Buildings of the Middle Kingdom

7   Temple of Sesostris III

8   Cenotaph to Sesostris III

9   Cenotaph to Ahmose

10   Temple of Ahmose

11   Pyramid of Ahmose

12   Chapel of Teti-Sheri

Part I

The Supreme Crime

1

Dawn was breaking over Abydos, the Great Land of Osiris, a dawn which had been both longed-for and feared, for this was the dawn of the new year. Would this special day see the beginning of the annual flood on which Egypt's prosperity depended? And would the flood be benign, devastating or inadequate? Despite their meticulous study of the archives and the initial measurements taken by the specialists at Elephantine, none of the experts felt able to make a confident prediction. People's hearts were full of anxiety, but everyone put their trust in Pharaoh Senusret. Since that impassive giant of a man had become Lord of the Two Lands, he had thwarted the attacks of evil forces, overcome the provincial governors' self-interest, reunited Egypt and restored peace to Nubia.

The commander of the soldiers guarding Abydos was unworried. According to his superior, old General Nesmontu, the pharaoh held sway over the spirit of the Nile: with the aid of rituals and offerings, the waters would be persuaded to rise in a harmonious way. All the same, the commander's confidence did not stop him performing his duties efficiently. Every morning he checked all the temporary workers who were allowed to cross the border of the sacred domain. From bakers to brewers, from carpenters to stone-cutters, he checked them one by one and noted down the days when they were present. Any man or woman who could not give satisfactory reasons for his or her absence faced immediate expulsion.

The next to enter was a tall man with strange, reddish eyes. His head and face were shaven and he was dressed in a white linen tunic: one of the temporary priests.

'What work will you be doing today?' asked the commander.

'Cleansing the permanent priests' official houses with purifying fumes.'

'How long will it take?'

'At least three weeks.'

'Who is your overseer?'

'Permanent priest Bega.'

That information was enough to inspire trust. Given Bega's sternness and his well-known rigour, those who worked for him were unlikely to have much spare time.

'Will you be leaving again this evening?'

'No,' replied the temporary priest. 'I have permission to sleep in official quarters.'

'You won't find much comfort there! Good luck to you.'

The commander was unaware that he had just admitted Egypt's greatest enemy, the Herald. Previously bearded and turbaned, he had taken the place of a temporary priest killed by his faithful henchman Shab the Twisted, in order to enter Abydos legally and there await his prey, Iker the Royal Son.

The Herald was the guardian of divine revelation and absolute truth, and he was going to impose them on the world, by force if necessary. Either unbelievers would submit or else they would be slaughtered. There were only two obstacles to the spread of the new belief: Pharaoh Senusret and the Mysteries of Osiris.

All attempts to assassinate the king had failed. He was too well protected, and seemed out of reach. So the Herald had decided to kill young Iker, whom many already saw as Senusret's successor. By committing this crime at the heart of

Osiris's realm, 'the Isle of the Just', he could desecrate a shrine reputed to be inviolable, pollute the wellspring of Egyptian spirituality, and ruin the system that had been so patiently built up.

The Herald walked slowly towards Wah-sut, 'Enduring Places', the little town recently built at Abydos by Senusret.

Another of the temporary workers, a jovial-looking gardener, fell into step beside him and asked, 'Do you like your job?'

'Very much.'

'That's just as well, my lad. We're well paid, it's true, but loafing around is out of the question, and the overseers take things very seriously. Still, we're serving the Great God – a sacred honour, eh? When I think how many people must envy us … What exactly are you doing at the moment?'

'Cleansing the houses.'

'That's nice work. You won't damage your hands, and you won't have trouble with your back, either. Well, go to it! We'll need your efforts with all this heat. Imagine the problems if the flood is too weak or too strong! May the gods protect us from misfortune.' And the gardener went off to tend his vegetable plot.

The Herald smiled. No god could protect Abydos.

Exploring this place fascinated him. While the guards and the army were searching for him all over Egypt, Syria, Canaan and Nubia, he was moving freely about in the realm of Osiris, which he was planning to destroy. The temporary priests knew nothing of his secrets, of course, and the Herald had scarcely brushed the surface of this spiritual fortress. Until now it had been indestructible, but he had the wholehearted support of one of the permanent priests, Bega, who had become a servant of evil, and that promised some fine tomorrows.

Enduring Places was not like other towns. Here lived ritual priests and priestesses, craftsmen and administrators, whose task was to ensure that the temples and their precincts functioned properly. These carefully chosen staff were directly attached to the Crown, and lacked for nothing. Imbued with the presence of Osiris, they were by nature serious folk and were still asking themselves a worrying question: had the Tree of Life really been healed once and for all?

The Herald let the optimists deceive themselves. The gold that the pharaoh's men had brought back from Nubia and Punt had worked its magic against the Herald's curse, and the great Acacia of Osiris had grown green again and was bursting with life. In itself it proved the god's capacity for resurrection. But a new curse might yet strike it down. Despite his great powers, the Herald could not attack it from a distance, but now that he was near it he would destroy the protective measures surrounding the tree and drain it of all life.

However, the atmosphere of Abydos disturbed him. The Great Land, which housed the Lake of Life, was the gateway to the heavens, a land of silence and righteousness, and it entered into the soul. Since the days of the very earliest pharaohs, the rites had made the powers of creation effective. No one, however indifferent, could escape their radiance.

There was no ambiguity about the Herald's mission: Osiris must never again come back to life. By putting an end to this miracle, he would spread the ultimate religion. Serving both as a doctrine and as a programme for government, it would submerge humanity. Each believer would repeat the unchanging words every day, and no freedom of thought would be permitted. Even if dictators arose here and there, determined to direct the destiny of one people or another, the system would still function, maintained constantly by credulity and violence.

The Herald shook himself like a wet dog. The energy emanating from the temples weakened him and might even compromise his actions. However, too much haste would be a mistake. Eating the salt of the god Set preserved his powers and his destructive fire. Aware that the outcome of the decisive battle was uncertain, the predator with the red eyes was advancing cautiously into enemy territory.

Built according to the laws of divine proportion, Enduring Places tried to repel the invader. As soon as he stepped into the main street, a hot wind stopped him in his tracks. He opened his mouth and drank it in.

'Is something wrong?' asked a serving-woman armed with a broom and some rags.

'I was admiring our beautiful city. It's going to be a beautiful day, isn't it?'

'But supposing the flood turns it into a disaster? Let's hope Osiris will save us.'

The Herald continued on his way until he reached Bega's house, which was at one end of a narrow street, sheltered from the sun. He pushed aside the mat that covered the entrance and entered a small room dedicated to the ancestors.

Bega, an ugly man with a prominent nose, leapt out of his chair. 'You didn't have any problems, did you?'

'None at all, my friend.'

'But the commander may have been suspicious.'

'I look sufficiently like the temporary priest I have replaced not to arouse any suspicions. Getting through the checkpoints amuses me.'

Bega's name meant 'Cold One', and indeed he was as icy as a winter's day. He had been a priest at Abydos for many years, and believed he should have been appointed High Priest and learnt the Great Mysteries, following the death of the previous incumbent. Senusret, though, had decided otherwise. He would pay dearly for humiliating Bega like that – the Cold One was enjoying each stage of his vengeance. Having become a devoted servant of Osiris's murderer, Set, he was in line for high office when the Herald was victorious.

7

He would rule the temples of Egypt with an iron fist: everyone would know his true worth and obey him unquestioningly. Until then, he would carry out the Herald's audacious plans, for only his new master could enable him to slake his hatred.

Bega burnt to destroy what once he had venerated. Nothing remained of his past as a ritual priest and servant of Osiris. Abydos, for so long the centre of his life, had become the focus of his resentment and bitterness. He would violate the Great Secret, and the destruction of this privileged domain would give him enormous pleasure. Once the pharaoh and the permanent priests had been wiped out, and women excluded from spiritual office, he would at last possess the treasures of Osiris.

'Have you seen Shab again?' asked the Herald.

'He's hiding in a shrine near the terrace of the Great God, awaiting your instructions.'

'Are there patrols in the area?'

'No – no outsiders are allowed to enter. From time to time, a priest or priestess might go there to meditate, but I chose a secluded shrine where Shab will not be disturbed.'

'Tell me about the measures taken to protect the Tree of Life.'

'They cannot be broken down.'

The Herald smiled strangely. 'Describe them to me,' he demanded in a soft voice.

That voice made Bega shiver, and the minuscule head of Set imprinted on the palm of his right hand flamed red. The pain made him rush into speech.

'Four acacias have been planted round the Tree of Life. They are impregnated with magic, and create a permanent protective barrier which no outside energy can cross. They embody the four sons of Horus, and a relic-holder shaped like four lions makes them even more powerful. These watchers, with their ever-open eyes, are nourished by Ma'at. The relic-holder is given life by the symbol of the province of Abydos, a pole whose top is shrouded, hiding the secret of Osiris. No one can touch it without being struck dead. And then there's the gold of Punt and Nubia, which covers the acacia's trunk and makes it invulnerable.'

'You seem very pessimistic, my friend.'

'Realistic, my lord.'

'Have you forgotten my powers?'

'Certainly not, but protection like that . . .'

'Any fortress, even a magical one, has a weak spot. I shall discover it. Is it possible to get inside the Temple of Senusret?'

'Provided you have a specific task to perform there.'

'When I have finished the cleansing, find me one.'

'That won't be easy, because—'

'No excuses, Bega. I must know everything about Abydos.'

'Even I cannot cross the threshold of every temple and shrine.'

'Which ones are forbidden to you?'

'Senusret's house of eternity, and also the Tomb of Osiris, whose door must remain sealed. That is the hiding-place of the vase containing the god's secret life.'

'Is it ever removed from the tomb?'

Bega shook his head. 'I don't know.'

'Why haven't you found out?'

'Because the priests have prevented me. Each permanent priest, myself included, is allocated specific duties. Our superior, the Shaven-headed One, sees that we carry out those duties meticulously, and anyone who makes a mistake, however minor, is expelled.'

'Then you must not make any. Failure would be tantamount to treason.'

Face to face with the Herald, Bega lost his composure and thought only of obeying him.

The charming voice of a young woman outside the door made him forget his fears for a moment.

'May I come in?' she asked. 'I've brought you some bread and beer.'

The Herald himself lifted the mat over the entrance to let her in.

A pretty brown-haired girl with small, round breasts appeared. Dressed in a skirt with a blue and black lattice pattern, held up by a blue belt, she wore simple bracelets at her wrists and ankles. She was sensual, alluring, full of life.

With her left arm, she steadied the basket she carried on her head; in her right hand, she held a pitcher. She set down her burdens, knelt before the Herald and kissed his hands.

'This is Bina, the Queen of the Night,' he said with obvious pleasure. 'Although she can no longer transform herself into a lioness, she still has the capacity to do considerable harm.'

'You have no right to be here!' protested Bega.

'I certainly have,' she replied sharply. 'I've just been appointed servant to the permanent priests, and I shall be providing them with food and clean clothes every day.'

'Has the Shaven-headed One given his consent?'

'The commander of the guards persuaded him that he couldn't hope to find a more dedicated or industrious temporary worker. That officer may be suspicious and rough-hewn, but he's still a man. My modesty won him over.'

'So,' observed the Herald, 'you will be able to get close to the highest-ranking priests of Abydos. Your prime target is to be the priest who watches over Osiris's tomb.'

'Be extremely careful, my lord,' advised Bega anxiously. 'The Shaven-headed One will undoubtedly have taken precautions I don't know about. Besides, there's no telling what powers you'll unleash if you violate that shrine.'

'On the first point, I shall await detailed information from you. Don't worry about the second.'

The Great Secret

'My lord, the radiance of Osiris—'

'Don't you understand yet that Iker and Osiris are going to vanish for ever?'

2

Iker had never known a woman before Isis, and would never know another. Isis had never known a man before Iker, and would never know another. Their first night of love had sealed an eternal pact, beyond desire and passion. A higher power had transformed their future into destiny. Indissolubly linked, united in mind, heart and body, from now on they would be as one.

Why had he been granted such happiness? wondered Iker. To live with Isis, in Abydos . . . But that was a dream which was sure to be shattered soon. So he opened his eyes, certain that he'd be cruelly disappointed: she was there, beside him, gazing at him with her enchanting green eyes.

He dared to caress her divinely soft skin, to kiss her face with its exquisite features. 'Is it . . . Is it really you?'

The kiss she gave him did not seem at all unreal.

'Are we really in your house, at Abydos?' he asked.

'Our house,' she corrected him. 'Since we're living together, we are now married.'

Iker sat up suddenly. 'But I cannot marry Pharaoh Senusret's daughter!'

'What can prevent it?'

'Reason and good sense.'

Her smile made those arguments seem trivial.

'But I'm nothing, a nobody, and I—'

'No false modesty now, Iker. You are the Royal Son and Friend of Pharaoh, and you have a mission to accomplish.'

He got up, paced the room, touched the bed, the walls and the storage chests, then took her in his arms.

'I'm so happy . . . I wish this moment could last for ever.'

'It will last for ever,' she promised. 'But we have vital work to do.'

'Without you, I'd have no chance whatsoever of success.'

Isis took his hand tenderly. 'I'm your wife now, aren't I? When we were far apart, you felt my presence and you lived in my thoughts. Today we are united for ever – not even the wind's breath can slip between us. Our love will lead us beyond the limits of our existence.'

'I'm not worthy of you, Isis.'

'Whether we face hardship or joy, we are one. Not even death can separate us.'

As they walked along the path that led to the Tree of Life, Isis told Iker that Senusret had asked her to watch for any suspicious behaviour among the permanent as well as the temporary priests. Her ritual tasks and path of initiation gave her little opportunity to keep watch on her colleagues, and she had seen nothing untoward. However, the pharaoh's anxieties must not be taken lightly: he could see through appearances, and he sensed treason at the heart of the most secret brotherhood in Egypt.

'How could an initiate of Abydos possibly become a son of the darkness?' asked Iker in astonishment.

'I used to ask myself that question constantly,' confessed Isis. 'However, the Way of Fire burnt away my naivety and made me understand that flawless rituals don't necessarily create flawless men.'

'And you really believe one of the priests may be cunning enough to deceive everyone?'

'Doesn't your mission imply that very thing?'

The pair stopped some distance from the acacia, and the young priestess asked the four trees and the four guardian lions to allow them to pass through into the enclosure. Almost immediately, Iker smelt a strange scent, sweet and calming. Isis gestured to him that they might go forward.

At the foot of the Tree of Life, whose trunk was covered in gold, the Shaven-headed One was pouring water.

'You're late, Isis,' he snapped. 'Take the vase of milk and perform your duties at once.'

She did so.

'Whatever is happening on the fringes of your life,' added her superior angrily, 'the rites must take precedence.'

'I am not a fringe,' cut in Iker. 'I am Isis' husband.'

'Family matters do not interest me.'

'My official function may interest you more. Pharaoh Senusret has ordered me to dispel the troubles that are corrupting the priesthood here, and to oversee the creation of new sacred objects for the celebration of the Mysteries of Osiris.'

A long silence followed this declaration.

Eventually, the Shaven-headed One said, 'Royal Son, Friend of Pharaoh, the king's envoy – they're merely high-sounding titles. Myself, I have always lived here; I preserve the House of Life and its sacred archives, see that the permanent priests perform their duties correctly and accept no excuses if they fail. I have not been criticized in any way, and the king retains his trust in me. As for the ritual priests, I stand as guarantor for them.'

'His Majesty is not so optimistic. Perhaps you have not been vigilant enough.'

'I will not permit you to speak to me like that, young man.'

'My age is of no importance. Will you agree to aid me in my investigation – yes or no?

The Shaven-headed One turned to Isis. 'What does the king's daughter think of this?'

'To fight among ourselves would be disastrous, because without your support Iker would get nowhere. And we must not forget that the Tree of Life is still under threat.'

The Shaven-headed One was outraged. 'It's glowing with health! Have you forgotten that it plunges its roots into the heart of the primordial ocean, in order to bring the righteous the water of regeneration?'

'Osiris is the only one in the acacia; life and death are united in him,' Isis reminded him. 'Today I sense a disturbance. It may presage new attacks by the forces of destruction.'

'But aren't the defences the king has put in place impregnable?' asked Iker.

She shook her head. 'We mustn't delude ourselves.'

'One more reason for eliminating any enemies within,' insisted the Royal Son.

The Shaven-headed One was deeply worried, and abandoned the futile argument. 'What do you wish to do?' he asked.

'Question the permanent priests one by one, and also gather together the craftsmen and tell them of the king's wishes. Everyone must have clean hands.'

'You're making trouble for yourself, Iker. You're a stranger to Abydos, and you'll arouse great resentment.'

'I'll help him,' promised Isis.

'Why should the Royal Son succeed where we have failed?' demanded the Shaven-headed One. 'We have found nothing to indicate that a permanent priest is guilty. And let us not forget our major concern. The star-sign of the god Sah* disappeared seventy days ago. If it doesn't reappear tonight, the cosmos will crumble and the annual flood we have been waiting for will not come.'

'I shall consult the Golden Palette,' announced Iker.

---

*The constellation of Orion.

The Shaven-headed One was stunned. 'The king has entrusted it to you?'

'I have that honour.' Iker indicated the case in which he was carrying it.

The old man shook his head. 'Use it with care. And don't forget: only the right questions produce the right answers. Now I must go to the king's Temple of a Million Years and prepare the offerings to the spirit of the Nile.' Grumbling, he left the enclosure.

'He hates me,' said Iker.

'He sees any stranger to Abydos as an undesirable. Nevertheless, you impressed him very much. He takes you seriously and won't hinder our work.'

'It's wonderful to hear you say "our work". If I were alone, I'd be certain to fail.'

'You will never be alone again, Iker.'

Together, they walked along the processional route, which was lined by three hundred and sixty-five small offering-tables bearing food and drink. Evoking the visible and invisible year, they sanctified each of its days. In this way an eternal banquet was celebrated, and offered to the *ka* of the divine powers. In return, they charged the foodstuffs with *ka*.

Because carrying out the daily libations was such a huge task, the permanent priest charged with this duty was assisted by several temporary priests. Today they found it hard to concentrate on their duties, for worrying rumours were circulating about the flood. Some went so far as to predict that it would not happen at all. The Shaven-headed One had offered no proof to the contrary, so they feared the worst.

Iker would have liked to explore the whole site and its monuments, but his whole mission might be called into question if the life-giving flood failed. Without the fertilizing silt, the fields would become barren.

'Why hasn't the star-sign of Sah appeared yet?' he asked Isis.

'The evildoer's power affects the heavens as well as the earth.'

'In that case, he can't be a human being.'

Isis didn't answer.

Her silence disturbed Iker deeply. No matter what powers the initiates of Abydos had, how could they triumph over such an enemy? The Tree of Life was only enjoying a respite; other storms were brewing. The Herald probably had one or more accomplices, so well-hidden that they had escaped the Shaven-headed One's notice. He, Iker, a novice, must identify them and prevent them from doing harm.

Isis took him to Senusret's Temple of a Million Years, where the permanent priests were chanting incantations linking the resurrection of Osiris to the rise of the Nile's waters. She introduced him to the seven female musicians whose task was to delight the divine soul; to the Servant of the *Ka*, who venerated and maintained the spiritual energy to strengthen the brotherhood's links with the Invisible; to the priest who poured the libation of fresh water on the offering-tables; to the priest who watched over the one-ness of the great body of Osiris; and to the ritual priest known as He Who Sees the Secrets.

They were all astonished to see that the Royal Son was holding the Golden Palette. Given the Shaven-headed One's respectful attitude, they realized that young Iker must exercise undeniable authority.

Ignoring their looks – some admiring, some suspicious – the young man explored the shrine. With the strange feeling that he had always known it, he passed through the pillared gateway, between the colossal statues of the king as Osiris, entered a pillared chamber whose ceiling was covered with stars, and meditated before scenes depicting Senusret communicating with the gods.

At the end of his long meditation, he addressed the priests. 'It is the second day of the month of Thoth, and the star-sign of Sah has still not appeared. This is exceptional, and underlines the determination of our great enemy, the Herald. So we cannot be content with patience and waiting.'

'What do you suggest?' asked the Shaven-headed One.

'We must consult the Golden Palette.' Iker took it from its case and wrote on it: '*What force can bring the flood?*'

The question vanished, and in its place appeared the answer: '*The tears of the goddess Isis.*'

'The permanent priestesses must invoke them,' decided the Shaven-headed One, 'by celebrating the appropriate rites.'

The priestesses of Osiris followed Isis up to the roof of the temple. There she spoke the first words of the love poem addressed to the cosmos: '"Sah, may your splendour light up the darkness. I am the star Sothis, your sister, I am faithful to you and will never abandon you. Light up the night; send the river down from on high upon our earth to quench its thirst."'

Iker and the permanent priests withdrew to the forecourt of the temple. Iker would have liked nothing better than to give himself up to contemplation of this magical place, Abydos, but he could not neglect the task he had been set. Besides, as he stood there, Iker had the feeling he was being watched – watched even here, in this world whose serenity should have been enlivened only by the search for sacred things. Carefully, he looked around but he could see nothing suspicious. He raised his eyes in silent prayer to the sky. The fate of Abydos and all of Egypt depended on him.

The Herald saw Iker turning to look his way. Lithe and quick despite his great height, he instantly ducked behind a wall. At worst, the young man would only have noticed a temporary priest and wondered why he was there. But the Royal Son was content to watch the setting sun.

The Herald knew that tracking his quarry, isolating him

and striking him down would be far from easy. If he infringed any of the rules of Abydos, he risked being spotted, even expelled. So he would have to move slowly and surely while he took the measure of the vast territory of Osiris.

Murdering Iker would not be enough. His death must shake people so much that it disheartened them and sowed utter desolation in a kingdom which thought itself protected from such a disaster.

The Herald took advantage of the gathering dusk to return to his modest sleeping-place. Shab the Twisted had given him plenty of salt, the foam of Set, gathered in the Western desert during the time of greatest heat. It quenched his thirst, fed him and maintained his predatory energy.

Enthralled by the beauty of the stars decorating the immense body of the sky-goddess Nut, Iker was wide awake. He thought of the sun's fierce fight against the dark powers, and of its perilous night journey, whose outcome was always uncertain. As it travelled across the body of Nut, it captured the light of the stars and passed through the doors leading to resurrection, one by one. Each life led to this voyage, giving it all its meaning.

Since his first death, in a wild sea, Iker had undergone many ordeals, known cruel doubts and made serious mistakes. But he had not turned aside from his path, the path leading to Abydos and to the wonderful happiness of living with Isis.

At the far edge of the night, on the fringes of the dawn, the sky suddenly changed in appearance, as if a new world were being born. A profound silence fell over the Great Earth. All eyes converged on a star-sign which, after more than seventy days' nerve-racking absence, had just reappeared, passing through the portal of flames. Once again, the miracle was taking place.

At Abydos the river rose and spread its waters wide, and

Hapy, the spirit of the Nile, leapt amorously to rejoin its banks. The tears of Isis had produced the flood and brought Osiris back to life.

3

At last Memphis allowed itself to give expression to its joy. The flood might have come rather late, but it would be abundant and not destructive. Every Egyptian, from the wealthiest to the most humble, sang the praises of the pharaoh, who had maintained the harmony between the heavens and the earth. The celebration of the rites had brought back the good star, and the normal course of the seasons would unfold according to the order of Ma'at. Once again, the Two Lands had avoided chaos.

Even this excellent news did not bring a smile back to the face of Sobek the Protector, commander of all the kingdom's security guards. A physically impressive and authoritarian man who loathed courtiers, diplomats and flatterers, he had venerated Senusret from the start of his reign, and protecting him remained Sobek's sole concern. Unfortunately, the king ran far too many risks and paid little heed to advice to be careful, so the Protector continued to take personal charge of training the soldiers who would form the king's bodyguard. At least, he thought, the palace, although not a fortress, was a refuge which could not be stormed by any rebel force, no matter how strong.

Sobek had not doubted for a moment that Senusret would ensure the flood's arrival, and his main concern was the ceremonies to mark the new year, the first of which was just beginning. During them many dignitaries and professional bodies would present gifts to the pharaoh. Ensuring his safety in such circumstances presented appalling difficulties. If an assassin mingled with the crowd and tried to rush at Senusret, Sobek's men would react instantly and stop him. But what if one of the prominent guests belonged to the Herald's network? How could he be intercepted? He would be near the king during the presentation of the gifts, and could strike before the Protector had time to intervene.

Searching all the participants and guests would have been the best solution but, alas, it was forbidden by protocol and propriety. All Sobek could do was be extremely vigilant and rely upon his lightning-swift reactions.

The first person to be presented to Pharaoh and the Great Royal Wife was Tjaty Khnum-Hotep, an elderly and corpulent man. There was nothing to fear from Egypt's first minister, for he was competent and respected. Nor was there from the commander of the country's armies, rugged old General Nesmontu, from High Treasurer Senankh, with his jovial appearance and strong character, or from the Overseer of Pharaoh's Works, the elegant and refined Sehotep. At the feet of the royal couple, the dignitaries laid a broad collar, symbol of the nine creative powers, a sword made from a mixture of silver and gold, a miniature gold shrine and a silver vase filled with water from the new flood, which was endowed with regenerative properties.

The ministers moved on and were succeeded by Medes, secretary of the King's House, bearing a small chest containing gold, silver, lapis-lazuli and turquoise. Sobek had no great liking for this short, fat man, but had to admit that his expert administration in Memphis merited the good reputation he had won. Medes's task was to draw up decrees and distribute them throughout Egypt, Nubia and the Syria–Canaan protectorate, and he carried it out with exemplary diligence. He was so devoted to the public cause that many dignitaries foresaw a brilliant career for him.

After him came over fifty members of the court, all rivalling each other in obsequiousness. As the ceremony progressed, the Protector grew slightly less tense, though he still watched everyone closely and tried to work out what they were thinking. Would a rebel be mad or drugged enough to attack Senusret?

Sobek glanced at the king: that huge man with a stern face and a gaze so intense that it rooted everyone who met it to the spot. His heavy eyelids drooped from the suffering and fallibility of humanity; his large ears heard the words of the gods and the supplications of his people.

Senusret was a born pharaoh. He was the guardian of a supernatural power, the *ka*, which was passed from king to king, and his very presence made ambitious men and rivals look ridiculous. He had performed such wonders as controlling the flood, abolishing the provincial governors' privileges, reunifying the Two Lands and pacifying Canaan and Nubia. The legend of the sovereign grew constantly, and his reign was already being compared to that of Osiris.

Indifferent to praise and detesting flattery, Senusret never vaunted his successes and thought only of the difficulties that must be resolved. Governing the country, keeping it on the way of Ma'at, strengthening unity, protecting the weak from the strong, and ensuring the presence of the gods would have been enough to wear out a giant. But the king could not rest and must ensure that his subjects could sleep peacefully.

He was facing a formidable enemy, the Herald, who was determined to spread evil, violence and fanaticism. Egypt and the office of pharaoh were major obstacles to the Herald's success, and he had tried to wound them in the heart by placing a curse upon the Tree of Life, the Acacia of Osiris at Abydos. It had recovered, but Senusret was still anxious and did not believe that the Herald had died in a remote corner of Nubia. On the contrary, his disappearance probably concealed a new manoeuvre, the prelude to a fearsome attack.

Senusret had built a pyramid at Dahshur, a Temple of a Million Years and a house of eternity at Abydos, and a magical barrier of fortresses between Elephantine and the Second Cataract, and had thus foiled his enemy's plans. Nevertheless, the Herald had created a permanent network of spies in Memphis, and knew how to coerce, bribe, and take advantage of weaknesses and shadowy areas. Far from being defeated, he was still a mortal danger.

It was the turn of the head sculptor of the craftsmen of Memphis to present his gift to the royal couple. The Protector did not lower his guard: the man seemed trustworthy, but that word was not part of Sobek's vocabulary.

'Majesty,' declared the sculptor, presenting the king with a small alabaster sphinx bearing his effigy, 'a hundred statues symbolizing the royal *ka* are now at your disposal.'

Each province would be given at least one, guaranteeing the country's unity. Diorite, whose hues varied from black to dark green, conferred power and austerity upon the statues. There was no vanity in these depictions of an elderly monarch with a serious face and large ears, only a wish to intensify the radiance of the *ka*. Thus, supernatural forces would continue to impregnate Egypt with their benefits, repelling the Herald's curses.

The ceremony was reaching its end.

Sobek wiped his brow with the back of his hand. Some people made sarcastic remarks about his constant suspicion and his obsessive concern for security. That mattered little to him; he would not alter his mode of conduct.

The last bearer of gifts was a puny fellow who held a granite vase in his outstretched hands. Suddenly, the surprisingly loud braying of a donkey rooted him to the spot, less than five steps from the dais where the royal couple were enthroned. Knocking over two soldiers, an enormous hound leapt at the puny man and bore him to the ground. A dozen vipers slithered out of the vase, causing panic among the guests.

Sobek and his men quickly killed the snakes with their staves, but the would-be assassin had been bitten several times and was already in his death throes. Under the protection of their personal bodyguard, the royal couple calmly withdrew.

The dog, obviously proud of himself, was being stroked by a square-faced fellow with thick eyebrows and a round belly.

Sobek went over to him. 'Good work, Sekari.'

'Congratulate North Wind and Flesh-Eater. The donkey sounded the alert, and the dog leapt into action. Iker's two friends have saved His Majesty's life.'

'They deserve to be promoted and decorated. Did you recognize the attacker?'

'Never seen him before.'

'His own snakes gave him no chance. I'd have liked to interrogate him, but anyone would swear that these bandits take a malign pleasure in cutting off our smallest lead. How are your underground investigations going?'

'My ears are wide open, but they haven't picked up anything interesting.'

Sekari, Senusret's special agent, could fit into any situation and background with ease: people confided in him, and he knew how to make himself almost invisible. He was trying to identify members of the rebel network, but since the death of a water-carrier and the arrests of a few underlings, there had been no notable successes. Wary now, the enemy had gone to ground.

'We must have made it harder for them to communicate with one another,' said Sekari, 'and so made it harder for them to attack us. This latest attempt may have been just a sudden, desperate act.'

'Unlikely,' replied Sobek. 'Protecting the pharaoh at that time and in that place was a real challenge, and that skinny fellow had a good chance of success. Their organization has taken a few hard knocks, but it's still very much alive.'

'I don't doubt that for a moment.'

'Are you convinced the Herald's dead?'

Sekari hesitated. 'Some of the Nubian tribes hated him ferociously.'

'Memphis has already suffered a great deal, and many innocent people are dead because of that evil demon. Making us believe he's dead would be a clever tactic. What can he be planning that's even worse?'

'I'm off to continue the hunt,' said Sekari.

Medes was fuming. Why had he not been informed about this new assassination attempt on the pharaoh? A robust forty-year-old, rather plump on account of his greed, with a moon-shaped face, black hair, short legs and pudgy feet, Medes was a senior official and tireless worker who gave complete satisfaction to the king and the tjaty. Charged with formulating and rapidly distributing the decrees promulgated by the pharaoh, he headed an army of qualified scribes and directed the movements of a flotilla of fast boats.

No one would ever have suspected Medes, secretary of the King's House, of serving the Herald. But, like his henchman Gergu, and Bega, the permanent priest of Abydos, he belonged to the conspiracy of evil. Each of the three conspirators bore on the palm of his hand a tiny head of Set, deeply imprinted, which became red and unbearably painful at the least thought of treason.

Why had he strayed from the path in this way? There was no shortage of reasons. The King's House ought to have co-opted an expert of his quality a long time ago. Naturally, the Herald had promised him the post of tjaty; that would be a simple step on the way to obtaining supreme power. To rule Egypt . . . Medes felt capable of it, for he was an exceptional administrator and leader. And yet he was still refused access to the covered temple and the secret part of the shrines, notably the one at Abydos, from where Senusret derived the major part of his strength. There was only one solution: to kill the king.

Quite apart from this legitimate ambition, Medes had to admit that evil fascinated him. As sole guardian of eternity, it struck down any and every opponent; so joining forces with the Herald, despite its terrifying aspects, had fulfilled all his hopes. That strange man was endowed with remarkable powers and, above all, had no fear of any attack by the enemy. In following his inflexible plans, he always calculated one step ahead, foresaw failure and integrated it into future successes.

Near his luxurious house in the centre of the city, Medes bumped into a stocky, visibly intoxicated man: Gergu, Egypt's principal inspector of granaries.

'Is Senusret unharmed?' asked Gergu.

'Unfortunately, yes.'

'Then the rumour was false. Did you know about the attack?'

'Unfortunately, no.'

Gergu's thick lips blanched. 'The Herald has abandoned us.'

A drunk who regularly resorted to prostitutes, Gergu owed his career to Medes and, despite a few disagreements, followed his instructions. Terrified of the Herald and of the punishment he meted out, he obeyed him unquestioningly.

'Don't jump to hasty conclusions,' said Medes. 'It may have been the Phoenician's idea.'

'We're done for!'

'You're still at liberty, and so am I. If Sobek the Protector suspected us, we'd already be in the interrogation cell.'

That argument reassured Gergu. But his reassurance was short-lived, for he was seized by a pang of anxiety. 'The Herald must be dead. His followers must have panicked and tried to do the impossible.'

'Don't lose your nerve,' advised Medes. 'A leader of his calibre doesn't disappear away like a common criminal. There was nothing panicky about the attack. The brave man who undertook it almost succeeded – if a donkey and a dog hadn't interfered, the vipers would have bitten the royal couple. The Memphis network has proved it can still act. Imagine the look on Sobek the Protector's face! He's been made to look ridiculous and incompetent. If the pharaoh dismisses him from office, we shall be rid of a major obstacle.'

'I don't think so. Even a tick hangs on less doggedly than that man.'

'An insect . . . A good comparison, my dear Gergu. We shall crush the Protector beneath our sandals. What successes has he had? A few miserable arrests, that's all. Our network is still intact, isn't it?'

Dry-mouthed, Gergu felt an intense need for a drink. 'Have you got any strong beer?'

Medes smiled. 'Not to have any would be a crime. Come in and make yourself comfortable.'

Entry to Medes's huge house was by means of a heavy double door. Next to it stood a hut occupied by a guard who roughly drove away any unwanted guests: he bowed very low before his master.

Behind the high walls lay a garden with a lake surrounded by sycamores. Wooden latticework doors opened on to it. As soon as Medes and Gergu sat down in the shade of a canopy, a serving-woman poured them some cool beer. Gergu drank greedily.

Medes was preoccupied. After a while he said, 'We still don't know what Royal Son Iker is really doing in Abydos.'

'But you drew up the official decree!' exclaimed Gergu in astonishment.

'The fact that he has been given full powers is surprising, but what will he use them for?'

'Can't you find out more?'

'Attracting the attention of the King's House would be catastrophic. But I can't bear things to be unclear. Go to Abydos, Gergu. Being a temporary priest, you'll be able to get reliable information.'

4

First, the raw materials. The stone, wood and papyrus had to be of an exceptional quality. Iker talked with the craftsmen every day, and never patronized them. In this way he was earning himself a reputation as a serious-minded, tenacious man who respected other people.

Observing the Royal Son with a critical eye, the Shaven-headed One noted his progressive integration into Abydos. Originally he had worried that the young man might be over-hasty and authoritarian, but now he was pleased by his understanding of the work to be done.

'The craftsmen think highly of you, Iker,' he said. 'That's quite an achievement, to tell the truth – those rather rough fellows do not grant their friendship lightly. But whatever happens, don't forget the time limit. In two months' time the celebration of the Mysteries of Osiris begins. Not a single item must be missing.'

'The sculptors are working on the creation of the new statue of Osiris, the carpenters on his ship, and they report to me every day. I check regularly on the manufacture of the mats, armchairs, baskets, sandals and kilts. As for the papyri that will be used for the ritual texts, they will last for generations.'

'Did you not wish to become a writer?'

'My other work takes up all my time at the moment, but my

taste for writing is as strong as ever. Hieroglyphs are the supreme art, aren't they? In them, the words of power passed on by the gods are written. No text surpasses the rituals. If I can one day take part in their creation, I'll have fulfilled my vocation.'

'But haven't you done so already? After all, you hold the Golden Palette.'

'I use it only in exceptional circumstances, and never for my personal ends. It belongs to the pharaoh, to Abydos and to the Golden Circle.'

The Shaven-headed One looked vexed. 'What do you know of the Circle?'

'That it embodies the highest point of our spirituality, which alone is capable of maintaining the creative energies and preserving the wisdom of the ancients.'

'Do you wish to belong to it?'

'A succession of miracles has strewn my life. I have hopes of this one, too.'

'Don't give yourself up to dreams. You must go on working unsparingly.'

When night fell, Iker rejoined Isis. Little by little, she was showing him the innumerable riches of the domain of Osiris. On this particular evening, they sat in contemplation beside the Lake of Life.

'It is unlike any other,' said Isis. 'Only the permanent priests are authorized to purify themselves in it and to impregnate themselves with the power of the *nun*. Linked to the fragrances of the Hidden God, that power is at its most powerful here. At major festivals and during the period of the great Mysteries, Anubis uses the water from this lake. He washes Osiris's viscera and renders them impervious to decay. No outsider may gaze upon this mystery.'

'But you have.'

Isis did not reply.

'Ever since I first saw you, I've known that you're more

than merely a woman, because the otherworld dwells in your eyes. You're showing me a path whose nature I don't know. I entrust myself unreservedly to you, my guide, my love.'

The lake glittered with a thousand reflections, from silver to gold. Arms entwined, the two young people shared an incredibly intense moment of happiness.

From now on, Iker belonged to Abydos. He had found his true homeland, the Great Land.

'Isis, why are you so anxious about the Tree of Life?' he asked.

'Its recovery isn't irreversible. A dark force is prowling round it. The daily rituals keep the evil at bay, but it never stops returning. If it gets stronger, will we be able to resist it?'

'Does the Shaven-headed One take the threat seriously?'

'He can't identify the source of the negative waves, and he's losing sleep over it.'

'Could the source be . . . in Abydos itself?'

Isis's expression darkened. 'We can't exclude that possibility.'

'So the king's fears are justified. One of the Herald's followers has got through the barriers and is preparing the ground for his master's next attack.'

The young priestess did not disagree.

'We must not look the other way,' advised Iker. 'I haven't questioned anyone yet, because first I had to get to know this world. Now I must start questioning each of the permanent priests and priestesses.'

'Spare no one – just find out the truth.'

The commander of the Abydos guards force prepared to search Bina himself. She was docile, and did not utter a word of protest.

'I'm sorry, my beauty,' he said. 'Orders are orders.'

'I understand, Commander. But you're getting to know me well, aren't you?'

'Security requires that we do some tasks over and over again. There are more unpleasant ones, I can tell you.'

Smiling and relaxed, Bina let him search her. 'What could I hide under my short skirt? As for my basket, you can see it's empty.'

Red with confusion, the officer stepped away. While fulfilling his office to the letter, he could not conceal his attraction to this pretty brown-haired girl, so gentle and submissive.

'Do you like your work?' he asked.

'Serving the permanent priests is a greater honour than I ever dared hope for. But forgive me: I don't want to be late.'

The Queen of the Night went to the door of one of the buildings in Senusret's temple complex. She was given fresh bread and a jar of beer, to be delivered to the priest who oversaw the oneness of the great body of Osiris and checked the seals on the door of the god's tomb.

No temporary worker was allowed to enter. Like the other serving-women responsible for looking after the permanent priests, Bina was restricted to meeting them in their houses, modest dwellings which were carefully maintained.

The checker of the seals was reading a papyrus.

'I've brought you something to eat and drink,' murmured Bina timidly.

'Thank you.'

'Where shall I put the things?'

'On the low table to the left of the entrance.'

'What would you like, dried fish, fillets of perch or grilled beef?'

'Today fresh bread will suffice.'

'Are you ill?'

'That is not your concern, little one.'

This priest was as crotchety as his colleagues: Bina's charm was not working. She said, 'I'd very much like to help you.'

'Don't worry, our medical services are extremely good.'

'Should I inform them?'

'If necessary, I'll do so myself.'

Bina lowered her eyes. 'Your work carries with it certain dangers, doesn't it?'

'What are you thinking of?'

'Doesn't the tomb of Osiris give off a fearsome energy?'

The permanent priest's face hardened. 'Are you trying to learn our secrets, young lady?'

'Oh no! I'm just interested – and a little bit frightened. People tell a lot of stories about Osiris and his tomb. Some of them talk about terrifying ghosts which pursue their enemies so as to drink their blood.'

The ritual priest said nothing. He was not going to criticize beliefs which contributed to the protection of the god's dwelling.

'I am entirely at your disposal,' said Bina, giving the sour-tempered priest her most beautiful smile. She need not have bothered: he did not even look up.

'Return to your baking and brewing, young lady, and to making your deliveries.'

Questioning the priestesses of Hathor was made easier because Isis was now their High Priestess. Iker interviewed each one of them, and found no cause for suspicion: they all performed their duties faithfully and well. They all spoke freely, and he was sure none of them was concealing anything. He concluded that the Herald's follower was not hiding among them.

While continuing his work with the craftsmen, therefore, he took a close interest in the permanent priests, who did not conceal their disapproval.

He Who Sees the Secrets was true to the title of his office. He listened to the Royal Son's questions but refused to answer them, because he would speak only to the Shaven-headed One. It was up to his superior to choose what should be passed on to Iker.

The Shaven-headed One did not have to be asked twice, and repeated the priest's declarations word for word. One main idea lay behind them: only those initiated into the Mysteries of Osiris had access to his secrets. Since Iker was not an initiate, the priests must keep silent.

'Don't you find this refusal to cooperate suspicious?' asked the young man.

'On the contrary,' replied the Shaven-headed One, 'this old travelling-companion respects his obligations to the letter, whatever the circumstances. All that matters to him is the preservation of secrecy. None of its essential aspects has been divulged. If the reverse were true, and he was betraying us to the Herald, the Tree of Life would have perished and Abydos with it.'

The argument convinced Iker.

The Servant of the *Ka*, whose task was to venerate the ancestors and keep alive their spiritual energy, invited the Royal Son to celebrate the ancestors' memory with him.

'Without their active presence,' he revealed, 'our links with the invisible world would dissolve little by little. If they were broken, we would become living dead.'

Together the old man and the young honoured the statues of Senusret's *ka*, in which the power born of the stars was concentrated. Slowly and solemnly, the priest spoke the words bringing to life the souls of kings and of those of just voice. Each day, the truth of his magical knowledge rendered his work fruitful.

'Like my colleagues,' he explained, 'I am just an aspect of the universal being of Pharaoh. Alone, I do not exist. Linked to his spirit and to the other permanent priests, I contribute to the radiance of Osiris, beyond the many forms of death.'

How could such a man be an accomplice of the Herald?

Iker next went to see the priest who watched over the oneness of the great body of Osiris, and asked, 'Will you show me the door of his tomb?'

'No.'

'The king has entrusted me with a delicate mission, and I am trying not to annoy anyone. Nevertheless, I must check that the sacred duties are being properly carried out. Your duties are part of them.'

'I am pleased to hear it.

'Will you reconsider your position?'

'Only those initiated into the Mysteries have access to the Tomb of Osiris. To doubt my competence, my commitment and my honesty would be an insult. Consequently, my word will have to suffice.'

'I am sorry, but I need more. Checking the seals does not take you the whole day. What do you do with the rest of your time?'

The priest stiffened. 'I am at the Shaven-headed One's disposal, and the day contains more tasks than there are hours. If he wishes, he will tell you what those tasks are. And now I must carry one of them out.'

Iker returned to the Shaven-headed One, who told him, 'I regard that priest as my right arm. He is a little sour-tempered, perhaps, but meticulous and devoted. I myself check the magical and material security of the seals, and have never noticed anything amiss. Here again, can you imagine the benefit the Herald would have derived from his betrayal? The only one left for you to meet is Bega, who is responsible for pouring the daily libations on the offering-tables.'

Tall, unattractive, cold and austere, Bega looked down at his visitor. 'The day has been arduous and I should like to rest.'

'Then we can talk tomorrow,' conceded Iker.

'No, I would rather dispense with this quickly. My colleagues and I respect your office and wish to give you complete satisfaction. However, your procedures offend us. Permanent priests of Abydos under suspicion: what an abomination!'

'Then isn't it important to prove their innocence?'

'No one doubts it, Royal Son.'

'My mission shows the contrary.'

Bega looked troubled. 'Is Pharaoh unhappy with our brotherhood?'

'He detects a certain disharmony.'

'What is causing it?'

'The presence, here in Osiris's domain, of an accomplice of our sworn enemy, the Herald.'

'That's impossible!' protested Bega in a rasping voice. 'In any case, if such a demon does exist Abydos will drive him away. No one can mar the unity of the permanent priests.'

'I find that belief reassuring.'

'Can it be that the Royal Son believed for a moment that one of us is a traitor?'

'I was obliged to consider the possibility.'

The trace of a smile appeared on Bega's grim face. 'It may be that the Herald is trying to trick us and divide us by spreading such tales. A lack of clear-headedness would lead us to disaster. How right the pharaoh was to appoint you. Despite your youth, you show an impressive maturity. Abydos will be grateful to you for that.'

This phase of Iker's investigation had ended inconclusively.

5

The priestess of Hathor named Nephthys – which meant
'Sovereign of the Temple' – was decked in a four-strand
necklace, narrow earrings and broad bracelets, a pleated dress
and a cape that left the right shoulder bare. The queen had
entrusted her with responsibility for running the weaving-
women's workshop in Memphis, but on the queen's orders
she had returned to Abydos in answer to an urgent summons.

She bowed before Isis, her High Priestess.

'One of the Seven has died,' Isis told her. 'Another
priestess must replace her at once in order to keep the ritual
number intact. Your knowledge of the rites has caused you to
be chosen.'

'Your confidence honours me, and I shall try to prove
worthy of it.'

Nephthys bore a curious resemblance to Isis: the same age,
the same height, the same shape of face, the same slender
figure. Straight away they felt a kinship and mutual
understanding. Some people regarded them as sisters, who
were happy to rediscover each other.

Isis initiated Nephthys into the final Mysteries. Like Isis,
she travelled the Way of Fire and passed through the
doorways leading to the Secret of Osiris. Then Isis set out the
dramatic events that had struck Abydos, hiding none of her
anxiety.

Instructed to prepare the god's shroud for the coming ceremonies, Nephthys immediately checked the quality of the linen-fibre harvested at the end of March. Only the very softest stems were used in the manufacture of beautiful fabrics. Soaked in water until the woody parts were eliminated, certain fibres survived decay. Their purification, which was finished off by the sun's rays, enabled a fine, flawless material to be produced.

Isis and Nephthys spun and wove. No shading or multi-coloured patterns would soil the tunic of white royal linen that Osiris would wear. This garment was both flame and light, and preserved the Mystery.

After preparing long strands, the two women knotted them into balls, which were placed in ceramic pots. They wove the linen with ancient distaffs used only by followers of Hathor, and kept to a strict rule: sixty-four warp threads to every forty-eight weft.

'When Ra felt great tiredness,' recalled Nephthys, 'his sweat fell to earth, germinated and was transformed into linen. Impregnated with the sun's brightness, nourished by the moon's radiance, it forms the newborn baby's swaddling clothes and the shrouds for those who are reborn.'

The precious garment was housed in a shrine of the Temple of Osiris.

'I have failed, my lord. Whatever the punishment may be, I accept it.'

Despite her charm, her feigned modesty and her total dedication, Bina had been unable to pierce the thick shells of the permanent priests. Not her smile, nor the finest beer, nor the most delicious food could sway them. She had gone from one to another so as not to attract the attention of the priest who checked the seals placed upon the door of Osiris's tomb – he had refused to engage in idle conversation and paid not the slightest heed to her alluring body.

The Herald stroked her hair. 'We are in enemy territory, my sweet one, and nothing will be easy. These priests don't behave like ordinary men. Your experience proves that they are more attached to their duties than to their desires. It is pointless to run ill-considered risks.'

'You mean . . . you forgive me?'

'You have done nothing wrong.'

Bina kissed her lord's knees. Although she preferred him bearded and turbaned, his new appearance took nothing away from his power. In a little while from now, the Herald would shatter the spiritual and material fortifications of the servants of Osiris.

'Will we soon violate the secret shrines?' she asked anxiously.

'Have no fear: we shall succeed.'

Iker had a long interview with the commander of Abydos's guards, to find out how the temporary workers were organized. Guards, sculptors, painters, artists, vase-makers, bakers, brewers, florists, bearers of offerings, musicians, singers and other servants were listed in a table according to their skills and availability, with no account taken of their age or social position. The duration of their work varied from a few days to a few months. They brought to life a veritable town and the temples in the service of Osiris, so that no material detail should spoil the harmony of the place.

It was impossible to summon them all and to check them individually, but the commander was adamant that no black sheep entered the sacred domain. Of course, some workers proved less efficient than others; in those cases the overseers took immediate action, and they showed no leniency. A complaint that reached the Shaven-headed One almost always resulted in permanent expulsion.

Iker was eager to meet the old workers and the most dedicated, and his conversations with them reassured him. It was clear that they were well aware of their duties, and never crossed the limits imposed on them.

Bina entered the room where the Royal Son was listening to the testimony of an old temporary worker who hoped to die in service. Although she saw Iker from behind, she recognized him instantly and drew back, almost dropping the basket she was carrying on her head.

Because of a slanting ray of sunlight, the old man saw nothing but her silhouette. 'Don't worry, little one,' he said. 'Just put the food down outside.'

She obeyed and hurried off. One more step, and Iker would have seen her. So he was not content with questioning the permanent priests and priestesses, but wanted to question every temporary worker as well. How was she going to avoid him?

Although Abydos intrigued Gergu, at the same time he loathed the place. It made him so uneasy and unsettled that he was on the verge of depression. He would gladly have settled for his post as principal inspector of granaries, his daily jar of strong beer, and the best prostitutes in Memphis, but Medes and the Herald demanded more of him. He couldn't help wondering whether all the risks he ran would really lead to success. But, though he longed to lead a less nerve-racking life, he could see no way out. He had no choice but to serve the Herald and to hope for the rapid downfall of the pharaoh and the coming of a new regime in which he would be one of the leading dignitaries.

He had brought to Abydos a consignment of goods for the permanent priests. The vessel berthed smoothly, and the commander of the guards greeted Gergu at the foot of the gangplank: 'Still fighting fit, I see.'

'I take care of myself, Commander.'

'I'm sorry, but orders oblige me to inspect your cargo.'

'By all means, but don't damage anything, will you? The permanent priests are very pernickety.'

'Don't worry: my men are experts.'

Gergu sipped some lukewarm beer while he waited; it was too sweet for his taste. As usual, nothing suspicious was discovered. As soon as the goods had been cleared, he headed for the place where he always met Bega.

Bega was ice-cold and grim-faced; he did not seem exactly delighted to see his accomplice again. 'What is the reason for this visit?'

'Just a routine delivery – it would look suspicious if we changed our routine, wouldn't it?'

Bega nodded. 'And why are you really here?'

'Medes hates not knowing everything, and he wants to know exactly what the Royal Son's instructions are.'

'Surely the secretary of the King's House is the person best placed to know that.'

'Normally, yes, but he says this time the official decree is very brief. You, on the other hand, undoubtedly have the information he wants.'

Bega reflected on this. 'I'm going to give you a new list of things to procure for us.'

'Are you refusing to tell me?'

'Let us go to the terrace of the Great God.'

'And start smuggling stelae again? That seems rather risky.'

The two men set off along a path bordered by offering-tables and shrines, whose number increased the closer one came to the Staircase of Osiris.

The little shrines, which were fronted by gardens, contained no mummified bodies. Instead they housed statues and stelae linking their righteous dedicators to the eternity of Osiris. The place was deserted and peaceful. From time to time, Bega burnt incense, 'that which makes divine'. The souls of the living stones used it in order to rise up to the heavens and commune with the Light.

Bega led the way to a shrine surrounded by willows whose low branches almost concealed the entrance.

We'll bring out one or two small stelae, thought Gergu, and sell them to the highest bidder. Another fine opportunity to get rich.

'Follow me,' commanded Bega.

'I'd rather stay outside.'

'Follow me.'

Reluctantly, Gergu obeyed. Even if the dead were not there, they seemed present. He was worried that disturbing their rest like this would provoke devastating anger.

At the back of the monument he saw a ghost! A very tall priest, with a shaven head and red eyes, was staring at him so intensely that he was rooted to the spot.

'No,' he gasped, 'it can't be! You're not . . .'

'Those who betray me do not live long, Gergu.'

The minuscule head of Set imprinted in Gergu's hand burnt so fiercely that he cried out in pain. 'You can trust me, my lord!'

'Your declarations are of no interest to me. All that matters is the results. Why are you here?'

'Medes is worried,' Gergu admitted immediately. 'He wants to know Iker's real objectives and he thinks Bega can tell him.'

'Do you think his concern is legitimate?'

Gergu's throat tightened, and he could scarcely swallow. 'That's for you to decide, my lord.'

'A good answer,' said Shab the Twisted's bitter voice.

Attacking from behind as he always did, he pricked the back of Gergu's neck with the point of his knife.

Shab had been a petty criminal with no future until he discovered the true faith through listening to the Herald's sermons. He hated all women and all Egyptians, and never hesitated to kill an unbeliever in order to please his master.

'Shall I execute this traitor, my lord?'

'I haven't betrayed you!' protested Gergu in panic.

'I grant him my pardon,' decreed the Herald.

The tip of the knife moved away, leaving a small, bloody mark.

'The time does not lend itself to the smuggling of stelae,' said the Herald. 'You will get very rich before long, my good Gergu, so long as you serve me unquestioningly. Bega, can you answer Medes's question?'

'The Royal Son has been called upon to play a major part in the celebration of the Mysteries of Osiris. By entrusting the Golden Palette to him, the king has granted him the ability to direct the brotherhoods of permanent and temporary priests. According to a reliable source, he is having a new statue of Osiris made and restoring the god's ship. It is up to him to acquire the goodwill of the craftsmen and to lead this work to a speedy conclusion. And there is another aspect to his mission: he has questioned each of the permanent priests and priestesses, because he suspects that one of them is in league with the Herald.'

Gergu started. 'Then we're lost!'

'Certainly not,' said Bega. 'On this point, the Royal Son has failed. His laborious investigations have yielded nothing that would enable him to make any specific accusations.'

'Unfortunately,' said the Herald, 'he is also interested in the temporary workers – he almost came face to face with Bina. And let us not forget his marriage to Isis, whose perspicacity might do us harm.'

'What is your plan?' asked Bega.

'To avoid doing anything hasty, and through you, my friend, to learn more about the secret places.'

Bega would have preferred to remain in the shadows and not be implicated in quite such a direct way.

'Do you disagree?' demanded the Herald.

'No indeed, my lord. But we must be extremely cautious,

and act only when we are certain the way is clear.'

'Our infiltration of Abydos has given us a decisive advantage. Several attacks will occur at the same time, and Senusret will not recover from them. When he accepts the final death of Osiris, his throne will crumble.'

The Herald's tranquil assurance reassured his followers.

He went on, 'Let us not forget our other goal: Memphis. What is happening there, Gergu?'

'My lord, we are facing a major danger: Sobek the Protector. I am afraid he may succeed in destroying our network. Killing him is vital, but how is it to be done?'

'Here is the solution to that problem.' The Herald displayed the acacia-wood box that had once contained the queen of turquoises, a jewel with strong magical powers. 'I am entrusting this to you, Gergu. Do not on any account open it. If you do, you will die.'

'What am I to do with it?'

'The box will leave Abydos by our usual route, and you will place it in Sobek's bedchamber.'

'That won't be easy, and—'

The Herald's eyes flamed. 'You are not permitted to fail, Gergu.'

6

Isis was playing a large, angular harp, whose melody rang out in the sweetness of the night. The instrument's twenty-one strings gave scope for many variations, and the young High Priestess used the two octaves with marvellous skill.

Iker let the music carry him away. This happiness would never fade, because he and his wife built and strengthened it day after day, well aware of the immense gift given to them by the gods; they strove constantly to perceive the extent of their good fortune. Sharing each other's thoughts and emotions, the lovers experienced the most intense communion.

Their earthly paradise was Isis' little house. Although the Shaven-headed One regarded it as unworthy of a Royal Son and the king's daughter, neither of them wished to live anywhere else. No doubt they would have to leave it sooner or later, but until then they wanted to enjoy the charm of the place where they had been united for the first time.

Iker loved the white walls, the front door with its limestone surround, the warm colours in which the interior was painted, and the simplicity of the furniture. Sometimes he wanted to believe that Isis and he were a couple like any other, leading a peaceful existence as ritual priest and priestess.

The gravity of the situation and the difficulty of his mission soon brought him back to reality. His results so far both reassured and worried him. To all appearances, there was no indication at all that the Herald had an accomplice inside the kingdom of Osiris, but that might be simply because Iker had been unable to flush him out.

A succession of chords, from high to low, ended the melody. Isis put down the harp and laid her head on Iker's shoulder.

'You look careworn,' she observed.

'I'm uneasy, because I'm certain I've been lied to. I should have seen, but I was blind.'

The young woman did not contradict her husband: she shared his unease. An evil wind was attacking Abydos, its negative waves troubling the serenity of daily life.

'Neither you nor the Shaven-headed One has found anything out of order in the rituals,' said Iker, 'and there are no incidents to report among the temporary workers. Yet I'm convinced that one of the enemy has slipped in among us. Should I begin my questioning again? No, that would be pointless. I must wait for him to act, and so place the Great Land in terrifying danger. I keep seeing the Island of the *Ka* again, and the great snake who was once master of the land of Punt, and I hear its warning: "I could not prevent the end of this world. Will you save yours?" Isis, I don't believe I'll be able to.'

'You aren't a castaway now, Iker, and the Isle of the Just won't disappear as the Island of the *Ka* did.'

'I've also been thinking about my old master, the scribe in my village, Madu, and about his final message, from beyond death: "Whatever ordeals may face you—"'

'"I shall always be by your side,"' cut in Isis, '"to help you accomplish a destiny of which you are as yet unaware."'

Iker stared at her in astonishment. 'The pharaoh . . . and now you . . . How do you know those words?'

'Many people develop according to the will of events, others answer the call of destiny, deciphering the real meaning of their lives. Their vocation is to live the Mystery

47

here below without betraying it and to pass on that which cannot be passed on. Your old master came from the Temple of Osiris. He identified those people and awoke them to themselves, through an apprenticeship in hieroglyphs.'

Overwhelmed, Iker saw that there had been no element of chance in the inexorable chain of his ordeals. 'Who killed him?'

'The Herald,' replied Isis. 'He was searching for you, too. By sacrificing you to the sea-god, he was strengthening his powers. Evil beings feed on their victims and are never sated.'

'My master, the pharaoh and you . . . you were all guiding me, protecting me!'

'You interpreted certain events wrongly, and wandered in the depths of the shadows, but you always sought the light again. So you fashioned yourself, creating a path for your feet.'

'Since I'm holding you in my arms, surely my destiny's been accomplished far beyond my hopes?'

'Our love remains the unshakeable plinth upon which you build yourself, and nothing can destroy it. But do you think you have passed through all the doorways of Abydos?'

Isis' smile disarmed him, and he said, 'Will you forgive me my self-importance?'

'When we no longer have a choice, we are free. We must still keep to the way of Ma'at.'

'Help me go further. The king opened up the house of eternity of the writers, at Saqqara, and I long to explore the library at Abydos.'

'It is not like any other.'

'Do you think I'm worthy to use it?'

'That is for the guardian of the threshold to decide. Do you feel able to face her?'

'If you guide me, what have I to fear?'

Iker followed his wife. No other woman moved with such

lightness and elegance. Barely touching the ground, she seemed to fly above the world of humans.

The high walls of the House of Life impressed Iker deeply. The entrance was very narrow, so as to admit only one person at a time.

'This is the place where the joyful word is devised, where one lives in righteousness, and where words are distinguished.'

From the offering-table before the entrance, Isis took a round loaf. 'Write the words "confederates of Set",' she ordered.

Using a fine brush, Iker drew the words in red ink.

'Now try to enter, and put aside your fear.'

Iker had barely crossed the threshold when he halted in his tracks, his blood turned to ice by a menacing growl. Looking up, he saw a she-panther, the incarnation of the goddess Mafdet, ready to pounce.

He held out the bread of the enemies of Osiris. The creature hesitated for a moment, then sank its teeth into the bread and vanished.

Now that the way was open, he set off along the passage-way and soon came to a vast hall lit by many smokeless oil-lamps. Carefully arranged in racks were hundred of rolls of papyrus, whose titles filled him with wonder. Almost intoxicated with excitement, he began with the great book revealing the secrets of the heavens, of the earth and of the world between, then consulted the book for preserving the sacred ship and the instructions for sculpture. A vision of unknown realities, paths to a completely new knowledge . . .

Iker had scarcely brushed the surface of these treasures when he came to himself with a start as Isis laid her hand on his shoulder,

'Dawn is about to break,' she said. 'We must go to the Tree of Life, for the Shaven-headed One wishes you to participate in the ritual.'

Calm and collected by the time they reached the sacred enclosure, Iker presented his wife and the priest with the vases containing water and milk. They poured the contents at the foot of the acacia, which was to all appearances in excellent health.

Isis handed the Royal Son a heavy silver mirror with a jasper handle decorated with the face of Hathor. 'Hold it so that the sun's rays are reflected on to the trunk of the acacia,' she said.

The ritual act was brief and intense.

'Last night and this morning,' said Isis, 'you passed through many stages. By accepting the touch of your hand, the goddess's mirror recognizes you as a servant of the Light.'

'That is not enough,' retorted the Shaven-headed One. 'This evening, I shall await you at Senusret's temple.'

As the three of them left the enclosure and walked away, the Herald watched them go. Thanks to Bega's intervention, and despite a delay due to administrative slowness, he had at last been transferred to Senusret's Temple of a Million Years, where he had been given charge of the vases and cups belonging to the gods and to the ritual priests. He was getting close to the nerve-centres of Abydos. Authorized to sleep in a building in the temple complex, the Herald had an excellent point of departure for destroying Osiris's protections one by one.

His predatory eye was quick to spot the four young acacias planted at the cardinal points round the Tree of Life. To his great surprise, no guard, priest or temporary worker was watching the area. So, he thought, its safety must be so assured that it does not require a human presence.

Going closer, he saw a relic-holder made of four lions, back to back. In the centre was a pole whose top was veiled and decorated with two ostrich feathers, the symbol of Ma'at.

He sat down in the scribe's position, which was conducive

to meditation. The Egyptians knew how to wield thought and adopt bodily positions favourable to its blossoming. By doing likewise, any outsider would have felt drawn towards the sacred. The Herald, though, was not subject to any influence. The sole and ultimate repository of the divine message, he turned the enemy's own weapons against him.

A strong protective force emanated from the symbolic arrangement of the lion relic-holder and the four acacias. The Herald must disable it, but that would require using exactly the right words, and he did not know them.

Where was he to find the vital clues? Where but in the temple? No doubt the texts dictated by Senusret would provide him with valuable information. Correctly equipped, he would then attack the Tree of Life.

The Herald returned to the shrine where he worked and received his superior's instructions. Not one to balk at hard work, he agreed to replace a sick colleague during the night – which would enable him to decipher the walls and search for the words of power.

When night had fallen, the Herald waited until he was alone to begin his exploration of the temple, armed with two alabaster vases. If he was taken by surprise, his explanation would be ready: he was cleaning the precious vases before placing them on an altar.

The spiritual intensity of this place angered him. Each hieroglyphic figure repelled him, each star painted on the ceiling gave off a hostile light. His suspicion proved right: having no trust in humans, the sages had charged symbols with the task of protecting the temple.

Any ordinary magician would have fled. Bruised and half-suffocated, the Herald extended his falcon's talons and beak. The magic of the signs slid over his predator's flesh without burning it.

Staying on his guard, the Herald scrutinized the scenes, studied the words of the gods and of the pharaoh. Offerings, more offerings, always offerings . . . And a perpetual, repeated communion between the otherworld and the king, who was thus promised millions of years and incessant festivals of regeneration.

The propagator of the new faith would shatter these promises. His paradise would welcome only warriors prepared to sacrifice themselves in order to impose their belief, be it at the cost of thousands of victims. The gods would leave Abydos and the land of Egypt for ever, giving way to a single, vengeful god whose will no one would contest.

But he still had to prevent Osiris from coming back to life and still had to bring about the death of the Tree of Life. Despite his keen sight, the Herald could not discern any tool that would enable him to pierce the magical defences. Patiently he persisted.

Halting before the huge statues representing the pharaoh as Osiris, arms crossed across his chest and holding two characteristic sceptres, the Herald smiled. Why had he not thought of it before? Everything here was inspired by Osiris; everything came from the god and returned to him. The key: he had found the key!

A hoarse voice startled him, and he slid hastily behind the half-open door of a nearby shrine. Looking cautiously out, he saw the Shaven-headed One and Iker enter the courtyard. If they spotted him, the outcome of the battle would be uncertain. Temporarily weakened by the hieroglyphs, the man-falcon did not possess his usual strength.

But the two men turned away from the shrine and gazed at one of the statues of Senusret-Osiris.

Although exhausted at the end of a particularly hard day's work, Iker had not been able to refuse the Shaven-headed One's invitation to visit Senusret's temple.

'The craftsmen were rather disagreeable today,' ventured the old priest.

'Indeed they were. However, they have almost completed their work. Did you by any chance advise them to do me harm?'

'There would be no point, for they know the Rule. You do not.'

'No, but I am eager to learn it and then practise it.'

'I hear that Memphis is a pleasant city where young people of your age enjoy a multitude of distractions. Don't you miss it?'

'Are you really hoping for a positive response?'

The Shaven-headed One muttered a vague insult. 'You cannot accomplish your mission without passing through a new doorway. The craftsmen know that and won't tolerate your being given preferential treatment.'

'I don't ask for it.'

'Look at this statue of Osiris. Who do you think created it?'

'The sculptors of Abydos, I assume.'

'Not all, Royal Son. Although all the craftsmen are highly skilled, few of them have been admitted to the House of Gold. That is where the secret work takes place that gives birth to the statue and transforms the raw material, wood, stone or metal, into a living work. The true creators, who have become Servants of God, are a very small group. They know the words of power, the magic incantations and the effective laws. So they fashion eternal materials which no fire can consume. Unless they accept you as one of them, you will have to leave Abydos.'

Since his offices would not spare him this ordeal, Iker did not protest. At the thought of discovering a new facet of Abydos, he began to burn with enthusiasm. 'Is the gold used in this house of eternity also that of the Circle?'

'During the celebration of the Mysteries, it alone enables Osiris to be resurrected. That is why, even when you did not know it, your life was dedicated to the search for it. When you brought the gold back to Abydos, you obliged yourself to continue on your path. Osiris revealed to the initiates the riches of the mountains and of the underground world; he showed them the hidden riches and taught them how to work metals. Be aware of an important reality: Osiris is the perfect accomplishment of gold.'*

Nefer n nub (Turin stele, 1640).

7

Gergu was in a hurry to leave Abydos. Armed with the list of supplies to be provided on his next trip, he was at the foot of the gangplank, about to board his boat, when a voice he knew only too well stopped him where he stood.

'Gergu! I didn't know you were here.'

He turned round. 'What a pleasure to see you again, Royal Son.'

'Were you going to leave without even speaking to me?'

'I didn't know you were here, either, my lord.'

'Have you had a pleasant stay?' asked Iker.

'Work, work and more work – Abydos is not known for its amusements.'

'Why don't you describe your work to me in detail? I might be able to suggest an easier way of doing things.'

'I'm afraid I must return to Memphis.'

'Is it an emergency?'

Gergu bit his lip. 'No, not exactly . . .'

'Then come and drink some beer at my house.'

'I wouldn't want to put you out, I—'

'It's getting dark: this is no time to begin a journey. You can leave tomorrow morning.'

Gergu dreaded having to answer Iker's questions – he might give himself away and put the whole network in danger. But running away would be an admission of guilt, so he had no choice but to follow Iker. Several temporary workers noticed this mark of the Royal Son's favour and immediately assumed Gergu was about to be promoted.

When they reached Iker's house, the cook had nearly finished preparing the meal: roast quail, lentils, lettuce and figs pounded to a paste. Although drawn by the appetizing smells, Gergu stared open-mouthed at Isis, who had just returned from the Lake of Life, where she had celebrated a rite with the permanent priestesses. How could a woman be so beautiful? When he was in power, he would make her his slave and she would have to satisfy his most twisted desires whenever he wanted. The Herald would assuredly approve of her humiliation.

'Is your friend dining with us?' asked Isis.

'Of course,' replied Iker.

Gergu smiled stupidly. Ravenous and thirsty, he behaved like a convivial guest, hoping that the conversation would not stray from banalities.

'Do you spend time with a lot of the temporary workers?' asked the Royal Son.

'No, only with a few. All I do is deliver the supplies to the permanent priests.'

'Are the orders given by different people?'

'No, they always come from Bega.'

'He's authoritarian and stern – he doesn't forgive mistakes.'

'That's why I don't make any,' said Gergu.

'Do you know any other permanent priests?'

'No, none at all. You know, Abydos frightens me a bit.'

'Then why do you go on coming here?'

Gergu choked. 'My office . . . the need to help. I mean – you know what I mean. I'm just a modest temporary worker, with no real responsibilities.'

'Have you by any chance noticed anything unusual or worrying lately?'

'Nothing, I assure you. After all, Osiris protects the place against curses, doesn't he?'

'Has Bega asked you to do anything unexpected or even shocking?'

'Never, absolutely never. For me, he's the embodiment of honesty. Now, I plan to leave at dawn, and I should like to get to sleep early. Thank you a thousand times . . . It was a delicious meal.'

As he walked back to his boat, Gergu realized that Isis had not said a word. But that didn't matter, because he had emerged unscathed from the trap.

At the end of a night filled with horrible dreams, Gergu was delighted to see the serving-woman coming with his milk and cakes.

Bina's vexed expression soon dispelled his cheerfulness. 'You ate at Iker's house last night,' she said accusingly. 'What did he want?'

'To renew our bonds of friendship.'

'He must have bombarded you with questions.'

'Don't worry, I fared extremely well. He isn't in the least suspicious.'

'What did he ask you and what did you tell him?'

Gergu gave her a brief report of the conversation, putting himself in a good light. He'd gladly have strangled this suspicious woman, but the Herald would never forgive him.

'Hurry back to Memphis and don't come here again unless our lord specifically orders you to.'

Bina prostrated herself and kissed the Herald's knees. 'The Royal Son suspects Gergu of being involved in something underhand,' she said. 'He doesn't yet know the nature of it or that it is connected to the central battle.'

'Excellent, my sweet.'

'Isn't Gergu becoming a danger to us?'

'On the contrary, he's luring our enemies towards Memphis, and so towards Medes. Neither of them is a true believer. All they want is more privileges, and they think they can use us to get them.'

Bina gave a predatory smile. 'And that mistake will cost them their lives.'

'Everything in its own time.'

She leant back and looked up at him. 'Iker knows there's a link between Gergu and Bega. If he orders the priest's arrest, won't we lose a key ally?'

'When it comes to deception, no one can match Bega – he'll be able to satisfy Iker. Anyway, the Royal Son won't live much longer.'

Bina pressed herself against her lord's thigh. 'You've foreseen every step, haven't you?'

'If I hadn't, I wouldn't be the Herald.'

Iker couldn't help thinking of Isis' judgment of Gergu.

Although he felt no great admiration for the man, the Royal Son regarded him as quite a friendly fellow, and one who enjoyed life. But all through the meal Isis had silently observed their guest, paying close attention to his words and gestures, and Iker's illusions were shattered by the judgment she delivered afterwards: 'Gergu is like a rotten fruit.'

Having complete faith in his wife's clear-sightedness, he reproached himself angrily for being too credulous. So Gergu was flattering him in order to insinuate himself into the good graces of the pharaoh's Royal Son and thereby rise in society. But did his tawdry, banal ambition conceal dark designs? Had the fat fool become a follower of the Herald?

The possibility astonished Iker, because Gergu's behaviour was always that of a lover of good food and wine, who paid no heed to matters of religion. Nevertheless, Gergu knew Bega, who was cold, stiff, narrow-minded in his learning – very different from him. Were their meetings merely circumstantial or a conspiracy?

Bega, the Herald's accomplice? Unthinkable! His ungracious manner and his ugliness in no way justified such an accusation. But Gergu did spend a lot of time with him . . .

In meditative mood, Iker headed for the Stairway of the Great God. The profound peace of the place might enable him to reach a definite opinion.

As soon as his instinct alerted him to danger, Shab stopped chewing his piece of dried fish. Pushing aside one of the low branches of the willow that masked the entrance to the shrine where he was hiding, the Twisted One spotted Iker.

How could that damned meddler have detected him? The scribe came slowly closer, and he seemed to be alone and unarmed. That was a fatal mistake, and a chance beyond Shab's wildest dreams. The Royal Son was taking a huge risk, and would pay dearly for his stupidity. Shab gripped the handle of his knife.

Iker sat down on a low wall about twenty paces from the shrine. Unfortunately, he was facing the Twisted One, and Shab never attacked from the front because that might give his victim time to react.

The scribe unrolled a papyrus and wrote a few lines, then pensively crossed them out. Clearly he was not looking for anyone. He seemed to be busy sorting out his ideas, trying to reach a decision.

Shab hesitated. If he took advantage of this unexpected situation and killed Iker, would it please the Herald? It was for him, not his follower, to choose the moment of the Royal Son's death. The Twisted One retreated to the back of his lair.

After he had finished thinking, Senusret's envoy went away.

In his final message, Iker's old master had spoken of a stranger who had come to Madu and had got on wonderfully well with the village headman, a corrupt fellow who wanted to get rid of the apprentice scribe. A stranger . . . It must have been the Herald! Both plotter and murderer, he was not only the leader of a band of fanatics but also the expression of evil, the implacable tendency to destruction that only Ma'at – at once the plinth of pharaonic civilization and the tiller of the righteous – could combat.

Now Iker could see the meaning of his life and the reason for the ordeals he had undergone: to fight with all his strength in this battle, and never to bend. Each day, he must begin again and look into the face of a world that was fragile, close to breaking-point.

By killing General Sepi, that great scholar of the magic spells that could drive monsters away, the Herald had shown the vast extent of his powers. Where did they come from if not from the opposite of Ma'at, *isefet*, which was constantly nourished by innumerable vehicles of decay and annihilation? It was impossible to eliminate *isefet* from the world of humans. Would the Great Land of Abydos remain sheltered from its devastating tide?

Isis' smile dispelled these sombre thoughts. Her love gave him unhoped-for power. Thanks to her, he felt no corrosive doubt or paralysing fear.

'It's time to prepare yourself for your next initiation,' she told him. 'You must know everything about Abydos.'

Iker shivered. Instead of filling him with joy, this declaration frightened him.

'Would you rather remain in ignorance?'

'Everything's moving so quickly! Before, I was on fire with impatience, but now I'd like to take time, a lot of time, and enjoy each stage.'

'The month of Khoiak is approaching, and you must conduct the ritual of the Mysteries of Osiris in the king's name.'

'Will I really be capable of it?'

'That will be the fulfilment of your mission. What does the rest matter? Come now. It is time.'

Once again, Isis was his guide as he trod the path towards the Mysteries. Her knowledge of the secret places of Abydos became Iker's as in his turn he explored the Ways of Fire, Water and Earth, passed through the seven doorways and saw the ship of Ma'at. During these blessed hours, they were truly one being: they gazed upon the same light with the same eyes and lived a single life.

Then Iker and Isis became husband and wife, brother and sister, for ever. Their pact was sealed in the most mysterious place in Abydos, the site of the Tomb of Osiris, which was surmounted by a great mound of earth planted with acacias.

Checked daily by the permanent priest charged with this duty, the seals held fast the door of the last and innermost shrine, where the murdered god was preparing for his resurrection. Only Pharaoh could break them and enter this house of eternity, the matrix of all others.

'This is where the primordial vase lies,' said Isis.* 'It contains the secret of undying life, beyond death. The innumerable forms of life come from it, so it remains with Osiris.'

'Is this the secret of the Golden Circle?'

'The goal of your journey is approaching, Iker. Although no human may either handle or open this vase, its mystery must nevertheless be revealed and passed on, while yet remaining intact. If the House of Gold recognizes you as a true Living One, if it opens your eyes, ears and mouth, if the vase of your heart is a pure, spotless receptacle, you will know.'

Fear was replaced by a feeling of unworthiness. He, the apprentice scribe from Madu, was attaining the centre of Egyptian spirituality, was benefiting from impossible

---

*The primordial vase was the *khetemet*, origin of the Grail.

happiness and realizing his ideal. Would he be able to climb the last step? Would he pass across this last threshold, which would probably exceed his abilities?

Iker swept away his anxieties, contemptible attempts at flight and turning back in the face of the destiny mapped out by Isis. It was here below and right now that he must live the Mystery whose source she had indicated to him. To show himself worthy of it implied launching himself into the invisible, like the ibis of Thoth with its immense wings, crossing the dusk to reach the light of the future dawn.

'Feeling ready means nothing,' he said. 'All I know is that I must go forward, and I will follow you to the end of the night.'

Strange glimmers pierced the dusk.

'The House of Gold is beginning to radiate light,' said Isis. 'It is waiting for you.'

8

Somebody was following Medes; he was certain of it.

Once his wife's sleeping-draught had taken effect, and his servants were also asleep, he had put on a coarse tunic and a hood which he pulled down over his face – no one would recognize the secretary of the King's House dressed like that – and slipped out of the house in the middle of the night. Despite the risk involved, he had to see the Phoenician and give him an up-to-date report. Medes was always wary when he visited his accomplice. He took a different route every time, he pretended to get lost, walked away from his destination just as he was about to reach it, retraced his steps and turned round at least a hundred times. Up to now nothing had gone wrong, but tonight he was being followed.

Given his carefulness and all the precautions he had taken, there was only one explanation: Sobek the Protector was having him constantly watched. Was it a special measure or something extended to all the leading figures at court? Since he had no way of knowing, Medes assumed the worst: he must have become the principal suspect, even though he had not made a single mistake.

This led to a worrying thought: Gergu must have been arrested in Abydos, and in his fear talked freely, betraying his master. There was one comforting thought: Gergu bore the mark of Set in the palm of his hand, and if he committed treason the Herald would kill him.

Medes sat down at the corner of a narrow street and pretended to go to sleep. Out of the corner of his eye, he saw the man following him walk past. He was a man of only medium height and quite slightly built. Medes could easily knock him down, but that might be seen as an admission of guilt.

Obliged to keep behaving like an ordinary passer-by, the guard walked away. As soon as he was out of sight, Medes rushed down the opposite street and ran as fast as his legs would carry him. Out of breath, he hid behind a bread oven and waited. Nobody appeared.

Warily, Medes walked in a large circle round the Phoenician's house before at last approaching it. He handed a piece of cedar-wood to the guard outside. Suspiciously, the guard held it up to the moon's light. Seeing the hieroglyph of the tree, deeply engraved, he opened the heavy wooden door.

The inner guard also checked the hieroglyph, then said, 'Go up to the first floor.'

Situated in the heart of a humble district, the Phoenician's expensive house was virtually invisible from the adjacent streets, and gave no clue to what it really was. Not even a close observer would suspect the riches contained within this squat, ordinary-looking building.

Medes ran up the stairs four at a time.

'Come in, my friend.' It was the Phoenician merchant's oily voice.

Over-perfumed and dressed in colourful robes, the trader was sprawled across equally colourful cushions and was guzzling cakes soaked in date wine. He had given up trying to follow diets that did not work, and simply went on getting fatter and fatter. He could never resist the delicious Egyptian food, which was the only thing that calmed him down when he was worried.

The robes hid a terrible scar across the Phoenician's chest.

Once, and once only, he had tried to lie to the Herald, and the man-falcon's talons had almost torn out his heart. Ever since then, the Phoenician had been his master's zealous servant. Talkative, charming and a peerless trader, he was sure he would be given an extremely important role when the new government of Egypt was formed.

The Herald's religion would demand numerous executions, followed by a pitiless purification process, which would be handled by the Phoenician. He was well used to moving in the shadows, and his ambition was to head a political guards force which no one would be able to escape.

'What is the current situation?' Medes asked aggressively.

'Because of the rigorous new checks, our trade with Phoenicia has been temporarily interrupted. Let us hope that this deplorable situation comes to an end as soon as possible.'

'I haven't come to talk about that.'

'That's a pity – I was hoping you might be able to intervene.'

'When will you order the killing to start?'

'When the Herald tells me to.'

'If he's still alive.'

The Phoenician poured red wine into two large cups. 'Calm down, my dear Medes, calm down. Why are you so anxious? Our lord is extremely well and continues to poison the heart of Abydos. Haste would be very damaging.'

'Do you know what Iker's real mission in Abydos is?'

'Won't Gergu tell you when he gets back?'

'I don't know if he'll ever come back.'

'Don't be pessimistic. It's true that, since the death of our best agent, communication between our groups in Memphis has been slow and difficult, but Sobek's investigators are getting nowhere, and not one fighter for the true faith has been caught.'

'I was followed,' said Medes. 'I'm sure he was one of Sobek's men.'

The Phoenician's expression darkened. 'Were you recognized?'

'Impossible.'

'Are you sure you threw him off the scent?'

'If I hadn't been, I wouldn't have come here; I'd have gone back home.'

'So Sobek's having you watched, and probably all the other courtiers, too. He trusts no one and is increasing his efforts. It's annoying, very annoying . . .'

'If we don't kill him, we'll fail.'

'He's a serious problem, I agree,' said the Phoenician, 'but it would be difficult to get to him. Must we sacrifice some of our people to bring him down?'

As head of the rebel network in Memphis, the Phoenician commanded a small army of shopkeepers, barbers and strolling traders, all well integrated into the Egyptian population. Some of them were married and had children, and all of them lived in perfect harmony with their neighbours.

'Sobek must die,' insisted Medes.

'I'll think about it.'

'Don't delay too long. That damned Protector may be getting closer more quickly than I realize.'

The Phoenician suddenly lost his jovial, carefree air, and the ferocity of his expression astonished Medes.

'No one will stand in my way,' he promised.

Sobek the Protector's wrath made the walls of his big office shake. There, every morning, he listened to the reports of his subordinates and of agents sent on special missions. It was one of those who was bearing the brunt of his commander's rage.

'Let us go back over this point by point,' demanded the Protector. 'At what time did the suspect leave Medes's house?'

'In the middle of the night, sir. The whole city was asleep.'

'What was he wearing?'

'A coarse tunic, and a hood pulled down over his face.'

'You didn't see his face at any time?'

'Unfortunately, no, sir.'

'From his pace, was he a young or an old man?'

'An energetic one, at any rate.'

'What route did he take?'

'It was incomprehensible. In my opinion, he was wandering.'

'He was trying to throw you off – and he succeeded.'

'When he sat down, I had to continue on my way. By the time I turned round, he'd disappeared. It was unavoidable, sir, I assure you.'

'Return to the barracks. You will sweep all the courtyards.'

Deeply relieved not to have been more severely punished, the man left.

When he had gone, Sobek sat in thought for a moment. Although the guard had failed, his report was an interesting one. By keeping a closer watch on as many notables as possible, Sobek had achieved his first results. He must inform Tjaty Khnum-Hotep at once.

After checking the budgets of several provinces with High Treasurer Senankh, Khnum-Hotep was planning to rest for a while. His legs and back were painful, and he no longer took his dogs for a walk himself, which saddened them deeply; he slept badly and had no appetite. The old tjaty could feel life trickling through his fingers, and all Dr Gua's care and remedies could not hold it back.

Each morning, he thanked Ma'at and the gods for granting him a wondrous life and uttered a final request: to die at work, not in his bed.

'Commander Sobek wishes to see you urgently,' his private secretary announced.

Rest was instantly forgotten. Sobek the Protector never disturbed him without good reason.

'Tjaty, you look exhausted,' said Sobek.

'Never mind that. What is the reason for this urgency?'

'There are two aspects to it: one instructive, the other . . . delicate.'

'Which would you rather begin with?'

'The delicate one. Conducting in-depth investigations, especially those involving prominent persons, sometimes implies crossing certain boundaries, and—'

'Come to the point,' interrupted the tjaty. 'Have you ordered that dignitaries are to be watched, without informing me and without official instructions?'

'That's a harsh way of putting it, but it's more or less right. In view of the quarry I'm hoping to flush out, I'd rather not have any problems.'

'Have you no regard at all for the proper way of doing things?'

'There was no better alternative. This way, he couldn't run away.'

'What is the name of this "quarry"?'

'I don't know yet.'

'If you want my support, don't play games.'

'This is the instructive aspect: the secretary of the King's House appears to be mixed up in shady dealings.'

'What kind of dealings?'

'In all honesty I don't know, but this is what happened,' and he gave Khnum-Hotep a detailed account.

'Yes, it's certainly strange,' agreed the tjaty, 'but it isn't enough to justify suspecting Medes of links with the rebels.'

'Perhaps not. But will you grant me permission to continue the investigation?'

'You'll continue with my permission or without it,' said the tjaty drily. 'Be very careful, Sobek. Accusing an innocent man would be an extremely serious matter. Medes would react forcefully, and he'd have your head.'

'I'll take that risk.'

*

From district to district, street to street and house to house, every day Sekari walked from one end of Memphis to the other, always ending up in a tavern where tongues grew loose. To gather as much information as possible, and perhaps even contact some of the Herald's sympathizers, he had become a water-seller, replacing a rebel who had recently been killed. North Wind carried the water-flasks, while Flesh-Eater watched over the merchandise. The modest trade paid well, as long as he didn't have too many naps. The difficult part was getting out of the grip of certain housewives, some bewitching, others insatiable gossips.

Alas, he had reaped a meagre harvest. If hearsay was to be believed, the rebels had left the city. Sekari did not believe it, and he persisted in his efforts. He was sure that, though shaken, the enemy had merely gone to ground and was keeping quiet, for the conquest of Egypt implied capturing Memphis. The great attack would begin here, where a band of fanatics and murderers would sow terror and desolation.

Every morning, he went to a different barber. His calm, cheerful manner attracted confidences, and conversation soon got under way. Grievances, plans, family stories, bawdy jokes . . . But not one slip, not one criticism of Senusret, not even a veiled comment in favour of the Herald. If there were still rebels among the barbers, they were superb actors.

The other strolling traders liked Sekari. They knew all the latest rumours, and to a man they praised the king, protector of the weak and guarantor of Ma'at. They were still deeply shaken by the murders the Herald's men had committed in Memphis, and hoped never to experience such a tragedy again.

Sekari visited the docks, where many foreigners worked. None of them hated the pharaoh; quite the contrary, in fact. Thanks to him, they had properly paid work, somewhere decent to live and could start a family. Some grumbled about the harshness of their employers, and one man said he missed his native Syria, though he did not want to leave Egypt. There was nothing there for Sekari, so he decided to try his luck in the north of the city, not far from the Temple of Neith.

His sandals were in a deplorable state, so on the way there he looked for a shop where he could buy some better ones at a reasonable price. Before long he spotted one; the shop-keeper was dozing in the sun outside.

Suddenly, North Wind stopped and Flesh-Eater growled menacingly. Sekari did not ignore their warnings, for he had good reason to know their worth.

'A suspicious shop?' he asked the donkey.

North Wind's right ear pricked up, indicating 'Yes'.

'A suspicious fellow?'

The ear remained vertical, Flesh-Eater bared his teeth, and Sekari regarded the sleeper in a quite different light.

'Turn back,' he ordered.

All at once, the atmosphere seemed heavy. If the shopkeeper belonged to the rebel network, his accomplices must surely be prowling around here. Fearing a trap, Sekari walked calmly away.

When a passer-by asked to buy some water, Sekari looked around, ready to defend himself, but the donkey and the dog were calm.

'This is a quiet district,' observed Sekari. 'You must like it here.'

'We can't complain,' agreed the customer.

'That sandal-seller . . . Has he lived here long?

'Yes, we've known him for a good long time. He's a helpful fellow – we could do with more like him.'

9

Iker had spent the night meditating before the House of Gold, which shone like the sun. Surrounded by a brightness which pushed back the darkness, he felt no tiredness. Hour after hour, he detached himself from his past, from events, from misfortunes and from happy times. All that remained was Isis, unchanging and radiant.

At dawn, the Shaven-headed One sat down in the scribe's position, facing the Royal Son. 'What must be known, Iker?'

'The shining of the Divine Light.'

'What does it teach you?'

'The words of transformation.'

'Where do they lead you?'

'To the gates of the world beyond and on to paths that the Great God walks.'

'What language does he speak?'

'That of the soul-birds.'

'Who hears his words?'

'The crew of the sacred ship.'

'Are you prepared?'

'I am not wearing anything metallic, and I am carrying the Golden Palette.'

'None may enter the House of Gold unless he becomes like the eastern sun, like Osiris. Do you wish to experience his fire, knowing that you risk being burnt?'

'I do.'

Two craftsmen undressed Iker and washed him thoroughly.

'No trace of unguent must remain,' said the Shaven-headed One. 'Be four times purified by Horus and Set.'

Two ritual priests wearing masks of the gods each picked up two vases. From their mouths emerged an energy whose glittering particles took on the shape of the *ankh*, the Key of Life.

'Be thus delivered from all that is bad within you and discover the way that leads to the source.'

The gods and craftsmen disappeared.

Left alone, the young man was not sure what to do. Doing nothing would probably be a fatal mistake, but so would acting at random. So he called upon Isis' help. Here as elsewhere, she would guide him.

Feeling her hand take his, he walked forward to a spinney of acacias, pushed aside the branches and climbed to the top of the small hillock that lay behind the trees.

'Gaze upon the mystery of "the first time",' commanded the Shaven-headed One's harsh voice, 'that is, this mound, which emerged from the primordial ocean. Here, creation takes place at every moment. To be initiated consists of perceiving this process and practising the transmutation of matter into spirit, and of spirit into matter. If you survive the ordeals, you will see the heavens upon earth. Before that, the sculptors will rough-hew you, for you are the raw mineral extracted from the entrails of the mountain.'

Three craftsmen hauled a wooden sledge to the foot of the mound.*

'I am the guardian of breath,' declared the first. 'The embalmer and the overseer assist me. Let us work the stone so that the journey may take place to the place where life is

*The rites described are those of the *tikenu*.

renewed.' He gripped Iker's chest. 'Let the old heart be torn out, and the old skin and hair burnt. May a new heart be formed, capable of accepting transformation. If not, the fire will consume the unworthiness.'

The Shaven-headed One covered the young man with a white cow-skin and made him lie down on the sledge, in a foetal position.

A long journey began.

Iker had the feeling that he had become a raw material, brought to the site where a temple would be built. One stone among others, he did not think of his location, but was only too happy to belong to the construction.

The Royal Son was now ageless. He had become an embryo, sheltered by this protective skin, and felt no fear.

The sledge halted.

The Shaven-headed One made Iker sit on his heels.

An immense papyrus was unrolled before him, covered in hieroglyphs arranged in columns. At the centre was a surprising depiction: Osiris, face-on, wearing the crown of resurrection, holding the 'Power' sceptre and the Key of Life. Around the Great God were circles of fire.

'This is the furnace of transformations. It contains death and life.'

Iker thought he was hallucinating, for General Sepi appeared, springing out of the text.

'Decipher these words and engrave them upon your new heart,' the general advised his pupil. 'He who knows them will shine in the heavens as Ra does, and the starry matrix will recognize him as an Osiris. Descend to the heart of the circles of fire; reach the burning isle.' His silhouette faded.

Iker's entire being, not only his memory, retained the words. He became a hieroglyph.

The papyrus was rolled up again and sealed.

Three hostile-looking craftsmen suddenly appeared: a sculptor, a rough-cutter and a polisher.

'Let those who must strike the father do their work,' ordered the Shaven-headed One.

Unable to defend himself, Iker saw a chisel, a mallet and a round stone raised.

'You shall sleep now,' announced the old priest. 'Let us pray to the ancestors that you will emerge from your sleep.'

After passing through the usual barricades and checks, Bina went to the temple complex, where she was given bread and fresh milk to be delivered to the permanent priests.

'Am I to begin with the Shaven-headed One?' she asked the temporary worker in charge of allocating tasks.

'No, he is not in his house,' he replied.

'Has he left Abydos?'

'Him? Never! Apparently he's busy initiating the Royal Son.'

Bina put on a look of astonishment. 'The Royal Son? Hasn't he already got all the powers he needs?'

'We're in Abydos, my little one. All that counts is the Rule of the Mysteries. Everyone submits to it, no matter how exalted he may be.'

'Very well, I shall take care of the other permanent priests. They are at home, I hope?'

'You'll soon see. No more chattering, now; don't waste time. Those old priests don't like waiting for their breakfast.'

Bina's last delivery was to Bega.

'What is happening to Iker?' she asked.

'The Shaven-headed One and the craftsmen are revealing the secrets of the House of Gold to him.'

'Do you know them?'

'I do not belong to the brotherhood of sculptors,' replied Bega dryly.

'Why is Iker being initiated by them?'

'Probably because it is vital to the success of his mission.'

Bina had to wait until late morning to meet the Herald, who

had been washing some of the large ceremonial vessels used during the purification of the altars.

'I'm worried, my lord,' she told him.

'About what?'

'Iker's being given new powers.'

'You mean his initiation into the House of Gold?'

'You know about it?'

'Since that damned scribe survived the wreck of the *Swift One* and the destruction of the Island of the *Ka*, he'll proceed to the end of his destiny.'

'Shouldn't he be killed straight away? Soon he'll be out of our reach.'

'Have no fear: he won't escape me. The higher he rises within the Mysteries, the more irreplaceable he becomes, the successor to Senusret. Eliminating insignificant people is of little interest. On the other hand, killing someone of such importance will break Senusret's back, for Iker is his weak spot. When the pharaoh sees the future of Egypt, which he has built so patiently, collapsing around him, he'll be distraught. And then he'll be vulnerable.'

The Shaven-headed One's hand touched Iker's brow, and Iker awoke.

'You were lying asleep. And now you have arrived at the port of transformations, safe and sound. The stone may be hauled to the site.'

Three craftsmen pulled the sledge.

It was neither night nor day, but a soft twilight. This new journey was a smooth one, like a happy return into a native land abandoned much too long ago.They came to the threshold of a closed door.

'Get up and sit on your heels,' ordered the Shaven-headed One.

Slowly, Iker managed to do so.

'Only Osiris sees and hears,' said the priest. 'However, the initiate participates in this sight and hearing, if his eye becomes that of the falcon of Horus and his ear that of the cow of Hathor. This eye acts and creates, this ear perceives the voices of all living beings, from the star to the stone. Such are the two doorways of knowledge. See into the depths of the darkness, hear the first words, cross the firmament and rise up towards the Great God. His sacred land absorbs the destructive, burning coals. Be clear-headed, cold and calm in the likeness of Osiris, go in peace towards the region of light where he lives for ever.'

The door of the House of Gold opened.

'Forge your path, Iker.'

The young man stood up, feeling an irresistible desire to walk forward. Very slowly, he crossed the threshold of the shrine.

'Now walk upon the waters.'

The silver floor seemed liquid, and his feet sank into it. Was he who walked upon his master's waters not acting as a perfect servant? Iker went further. The surface hardened. A silver radiance flashed from it, enveloping him.

'Be brought before the Great God,' declared the Shaven-headed One, tying round Iker's brow a band of fabric.* 'You now possess the symbol that can bring your gaze into the world, can extract the living from the darkness and can give you illumination.'

The touch of the fabric revived the astounding power of the crocodile, which had lived within Iker ever since he had dived down into the depths of a lake in Faiyum. The union of the band of fabric and this force unleashed a lightning-bolt of fearsome intensity.

Freed from the white cow-skin, Iker touched the heavens, brushed the belly of the stars and danced with the constellations.

When the dazzling light faded, he made out Sehotep,

*The *seshed*, mentioned in the Pyramid Texts.

Overseer of Pharaoh's Works and head of all craftsmen.

'Now you are the successor of Osiris,' he announced. 'It is up to you to venerate him and to continue his work.'

He dressed Iker in a robe decorated with five-pointed stars. 'With pure hands, you become a permanent priest of Abydos and a servant of the Great God. Discover the hidden work of the House of Gold. It brings to birth statues and transforms matter into a living work.'

'What are the names of Osiris?' asked the Shaven-headed One.

The words of knowledge passed through Iker's mind. 'The place of creation, the accomplishment of the ritual deed and the seat of the eye.* The source of life, he establishes Ma'at and reigns over those of just voice.'

'Build the new throne of Osiris.'

One by one, Iker lifted up the materials required: gold, silver, lapis-lazuli and carob-wood. They assembled themselves, forming a plinth on which Sehotep placed a statue of Osiris.

'Decorate the breast of the master of Abydos with lapis-lazuli, turquoise, and gold mixed with silver – all the elements that protect his body.'†

The Royal Son's hands did not tremble, and the pectoral placed Osiris beyond the reach of danger.

'As priest of the secrets, place the god's crown upon his head. Surrounded by ostrich feathers, covered with gold leaf, it pierces the heavens and mingles with the stars.'

Iker set the crown on the head of the statue. Then he placed in its hands the two sceptres, the farmer's flail, symbol of the threefold birth, and the shepherd's crook, used to gather the animals together.

*These are the principal interpretations of the word *Usir* (Osiris).
†These details are given on the stele of Iker-nofret, a major testament to his offices at Abydos.

'The first part of the Royal Son's mission has been accomplished,' said the Shaven-headed One. 'The new statue of Osiris will bring life to the next celebration of the Mysteries. But the Lady of Abydos has still to be awakened.'

Three lamps lit up a shrine housing the ancient ship of the Great God.

'Because of the curse, it does not move about freely any more, so it must be restored and brought back to life.'

Using gold, silver, lapis-lazuli, cedarwood, sandalwood and ebony, Iker built an innermost shrine, which he placed in the centre of the portable ship. The stars on the ceiling of the House of Gold sparkled, and all the areas of shadow gave way to light.

'Ra built the ship of Osiris,' said Sehotep. 'The Word builds the resurrection. Ra lights up the day, Osiris the night. Together, they make up the reunified soul. Osiris is the place whence the light springs forth, the essential material of the Mysteries.'

'The ship is moving again,' said the Shaven-headed One. 'The junction between the world beyond and the world below has been re-established. The spirits of the initiates may pass through the doorways of the heavens. The second part of the Royal Son's mission has come to an end. Thus he becomes worthy of directing the ritual of the Mysteries.' He embraced Iker.

For the first time, Iker felt the old priest's deep emotion.

10

Sobek the Protector received Medes in the first hour of the day.

Medes found it difficult to control his anger. He said, 'I demand a thorough investigation. Thieves came to my house and stole several valuable things.'

'I thought your house was well protected?'

'My doorkeeper was asleep, the imbecile! The thief was particularly skilful, and might come back again, so I've engaged two guards to watch my house day and night.'

'That's an excellent idea.'

'This thief must be caught, Sobek.'

'Without any clues, that won't be easy.'

'I have a clue.'

'Who gave it to you?'

'A servant who couldn't sleep. He was looking out over the garden and saw a man pass by. The man was of average height, athletic, and was dressed in a coarse tunic, with a hood over his head.'

'Did the servant catch a glimpse of his face?'

'I'm afraid not. But you must send some of your men out to search for him.'

'You can depend on it,' said Sobek.

Medes looked sombre. 'I have a feeling that this was no ordinary thief.'

Sobek frowned. 'What makes you say that?'

'It's only a theory, but it should perhaps be taken into consideration. The rebels want to kill Egypt's highest dignitaries, including the members of the King's House, don't they? This man could be an emissary, sent to survey the area in order to prepare for an attack. The theft was a deception.'

'I shall take that idea seriously,' nodded Sobek, 'because there have been other attempts at burglary at the homes of Sehotep and Senankh.'

Medes looked devastated. 'Then the rebel attack must be imminent.'

The Protector clenched his fists. 'The King's House will remain intact, I promise you.'

'You're our last defence, Sobek.'

'You may rely upon me to stand fast.'

When Medes had gone, the Protector remained alone for some time. Was he wrong to suspect Medes? Once again, Medes had proved his clear-headedness and his loyalty to the king. If his forebodings proved true, the rebel network was indeed preparing to strike.

Medes was having a nightmare in which he was pursued by ten Sobeks, each more ferocious than the last, when he was awakened by his wife's hysterical shrieks. Soaked with sweat, he burst into her bedchamber and slapped her.

'Call Doctor Gua quickly,' she begged, 'or I shall die – and you'll be responsible.'

Medes often thought of strangling his wife, but in the present circumstances he did not want to draw attention to himself. As soon as he ruled Egypt, he would get rid of this tiresome burden.

'Call Doctor Gua – quickly!' she repeated.

'I'll call him straight away. In the meantime, your serving-women can make you look presentable.'

Medes sent his steward to fetch the famous doctor. There was no point in offering him an enormous fee, because, despite his fame, Gua was incorruptible. He often put off examining someone of high rank in order to treat a humble person whose case seemed more urgent. No pressure could change his behaviour, and it was better not to get on the wrong side of him.

Although she was elegantly dressed, Medes's wife was still crying so much that her maid had to dress her hair all over again. The maid dared not make the slightest protest, or she would have been instantly dismissed and Medes's wife would have taken a sly revenge – all her staff were afraid of her malice.

To Medes's astonishment, Dr Gua arrived before lunch; as always he was carrying his leather bag of remedies and potions. Without even glancing around at the beautiful garden and house, he went straight to his patient's bed-chamber.

Medes was waiting for him outside the door. 'Thank you for coming so quickly, Doctor,' he said warmly. 'I think the doses ought to be doubled.'

'Who is the doctor, you or I?'

'I didn't mean—'

'Stand aside and let me enter. And make sure no one disturbs us.'

Gua asked himself two questions. First, Medes was a conscientious official, honest, jovial, open and of excellent reputation, but he suffered from a liver which did not correspond to that description. The liver was the seat of the character and did not lie; therefore Medes was pretending. Was it merely a politician's ploy, or did he have motives he could not admit? Second, what was the real cause of his wife's illness? Certainly she was self-centred, aggressive, twisted, excessively nervous – she had accumulated an impressive number of failings – but Gua's treatment ought to have improved her condition and stopped her attacks. His professional failure irritated him.

'Ah, Doctor, at last!' she cried. 'I thought I was going to die.'

'You seem very much alive to me – and still too fat.'

She blushed and put on a little girl's voice. 'Because of my anxieties, I haven't been able to resist pastries and food cooked in rich sauces. Forgive me, I beg you.'

'Lie down and give me your wrists. I'm going to listen to the channels of your heart.'

Relaxed at last, she smiled at him. Her simpering exasperated him, but he continued the examination.

'Nothing alarming,' he concluded. 'Proper drainage will maintain a good general condition.'

'And my nerves?'

'I no longer wish to treat them.'

She sat up with a start. 'You . . . you're not going to abandon me?'

'The remedies I've used ought to work but they don't, so a new diagnosis will have to be made in order to understand why not.'

'Well, I don't know . . .'

'You do know.'

'Doctor, I'm ill!'

'Something is obsessing you, something so intense and so profound that no treatment works. Search your conscience, relieve it and you will recover.'

'It's my nerves, just my nerves.'

'Certainly not.'

She gripped the doctor's arm. 'Don't abandon me, I beg you!'

He freed himself immediately. 'Renseneb the remedy-maker will prepare some very powerful pills, capable of calming the wildest hysteria. If they do not work, I shall be sure of my diagnosis. You are hiding deep within yourself a serious sin, it is gnawing away at you and leading you to madness. Confess and you will be freed.'

Retrieving his leather bag, Doctor Gua left Medes's house. A little girl with a respiratory problem awaited him.

'What did you talk about?' Medes asked his wife.

'My condition . . . I may not live much longer, my darling.'

Excellent news, thought her husband.

'Doctor Gua prescribes a shock treatment,' she went on anxiously.

'We must trust him.'

She clung to him. 'What a wonderful husband I have! I need perfumes, ointments and new dresses. And then we'll change cooks – and other servants, too. Those people bore me and don't do their work well – it's largely because of them that my health's getting worse.'

Although Medes's steward was grossly overpaid and devoted to his master, he sometimes suffered humiliations which were difficult to bear. A case in point was the insults being hurled at him by Gergu, who was completely drunk and demanding to see Medes immediately.

The steward went to inform Medes. 'I warn you, my lord, his breath is pestilential and his clothes stink.'

'Have him washed, perfumed and dressed in a clean tunic. Then he may join me under the pergola.'

When Gergu appeared he was still unsteady on his feet, but he was at least clean and presentable. He collapsed into a chair.

'You seem worn out,' said Medes.

'It was an interminable journey, and the stages were too much long—'

'You stopped to drink and you planned to disappear. But the sign of Set called you back to order, so you came back to Memphis.'

Gergu lowered his eyes.

'Let's forget this childishness and attend to what really matters: Iker's true intentions.'

'According to Bega, he must restore the ship of Osiris and create a new statue of the god. Once he's been initiated into the House of Gold, he'll probably become a permanent priest, conduct the ritual of the Mysteries and never leave Abydos again. It'll be a sort of golden, definitive exile.'

'What does the Herald think of this?'

'He is certain he'll succeed in the end.'

'So he will kill Iker and smash Abydos's defences.'

'Probably.'

'You display a singular lack of enthusiasm, Gergu. Have you committed some grave error?'

'No, don't worry.'

'Then the Herald must have entrusted you with a mission which frightens you.'

'Shouldn't we stop while we still can? One step further, and we'll fall.'

Medes filled a cup with a fruity white wine that lingered long in the mouth, and offered it to his henchman. 'This is the best medicine. It will bring you back to reality and give you back your confidence.'

Gergu drank greedily. 'Wonderful! At least ten years in the wine-jar, I'd say.'

'Twelve.'

'One cup isn't enough to do it justice.'

'You may have some more when you've given me the Herald's instructions.'

'Believe me, they're completely insane.'

'Let me be the judge of that.'

Knowing he couldn't escape Medes, Gergu told him. 'The Herald wants to kill Sobek.'

'How?'

'He gave me a box that I mustn't open under any circumstances.'

Medes's eyes narrowed. 'You have suppressed your curiosity, I hope?'

'The thing terrifies me! It contains a thousand and one deathly curses.'

'Where is it?'

'I brought it here, of course, wrapped up in a piece of coarse linen.'

'What were the Herald's orders?'

'To put it in Sobek's bedchamber.'

'Is that all?'

'It seems impossible to me.'

'Don't exaggerate,' snapped Medes.

'That damned snooper's under constant guard, isn't he? If he feels under threat, he surrounds himself with a few hand-picked men who can thwart any attacker, no matter who he is.'

'Show me this unexpected weapon.'

Gergu went and fetched the box.

Medes unwrapped it from the cloth. 'It's a real little work of art – the finest acacia-wood and made by an exceptionally gifted carpenter.'

'Don't touch it! It might strike us dead!'

'The Herald surely doesn't want that. His target is Sobek.'

'If I take it to Sobek he's bound to be suspicious.'

'I'm not asking you to take that risk, my friend. No one must suspect us of the Protector's killing. But can you imagine what things will be like once we're at last rid of him? He's been causing us problems far too long. I even fear he may be closing in on us, because he's having me followed and watched.'

Gergu blanched. 'Do you think you may be . . . arrested?'

'Sobek was probably thinking of it, but I managed to allay his suspicions and reassure him as to my loyalty. Nevertheless, he'll continue to have me watched.'

'While there is still time,' said Gergu earnestly, 'let's leave Egypt with as much wealth as we can carry.'

'Why should we lose our composure? All we have to do is obey the Herald to the letter and prepare our plan correctly.'

'Neither you nor I can take this box to Sobek,' insisted Gergu.

'Then someone else will have to do it.'

'I don't see who.'

Medes did not have to think for long. The solution seemed obvious.

'We have one ally whose opinion we needn't even ask for,' he said. 'I'm going to use my dear wife's one and only talent for a second time.'

11

Sekari had spent the whole night watching the comings and goings around the suspect sandal shop. At first he was disappointed. All he saw was a few passers-by, who were having more or less lively conversations, some drunken loiterers, dogs on the hunt for bitches in heat, cats out hunting – in short, the ordinary life of a workers' district.

However, his trained eye soon noted something unusual: hidden behind the plants in the corner of a terrace, a man was watching the square and the adjacent streets. This was no resident taking the air, but an alert lookout. At regular intervals, he made a hand signal to an accomplice, whom Sekari had great difficulty in spotting; and there would certainly be others. It was a clever arrangement – clearly, the people watching the area knew what they were doing.

Sekari realized he was in danger: one of the rebels might well have spotted him. Instead of trying to get away, he headed slowly for the centre of the square and joined a group of night-owls who were chatting there.

'A fine night, isn't it, lads?' he said. 'I'm not sleepy. Don't suppose you know any obliging girls around here?'

'You don't live here,' snapped one surly fellow.

'I know him,' cut in a man with curly hair. 'He's the new water-carrier – he sells at good prices. There are plenty of obliging girls, friend.'

Out of the corner of his eye, Sekari saw one of the lookouts moving about. The arrival of an intruder had obviously disturbed the place's usual calm.

'One good turn deserves another,' he said to Curly-Head. 'If you take me to a welcoming professional, you won't regret it.'

Curly-Head licked his lips greedily. 'How about a Syrian girl? Would that suit you?'

'Does she give you a good time?'

'I wouldn't know – I've just got betrothed! But the men who go with her say good things about her.'

'Then let's go.' Curly-Head set off along a dark, silent alleyway.

As Sekari fell into step he felt several pairs of eyes watching them, and he noted that Surly was following. But nothing happened, and eventually his guide stopped on the threshold of a pretty two-storey house.

'Is Surly coming with us?' asked Sekari.

'No, he's going home.'

'Oh, so he lives near here, does he?'

'Let's go upstairs, and I'll introduce you,' said Curly-Head. He closed the door carefully behind them.

There were no sensual perfumes, no decorations evoking the games of love, no welcoming room furnished with mats and cushions, no cups of beer for the new customer. The place hardly seemed designed for pleasure.

'You won't be disappointed, you'll see,' predicted Curly-Head, pausing at the foot of the stairs.

Sekari knocked him flying and rushed upwards. At the first landing a killer was waiting for him, armed with a club. Butting him in the stomach, Sekari knocked him down and raced up to the second floor, four steps at a time.

As he emerged on to the terrace a dagger-blade brushed his cheek. Sekari knocked his attacker out and looked quickly around. There was only one way to escape: to leap from roof to roof, at the risk of breaking his neck.

Down in the street Surly was giving the alert, and behind Sekari dark silhouettes were pouring out on to the terrace and converging on him. Sekari's speed and agility took his pursuers by surprise. The swiftest of them missed his jump and fell between two houses. Dismayed, the others stopped and drew back.

Curly-Head ordered his men to return to their lairs. Too much activity would attract attention from the city guards.

Sobek ate a grilled rib of beef, a salad, some fresh fruit, and drank a cup of wine as he studied the reports from his senior officers. The quiet of the night was conducive to thought, and enabled him to take a step back, separating the important from the less so.

There had been a new and perhaps decisive development: Sekari thought he had a serious lead but, prudently, was carrying out a final check. As soon as he returned and made his report, Sobek would take the necessary measures.

Someone knocked at the door.

'Enter.'

'Sorry to disturb you, sir,' apologized the guard. 'This box has been delivered to you, with a message marked "Urgent".'

Sobek broke the seal and unrolled a small papyrus of excellent quality.

'*Here is a storage chest for your confidential records, the work of one of our finest craftsmen. You will appreciate the excellent workmanship, as will the other officials to whom His Majesty is making this gift. Until the Great Council tomorrow,*
      Sehotep'

'It is indeed excellent workmanship,' agreed the Protector. 'That's all; you may go back to your post.'

When the man had gone, Sobek put the box down on his desk and lifted the lid. To his surprise the box was not empty. It contained six small terracotta figures resembling the 'Answerers',* who in the otherworld carried out various tasks in the place of those of just voice, notably irrigation, transport of the fertile Nile silt from east to west, and tilling the fields. But these 'Answerers' had some surprising peculiarities. Instead of holding hoes and adzes they were brandishing daggers, and their bearded, menacing faces did not look at all Egyptian.

'This isn't a gift from the pharaoh,' he said. 'It must be a malicious joke.'

As he picked up one of the statues to examine it, it plunged its dagger into his hand. Caught off guard, he let go of it. All six figures rushed at him together and struck him again and again.

Although he could not parry all the blows, Sobek thought he would certainly be able to defeat his miniature attackers, but the statuettes moved about so fast that he could not even damage them. Bleeding from dozens of wounds, he felt his strength ebbing away. Tirelessly, the dagger-points kept piercing his flesh, allowing him not an instant's respite. The attackers even seemed to smile at the thought of destroying their giant opponent.

Sobek slumped forward heavily over the box. In a frenzy of excitement, the figurines attacked his neck and his head. He was almost losing consciousness, but still managed to protect his eyes with his hands. Furious at dying like this, he howled like a wild beast, so loudly and desperately that the guard outside summoned up the courage to re-enter the office without permission.

'Sir,' he said nervously, 'is something the matt—*Sir!*'

The astounded man kicked the figurines hard as he tried to

*The *ushebtis* or *shauabtis.*

free Sobek, but they were unbreakable and returned immediately to the attack. In a desperate attempt to get the Protector out of this hell, he tried to drag him by the arm. As he did so, he bumped into a lamp and overturned it. The burning oil splashed over a statuette, which immediately burst into flames.

'Help!' shouted the guard.

Several of his fellows came rushing in, to be met by the incredible sight of their commander and the ferocious statuettes.

'Burn these horrors!' he roared.

His colleagues instantly did so, and flames began to swallow up the attackers. As they cracked, the terracotta figures emitted sounds like terrible moans.

Sobek was drenched in blood and no longer moving.

The guard dared not touch his commander's tortured body. 'Fetch Doctor Gua!' he ordered.

Once out of immediate danger, Sekari leant against the front wall of a house, closed his eyes and breathed deeply. He had had a very close brush with death. Never before had he encountered a gang like this – the speed of its reaction showed how well-organized and well-led it was.

No wonder Sobek's men had not been able to flush the rebels out. Deeply embedded in the district – and no doubt elsewhere, too – they worked, started families, forged friendships and were indistinguishable from the native Egyptians. Nobody regarded them as foreigners, and nobody suspected them.

He came to a worrying conclusion: the Herald was applying a plan which had been devised a long time ago. How many years had his killers lived in Memphis? Ten, twenty, perhaps even thirty. Forgotten, anonymous, they had become ordinary fellows liked by their neighbours. They awaited their master's orders, and never struck unless the outcome was certain.

No investigation would ever get anywhere, because some of the guards' informants were bound to be the Herald's men. They would lie, give reassurance and provide unimportant information, enabling minor criminals to be arrested, but never a fanatic.

Each of these districts was as secure as a fortress. Lookouts would spot anyone showing signs of curiosity, and would instantly alert the network. By behaving as he had, Sekari had shown himself to be no mere passer-by. The rebels now knew he was an enemy and would be determined to eliminate him.

What a fool I've been, he thought. They don't stir up the neighbourhood – they're too discreet for that – but they won't give up trying to kill me. There'll be no mob at my heels, just a murderer or two, quick and silent.

At that moment a rebel jumped from the first floor of the house and smashed Sekari to the ground. Knocked half unconscious, he reacted slowly and could not get free. The rebel wound a leather thong about his victim's neck and pulled with all his might. He was amused by the resulting death throes: larynx crushed, the Egyptian was suffocating to death.

A violent blow to the head made the assassin let go of the thong. At first, he did not understand what was happening; then he felt the fangs of a giant hound sinking into his skull and crushing it.

His work done, Flesh-Eater licked Sekari's hands as he fought for breath.

When he could speak again, Sekari croaked, 'You have a fine feeling for the right moment, my friend.' He stroked and patted his rescuer for a long time, and the hound's eyes shone with pleasure.

Although he was still unsteady on his feet, Sekari recovered rapidly. One thought tormented him: had the enemy sent out more than one killer?

'I must warn Sobek,' he said, and he and Flesh-Eater set off urgently.

They soon emerged from the maze of narrow streets into a broader street, and North Wind was waiting for them, carrying several water-flasks. Sekari took one and drank hastily; the cool water soothed the burning in his throat. Then the trio hurried on towards the palace.

As they neared it they saw an unusual amount of activity around the wing where Sobek had his office. There was smoke rising, and water-carriers were rushing into the building.

'What's happening?' Sekari asked one of the duty guards.

'A fire broke out. Go on home – we're dealing with it.'

'Is Commander Sobek safe and well?'

'What's that to do with you, friend?'

Given the urgency of the situation, Sekari realized he would have to break his rule of absolute secrecy. 'I have an important message for him.'

The guarded took a close look at him. 'That's odd, that mark on your neck . . . Have you been attacked?'

'It's nothing serious.'

'I need more details.'

'I'll give them to Sobek.'

'Don't move a muscle, do you hear?' and the guard raised his club.

Immediately, North Wind and Flesh-Eater confronted him. The donkey pawed the ground and the hound growled menacingly.

'It's all right, my friends,' said Sekari quickly. 'He means me no harm.'

Prudently, the guard drew back. 'Keep those two monsters under control.'

Several other guards came to his aid.

'Is there a problem?' asked their officer.

'I'd like to see Commander Sobek,' Sekari said humbly.

'What about?'

'That's personal and confidential.'

The officer hesitated. He could either throw this peculiar character into prison or take him to one of the Protector's bodyguards, who would check his identity and decide whether to let him see the commander. After a long moment's hesitation, he chose the second course of action.

The bodyguard recognized Sekari, and drew him discreetly aside.

'You must warn Sobek immediately,' said Sekari. 'We must take over a district to the north of the Temple of Neith.'

'Why? What's happened?'

'That area is home to a whole nest of rebels.'

His voice cracking, the officer said, 'Sobek can no longer give orders.'

'Administrative problems?'

'If only that's all it were!'

'You don't mean . . . ?'

'Follow me.'

In a room near his office Sobek was lying on a mat, his head resting on a soft cushion. Dr Gua was cleaning his innumerable wounds.

Sekari went over to them. 'Is he alive, Doctor?'

'Barely. I've never seen a man with so many wounds.'

'Can you save him?'

'At this stage, that is for destiny to decide.'

Sekari turned back to the officer. 'Do you know who attacked him?'

The officer summoned the man who'd been on guard. In halting sentences, he described the horrible spectacle he'd witnessed.

The officer showed Sekari a small papyrus, splattered with blood. 'We know who the criminal is. He made the statuettes, sent the chest, and even signed his name here.'

12

Knowing all about Senusret's Temple of a Million Years, the Herald did not judge it necessary to destroy texts, sully ritual objects or cast spells on statues. This whole unceasing ritual process served solely to maintain the pharaoh's *ka* and to produce an energy reserved for Abydos. To reduce it would produce insignificant results. What must be done now was to strike the enemy down.

He performed his morning duties as meticulously as usual, then handed over to the other temporary priests who tended the shrine, and set off as if for home. Having checked that nobody was watching him, he changed direction and made for the Tree of Life.

There was not a single guard or priest there. Following the dawn ceremony, the Acacia of Osiris was alone, bathed in sunshine. The protective barrier produced by the four young trees was enough to protect it.

From the pocket of his tunic, the Herald took four phials of poison. During the nights he had spent at the temple, he had entered the workshop and, taking care to leave no traces, had made up a mixture that would be deadly after a while. The trees would look in good health, but would dry out from the inside and cease to function. By the time the Shaven-headed One noticed, it would be too late.

First, the east. The Herald poured the colourless, odourless poison at the foot of the young acacia tree. 'May the reborn light no longer warm you. May it wound you, like the frozen winter wind.'

Next, the west and the second phial. 'May the glimmers of the setting sun inflict a bad death upon you and envelop you in darkness.'

Then the south and the third phial. 'May the sun's noontime rays burn you and destroy your sap.'

Finally, the north and the fourth phial. 'This is the cold of nothingness. May it burden and eat away at you.'

The very next day, the Herald would be able to see the effects of the poison. If it was as effective as he hoped, the protective barrier would disappear.

And then he would attack the four lions.

Iker was reliving every moment of the ritual of initiation into the House of Gold, whose sheer scale still dazed him. How could a mere man perceive so many dimensions and grasp all the many meanings of all the symbols? Perhaps by not dissecting or seeking to analyse, but by developing an intelligence of the heart and by entering vigorously into the heart of the Mystery.

The universe could not be explained. And yet it had a meaning, an eternal meaning, ceaselessly springing forth from itself and leading beyond the limits of the human race. Born of the stars, life that had been made aware returned there, thanks to initiation. And he, the apprentice scribe from Madu, had passed through a doorway opening on to fabulous landscapes.

Isis had risen very early and was celebrating a ritual with the servants of Hathor. Since leaving the House of Gold, where the statue and ship of Osiris were being charged with energy, she had not said a word. She had herself faced ordeals like Iker's, and knew the importance of contemplation after an experience of such intensity. Scattered forces gathered within the initiate, presiding over the birth of a new vision.

Iker was progressively coming back to earth, but had forgotten nothing of his voyage beyond time and space. Emerging from their small white house, he gazed for a long time at the sky. He knew he would never again look at it as he had before his initiation. From this matrix came works steeped in immortality, made visible by the craftsmen.

Unfortunately other realities existed, and they were far less worthy of enthusiasm. It was up to the Royal Son, Friend of the King and pharaoh's envoy, to confront them.

'The milk is foul-tasting and the bread is dry,' declared Bega. 'Pay more attention to the quality of the food you deliver to the permanent priests. If one of them complains, you will be dismissed.'

Bina bridled. 'Are you the one who decides whether the food tastes good?'

'Everyone here respects my judgment.'

'Perhaps that's why Abydos is decaying!'

'Don't overstep the limit, girl. Just do your work properly.'

Bega hated women. Frivolous, insolent, manipulative, perverse, they had a thousand incurable faults. As soon as he rose to supreme power, he would drive them out of Abydos and forbid them to take part in any of the rites and cults. No more priestesses would sully the temples of Egypt, which would be reserved for men, who alone were worthy to address the gods and to gather in their favours. The Herald's doctrine was an excellent one: keeping women away from all religious office, excluding them from the schools, covering their bodies entirely so that they no longer tempted the opposite sex, and confining them inside the family home, in the service of their husbands. Pharaonic civilization permitted them so many freedoms that they behaved like independent beings – they could even reign!

Bina fixed the priest with a sarcastic glare. 'Are you going to eat and drink, or shall I take the bread and milk away?'

'They'll do this time, but tomorrow they must be better and—Go, quickly! Iker's coming!'

In the twinkling of an eye, she made good her escape.

Bega concentrated hard on his food.

'Forgive me for disturbing you so early in the morning,' said Iker.

'We are all at the disposal of the Royal Son. Have you eaten?'

'Not yet.'

'Then will you not share my meal?'

'Thank you but I'm not hungry.'

'But you must keep your strength up.'

'Don't worry, ordeals make me healthier.'

'Congratulations on your initiation into the House of Gold. Such a privilege is rarely granted, and it confers immense responsibilities upon you. We shall be proud to see you conducting the rites of the month of Khoiak.'

'The date seems very close, and I feel utterly incompetent!'

'All the permanent priests, beginning with me, will help you to prepare for this great event. Have no fear, you will master the situation. Is your mission going any better?'

'The House of Gold is bringing into the world a new statue and ship of Osiris, and I hope that all is now well within the priesthood. My investigation shocked you and your colleagues, I know, but it was vital.'

'It's all over and forgotten,' Bega assured him. 'We appreciate your discretion and the fact that you were free from all arrogance. You had to make sure that the permanent priests were deeply and sincerely devoted to the rites of Osiris. As the spiritual centre of Egypt, Abydos must remain spotless, so of course it necessary to check regularly that all is well. His Majesty proved his clear thinking by instigating this examination and by choosing a man capable of conducting it properly.'

Bega seldom expressed satisfaction or paid compliments. Even now his manner was still cold, and his voice still a hoarse rasp, but his words comforted Iker, for his judgment was an echo of all the permanent priests', manifesting their approval and easing the tension.

Bega went on, 'When we learnt that the Golden Palette had been entrusted to someone so young and so unfamiliar with our rites and our Mysteries, we were very surprised – in fact, I've seldom seen the Shaven-headed One so disturbed. But we were too closed in upon ourselves and made the mistake of underestimating the scope of Senusret's vision. That was contemptible vanity, and inexcusable: our age and experience had made us less aware. Each day the work of God is accomplished, and our duty is humbly to prolong it, forgetting our own ridiculous ambitions. Your coming, Iker, has taught us a valuable lesson. There was no better way to revive our vigilance and remind us firmly of the demands of our offices. If a pharaoh distances himself from Abydos, Egypt is at risk of death; if he comes closer, the ancestors' inheritance dispenses countless benefits and the Two Lands know prosperity. Senusret's choices are exemplary, his reputation and his popularity well deserved. You and we are fortunate to serve an exceptional king, whose decisions illuminate our path.'

Iker would never have expected such confidences from the austere, deeply reserved Bega, and he appreciated his sincerity, which bore testimony to the priest's irreversible commitment to Abydos.

However, he did not omit to ask the questions that had haunted him since Isis' declaration that 'Gergu is like a rotten fruit.'

He said, 'The permanent priests don't often leave Abydos, I understand.'

'Almost never. That isn't because the Rule imposes a reclusive life upon us, merely because to us the outside world has little to offer. We have chosen our way of life freely, love the domain of Osiris, and are in contact with the very essence of life. What more could anyone wish for?'

'Then perhaps you can explain something that's been puzzling me: how did you come to meet Gergu?'

Bega stiffened. 'By chance. I supervise the ordering and distribution of food and other necessities for the permanent priests. Gergu was appointed to deliver the things I order, and I wanted to test his skills.'

'Who sent him to Abydos?'

'I don't know.'

'Didn't you ask him?'

'I am not by nature curious. He had passed all the checks, so why should I need to know more? All I demand is that everything I order is delivered punctually, and Gergu hasn't disappointed me so far.'

'Does he ever ask . . . inappropriate questions?'

'If he did, I'd have him expelled from Abydos. No, he confines himself to receiving my lists and delivering the supplies as quickly as possible.'

'Does he always bring them himself?'

'He's very conscientious – he never lets anyone else check the consignments or bring them here. In fact, because of his good and loyal service, he's been appointed a temporary priest. His manner is somewhat uncouth, I grant you, but that doesn't prevent him from admiring Abydos and valuing his office.' Bega rubbed his jaw. 'But why all these questions? Do you suspect Gergu of having done something wrong?'

'I've no proof that he has.'

'But you're suspicious of him nevertheless?'

'Shouldn't his post as principal inspector of granaries take up all his time?'

'Senior officials often come here from Memphis, Thebes or even Elephantine – in view of Abydos's importance, distance is of no consequence. Some stay for only a week or two, others for longer. None of them would give up his post here, no matter how modest. Gergu is one of that community of faithful, dedicated temporary workers.'

'Thank you for your help, Bega.'

'You lead us now. Don't hesitate to ask if you need my help again.'

As he watched the Royal Son walk away, Bega nervously chewed a piece of bread. He regretted having defended Gergu, but criticizing or accusing him would have prompted a detailed investigation, which would inevitably have led back to him, Bega.

Would his declarations convince Iker of Gergu's innocence? Probably not.

Iker was becoming very dangerous. Now invested with considerable powers, and recognized as worthy of the Mysteries of Osiris, he had acquired an unexpected dimension. In believing that Abydos would reject him, Bega had been badly mistaken. A strange light burnt within the young man, and the rites of Osiris were feeding it.

For a moment, a brief moment, Bega wondered if it might not be better to renounce the conspiracy and betrayal, become a real permanent priest again and return to the way of the Rule. Angrily, he rubbed his eyes. Iker's purity, idealism and respect for traditional values were leading him to a dead end. The Herald alone represented the future.

Besides, Bega had gone too far to turn back now: he had denied his past and his oath, and was committed to the conspiracy of evil. This choice had liberated impulses which had long been contained, the desire to gain wealth and the will for power. People like Iker must disappear. The Herald must act swiftly.

The sunset rituals had been carried out, and the lamps were being lit in the houses of the permanent priests and of those temporary workers permitted to sleep in Abydos. After the evening meal, the star-watchers would climb up to the roof of Senusret's temple, note the position of the stars and try to decipher the message being sent by the goddess Nut.

Shab the Twisted met his master near the Stairway of the Great God, out of sight of the soldiers who patrolled in the desert outside the site.

The Herald asked, 'Have you tried to get near the tomb of Osiris?'

'There's no apparent protection,' replied the Twisted One, 'just an old priest who checks the seals and speaks the ritual words.'

'No guards?'

'None at all. I did as you told me and kept at least thirty paces away from the door of the tomb. There must be some kind of invisible protection – a monument of that importance can't possibly be so easily accessible.'

'The sacred nature of the place and the radiance of Osiris are enough to deter the curious,' replied the Herald. 'They're afraid of arousing the god's anger.'

'But have the priests set up a magical barrier?'

'If they have it won't stop me, my friend. Little by little I'm breaking down the walls of Abydos.'

'Must I go on hiding in that shrine, my lord?'

'Not for very much longer.'

The Twisted One gave an evil smile. 'Am I to have the privilege of killing Iker?'

The Herald's eyes became fiery red, and a furnace-like heat began to emanate from his body. Shab recoiled in fear.

'My figurines are emerging from the chest,' said the Herald in a menacing voice. 'By opening it, Sobek the Protector has made his last mistake. This evening we shall be rid of him and our Memphis network can launch its attack.'

13

Senusret rejoiced at the happy outcome of Iker's initiation into the House of Gold. According to the Shaven-headed One, the young man had behaved in a remarkable manner and accomplished his mission with care and skill. Without knowing it, he had passed through the first doorway of the Golden Circle of Abydos and was therefore, little by little, becoming an Osiris. Soon, as he conducted the vital rituals during the month of Khoiak, he would also become its centre, and would quite consciously enter the heart of Egypt's most secret brotherhood.

Thus Iker was building himself like the Stone of Light, from which every pyramid, temple and house of eternity was born. On this stone Pharaoh strengthened his kingdom, not for his own glory but for that of Osiris. For as long as the Two Lands carried on his work, death would not kill the living.

There was a persistent rumour that Senusret would soon appoint Iker co-regent and link him to the throne, so as to prepare him to reign. But the king's vision, though not excluding this eventuality, went beyond it. Following the example of his predecessors, he must pass on the *ka* of Osiris to someone worthy of receiving it, preserving it, making it grow, then passing it on in his turn. As the creator of the god's ship and statue, Iker would play this essential role. By attaining knowledge of the Mysteries, he would celebrate them. In his very exceptional case, there was no difference between contemplation and action, discovery and implementation. The succession of hours would be abolished, and the Royal Son would experience Osiris's time, which was at the origin of the supernatural duration of the symbols, steeped in matter and spirit. He would join Isis beyond the Way of Fire and would see the interior of the Tree of Life.

The Herald's threats meant that the young couple's role was of prime importance. To his fanatical doctrine and his will to impose his sinister beliefs, Isis and Iker would oppose a joyous spirituality, free from dogma, made up of incessant transformations and reformations, nourished by a creative light.

But victory was not yet won.

Senusret did not believe the Herald was dead. Like a sand-viper, he was merely hiding and preparing to strike. Had he understood Iker's real importance, or was he bent solely on fighting the pharaoh by killing more people in Memphis? Despite a few successes, Sobek the Protector feared the rebel network's capacity to do harm, for it was so deeply embedded that even Sekari had difficulty in finding the right leads.

In the middle of the night, General Nesmontu interrupted the king's thoughts. 'I bring very bad news, Majesty. Sobek has been the victim of a murderous attack. Magical figurines transported in a chest delivered to him inflicted an incredible number of wounds upon him – the only thing that defeated them was fire. Doctor Gua is trying to save him, but the outlook is not encouraging. And our misfortunes do not end there. When he was called, the doctor was at the bedside of the tjaty, who is seriously ill. According to Gua, Khnum-Hotep is at the end of his strength.'

'We must take immediate action,' urged Sekari. 'If we wait too long, the rebels will escape.'

The handpicked men who guarded Sobek were distraught.

'Only the Protector can take a decision like that,' his second-in-command declared.

'Face reality! Sobek's on his deathbed. He knew the details of my investigations and was awaiting my report. It can be expressed in three words: we must act. The Protector would have used any and all means – you can be sure of that.'

The shattered officer seemed unable to react properly. 'Only Sobek knew how to coordinate all our forces and mount an operation of that size. Without him, we're at a loss. He didn't delegate anything; he studied every case in detail and then acted accordingly. By killing him, the enemy has immobilized us. We'll never find another leader of his calibre.'

'We won't have an opportunity as good as this for a long time,' said Sekari. 'I insist: give me all the well-trained men you have. There's still a slight chance of destroying at least one branch of the Herald's network.'

Doctor Gua emerged from Sobek's office. 'Go and fetch me a jar of ox's blood.'

'Is he . . . Do you mean he's still alive?' asked Sobek's deputy.

'Hurry!'

Two soldiers dashed off, awoke the master-butcher from Senusret's temple and waited while he sacrificed two fat oxen. They hurried back with the precious blood, which Dr Gua poured into the wounded man a little at a time.

'Can you save him?' asked Sekari.

'Medicine cannot perform miracles, and I am not Pharaoh.'

At that moment the king appeared on the scene. 'I can help you,' he declared.

Immediately he magnetized the Protector for a long time, thus repelling death's talons.

The injured man stirred and slowly regained consciousness. 'Majesty . . .'

'Your work is not yet done, Sobek. Allow yourself to be treated, sleep and recover.'

Dr Gua could not believe his eyes. Without the king's intervention, the Protector would have died, despite his great strength. Magnetism and ox blood had already given him a little colour back.

'Tell Renseneb to send me his best fortifying remedies,' commanded the doctor.

The king and Sekari withdrew.

'Sobek's men are in disarray, Majesty,' said Sekari, 'so I need General Nesmontu's help to surround an area of the city where rebels are hiding.'

'Go to him and act as guide for his soldiers.'

Sobek's deputy came up to them and bowed deeply. 'Majesty, we know who was responsible for the attack.'

'Was it not the Herald?'

'No, Majesty.'

'How can you be certain?'

'The crime bears a signature.'

'What do you mean?'

'There is a signature on this papyrus, which is written in the hand of the assassin who sent the chest to Sobek, pretending to be acting on your behalf.'

Senusret read the document. It pointed directly to Sehotep.

Rejuvenated at the thought of arresting rebel fighters, Nesmontu directed the operation energetically. He himself awoke his soldiers in the principal barracks at Memphis, and took command of the operation, deploying them in accordance with Sekari's advice.

It was the middle of the night, and the squares and narrow streets were deserted.

'We must be on the alert for ambushes,' Sekari warned the general.

'These criminals won't trick me the way I tricked them at

Sichem,' promised Nesmontu. 'First we'll surround the area, then small groups of footsoldiers will search each house. Archers positioned on the rooftops will cover them.'

The general's orders were carried out quickly and efficiently.

The district began to come to life. There were loud cries of protest and children cried, but there was no fighting and nobody tried to run away.

Accompanied by ten footsoldiers, Sekari searched the house where he had so nearly been killed. All they found was leftover food, used lamps, old mats . . . The place had clearly been abandoned in haste, but not a single thing of significance had been left behind.

However, there was still the suspect sandal-seller's shop.

Along with his wife and frightened young son, the shop-keeper protested his innocence.

'Search the place,' ordered Nesmontu.

'On whose orders?' demanded the suspect.

'It's a matter of state.'

'I shall complain to the tjaty. In Egypt, people aren't treated like this. You must respect the law.'

Nesmontu looked the man squarely in the eyes. 'I am the supreme commander of the Egyptian army, and I am not here to be taught a lesson by an accomplice of the Herald.'

'An accomplice of the Herald? I don't understand.'

'Would you like an explanation?'

'I demand one.'

'We suspect you of being a rebel and of wishing to murder Egyptians.'

'You . . . you're talking rubbish!'

'Show some respect, my lad. Experts will deal with you while I search your shop from top to bottom.'

Despite his vociferous protests, soldiers dragged the man away.

Sekari joined in the search, looking eagerly for proof of the shopkeeper's guilt. He turned up average-quality leather, dozens of pairs of sandals, accounting papyri and numerous items needed in the daily life of a family . . .

'We shan't find anything here,' he said gloomily.

'There may be caches of weapons,' suggested Nesmontu.

'The Herald's people had time to move them.'

'Then we'll question every single inhabitant of the district, and they'll talk, believe me!'

'No, General. If there are any rebels still here, they've let themselves be caught. They're well trained, and they'll either say nothing or else lie.'

The old general did not argue the point. Nevertheless, he continued with the operation until the whole area had been searched. The result was a dismal failure. They found no trace of Surly or Curly-Head, and they had not only to release the sandal-seller but to make a formal apology to him.

At the end of the dawn rite, Senusret summoned Dr Gua.

'Sobek will recover,' predicted the doctor. 'My medicine would suit a wild bull – and fortunately he has the constitution of one! The only problem will be making him stay in bed until the deep wounds have scarred over. None of his vital organs was seriously damaged, so he will recover all his strength and vigour.'

'And what of Khnum-Hotep?'

The doctor did not try to hide the truth. 'There is no hope for him, Majesty. Because of overwork, the tjaty's heart will soon simply stop beating. My treatment now has only one aim: to prevent him suffering.'

'His care is to take priority over everything else,' ordered Senusret.

The next person the king saw was General Nesmontu, who gave him an unvarnished account of the previous night's operation. The guards would have to investigate the past of every single person who had been questioned, and check what he or she had said. It would be a long, painstaking task, and there was no telling what the outcome would be. The rebels were so well mingled with the population that they had become virtually invisible.

'Sobek's deputy is demanding that Sehotep be arrested,' said the king.

'Neither I nor Sekari believe he is guilty, Majesty,' protested the general. 'No member of the Golden Circle of Abydos could so much as think of killing the Protector.'

'We have a document incriminating him.'

'It's a forgery – someone is again trying to discredit the King's House.'

'The Great Council will not meet this morning,' decided Senusret. 'I must hear what Sehotep has to say.'

'He won't give his name, sir,' said the general's assistant, 'but he claims he has serious and urgent information.'

'Deal with it,' said Nesmontu.

'He won't talk to anyone but you, sir. Apparently, it concerns the pharaoh's safety.'

If the man was a timewaster, he would soon find himself in court, charged with insulting the army and propagating false information.

The man was aged about thirty, tall, with a scar running across his left forearm. He seemed level-headed and anxious. He spoke in measured tones. 'I'm an officer in Commander Sobek's guards, General,' he explained. 'On the commander's orders, I infiltrated the secretariat of the King's House in order to keep watch on Medes and his staff.'

Nesmontu gave a sort of grunt. 'The Protector really doesn't trust anyone! Has he got watchers in every government secretariat?'

'I don't know, General. At the first sign of anything untoward I was to inform Sobek immediately. Now something has happened, and since Sobek cannot see me I thought I ought to inform you.'

'You thought right. Go on.'

'I occupy a post of considerable responsibility, so I have access to most of the documents dealt with by Medes and his most senior officials. Winning and keeping his trust has been difficult. He's an absolute tyrant: he demands that everyone works extremely hard, and he hands out severe punishment for even the smallest mistake.'

'That's why his department is working so well,' said Nesmontu. 'The secretariat of the King's House has never been so efficient.'

'Medes leads by example,' said the officer. 'Professionally, I've nothing to say against him, and I saw nothing abnormal or suspicious until yesterday. Last night it was my task to close the offices when work was finished for the day. While doing so, I examined the papyri Medes would have to consult this morning. Among them there was an anonymous letter which said, "*A traitor is manipulating the King's House. He invented the legend of the Herald, a Syrian rebel who in fact died a long time ago. This cold and determined monster leads the Memphis rebel network, has committed appalling crimes, and plans to kill the commander of the city guards. Next, he will organize a new attempt on the pharaoh's life, to be carried out by an assassin no one would ever suspect: Sehotep.*"'

'Did you seize the document?'

'No, General, because it will be instructive to see what Medes does – whether he reports it or keeps quiet about it. However, that is no longer my concern, because I've tendered my resignation for reasons of health. I want to rejoin my unit before I'm identified as an informer.'

Nesmontu hurried off to see the king.

14

The Phoenician merchant was worried about how slow communication among the rebel groups in Memphis had become since the death of the water-carrier, his best agent. Now, instead of the water-carrier passing on orders throughout the city, each group's representative had to don the disguise of a delivery man, contact the Phoenician's door-keeper and receive the necessary instructions.

The Phoenician had had to take on a replacement for the water-carrier, but was wary of the Herald's followers and would not receive in his house anyone whose reliability had not been proven. In fact, the only person granted that privilege was Medes, who was marked with the sign of Set and therefore could no longer draw back.

Today the door-keeper had brought him a coded message, which filled him with delight: Sobek was bleeding to death from the wounds inflicted by the magical figurines. The Herald had struck a devastating blow. Without their leader the Memphis guards would lose their cohesion, and it would be much easier to arrange murders and other crimes.

In his excitement, the Phoenician swallowed three creamy cakes, one after the other.

The door-keeper reappeared. 'My lord, Curly-Head wishes to see you urgently at the market.'

The request implied a serious or worrying situation, for the leader of the Memphis rebels rarely left his hideout. The Phoenician therefore set off at once.

His ever-increasing weight slowed him down, and it seemed a long walk to the market. He stopped before a fig-stall; the seller belonged to the network.

Curly-Head came up and stood beside him.

'Are there any guards around?' asked the Phoenician.

'Two at the entrance to the market, two others mingling in the crowd. We're watching them. If they come this way, we'll be warned.'

'What has happened?'

'An Egyptian spy detected us,' said Curly-Head. 'We tried twice to kill him, but failed. I was sure the guards would mount a raid at any moment, so I and my men immediately left the district, taking care to leave no traces behind us. Much to our surprise, it was the army, not the city guards, who carried out the raid and searched the houses.'

'What was the result?'

'Total failure for the soldiers and vigorous protests by the townsfolk, including our brave fellows who stayed in place. The sandal-seller even received an official apology! In Egypt, everyone takes the law seriously and people aren't dealt with high-handedly – that weakness will lead to the pharaoh's downfall.'

'Have any of our men been arrested?' asked the Phoenician.

'No, not one. The rumours that Sobek's dead seem to be true, because the authorities had to use the army not the guards, whose organization is completely disrupted. I can just imagine the authorities' disarray! They deploy their forces, try to infiltrate us, carry out detailed investigations, and nothing works – they still can't lay hands on us. It's all thanks to our master, the Herald. His protection makes us invulnerable.'

'Of course, of course,' said the Phoenician, 'but we must

go on keeping the different groups separate, and we must go on being careful.'

'But surely Sobek's death gives us a tremendous advantage?'

'We mustn't forget General Nesmontu.'

'That old man can't do anything any more – except address his troops! They won't be able to repress our activities in the city.'

'Where are you and your men intending to hide?'

'Where nobody will ever think of looking for us: in the district that's just been searched from top to bottom. With our new system, it will be impossible to find us.'

The Phoencian nodded approvingly. The plan did indeed guarantee the safety of the rebels who would launch the first attacks.

'Don't make us wait too long,' said Curly-Head. 'Living like this is rather uncomfortable.'

'I'm simply awaiting the order from the Herald.'

The answer pleased and reassured Curly-Head, who had sometimes doubted the Phoenician's commitment, slave as he was to good living, and wondered if his position as leader of the network was going to his head. He said, 'When the time comes, my men and all the others will strike in the name of the Herald and of the new faith. We shall wipe out the unbelievers; only converts will be spared. The law of God will be imposed, and religious courts will pursue impious and immodest women.'

The Phoenician tried to dampen his enthusiasm. 'Taking Memphis is unlikely to be easy. Coordinating all our different groups presents serious problems.'

'Then solve them. Whatever happens, the Herald will choose the right time. The Egyptians are so devoted to happiness and the pleasures of life that they'll be helpless in the face of our purifying wave. Hundreds of city guards and soldiers will kneel and beg for their lives. When we display their severed heads on the points of our spears, their officers will run away and abandon the pharaoh. And we shall hand Senusret over, alive, to the Herald!'

Although he fully appreciated that splendid prospect, the Phoenician did not underestimate the enemy and had reservations about his own men. After the victory, and as soon as he was appointed head of the religious guard forces, he would accuse Curly-Head and those like him of depravity and have them executed. Such zealots were extremely useful during the period of conquest, but afterwards became uncontrollable and dangerous creatures.

Two pills in the morning, one at noon, three in the evening, and several infusions during the course of the day: Medes's wife followed Dr Gua's instructions to the letter. The moment she took the remedy prepared by Renseneb, she felt light and relaxed. Her sleep was almost peaceful, she had no attacks of hysteria, and she was calm for long periods. Her new hairdresser and cook satisfied her every whim. The cook prepared the most delicious dishes and wonderful desserts, with which she stuffed herself.

Full of unaccustomed energy, she attended to her home once more. At the crack of dawn, she summoned an army of craftsmen and set them several tasks: they must repaint the outside walls, clean the washroom, prune the trees and check the channels that carried waste water away. This spate of activity enabled her to forget the serious crimes that weighed upon her, so she would not have to confess them to Dr Gua, breaking the silence her husband had imposed on her.

'How well you are!' exclaimed Medes in astonishment.

'Doctor Gua is my good spirit. I hope you'll be proud of me. The house needed a great many improvements, and I'm dealing with them at last.'

'Congratulations, my darling. Exercise your authority to the full, and don't let them walk all over you – all workmen ever think of is stealing from their employers.'

When Medes set off for the tjaty's offices, to receive his instructions for the day, he was smiling. By now Sobek's spy must have read the anonymous letter slipped in among the confidential documents. The last to leave the offices, the officer would have searched everywhere. A discovery of such importance would be a fitting reward for his patience.

Of course, the spy was awaiting Medes's reaction. If he was secretive and silent, that would prove his complicity with Sehotep and his participation in an exceptionally dangerous conspiracy.

The atmosphere in the tjaty's secretariat was tense.

'Khnum-Hotep's health is giving cause for great anxiety,' a senior scribe told Medes. 'He was so ill that we thought we were going to lose him, but fortunately Doctor Gua has revived him.'

'Is he at last consenting to rest a little?'

'I'm afraid not. Go in now – he's expecting you.'

Medes had not seen Khnum-Hotep for some days, and was astonished by the change in him. Normally an imposing man, he had got very thin; his face was hollow, his complexion grey, and he was having difficulty breathing.

'It is not my place to counsel you,' said Medes, looking very upset, 'but would it not be advisable to lighten your heavy workload a little?'

'You seem to have forgotten that work is pronounced *kat* and gives us *ka*, the energy vital to life. Dying while working is the best possible way to go.'

'Don't say such things, Tjaty!'

'Let us not hide from reality. Even Doctor Gua has given up trying to cure me. Another man loyal to Senusret will replace me and serve our country to the utmost.'

Medes assumed an embarrassed air. He said, 'I've received a strange anonymous letter. It is obviously a tissue of lies, intended to besmirch the name of a member of the King's

House. It angered me so much that I almost destroyed it, but I thought it better to bring it to your attention.' He handed it to the tjaty.

Khnum-Hotep read it quickly and said, 'You did the right thing.'

Sehotep had spent a wonderful night in the company of a young woman who was expert in the games of love: amusing, fond of jokes, and thoroughly uninhibited. Strongly opposed to marriage, she intended to take full advantage of her youth before succeeding her father and managing the family estate. The lovers had parted on excellent terms, after a copious breakfast.

While he was being shaved, Sehotep thought about what he would say at the meeting of the Great Council. He would set out the progress being made at each of the construction sites across the land.

When he arrived at the palace, a security guard took him not to the chamber where the King's House convened but to Senusret's office. Every time they met, the elegant Sehotep felt more and more admiration for this giant of a man who defied fatigue and was undaunted by all the difficulties he faced. The pharaoh dominated his time and his subjects, and was entirely committed to his office.

'Is there anything you wish to tell me?' asked the king.

Sehotep was surprised. 'Am I to make my report to you in private?'

'Do you disapprove of Sobek's conduct?'

'Although he was wrong about Iker, I consider him an excellent commander of the guards.'

'Did you send him, in my name, an acacia-wood chest containing magical figurines?'

The usually quick-thinking Sehotep was nonplussed for a moment. 'Certainly not, Majesty. Who was behind this sinister joke?'

'Animated by an evil spirit, the figurines tried to kill Sobek. He suffered numerous wounds, and lost a great deal of blood. We think he is out of danger, but the would-be assassin must be caught and punished. Now, he put a signature to his crime – and that signature is yours.'

'That's impossible, Majesty!'

'Look at this papyrus.'

Deeply troubled, Sehotep read the blood-spattered document. 'Majesty, I did not write these lines.'

'Do you not recognize your own handwriting?'

'The resemblance is astonishing. Who could have created such a perfect forgery?'

'There is another accusation against you,' added the king. 'According to an anonymous letter, you are the leader of the rebel network in Memphis, and are determined to kill me. To ward off suspicion, you invented the spectre of the Herald, inspired by a bandit who is now dead.'

Sehotep was so stunned that he could not find a single word to say.

'Sobek's second-in-command and all the senior guard officers are demanding your arrest,' said Senusret. 'This papyrus is sufficient grounds for them to lodge a complaint with the tjaty.'

'But is it not a rather clumsy attack on me? If I were guilty, I would never have been so stupid as to sign my own death-warrant! And an anonymous letter has no worth in the eyes of our legal system.'

'Nevertheless Khnum-Hotep feels obliged to open a case, lodge the complaint against you, and suspend you from your duties.'

'Majesty . . . do you doubt me?'

'If I did, would I speak to you like this?'

Intense joy lit up Sehotep's eyes. So long as he had the king's trust, he would fight. But how was he to find the author of the forgery?

'Because you have been accused,' Senusret went on, 'I cannot bring together the entire Golden Circle. Your seat will remain empty until the proclamation of your innocence.'

'My worst enemy will be rumour. Evil tongues will be at work, and the guards' hostility will not make our task any easier. Perhaps the attack is not so clumsy after all. The tjaty, Senankh and Nesmontu must be the Herald's next targets.'

'Khnum-Hotep's health is declining irreversibly,' said the king.

'Doctor Gua . . .'

'This time, he is admitting defeat.'

Although optimistic by nature, Sehotep faltered for a moment. 'It is you that the Evil One wants to strike, Majesty. By isolating you, driving away those faithful to you, disrupting the state secretariats one by one, and breaching the integrity of the Golden Circle, he is trying to make you vulnerable. No massive action, no frontal attack, but a cunningly distilled poison of fearsome effectiveness. Urgency demands that I am replaced, for the reputation of the King's House must not be sullied. The construction works in progress must also be continued.'

'I shall not replace anybody,' decreed the pharaoh,' and each man shall remain at his post. Dismissing you would be an admission of your guilt before the tjaty's court has even pronounced its verdict. We shall therefore follow the normal procedure, applicable to the great as well as the small.'

'But what if my innocence cannot be proved, Majesty? Assuming that the Herald has suborned some of the guards and is using them against me, my chances of success look extremely small.'

'Let us continue to follow the way of Ma'at, and the truth will shine forth.'

Sehotep shivered. An evil wind was blowing across the

land and threatening to ravage it. The imperturbable pharaoh was preparing for a battle whose scope and ferocity would have terrified even the bravest man.

15

The commander of the Abydos guards stopped Bina. 'Where are you off to in such a hurry?'

She smiled at him. 'To the temple as usual, to fetch food for the permanent priests.'

'You're punctilious, aren't you?'

'I like my work very much and wouldn't want to change it.'

'People don't talk like that at your age. Go on working well like this and you'll be promoted.'

'I only want to make myself useful.'

'Come, come, don't play the timid little creature. I have a strong wish to give you a body search.'

Bina took a step backwards. 'Why?'

'Can't you guess? A beautiful girl like you can't be happy to serve the morning meal to old priests who care about nothing but rites and symbols. In my opinion, you're really going off to meet your lover. I'm responsible for security here, and I want to know his name.'

'I'm sorry to disappoint you, but I don't go and meet anyone.'

'That's hard to believe, my pretty. I can understand that you want to protect the lucky fellow, but I must know everything that happens in Abydos.'

'How can I convince you that you're wrong?'

The commander folded his arms. 'Let's suppose . . . In that case, you must be planning to get married.'

'I'm in no hurry to marry.'

'Don't deceive yourself. Whatever you do, don't throw yourself into the arms of just any man – take advice from a man of experience.'

'Like you, for example?'

'Lots of attractive young women are interested in me. I only hold out because of you.'

Bina pretended to be moved. 'I'm very touched. Unfortunately, though, I earn only a small wage and wouldn't be worthy of an important man like you.'

'Important men sometimes marry ordinary girls, don't they?'

The pretty brunette lowered her eyes. 'You've taken me by surprise. I can't answer you.'

He patted her shoulder. 'There's no hurry, sweetheart. We'll have all the time in the world to be happy.'

'Do you really think so?'

'Trust me, and you won't be disappointed.'

'Will you give me time to think?'

The commander smiled beatifically. 'Decide freely, my little quail. I hope I shan't have to wait too long.'

Bina made good her escape. The situation was getting worse. She could not hold him off for very long. He said the same thing to every girl he took up with. Easily bored, he went on from one to another, proposing marriage in the evening and forgetting his promises in the morning.

Bina hoped the Herald would act soon. When he launched the final attack on Abydos, she would kill the commander with her own hands.

The four young acacias were so weakened by the Herald's poison that they emitted only a feeble defensive barrier, which the Herald easily penetrated. He was amused by the sensation of pins and needles in his legs.

The Tree of Life had one final protection: the four lions whose eyes never closed. Tireless watchers, they would strike dead anyone who tried to harm the Acacia of Osiris. A pole with a covered top, the symbol of the Great Land, endowed them with fearsome strength. The Herald was careful not to touch it. Until he had killed Osiris, the fetish would give off dangerous energy.

On the other hand, having transformed Bina into a terrifying lioness, he had no fear of confronting the watchers. His only uncertainty was about what would be the best strategy.

Each guardian lion had a different expression. The Herald chose the most austere, at the north, and covered its eyelids with a reddish liquid made from rye-grass, Nubian sand, desert salt and Bina's blood. He rubbed the limestone patiently until the substance penetrated it and made the lion blind. Then the three others suffered the same fate. South, east and west all lost their sight.

Soon their teeth and claws would be powerless, and the guardians reduced to the state of inert stones.

Iker, the Bearer of the Golden Palette, celebrated the morning rite, assisted by the Shaven-headed One. Afterwards they checked the work of the permanent priests, then meditated before the tomb of Osiris.

'You have not made a single error,' observed the old priest, 'and you have truly become the leader of our brotherhood.'

Iker shook his head. 'I am merely the king's envoy. It is you who lead them.'

'Not any longer. In a very short time you have travelled an immense distance, avoided a thousand and one pitfalls, thrust aside many obstacles and fulfilled a delicate mission. Age matters little. The permanent priests now recognize you as my successor, and I cannot imagine a better one.'

'But isn't that decision premature?'

'Some people have the leisure to prepare themselves for

their future tasks, others learn how to master them while carrying them out. Your destiny obliges you to create your path as you go along. You wanted Abydos, and Abydos has answered you.'

'The Golden Circle . . .'

'You are already inside it. There is only one last doorway to pass through, during the celebration of the Mysteries. The preparations for them must be rigorous, so, beginning this evening, we shall draw up a list of everything that will be required. Then we shall examine the phases of the ritual.'

When Iker returned home, Isis welcomed him with a radiant smile and they fell into each other's arms.

'I'm worried, Isis,' said Iker. 'Will I be able to do what's required of me?'

'That's a question which shouldn't be asked. Who could ever think himself worthy of the great Mysteries? The spirit of Abydos calls us, our hearts open to its light and we perform the rites, setting our feet in the footprints of the ancestors. Faced with that vital duty, what do our worries matter?'

They climbed the stairs to their terrace, which was protected from the sun by a sheet of linen fixed to four small wooden pillars.

This was happiness, the perfect union of the ordinary and the sacred, the ideal and its accomplishment. Living by the same gaze and the same breath, Isis and Iker thanked the gods for granting them such fortune.

'Does my sister in the Golden Circle truly welcome me without reservation?'

'I've thought about it a lot,' she joked, 'and I hesitated for a long time. But you seemed the least bad of the candidates . . .'

He adored the lightness of her laughter and the gentleness in her eyes. The love that had been born at their first meeting was continually growing and expanding. Both knew that time would not damage it – quite the contrary.

Eventually, though, Iker's worries crept slyly up on him again. He said, 'Bega praised Gergu to the skies, but I didn't hide the suspicions that your immediate judgment of Gergu roused in me.'

'I'm surprised. Bega never praises anyone.'

'His coldness makes him rather disagreeable, I agree, but he seems honest. Gergu supplies all the provisions Bega orders and gives complete satisfaction. However, a shadowy area does still exist: did Gergu come to Abydos of his own accord, or did someone send him?'

'What does Bega think?'

'He doesn't care, because Gergu works well and has passed all the security checks without any queries being raised.'

'That's a strange attitude in such a meticulous man.'

'Would you go so far as to say it's suspicious?'

'No, I have no criticism of him – except that his heart is dry.'

'Is that appearance or reality?'

'Bega has hardly anything to do with the priestesses,' replied Isis. 'He did once try to strike up a friendship with me – in vain, of course.'

'Given your rank, is that likely to be rankling with him?'

'Given his constant moroseness, that's hard to say. Dedication and respect for the Rule shouldn't cause such an utter lack of joy. Even the Shaven-headed One, for all his sternness, isn't wholly without warmth or jollity.'

'Bega promised to help me. He admits that my arrival and my investigation caused serious upheavals, but they've calmed down now.'

'Let us hope so,' said Isis.

'You don't sound convinced.'

'You don't know your own power, Iker. Experienced priests bow before you because it is imposed on them. Although you're young, they know they can't oppose you openly. Some of them are resigned to it, but others feel frustrated. And we mustn't forget the king's warning. Not for a moment must we relax our vigilance.'

'I'm going to ask Sobek the Protector to carry out a thorough investigation of Gergu's actions and relationships – if he's involved in anything underhand, we'll soon find out. And I shall pay Bega special attention. Throughout the preparations for the Mysteries, I shall ask his advice. Will the High Priestess of Hathor help me, too?'

'The Rule obliges me to,' she reminded him with a smile.

Beautiful Nephthys had hardly slept since arriving in Abydos. Taking part in the rites, preparing the many lengths of cloth needed for the celebration of the Mysteries, checking the symbolic material along with the permanent priests – she did not notice time passing, and was living unforgettable days, beyond her wildest dreams.

Meeting Isis had been a sort of miracle. The High Priestess guided her, helped her to avoid doing the wrong thing, and made her work easier in all kinds of ways. Between the two ritual sisters there was such a communion of thought that they scarcely felt the need to speak.

Nephthys went to Senusret's Temple of a Million Years to check the condition of the cups and vases, some of which were to be used during the month of Khoiak. She spoke to a temporary worker and asked to see the person responsible for their care.

He took her to a shrine where a tall, handsome man was working. He looked haughty and distinguished. A strange charm emanated from his strong personality, and the young priestess immediately responded to it. Carefully shaven, tastefully perfumed, dressed in an immaculate long linen apron, he did everything gently and meticulously. He was cleaning a fine alabaster vase, dating from the days of the earliest pharaohs.

'May I interrupt you?' she asked.

The temporary priest raised his eyes slowly; they were a surprising and enchanting shade of orange.

'I am at your disposal,' he replied in a smooth voice.

'How many ancient masterpieces like that one are there in the temple's treasury?'

'At least a hundred, most of them made of granite.'

'Are they in good condition?'

'Excellent.'

'So they would be usable in a ritual?'

'All except one, which I've given to the master sculptor for restoration. Forgive my curiosity, but are you the twin sister of the High Priestess of Hathor?'

She smiled. 'No, though we do look very alike. My name is Nephthys, and the queen has granted me the tremendous privilege of replacing a priestess who died recently.'

'Did you live in Memphis?'

'Yes, and it's a wonderful city, but I don't miss it. Everything I could ever want is here in Abydos.'

'I don't know Memphis,' lied the Herald. 'I come from a small village not far from it, and have always dreamt of serving the Great Land.'

'Do you want to become a permanent priest?'

'That takes qualities I haven't got. I earn my living by drilling stone vases. For two or three months each year, I have the great good fortune to work here. The tasks I'm set aren't important. What matters is to feel close to the Great God.'

'I'll mention you to the Shaven-headed One. Perhaps he'll employ you for a little bit longer.'

'That would be wonderful! Thank you for your help.'

'What is your name?'

'Asher.'

Asher meant the 'boiling one'. The name suited him, despite his calm manner, thought Nephthys. His strange charm must arouse passion in many women.

She said, 'It's my turn to be indiscreet: are you married?'

'I don't earn enough to feed a wife and children, and I couldn't bear not being able to support them and make them happy.'

'Your selflessness does you credit. But supposing you met an independent woman who earned her own living, perhaps a temporary worker at Abydos?'

The Herald looked astonished, almost shocked. 'I concentrate on my work, and . . .'

'I congratulate you, Asher. I've always been interested in the way stone vases are made. Would you be willing to talk to me about it over the evening meal?'

The woman's effrontery was typically Egyptian. Under the reign of the true God, such a serious offence would be punished by a whipping, followed by a beating with sticks and then stoning.

The Herald held back his rage and said smoothly, 'You're a priestess, and I'm only a humble temporary worker. I wouldn't want to inconvenience you.'

'Would tomorrow evening suit you?'

Although determined to punish this insolent female, the Herald found her very attractive. He agreed.

16

'I don't believe it,' Sobek told his deputy. 'Give me some more beef and a cup of wine.'

Although in bed and officially near to death, he was regaining his strength remarkably fast. The ox-blood and Renseneb's tonics were succeeding.

'With respect, sir, you're mistaken. The proof is glaringly obvious. We have Sehotep's own signature.'

'Do you take him for a fool? He is not the man to behave so stupidly.'

'If the chest hadn't been sent to you by a friend, you'd have been suspicious. After killing you, the figurines were meant to destroy the papyrus so that there'd be no clue to who was responsible.'

The argument was a reasonable one, Sobek had to admit.

His deputy went on, 'The gods protect you, sir, but don't tempt fate too far. We now have a chance to destroy the destructive power of the criminal within the King's House.'

'Sehotep, leader of the Memphis rebel network? That's unthinkable.'

'On the contrary, sir, that's precisely why we haven't been able to dismantle it. Sehotep was the first to learn the pharaoh's plans, and he warned his accomplices of any danger. You had to be killed because he was afraid you were getting close to him, through our investigations of all the courtiers. By eliminating you, he cut off the head of the guards force and put an immediate stop to the investigations. A member of the King's House would certainly know how to use magic and bring killer statuettes to life.'

Perturbed, Sobek ate some more bloody meat. 'What are your plans?'

'I and my comrades in the guards are lodging a complaint with Tjaty Khnum-Hotep. The facts have been established, there is material proof, and the case is clear and solid. We demand that Sehotep be placed in custody and appear before a court, on the charge of attempted murder.'

'Which carries the death penalty.'

'A fitting punishment for such an appalling crime.'

The King's House dishonoured, Senusret weakened, the very foundations of Egypt shaken . . . The consequences of such a sentence were likely to be disastrous.

But there would be one good consequence: without their leader, the rebels would either have to disperse or else have to act individually, in an uncoordinated way which would be much easier to combat. And the nightmare would disappear.

There was no possible doubt: the watch on Medes's house had been lifted. Thanks to his wife's talents as a forger, all suspicions were converging on Sehotep. The guards were concentrating solely on him, and believed it unnecessary to follow or investigate anyone else.

Medes was triumphant. Sehotep made a splendid scapegoat and an irresistible false lead. Sobek's men were fiercely determined to avenge the attack on their commander, and would never let go of their prey. As for Medes himself, he would continue to play the part of an irreproachable official and a perfect servant of the king.

Warily, he checked and rechecked several times, to make sure there really were no guards prowling around, not even after nightfall. Once reassured, he waited until the household was asleep, then put on a brown tunic – different from the one he usually used – and covered his head with a hood. Despite the risks, he had to see the Phoenician.

All was quiet in the streets. Memphis, too, was asleep. Then, suddenly, he heard footsteps. A patrol! Medes flattened himself against the door of a storehouse set back from the houses. The soldiers might pass without seeing him.

He closed his eyes, thinking of what he would say if he were spotted.

Interminable minutes went by. Silence fell again. The patrol had gone.

Medes changed his route ten times, until he was certain he was not being followed. Calm once more, he went to the Phoenician's house, where he followed the usual identification procedure.

Once inside, he was surrounded by three loathsome-looking men.

'Our master has ordered us to search every visitor,' said a bearded man.

'That's out of the question!' snapped Medes.

'Are you hiding a weapon?'

'Of course not.'

'Then don't resist, or we'll use force.'

To Medes's relief, the Phoenician appeared.

'Tell these brutes to take their hands off me!' demanded Medes.

'They are to follow my orders,' replied the fat man.

Astounded, Medes permitted the men to search him.

When he entered the reception chamber, where for once there were neither cakes nor fine wines set out, he rounded on his host. 'Have you gone mad? Treating me – *me* – like a suspect!'

'The circumstances oblige me to be extremely careful.'

For the first time since he had known him, Medes sensed

that the Phoenician was very nervous. 'Is the attack imminent?' he asked.

'That is for the Herald to decide. As for myself, I'm ready. Not without difficulty, I have at last managed to link together my different groups.'

'My plan worked,' said Medes. 'The guards are concentrating solely on Sehotep, who's been accused of heading our network and trying to kill Sobek.'

'"Trying"? Did he survive?'

'He's mortally wounded, and his men's anger will be an advantage to us. By incriminating Sehotep, we're undermining the foundations of the King's House. Even if Senusret believes his friend innocent, the tjaty will apply the law and thus paralyse one whole arm of the government.'

The Phoenician became somewhat calmer. 'This is the ideal time – provided the Herald's order isn't too long in coming. You must help me again, Medes.'

'How?'

'My men need weapons – daggers, swords and spears – and plenty of them.'

'That will be difficult, very difficult.'

'We're nearing our goal. There must be no half-heartedness.'

'I'll see what I can do, but I can't guarantee anything.'

'This is an order,' snapped the Phoenician. 'Failure to obey it would be tantamount to defection.'

The two men glared at each other.

Medes did not take the threat lightly. For the time being he must agree, and accept the resulting loss of face. Once the victory was won, though, he would have his revenge.

He said, 'Bribing the sentries at the main weapons store would be impossible. I suggest a raid on the port storehouse where the weapons produced in the workshops are held before being delivered to the army. Gergu will recruit some men to distract the sentries; then it's up to your men.'

'No, that would attract too much attention. Find another solution.'

'We might be able to steal some weapons being shipped to a provincial town. Yes, that wouldn't be impossible. I'd have to falsify the documentation and alter the nature of the cargo. I couldn't do it more than once, though, because the error's bound to be discovered and those responsible punished. Once, and once only, I can extract myself from trouble by having someone else accused.'

'Do it – and don't fail. Now, there's one other thing we must discuss. It wasn't the city guards who nearly rounded up one of my groups, it was the army. With Sobek no longer a threat, we have only one major obstacle to eliminate in order to dismantle the rest of Memphis's protection. Without their legendary general, the army's senior officers will tear each other apart.'

'Would you dare to attack Nesmontu himself?'

'Surely you don't admire one of our worst enemies?'

'But he'll have the closest, strictest protection.'

'Not at all. Old Nesmontu thinks he's invulnerable, and he takes no more precautions than an ordinary footsoldier does. His death will be like an earthquake. The army and the city guards both in crisis – what more could we want?'

Faithful to custom, Nesmontu gave the army's new recruits a fine feast: red wine, stewed beef, vegetables pounded to a paste, goat's cheese and cakes soaked in alcohol, among other things. The general recounted a few memories of battles and praised the merits of discipline, the mother of victories. Assailed by questions, he answered them gladly and promised an exciting career to those who trained hard and did not balk at any exercise, however taxing. The feast ended with the singing of several bawdy songs.

'Tomorrow you'll get up at dawn and sluice yourselves down with cold water,' announced Nesmontu. 'Then there'll be a footrace and weapons training.'

A broad-shouldered young fellow came up to him. 'General, would you grant me an immense favour?'

'What is it?'

'My wife's just given birth. Would you consider becoming my boy's sponsor?'

'An old fellow like me?'

'Actually, my wife thinks that your longevity will be a blessing for the little one. She'd love to present our son to you. We live very near the barracks, and it wouldn't take much of your time.'

'Very well, but we must be quick.'

The recruit strode out briskly, and was soon a pace or two ahead of the general. He led the way down a narrow street, then down a second on the right, and a third at an angle, this one very narrow indeed.

When a sinister cracking noise tore through the silence, the false soldier ran off.

'Look out!' roared Sekari, who was following the two men precisely because he feared Nesmontu might be attacked.

The general was torn between chasing the rebel and retreating to a safer place. His hesitation was his undoing. The beams of some scaffolding, loosened earlier by other rebels, crashed down on to him and he disappeared under a shroud of wood and dust.

Sekari tried frantically to free him. 'General, can you hear me? It's Sekari! Answer me!' Heaving aside beam after beam, he toiled on. At last he found the general's body.

Nesmontu's eyes were open.

'You're losing your touch, my boy – that little piece of filth got away,' he murmured. 'As for me, my left arm's broken and I've got a fair few cuts and bruises, but I can stand up on my own.'

'The attack was well prepared,' said Sekari. 'It's pure luck that you survived.'

'Officially, I didn't. The rebels wanted to kill me, so let us give them the satisfaction of thinking they have – the news of my death will bring them out into the open.'

Signing the official accusation against Sehotep, his brother in the Golden Circle of Abydos, was heart-rending for Khnum-Hotep, but he had to apply the law without indulgence or personal favour. The evidence did not permit him to overlook the matter, even though he was in no doubt of Sehotep's innocence.

The enemy had shown remarkable talent in manipulating the guards and using the legal system to crack open the King's House and render Senusret vulnerable. The tjaty could not bear this defeat. So he would try to convince Sobek that his deputy and his colleagues were actually helping the Herald by lodging their complaint.

There was a flash of light inside Khnum-Hotep's head, and for a few moments, he lost consciousness. When he came to, he staggered to a window, propped himself up on his elbows and fought for breath. There was an unbearable pain in the centre of his chest, which compelled him to sit down again. Unable to breathe, and so unable to shout for help, he knew that he would not survive this attack.

The tjaty's last thoughts flew to Senusret, begging him not to abandon the struggle and thanking him for having granted his first minister so much happiness.

Together, his dogs bayed at the moon.

Built about a hundred cubits to the north of the pyramid of Dahshur, Khnum-Hotep's splendid house of eternity welcomed his mummy in the presence of all the members of the King's House, including its secretary, Medes. General Nesmontu's death in a tragic accident added to their profound sadness.

The heat hung heavy over the site. The mummy, prepared

quickly but with great care, was lowered to the bottom of a shaft and laid in a sarcophagus. The king himself performed the funeral rites. After opening the mummy's mouth, eyes and ears, he brought to life the scenes and hieroglyphic texts in the shrine inside the tomb, where a priest of the *ka* would keep the memory of Khnum-Hotep alive.

His death filled Medes with hope. With Sehotep out of the way, and High Treasurer Senankh absorbed by his work and considered irreplaceable, there were no other competitors for the post of tjaty. Senusret considered the secretary of the King's House to be a tireless worker and model official, and so was bound to raise him – one of the Herald's accomplices! – to the position of tjaty.

The only thing that spoilt the occasion was that, to Medes's astonishment, Sobek was there. He was obviously still unwell, and leant heavily on a stout cane, but he was there. It took a great effort for Medes to maintain his solemn expression.

When Senusret emerged from the shrine, he gazed for a long time at Khnum-Hotep's tomb. Then he turned to his courtiers.

'I must go to Abydos immediately,' he said. 'After so many tragedies, we are all aware of the dangers threatening Memphis. In my absence, the new tjaty will ensure the city's safety and show extreme firmness in dealing with any disturbances. May he prove a worthy successor to the great Khnum-Hotep. Sobek the Protector, be inspired by Khnum-Hotep's example and fulfil this office, which is as bitter as bile.'

17

As he sipped a smooth, sweet wine, the Phoenician congratulated himself on having treated Medes with suitable harshness. The man was too accustomed to being comfortable; in fact, he was almost asleep. By puncturing his inordinate vanity, the Phoenician had compelled him to show the true extent of his commitment and his readiness for action. And the result had been no disappointment.

From district to district the news ran, stunning all Memphis: Nesmontu was dead. It was murder, said some people; no, it was an accident, said others. The death of Tjaty Khnum-Hotep, the charges against Sehotep, and now the death of the old general: destiny was attacking the men closest to Senusret, who was becoming isolated and vulnerable. The appointment of Sobek as tjaty did not reassure anybody. Even if he recovered from his physical and mental wounds, which many doubted, he would be unable to cope with the full extent of his formidable new office. A guard officer was only a guard officer; he could deal with security and repression, but not social and economic matters.

This absurd choice proved that the king was afraid. In normal times he would have appointed Senankh or Medes. Forced to defend himself against an elusive enemy, he had abandoned real power to a diminished man whom only he believed capable of preventing the worst. His regime was falling apart.

136

Curly-Head and his men had returned to their base in the district north of the Temple of Neith. There were the usual patrols, and informants who had long since been identified, but no further military presence. Sobek's emissaries could search the houses and shops and search them again, but they would find nothing.

Knowing that the water-carriers, barbers and sandal-vendors were being closely watched, the Phoenician had information and his instructions circulated by housewives ostensibly chatting at the market. In this way, swift communication was established between the different groups, which were already on a war footing. Impatient for action, the Herald's followers dreamt of conquering Memphis and killing as many unbelievers as possible. The slaughter of women and children would spread such terror that the soldiers and guards would be unable to stem the destructive tide of the faithful.

The Phoenician, too, was becoming impatient. When was the Herald going to launch his attack? His plan to strike at the heart of Abydos must be encountering serious difficulties, perhaps so serious that they were enforcing this inaction.

The scar across his chest began to burn painfully, as it did whenever he doubted his supreme leader. He emptied his wine-cup in a single draught.

Abydos and Memphis, the sacred city of Osiris and the capital, the centres of spirituality and prosperity: if they were mortally wounded, it would lead to the collapse of the entire country. The Herald, the envoy of God, knew the day and the hour. Failure to follow him unquestioningly would draw down his fury.

For High Treasurer Senankh, director of the Double White House, there was only one reason for satisfaction: on the worldly level, Egypt was doing exceptionally well. Officials were paid on merit, and no privileges were granted for life, the emphasis being on duties rather than rights. Crafts, trade and agriculture were flourishing, there was unity between trades and age groups; everyone had the will to respect the Rule of Ma'at at all levels of society, and to punish fraudsters, corruptors and the corrupt. Little by little, the pharaoh's programme was being applied and it was producing good results.

But Senankh was not fully satisfied, for many problems still persisted. He had to remain implacably opposed to laxity and laziness, and to see that everyone worked as hard as they could.

In any case, how could he rejoice at his successes when his friend and brother Sehotep stood accused of attempted murder? And the victim, Sobek, was now the tjaty, who must preside at the trial! Obliged to respect the law, he would direct the deliberations and pronounce the sentence. Invoking a procedural error or alleging partiality would demand a major error on the part of the new tjaty.

Senankh would not abandon Sehotep to his unjust fate. Despite the evidence of forgery and deceit, there was a risk that the workings of the law might crush him. There was only one hope: Sekari.

The two men met in an ale-house in the southern district, where they knew no one would pay them any attention.

'We must get Sehotep out of this devil's trap,' said Senankh. 'You must have some ideas on how we can.'

'Unfortunately, I haven't.'

'If you give up, he's lost.'

'I'm not giving up, but other things must come first. I'm hoping that I'll soon be able to dismantle part of the rebel network.'

'So you'll forget about Sehotep?'

'The accusation won't hold water.'

'Don't deceive yourself. Tjaty Sobek will pursue the case with vigour. We'll have to make our own enquiries.'

'That won't be at all easy without the guards' help, and they'll stand united behind the Protector.'

'We can't simply do nothing!'

'A false move would make the situation even worse. The king's departure for Abydos leaves the field open for Sobek.'

Medes's anger was unabated. In view of his skills and personal qualities, the post of tjaty should have been his. In failing to recognize his merits, Senusret had again inflicted unbearable humiliation on him. So Medes would take great pleasure in witnessing the king's downfall and the birth of a new regime, with himself at the centre.

The elimination of the Phoenician would pose no problems. That of the Herald, on the other hand, would be delicate. Despite the Herald's immense powers, he must have weaknesses. Perhaps he would be weakened by the battle at Abydos and the final struggle against Senusret.

Medes knew he was destined for great things, and nobody was going to prevent him from acquiring supreme power. In the meantime, he would carry out his new assignment: providing the rebels with more weapons. The announcement of Nesmontu's death made his task easier, for the senior army officers were demoralized and were starting to give contradictory orders. Many soldiers who had been on security duty had been recalled to the central barracks, and one of the storehouses for swords and daggers, which was temporarily closed, was now unguarded.

Taking advantage of this opportunity, Medes entrusted Gergu with the job of lavishly bribing some dishonest dock-workers to empty the place and hide the weapons in an abandoned storehouse, from where the rebels could fetch them. Medes would thus demonstrate to the Phoenician his capacity for action; he would omit to mention that he was keeping some of the weapons, which he would use to equip his own men.

There was no need to organize the complicated theft he had described to the Phoenician. Fortune was definitely smiling on him.

Although deprived of his work and confined to his luxurious house, Sehotep was not idle. Every morning he had himself washed down and shaved, perfumed himself and chose elegant clothes.

Until now he had spent many enjoyable evenings in the company of charming women, had attended receptions enabling him to learn of any grievances felt by Memphis as a whole, had travelled throughout the provinces, overseeing the restoration of ancient structures or opening up new construction sites. Now he spent much very agreeable time rereading the classics, and rediscovering a thousand and one forgotten marvels. The style of the great authors never drowned the ideas, and form never became an artifice. The grammar itself served the expression of a spirituality which had been passed down since the golden age of the pyramids and had been ceaselessly reformulated.

These treasures gave Sehotep the strength to confront adversity. And in his memory he retained the teaching of the Golden Circle of Abydos, which had taken him to the other side of reality. Compared to initiation into Osiran resurrection, what did his misfortunes matter? During the rite of the inversion of the lights, his human part and his celestial part had been both married together and exchanged. The human part was not restricted to its pleasures and its sufferings, and the divine part was not confined to that which could not be spoken. The temporal dimension became the small side of existence, the eternal the great side of life. Whatever ordeals might lie in store, he would try to face them with detachment, as if they did not concern him.

A ray of sunshine lit up an acacia-wood box decorated with finely chiselled lotus flowers. Sehotep smiled as he mused that a similar box had caused his downfall. This modest work of art, however, bore witness to pharaonic civilization, attached to the incarnation of the spirit in many forms, from a simple hieroglyph to a giant pyramid.

'Tjaty Sobek wishes to see you,' his steward informed him.

'I'll meet him up on the terrace. Escort him there, and serve us some cool white wine from Year One of Senusret's reign.'

The Protector could have summoned Sehotep to his office but preferred to question him at his home, hoping to drive him into a corner. Sobek did not care much for this thirty-year-old aristocrat with the narrow face and eyes glinting with intelligence. Something was troubling him: why had Khnum-Hotep not signed the official warrant?

The simple explanation, of course, was that he had been in his death throes, and his hand had been contracting, unable to express his wishes. But there was another possibility: that Khnum-Hotep had not believed Sehotep guilty and wanted to investigate further before bringing a member of the King's House before Egypt's highest court.

As soon as the steward had announced Sobek and withdrawn, Sehotep asked, 'Is the judge questioning a guilty man, condemned in advance, or is there still a shade of doubt?'

Grim-faced, Sobek paced the terrace in silence.

'At least enjoy the view,' advised his host. 'From here you can see the White Wall of Menes, unifier of Upper and Lower Egypt, and all the many temples of this city with their unequalled charm.'

Sobek halted with his back turned to Sehotep. 'I shall admire the view another time.'

'Shouldn't one take advantage of the moment?'

Sobel turned. 'Am I or am I not face to face with the head of the rebels in Memphis, a man guilty of many appalling murders? That is my only question.'

'To impose his authority, the new tjaty has to make an example of somebody. Since my fate has been settled in advance, I'm enjoying my last hours of relative freedom.'

'You don't know me very well, Sehotep!'

'I know you accused Iker of treachery and imprisoned him.'

'That was a regrettable mistake, I admit. My new office obliges me to be more prudent and demands the very clearest thinking.'

Sehotep held out his wrists. 'Place the shackles on me.'

'Are you confessing?'

'When the death penalty is pronounced, you'll have to kill me with your own hands, Sobek, because I shall refuse to kill myself and will declare my innocence until the very last second.'

'That position is untenable – you're forgetting the facts.'

'When it comes to artifice and falsehood, our enemies are truly remarkable. Subjected to our own legal system, we become its victims!'

'Are you saying our laws are unjust?'

'All legislation has its weak points. It is up to the judges – particularly the tjaty – to minimize them by seeking the truth behind appearances.'

'You tried to have me killed,' said Sobek hotly.

'No.'

'You yourself made the magical figurines intended to kill me.'

'No.'

'After killing me, you would have killed His Majesty.'

'No.'

'For months you have been both informing your fellow conspirators of decisions made by the King's House and also enabling them to avoid arrest by the guards.'

'No.'

'Rather short answers, don't you think?'

'No.'

'Your intelligence won't protect you from the ultimate punishment. And the evidence is overwhelming.'

'What evidence?'

'The anonymous letter worries me, I'll concede that. Nevertheless, it respects a certain logic, in agreement with the rebels' intentions.'

Sehotep simply looked the tjaty straight in the eyes. The two men looked at each other with steady, honest, direct gazes.

'You signed your attempt at murder, and my survival changes nothing. Intention is the same as action, and the court will show no lenience. It would be better to confess and give me the names of your accomplices.'

'I'm sorry to disappoint you, but I am loyal to Pharaoh and I have committed no crime.'

'Then how do you explain the fact that the papyrus the figurines should have destroyed was in your writing?'

'How many times must I repeat it? The enemy is using a remarkably talented forger, who knows the members of the King's House very well. He thinks he's striking us a fatal blow. I hope the tjaty will not allow himself to be deceived.'

Sobek was surprised by how calm Sehotep seemed: he was obviously an extremely good actor.

'However effective it may be,' the accused man continued, 'this plot may actually be a mistake. Don't omit to keep a close watch on everyone close to me. Only one of them could have had access to my writing.'

'Including your mistresses?'

'I'll give you an exhaustive list.'

'Do you also suspect courtiers or dignitaries?'

'It is up to the tjaty to apply the Law of Ma'at by finding out the truth, whatever the consequences.'

18

The protection given to the Acacia of Osiris by the four young trees and the four lions had been destroyed, but two formidable defences remained: the fetish of Abydos and the gold covering the acacia's trunk. The gold, from Nubia and the land of Punt, would lose its effectiveness the moment the Herald removed the cover from the top of the pole at the centre of the relic-holder formed by the four back-to-back lions.

It would be impossible to carry out this profanation before killing the new Osiris designated by the rites – in other words, Royal Son Iker. The young man did not know it yet, but the Herald had been preparing for this moment for long years.

In choosing this solitary boy, so devoted to studying the sacred language, indifferent to honours and capable of undergoing a thousand and one ordeals without losing his resolve or enthusiasm, the Herald had made no mistake. However, he had not dealt gently with him, sending him several times to a certain death in order to check his abilities.

Nothing and no one, not even a raging sea, a frenzied wild beast, an attempt on his life, a conspiracy or any other destructive force, could strike Iker down. Scared stiff, beaten, humiliated, or wrongly accused, he always got up and continued on his way.

That way had led him to Abydos, the temple of eternal life. For him, though, it would be the lair of death.

This annihilation would require action by the Herald himself and the confederates of Set. By putting an end to the process of Osiris's resurrection, and by cutting off all links with the world beyond, they would kill Egypt's future and destroy her work. Despite his courage, Senusret would be powerless.

The king had not been wrong, either, in choosing Iker as his spiritual son, the new incarnation of Osiris and future master of the great Mysteries of Abydos. His age mattered little, since his heart possessed the capacity for the office. Guided by long experience, the Shaven-headed One had admitted him and was easing his ascent.

Although aware that danger threatened, Senusret would never be able to guess what the Herald planned: that Iker should become both the sworn enemy of the confederates of Set and a major weapon in the decisive battle against the pharaoh – against all pharaohs. By building up the boy in the manner of a temple, the king thought he could raise a magic wall capable of containing the attacks of evil. Once Iker was dead and Abydos defenceless, the Herald would strike the fatal blow.

Once his morning duties at the temple were done, the Herald went to the dining chamber and ate his midday meal there with the other temporary workers, all of whom were delighted to be working in Abydos. He took care to be friendly to them, and always ready to lend a hand, so he had gained an excellent reputation. Rumour had it that the Shaven-headed One would soon offer him a better post.

Walking quietly home afterwards, the Herald thought of the meal at Nephthys's house. The food had been excellent, and in addition there was the charm of the young woman, who was at once serious and lively, and exceptionally intelligent. He would soon take her into his bed, and derive the greatest pleasure from doing so.

But if she rejected the true belief, he himself would throw the first missile when she was stoned in the public square. Any unbelievers who demanded their continuing freedom must be wiped out. The female converts, however, would be cruel warriors, even more fanatical than the males. Strangers to pity, they would be inspired by Bina's example and gaily slaughter all those who resisted. Then the Herald's legions would emerge from their bellies. There would be no more wicked Egyptian potions, no more limiting the number of births, but instead a rapid increase in population. The sole ruler would be the howling mob, which was easily controlled.

When he reached his house, Bina came to greet him.

'Would you like some salt?' she asked.

'No, thank you.'

Rage suddenly filled her eyes.

'Is something wrong?' he asked.

'That girl Nephthys – she's trying to seduce you!'

'Does that shock you?'

'I am the Queen of the Night, and I should be the only woman admitted into your company.'

The Herald looked at her condescendingly. 'Your dreams are making your mind wander. Have you forgotten that woman is an inferior creature? Only man may take decisions. Moreover, one man is worth several women and so cannot be satisfied with only one. A wife, on the other hand, owes absolute fidelity to her husband, on pain of being stoned. Such are the commandments of God. The pharaohs' state is wrong to reject polygamy and give females a place which they do not deserve and which makes them dangerous. The reign of the new belief will soon wipe away these errors.'

He stroked Bina's hair. 'God's law imposes on you the presence of Nephthys – and of any other woman I choose. You will submit, because your spiritual progress demands it. You and those like you must evolve, beginning by obeying your guides, of whom I am the supreme leader. You aren't having any doubts, I hope?'

Bina knelt and kissed his hands. 'Do with me as you will.'

The answer to Iker's request that Gergu be investigated was deeply worrying: it informed him of the attack on Sobek, who was seriously wounded and unable to command his men. So the Memphis rebel network was on the offensive again! He told his wife the bad news immediately.

'Sobek will recover,' she prophesied. 'The king will expel the bad energy from his body, and Doctor Gua will heal him.'

'Our enemies are becoming dangerous again.'

'They never stopped.'

'If Sobek recovers he'll follow Gergu's trail, and perhaps it will at last lead us to the rebel leaders.'

'How is Bega behaving?'

'He's always friendly and respectful. He answers my questions directly and makes my task easier. One more day's work, and the preparations for the ritual will be finished.'

They gazed lovingly at each other.

'For the first time,' whispered Isis, 'you are going to direct the ceremony of the Mysteries. Remember, you must not speak or act in haste. Become the channel along which the words of power pass, the instrument that plays them in harmony.'

Iker knew he was unworthy of such a responsibility, but he did not try to hide from it. His life seemed to have been a succession of miracles; every day he offered thanks to the gods. To live with Isis, here in Abydos, to have the king's trust, to progress along the path of knowledge: what more could he ask for? From the ordeals he had undergone, he retained an acute awareness of the happiness whose every facet he savoured, from a sunset beside his wife to the proper celebration of a rite.

*

Nephthys was an exceptionally gifted spinner and weaver. The fabrics and garments used during the Mysteries of the month of Khoiak would be of superb quality. Even the Shaven-headed one, usually so sparing with compliments, recognized her talent.

Isis and Nephthys checked the list of items required. Everything must be right; nothing must be missing.

'You know most of the temporary workers well, don't you?' said Nephthys.

'More or less, especially the loyal ones who have been here a long time.'

'I'm thinking of a new employee in Senusret's Temple of a Million Years. He's a handsome man, tall, very stylish and distinctive, and extremely charming. Outside Abydos, he drills vases from hard stone. It is a difficult profession, and he has an excellent mastery of it. Here he's entrusted with the cleaning and maintenance of the ritual cups and vases. In my opinion, he deserves better. He might even have the stamp of a permanent priest.'

'What enthusiasm! Are you perhaps a little . . . smitten?'

'Perhaps.'

'Definitely!'

'We took our evening meal together,' admitted Nephthys, 'and we'll see each other again soon. He is intelligent, hard-working and attractive, but . . .'

'Is there something about him you're uncomfortable with?'

'His gentleness seems overdone, as if it's masking carefully hidden violence. But I'm probably wrong.'

'Heed your intuition before you go any further.'

'What about you? Did you feel anything like that about Iker?'

Isis shook her head. 'No, I knew only that his love was serious, absolute, and that it demanded total commitment. That power frightened me. I couldn't see within myself clearly, and I didn't want to lie to him. But I often thought of him, and I missed him. Little by little, this magical bond was transformed into love, and I realized he would be the only man in my life.'

'And nothing shakes your certainty?'

'Quite the opposite: it grows stronger every day.'

'You're very lucky,' said Nephthys. 'I don't know if my handsome temporary worker will bring me such happiness.'

'Do not ignore your intuition.'

Like a wild animal forever on its guard, Shab the Twisted sensed that someone was approaching his hiding-place. Pushing aside one of the low branches that hid the entrance to the shrine, he saw the large figure of Bega.

The Twisted One had no liking for the tall, ugly fellow and wondered how he managed to deceive the permanent priests. In their place, he would have been suspicious of this rigorous man with the suppressed ambitions. Bega thought he had a brilliant future at the head of a purified priesthood, but he was badly mistaken. Shab would take care of the purification, and the priest would be among the first condemned to death. All traces of the past must be wiped away, so as to build a world answering to the wishes of the Herald.

'Are you alone?' Shab asked warily.

'Yes. You can come out.'

Dagger in hand, his nerves on edge, Shab did so.

'A wonderful opportunity has arisen,' said Bega. 'Prepare yourself to kill Iker.'

Wearing jackal masks, two ritual priests played the part of Wepwawet, the Way-opener, one in relation to the North, the other to the South.

'May your emergence occur,' ordered Iker. 'Advance and care for your father, Osiris.'

Charged with bringing back the far-off goddess who had

fled into the depths of Nubia, and transforming the terrifying lioness into a peaceable she-cat, a spear-man, Onuris, protected the jackals. Near them, ibis-headed Thoth held the magical texts needed to keep away the dark forces that were determined to destroy Osiris's procession.

At the centre was the *neshemet*, the ship of Osiris. It would cross a good part of the site, would sail upon the sacred lake and would link the visible world to the invisible. 'In truth,' proclaimed Thoth, 'the Lord of Abydos will come back to life and will appear in glory.'

His crowns strengthened, the god rested inside the shrine constructed in the middle of the ship.

'Let the way to the sacred wood be made sacred,' commanded Iker.

A large wooden sledge was brought, and the ship was placed on it so that it might travel the Way of Earth, thus opening up the hearts of the inhabitants of East and West. They would see its beauty when it returned to its house of eternity, purified and regenerated. During 'the Night of Taking the God Forth and Offering Him Joy', the work of the House of Gold would take on its full meaning.

It still remained to mime the confrontation between the followers of Osiris and the confederates of Set. Arming himself with a pointed stave called 'Great of Strength', Iker assembled the former, facing the cohort of their enemies.

With his eyebrows and moustache dyed to match his red wig, and wearing a tunic of coarse linen, Shab the Twisted was unrecognizable as he mingled with the temporary workers who were practising their roles as the followers of Set.

He had eyes only for Iker. First, with the short staff he carried he would strike the Royal Son hard on the back of the neck. Then, while pretending to help him, he would strangle him with a leather thong. He would have to act quickly, very quickly. But he would have the advantage of surprise, and would manage to get away.

'Let us overthrow the enemies of Osiris!' ordered Iker. 'May they fall upon their faces, never to rise again.'

On both sides, the parts were taken seriously, but no blows were struck. The staves rose and fell in unison, following the rhythm of a sort of dance.

The Twisted One was obliged to copy the men around him as, one by one, the supporters of Set collapsed. He was furious at allowing himself to be caught in the trap of this ritual, whose form he did not know. He would have to force his way through the supporters of Osiris and strike Iker down.

Unfortunately, the Royal Son had a formidable weapon, and the Twisted One never attacked a victim face to face. Forced to give up, he dropped his staff and lay down on the ground.

Defeated, the confederates of Set no longer opposed the procession, which moved off towards the Tomb of Osiris.

The losers got up and dusted themselves down.

'You took your time falling!' commented a ritual priest in surprise. 'Don't take so long in the real ceremony.'

'Shouldn't we fight more determinedly?' asked Shab.

'Your role's going to your head, my lad! All that matters is the meaning of the ritual act. Go home, wash yourself and get rid of all that red dye. Here, nobody likes that colour very much.'

The Twisted One would gladly have strangled this giver of lessons, but he had to show patience. He swallowed his disappointment and returned to his hiding-place, hoping that the Herald would forgive his failure.

19

A sandstorm covered Abydos with an ochre-yellow mantle. It became difficult to move around, and visibility grew more and more limited.

However, Iker went to see Bega, who had invited him for the evening meal in order, he had said, to pass on information vital for the future of Abydos.

'You should take shelter, my lord,' advised the guards' commander, who was inspecting the town's perimeter defences. 'I've never seen such a severe storm.'

'Bega is waiting for me.'

'Hurry, then.'

The officer feared there might be accidents and injuries. Confined to their barracks by the storm, his men would not be able to help.

As he was returning to his post, he noticed the silhouette of a woman. He went closer. 'Bina! Don't stay outside – it's dangerous.'

'I wanted to see you.'

Flattered, he smiled. 'Is it urgent?'

She swung her hips seductively. 'I think . . .'

'Come with me. I'll help you.'

The pretty brunette put her arms round his neck and begged a kiss.

'Not here,' he protested, 'in this storm.'

'Yes, here and now.'

Utterly seduced, the officer slid the straps of Bina's dress down over her golden shoulders, and kissed her breasts. Shab the Twisted's leather thong encircled his neck from behind, and tightened. The commander died quickly and painfully.

He had been condemned to death because he knew Iker's destination. But Bina had wanted him dead anyway: she could no longer bear his lustful looks.

Bega's modest house was thoroughly unwelcoming and definitely in need of redecoration. To Iker's surprise, the austere priest had prepared what for him was a virtual banquet. On a long wooden table, which was covered with a white sheet, were two jars of wine, and dishes of meat, fish, vegetables and fruit.

'I am glad to see you, Royal Son. This evening, we shall feast.'

'What are we celebrating?'

'Your triumph, of course. Have you not just conquered Abydos? Let us drink to that great victory.'

Iker accepted a cup. He thought the wine rather sour, but did not like to criticize it. 'I confess I find those words surprising and even shocking,' he said. 'I am not a conqueror, and this is not a war. My only wish is to serve Osiris and Pharaoh.'

'Come, come, don't be so modest, my lord. To be superior of the permanent priests of Abydos at your young age – what a truly remarkable achievement! But do please eat and drink.'

Iker did not care for his host's biting sarcasm, but he picked at some dried fish and a few salad leaves, and drank a little more wine, which was still just as sour. 'What did you want to tell me?' he asked.

'You seem in a great hurry. If this storm worsens, you won't be able to get back home. I am happy to offer you hospitality.'

'I ask you again, what is this vital information?'

'It is absolutely vital, believe me.' The expression in Bega's eyes became openly hostile. He was filled with an icy wickedness, as if he was at last attaining a perverse goal, which he had for a long time believed inaccessible.

'Please explain yourself.'

'Don't be so impatient; you'll get your explanation. Let me enjoy this moment. Your triumph is an empty one, you ambitious little man. By stealing the post that rightly belonged to me, you committed an unforgivable sin. Now you are going to pay.'

Iker stood up. 'You must have lost your mind!'

'Look, here in the hollow of my hand.'

For a moment, Iker's vision blurred – it must be the effects of tiredness and bad wine, he thought.

Then Bega's hand came back into focus. A tiny and surprising figure was imprinted in the palm.

'It looks like . . . No, that's impossible! It's the head of Set!'

'Correct, Royal Son.'

'What does this mean?'

'You're swaying on your feet. You'd better sit down.'

Iker did so, and felt a little better.

Bega gave him a look of ferocious hatred. 'It means that I'm a confederate of Set and a member of the conspiracy of evil, as are Medes and Gergu. That's vital information, eh? And it isn't the last surprise I've got for you.'

Iker was dazed. He could hardly breathe, and his blood burnt. He put this down to Bega's incredible revelations. How could anyone possibly have imagined such wickedness in a permanent priest? Pharaoh was right: evil was flourishing at the very heart of Abydos.

A tall, beardless man with a shaven head appeared and fixed his red eyes on Iker.

Bega bowed. 'This time, Master, nothing and nobody can save the Royal Son.'

'Who are you?' asked Iker.

'Think,' advised a gentle voice. 'The riddle isn't very difficult to solve.'

'The Herald! The Herald, here on the sacred earth of Abydos . . .'

'You have survived terrible ordeals, Iker, and overcome many dangers. I made no mistake in choosing you. No other man could have accomplished what you have. But now you have fulfilled your destiny: you are the heir and successor to Pharaoh, heir to the great Mysteries, the irreplaceable spiritual son. For that reason, you must die. Deprived of a future, Senusret will collapse and drag Egypt down with him as he falls.'

Summoning the last of his strength, Iker seized his cup and tried to strike the evil monster. But Shab the Twisted leapt on him from behind, made him drop his makeshift weapon, and forced him to sit down again.

'Your power is fading away,' said the Herald. 'The texts in the workshop of Senusret's temple taught me a great deal. Egyptian scholars have a remarkable knowledge of animal and plant poisons, and one must admire their medicinal use of the venom of snakes and scorpions. I spoilt the taste of this fine wine by pouring a deadly poison into it. The new religion will ban all alcoholic drinks – you will die because of the depraved customs of this accursed land.'

Now Bina appeared. 'At last you're helpless and unable to fight! You thought you could reach the top, but you've failed – and I'm delighted to see it.'

Paralysed and covered in sweat, Iker felt life ebbing out of him.

'Before nothingness engulfs you,' went on the Herald, 'I must describe the near future to you. Thanks to your death, the foundation stone of the Two Lands will suffer irreparable cracks. The devastated Senusret will fall victim to misfortune, all those close to him will abandon him, and

Memphis will suffer the anger of my disciples. The only people to survive will be the converts to the true religion; all infidels and unbelievers shall perish. Sculpture, painting, literature and music will be banned. My words will be copied down, and will be spoken unceasingly – there will be no need for any other knowledge. Whoever dares doubt my truth will be executed. As inferior creatures, women will remain confined in their homes, will serve their husbands and give them many male children in order to form an army of conquerors, which will impose our faith on the entire world. Not an inch of a woman's body shall be uncovered. Each man shall take as many wives as he likes. The gold of the gods will enable me to develop a new system which will ensure wealth for my faithful. And above all, Iker, Osiris will no longer return to life.'

'You're wrong, you vile demon! My death will change nothing. The pharaoh will destroy you.'

The Herald smiled. 'You won't save your world, little scribe, for I have sentenced it to death. And I am indestructible.'

'No, you aren't . . . The Light . . . the Light will defeat you.'

Iker's lips clenched shut. The fire burnt more fiercely in his veins, his limbs were stiffening, and his sight fading. He called upon the pharaoh, his father, and addressed his last thoughts to Isis, so close and so far away. He engraved his love in a final sigh, certain that she would never abandon him.

Bega was the first to examine the corpse. 'He won't hinder us any more,' he noted icily.

In a brutal movement, he tore off the Royal Son's collar and trampled on the amulet representing the 'Power' sceptre. Then he took the sheet off the wooden table on which the meal had been set, revealing that the 'table' was in fact a wooden sarcophagus. With Shab's aid, he laid Iker's body in it.

'Take it away,' ordered the Herald, 'and place it close to Senusret's temple. I still have much work to do.'

'The storm's getting even stronger,' said Bina anxiously.

He stroked her hair. 'Do you think a mere sandstorm will stop me violating the tomb of Osiris?'

'Be careful, my lord. People say that place has magical protection which prevents anyone from approaching.'

'With Iker dead, and the spiritual transmission shattered, no wall, visible or invisible, will resist me.'

The sand was getting in everywhere, even though all the windows and doors were closed. In the end, Isis gave up trying to drive it out. She would have to wait for the bad weather to end before she attacked the dust.

The howling wind made her shiver. It carried wailing and moaning sounds, charging at the buildings without respite.

Isis felt suddenly worried. Why hadn't Iker returned? She told herself that he must be busy sorting out many details of the rites, so perhaps he had decided to stay in the temple until the storm subsided.

Suddenly she felt a violent pain which tore her heart open. She had to sit down, and could scarcely get her breath back. Never had she been afflicted with such anxiety.

On a low table, the Golden Palette was shining strangely. Overcoming her pain, Isis picked it up. The hieroglyphic of the throne was there, serving to write her name. Iker was calling her.

Anguished memories filled her mind. The former High Priestess had told her that she was not a priestess like the others and that a perilous mission would fall to her. No, she must not let herself be afflicted. A simple sandstorm, a simple delay in her husband's return, a simple moment's sickness due to too much work . . . Isis moistened her face with cool water and lay down on her bed.

The Golden Palette, her name, Iker's call . . . She could not just lie here. She got up, put on the long white robe she wore as a priestess of Hathor, tied a red belt about her waist and donned leather sandals.

When she left the house, the wind was still fierce and the sand stung her face. She could not see more than five paces ahead of her. She ought to have given up, but she knew Iker needed her. Their spirits and their hearts were so intimately linked that, even when they were apart, they remained close to each other. But in the last few minutes Iker had been getting further away. Was she in danger of of losing him?

Braving the storm, she headed for Senusret's Temple of a Million Years. The Royal Son must have encountered unexpected difficulties, and was trying to resolve them, losing track of the time. Surely he must be going into each episode of the Mysteries in depth with the ritual priests?

None of these thoughts calmed her. At each step, she perceived a tragedy more acutely. Evil had just struck Abydos. Never had the night been so dark.

"You will live through terrible ordeals,' the Great Royal Wife had predicted. 'You must know the words of power in order to fight visible and invisible enemies.'

She reached a paved area: the path leading to the temple. She knew this place better than anyone. And yet she hesitated to go on.

Near the first gateway, her foot hit a sarcophagus. On the cover, painted in red ink, was a head of Set. Feverishly, she slid the lid off. Inside lay a corpse.

Hoping that she was mistaken, Isis closed her eyes for a few moments.

'No, Iker, no . . .' She dared to touch and kiss him.

Taking off her belt, she tied a magic knot in it and laid it on the body, in order to maintain the link between her soul and that of the dead man. Then she placed an *ankh*-shaped ring on the middle finger of her husband's right hand.

A huge figure emerged from the mass of ochre brown sand.
'Majesty . . .'
Senusret held his daughter tightly. She wept, as no woman
had ever wept before.

Part II

Isis' Quest

20

The pharaoh had had a premonition of disaster, and feared he would arrive too late. Difficult conditions on the river had prevented him reaching Abydos in time.

The enemy had stabbed him through the heart. By killing Iker, he had murdered Egypt's future.

Isis gazed up at the sky. 'He who tries to separate the brother from the sister shall not triumph. He wants to break me and hurl me into despair. I shall crush him, for he destroys happiness and the righteous moment. Iker must be brought back to life, Majesty, by using the Great Secret.'

'I share your pain, but you are asking the impossible.'

'Does the *ka* not pass from pharaoh to pharaoh? Is it not true that only one pharaoh exists? If this power was within Iker, we can try to bring it to rebirth. In at least one case, that of the master-builder Imhotep, who has been alive since the time of the pyramids, his *ka* has been ceaselessly passed from initiate to initiate, and he remains the sole founder of temples.'

'The most urgent thing is to remove the causes of death and halt the process of decay. Bring the Shroud of Osiris prepared for the celebration of the Mysteries and join me at the House of Life.'

The sandstorm was at last subsiding. The guards escorting the king carried the sarcophagus as far as the entrance to the building.

'Majesty,' an officer informed him, 'we have found the body of the commander of the security guards. He was strangled.'

The king's face remained unreadable. So, as he had assumed, the enemy had entered the very heart of the city of Osiris.

'Wake all the guards, request reinforcements from the nearest towns, and surround the entire area of Abydos, including the desert.'

Dishevelled and limping, the Shaven-headed One bowed before the king. As he did so, his eyes fell on the sarcophagus. 'Iker! Is he . . . ?'

'The Herald's accomplices have murdered him.'

The Shaven-headed One suddenly looked very old. 'So they are hiding among us, and I saw nothing!'

'We are going to initiate the rites of the Great Secret.'

'Majesty, they are applicable only to the pharaoh and to exceptional persons like Imhotep or—'

'Is Iker not exceptional?'

'If we are wrong, he will be annihilated!'

'Isis wishes to fight this battle. And so do I. We must hurry – I must repel death.'*

The Shaven-headed One opened the door of the House of Life.

When she saw the pharaoh the she-panther, guardian of the sacred archives, showed no sign of aggression.

As soon as Isis joined him, bearing a chest of ivory and blue glazed porcelain, the king picked up Iker's body and carried it into the building. In this place where the words of joy flourished, where one lived by the Word, where words were distinguished and given all their meaning, the pharaoh had often meditated, read and performed the rituals refined by the permanent priests through the ages.

*All the rites mentioned below are described in Egyptian sources (temples, tombs, stelae and papyri).

He laid the body of his spiritual son on a wooden bed decorated with divine figures armed with knives. No evil spirit could attack the sleeper.

'Dress him in the tunic of Osiris,' the king ordered Isis and the Shaven-headed One. 'May his head rest on the bedhead of Chu, the radiant air that is at the origin of all life.'

Isis opened the chest and unfolded the garment of royal linen that Iker would have offered Osiris during the celebration of the Mysteries. She herself had washed and smoothed the precious tunic. Only a woman initiated into the Mysteries of Hathor could handle this fabric, which was as bright and sparkling as a flame. As the sweat of Ra, the expression of the Divine Light, this shroud purified the wearer and rendered him proof against decay.

To the Shaven-headed One's amazement, Iker's face, with its wide-open eyes, remained peaceful when he was dressed in the tunic of Osiris. The flame of the sacred fabric ought to have consumed his flesh and put an end to Isis' mad hopes.

She looked at him and spoke to him, although no word emerged from her mouth. Having passed successfully through this first ordeal, Iker was continuing to fight in a place that was neither death nor rebirth.

His wife could have confined herself to the rites permitting the souls of the righteous to live again in the paradise lands of the world beyond. But this death, this murder, was the work of evil. Not content with killing a man, it aimed to destroy Pharaoh's spiritual son and the destiny he embodied.

Isis saw the Shaven-headed One's disapproval and knew the extent of the risks. Yet the ordeal of the shroud surely indicated Osiris's support and Iker's consent?

When a huge man appeared wearing the mask of Anubis, the jackal who knew the beautiful paths of the West and the roads of the otherworld, Isis and the Shaven-headed One withdrew and went to the treasury of the House of Life to fetch the items needed for the ritual.

'I bring together the bodily tissues of the complete soul,' proclaimed Senusret. 'I heal from death, fashion the sun, the golden stone with its fertilizing rays, and shape the full moon in its incessant renewal. I pass on their strengths to you.'

Until dawn, the pharaoh laid on his hands and magnetized Iker. Mummified, stabilized between two worlds, the corpse would not decay.

The Shaven-headed One handed the king a cubit stick painted white and decorated with red rings. Senusret placed this *Pedj-aha*, or 'right extensor', under Iker's back. It took the place of his vertebral column and spinal cord, so that the magnetism could continue to circulate and ward off the cold of death.

Isis handed her father an animal skin, which Anubis slashed before using it to wrap the body of his son.

'Set is present,' he declared. 'After killing you, he is now protecting you. Henceforth, he will inflict no wounds upon you. His destructive fire preserves you from itself and retains the warmth of life. Let the seven sacred oils be applied.'

Brought together, they recreated the eye of Horus, the triumphant unification of dispersion and chaos. With her little finger, Isis touched Iker's lips and endowed him with the energies of these oils: 'festival perfume', 'jubilation', 'punishment of Set', 'union', 'support', 'finest of the pine', and 'finest of Libya'.

Anubis uncapped the vase the Shaven-headed One gave him. It contained the quintessence of minerals and metals, resulting from the alchemical work of the House of Gold.

'I anoint you with this divine substance, measured out for your *ka*. Thus you become a stone, the place of metamorphoses.'

Using an adze made of sky-iron, Anubis unblocked the channels of Iker's heart, ears and mouth. New senses were awakened; twelve channels joining at the heart produced breath and formed a protective envelope.

However, although he had become a body of Osiris, shielded from corruption, Iker was still a long way from resurrection. His being must be made to shine forth, it must be filled with a light that came from a time before birth. Taking off his jackal's mask, the pharaoh spoke the first words of the Pyramid Texts, beginning the process of resurrecting the royal soul: "'Truly you did not depart in a state of death; you left alive.'"

And Isis added: "'You left, but you will return. You sleep, but you will awake. You reach the shores of the world beyond, but you live.'"

The Shaven-headed One left father and daughter alone.

'Death was born,' declared Senusret, 'therefore it will die. That which shines forth beyond the seeming world, beyond what we call "life" and "death" is not subject to nothingness. "Beings from before creation escape the day of death."* Only that which was not born can come back to life. So initiation into the Mysteries of Osiris is not merely a new birth and the journey across a death. Human beings die because they do not know how to reunite themselves with the beginning and do not listen to the message of their celestial mother, Mut. Mut implies death, righteousness, precision, the right moment, a fertilizing channel and the creation of a new seed.†

'Is the dwelling of the dead not too deep and dark?' asked Isis anxiously. 'It has no door or window – no ray of light illuminates it, no northerly wind cools it. The sun never rises there.'

'That is the hell of the second death. A person with knowledge can escape it; no magic chains him there. Remember your initiation, during the ordeal of the sarcophagus. At that moment, you perceived the Great Secret: initiates into the

---

*The three quotations are from Pyramid Texts 134a, 1975a–b and 1467a respectively.
†All these notions are contained in the root, '*m(ut)t*'.

Mysteries of Osiris can come back from death, provided they are free from evil and have been identified as being of just voice.'

Isis remembered. The human body was made up of a perishable body, a name which influenced its destiny, a shadow which remained after death to carry out an initial regeneration, a *ba*, the soul-bird that flew up to the sun and brought back the radiance of the Osiran body, a *ka*, the indestructible vital energy to be won back after death, and an *akh*, the radiant spirit awoken during initiation into the Mysteries.

Iker had all these elements. However, death had separated and scattered them. If the court of Osiris judged him favourably, they would be brought back together on the other side and reassembled in a new individual able to experience two kinds of eternity, the eternity of the moment and the eternity of time, nourished by the cycles of nature.

Isis demanded more.

'The world is made up of three spheres,' said the king. 'They are the sphere of chaos and darkness, where the damned are punished, the sphere of Light, where Ra and Osiris are united in the present of the righteous, and, lying between those two, the sphere of filtration, where evil must be caught in a net. You and Nephthys must conduct the rites of this intermediate world.'

Isis and Nephthys painted each other's faces. A line of green kohl, emanating from the eye of Horus, decorated the lower eyelids. A line of black, from the eye of Ra, adorned the upper ones. These face-paints, which were kept in the box called 'Opener of the Eye', were masterpieces made by specialists in the temple, and took care of the divine eye. Red ochre emphasized the two priestesses' lips, and oil of fenugreek softened their skin.

On Nephthys's heart, Isis drew a star; on her navel, a sun.

Thus they became the two mourners, Isis the Great, who was compared to the deck of the celestial ship, and Nephthys the Lesser, compared to the prow.

Nephthys presented Isis with seven robes of different colours, embodying the stages the High Priestess of Hathor had passed through in the House of the Acacia. Then the two dressed in tunics of finest linen, as white as the purity of the newborn day, as yellow as the crocus and as red as flame. Upon their heads they wore golden diadems decorated with cornelian flowers and rosettes of lapis-lazuli, and covered their chests with broad collars of gold and turquoise, whose clasps were shaped like falcons' heads. On their wrists and ankles they wore bracelets of bright red cornelian, stimulating the vital fluid. Their feet were clad in white sandals.

Nephthys embraced her sister priestess. 'Isis, you cannot imagine how much I share your pain. Iker's death is an unbearable injustice.'

'Therefore we must set it right. I need your help, Nephthys. The pharaoh's magnetism and the words of power have stabilized Iker's existence in the intermediate sphere. It is up to us to bring it forth from there.'

The two young women entered the mortuary room, which was dimly lit by a single lamp. Isis positioned herself at the foot of the coffin, with Nephthys at its head. Holding their hands out over it, they magnetized it. Undulating waves emerged from their palms and enveloped Iker's body in a gentle light.

In turn, the mourners chanted ritual lamentations handed down since the time of Osiris. The vibrations of these rhythmic words imprisoned destructive forces and drove them away from the mummy. Stretched out between the world of the living and the world of the dead, the net of magical words acted as a purifying filter.

And then came the moment of the final supplication.

169

'Return to your temple in your original form,' Isis implored him, 'return in peace! I am your sister who loves you and drives away despair. Do not leave this place; unite yourself with me; I shall drive out misfortune. The light belongs to you; you shine forth. Come to your wife; she embraces you. Reassemble your bones and your limbs, and become a complete and whole individual. The Word remains upon your lips; you drive back the darkness. I shall protect you for ever. My heart is full of love for you; I desire to embrace you and to remain so close to you that nothing can separate us. Here I am at the heart of your mysterious shrine, determined to defeat the evil that afflicts you. Place your life in me, I enclose you in the life of my being. I am your sister; do not depart from me. Gods and men weep for you. I call you to the summit of the heavens! Do you not hear my voice?'*

The pharaoh, the Shaven-headed One, Isis and Nephthys were standing around the coffin at the end of a long vigil.

'Osiris is not the god of all the dead,' recalled the king, 'but the god of those faithful to Ma'at who followed the path of righteousness during their lives. The judges of the world beyond see our lives in a moment and take into consideration only our deeds, which are placed in a heap beside us. They show us no indulgence, and only the righteous will walk freely upon the beautiful paths of eternity. First, the human court is convened. I represent Upper and Lower Egypt, the Shaven-headed One the permanent priests of Abydos, Isis the priestesses of Hathor. Do you consider Iker worthy to appear before the Great God and step aboard his ship?'

'Iker committed no sin against Abydos or initiation,' declared the Shaven-headed One, with great emotion.

*The long version of the 'Lamentations of Isis and Nephthys', notably translated by R. O. Faulkner and S. Schott, can be found in the Bremner-Rhind papyrus.

'Iker's is a great heart; no mortal sin sullies it,' stated Isis.

There remained the king's sentence. Would Senusret reproach Iker for his past errors and his lack of clear thinking?

'Iker followed his destiny without cowardice or weakness. He is my son. May Osiris receive him into his kingdom.'

21

When favourable, the judgment of the court of Osiris often manifested itself to watchers in the form of a bird, a butterfly or a scarab beetle.

As soon as the ritualists emerged from the House of Life, Isis looked up at the sky. She herself knew Iker's heart, his purity and his righteousness, but what would the Invisible powers decide? The continuation of the ritual process depended upon their verdict.

Suddenly, a large ibis with long, elegant wings flew slowly across the blue sky. Its gaze met Isis'.

She knew then that Iker had spoken the correct words, assisted by Thoth, the patron and protector of scribes. Light as the goddess Ma'at's ostrich feather, his heart continued to live. By proving that he had put into practice the words taught by the master of hieroglyphs, the Royal Son had traced his path towards the afterlife.

On the Golden Palette the words '*Of just voice*' appeared.

'The most difficult part is still to come,' said Senusret. 'Now the death of Iker must be transferred into the mummy of Osiris. When it has overcome that death, Iker's Osiran body will be reborn.'

The backbone of Egypt, the foundation of everything that was built, both spiritually and materially, Osiris served as a basis for temples, houses of eternity, houses, canals . . . No space was empty of him, no form of death could touch him. Could this transfer succeed, reserved as it was for pharaohs and those few sages of the stature of Imhotep?

While the Shaven-headed One was pouring the libations of water and milk at the foot of the Tree of Life, Senusret and his daughter went to the tomb of the Great God.

The permanent priest charged with watching over it ran to meet them. 'Majesty, something terrible has happened! Last night, the seals on the door were broken.'

The pharaoh crossed the sacred wood to reach the entrance to the monument, which was hidden among the vegetation. Near it the acacia trees were burnt. A violent battle had taken place between the profaner and the shrine's magical defences. Before the entrance lay the broken seals.

Senusret crossed the threshold. Jewellery, vases, dishes and other ritual objects important to Osiris's eternal life lay scattered, broken and trampled underfoot. The banquet of the world beyond could no longer be celebrated.

The king advanced, fearing the worst. Several lamps were still burning in the chamber of resurrection. It, too, had been laid waste.

Formerly, the mummy of Osiris had lain upon a bed of black basalt shaped like the bodies of two lions. It had worn the White Crown, and held the sceptre called 'Magic' and the sceptre of threefold birth. These symbols had been broken into a thousand pieces. Violating this place of peace where the Great God, master of silence, had reposed, the Herald had penetrated the seven walls protecting the sarcophagus. As for the mummy, the basis for resurrection, nothing remained of it. The Herald would disperse the parts of the god's body so that nobody could put it back together.

One hope remained.

Senusret lifted a heavy flagstone, uncovering a flight of steps leading down to a vast underground chamber. It housed a sealed vase, the *khetemet*, surrounded by a ring of flame.

173

This vase contained the mystery of the divine work, the lymphatic fluids of Osiris and the source of life.

The fire still burnt, but the vase had gone.

Isis saw the distress in her father's eyes. For the first time, the giant swayed.

'Hide nothing from me,' she demanded.

'Only the Herald could have profaned Osiris's house of eternity in this way.'

'His mummy . . . ?'

'Unwrapped and destroyed.'

'And the *khetemet*?'

'Stolen and destroyed.'

'Then we cannot transfer Iker's death to Osiris and use the divine fluid to bring him back to life.'

The Shaven-headed One ran up in terrible distress. 'Majesty, the Tree of Life is dying again! The four guardian lions have been blinded and the protective barrier created by the four acacias has been destroyed. The healing gold is tarnished.'

'What of the fetish of Abydos?'

'The pole has been torn out and the cover ripped up.'

'And the relic of Osiris?'

'Horribly damaged.'

The Herald had not hesitated to disfigure the god.

'Should we not convene the Golden Circle?' suggested the Shaven-headed One.

'We cannot,' replied Senusret. 'The new tjaty, Sobek the Protector, fears there will be killings in Memphis. In order to lure the rebels out into the open, he is spreading the news that Nesmontu is dead. The general must remain in hiding and act as he sees fit. In addition, Sehotep is confined to his house and faces the death penalty if he is found guilty to trying to murder Sobek.'

'Are we bound hand and foot, finally defeated?'

'Not yet,' the king assured him. 'We must immediately strengthen our protection of Iker. The master-carpenter and the initiated craftsmen must place the ship of Osiris inside the House of Life. Then guards will surround it and will forbid anyone to enter, with the exception of the two of you and Nephthys. They will be ordered to kill without warning anyone who attempts to force their way through. You, Shaven-headed One, must try to find out if anyone witnessed the murders of Iker and the commander of the security guards.'

'But won't the murderers have left Abydos?'

'Even if they have, we shall prevent them from escaping.'

'Perhaps they have not yet achieved all their goals,' suggested the old priest, chillingly.

The king and the two priestesses laid Iker's mummy in the recently completed ship intended for the celebration of the Mysteries. It symbolized Osiris made whole again and, thanks to the precise assembly of its various parts, it enabled the Lord of the West to bring together all the gods.

'May you set sail and take the oars,' said the king to Iker, 'travel wherever your heart desires, be welcomed in peace by the Great of Abydos, participate in the rites and follow Osiris on pure paths across the sacred land.'

'Live with the stars,' Isis told him. 'Your soul-bird belongs to the community of the thirty-six decans; you can transform into each one of them at will and you feed upon their light.'

Nephthys watered a little garden close beside the boat. The soul-bird would come there to quench its thirst before setting off again for the sun.

In accordance with the royal instructions, the master-sculptor of Abydos created a cubic statue of Iker. It depicted the scribe seated, with his legs drawn up in front of him and his knees almost at the level of his shoulders. The body was wrapped in a shroud of resurrection, from which the head emerged, its open eyes directed towards the afterlife.

The initiate who was embodied in this way escaped being fragmented and became one with an unchanging order, for the cube contained all the geometric figures relating the construction of the universe. This sculpture might anchor Iker's soul in a Stone of Light, but formidable tasks still awaited the king and his daughter.

Forgetting to eat or sleep, Isis never left the sarcophagus. As for Nephthys, she rested only a little.

When her father took her gently in his arms, Isis feared the worst. 'Is there no more hope?'

'There is still a tiny chance of success, Isis. Tiny, but real.' Senusret never spoke lightly and did not try to deceive her. 'We cannot free Iker from the prison of the intermediate world without the *khetemet*.'

'Finding it intact . . . No, that is an impossible dream.'

'I fear so.'

'Then death has triumphed.'

'Perhaps another *khetemet* vase exists, and also contains the lymph of Osiris.'

'Where would it be hidden?'

'In Madu,' said the king.

'Iker's village?'

'Chance plays no part in the battle we are fighting against the Herald. Destiny chose Iker to be born in that place, which is so ancient that it fell into oblivion. I am therefore going to Madu, though I may well fail in my quest. No one knows the precise location of the primitive shrine of Osiris. The last person who did know the secret was an old scribe, Iker's protector and teacher. That is why the Herald murdered him.'

'How will you find the shrine again?'

'By undergoing a form of death that will put me in contact with the ancestors. Either they will guide me or the royal power will be insufficient and will die. If Iker's resurrection does not take place, Osiris will pass away for ever. The Herald will then have free rein, and the era of fanaticism, violence and oppression will begin. My duty is to find that *khetemet*, always supposing that it has survived. Your own task will be no easier.'

Senusret handed his daughter the Basket of Mysteries, made of reeds coloured yellow, blue and red. Its base was reinforced with two wooden bars laid across each other in the form of a cross. Within this basket, that which was scattered could be brought back together, and the soul of Osiris reconstituted. Iker had had the good fortune to see it once, during the harvest ritual.

'The Herald and the confederates of Set want to tear apart the Great Word, the expression of the Light embodied in Osiris. Travel the provinces, visit the towns, seek out the secret parts of temples and burial sites, gather up the divine limbs and bring them back to Abydos so that they may be reunited. Osiris is life. In him, those of just voice are safeguarded from death, the heavens do not collapse and the earth remains stable. But his integrity and cohesion must still be ensured, so as to pass on this life. Since your initiations, you now possess a new heart, able to perceive the Mystery of the shrines spread out across the Two Lands. If you reach the end of your quest before the start of the month of Khoiak,* we shall have thirty days left in which to bring the Osiris Iker back to life.'

Senusret took his daughter to his house of eternity. He went into the treasure chamber and brought back a knife made of solid silver.

'This is the Blade of Thoth, Isis. It cuts through reality, detects the correct path and penetrates the veils that conceal the scattered parts of Osiris's body.'

'Will there be enough time?' she asked worriedly.

'Have you forgotten the ivory sceptre of the Scorpion

*Around 20 October.

King? Fashioned by the gods' magic, it will deflect evil's attacks away from you, will inspire your words and will enable you to move with the winds. Explore the sacred lake; go to the bottom of the primordial ocean. If the gods have not abandoned us, you will discover there the leather scroll that Thoth wrote in the time of the Servants of Horus. It describes each province of Egypt, drawn in the heavens' image, and will reveal the stages of your journey to you.'

Isis had already seen the *nun* at the heart of the lake, where she came daily to draw the water needed for the acacia's survival. She walked slowly down the stone steps and under the surface, armed with the Blade of Thoth and the 'Magic' sceptre.

As thick darkness enveloped her, a ray of moonlight lit her way. Deep in the blackness, it shone upon an iron chest. Isis placed the tip of the knife in the lock. The lid opened automatically. Inside was a bronze chest. It contained a third made of wood, which housed a fourth of ivory and ebony, surrounding a fifth of silver. As this seemed sealed, Isis used the sceptre.

A gold chest appeared, surrounded by snakes. Hissing furiously, they protected the treasure. The shining blade of the knife calmed them. They moved aside and formed a wide circle round the priestess.

When she opened the gold chest, a lotus blossom sprang forth with lapis-lazuli petals surmounted by a peaceful, strikingly young face.

The face of Iker.

Taking the scroll of Thoth from the chest, she shut the lotus inside it and returned to the surface of the lake.

'Here is the head of Osiris,' she told the pharaoh, handing him the relic. 'The gods have not abandoned us and are continuing to support us. Iker has become the new basis of resurrection. Our destiny shall henceforth be played out through his.'

Senusret reopened the eyes of the four lions, brought the four young acacias back to life, set the fetish of Abydos back at the top of its pole and covered it with a cloth woven by Nephthys.

The sky grew clear, and the sun shone. Hundreds of birds flocked above the Tree of Life, whose golden covering regained all its brightness.

'Listen to them,' said the king. 'They, too, will guide you.'

Isis could understand their language. With one voice, the souls of the other world were calling upon her to recreate the body of Osiris.

The provinces of Lower Egypt

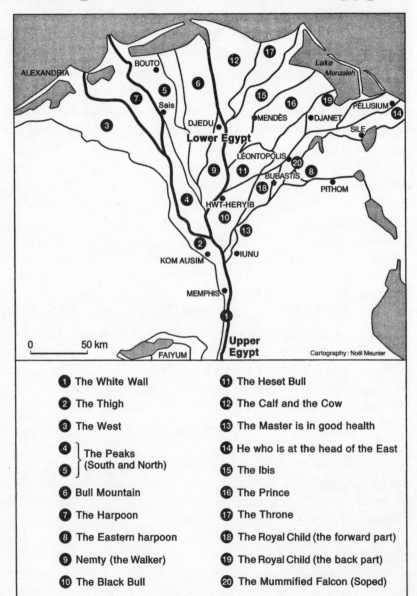

Cartography : Noël Meunier

1. The White Wall
2. The Thigh
3. The West
4. / 5. The Peaks (South and North)
6. Bull Mountain
7. The Harpoon
8. The Eastern harpoon
9. Nemty (the Walker)
10. The Black Bull
11. The Heset Bull
12. The Calf and the Cow
13. The Master is in good health
14. He who is at the head of the East
15. The Ibis
16. The Prince
17. The Throne
18. The Royal Child (the forward part)
19. The Royal Child (the back part)
20. The Mummified Falcon (Soped)

22

The pharaoh and his daughter spoke at length with the Shaven-headed One and Nephthys. In the name of the king, the old priest would ensure the safety of Abydos, and the continuation of the rites together with Nephthys, who was also involved in the investigation. The new commander of the security guards, a member of the king's personal bodyguard, would assist them.

'Apart from the two of you,' ordered Senusret, 'no one is to enter the House of Life. Our best men will watch it night and day. Spread the news of Iker's death. If his murderers are still here in Abydos, they will believe they have won and may perhaps make a mistake.'

'Won't they be suspicious when they see the House of Life so closely guarded?' asked Nephthys worriedly.

'It will be proof of our distress – we shall do the same for all the monuments and vital centres of Abydos. The first priority is the preservation of Iker's mummy – you are to speak the words of power every day. Your second priority is to prevent anyone from leaving or entering the land of Osiris.'

'Are you planning to return soon, Majesty?' asked the Shaven-headed One.

'Either I shall bring back the sealed vase containing the Great God's lymph, or I shall not return at all.'

When the pharaoh walked away, the Shaven-headed One thought he was living through the last hours of Abydos.

Isis said goodbye to Nephthys and advised her to exercise the greatest caution. Their enemies had already resorted to murder several times, and would not hesitate to kill a woman.

According to the Scroll of Thoth, the Widow – in this case, Isis – must go first to Elephantine, the head of Egypt, then travel down the Nile. She boarded a fast boat whose captain was extremely skilful and whose crew, made up of experienced men, knew all the river's traps. Ten elite archers escorted her.

As soon as the sails had been unfurled, the young woman pointed the 'Magic' sceptre towards the sky. In a few moments, a strong north wind began to blow. The captain had never known his boat go so fast, and the crew found it took only the minimum of effort to handle the sails and ropes for best results.

'We shall sail by night,' announced Isis.

'That is very dangerous, my lady,' said the captain.

'The moon's rays will light our way.'

Shab the Twisted emerged cautiously from his hiding-place: there was nobody about. He wanted to know if the whole site was surrounded or if there were still weak points.

Beyond the last shrines lay a desert area, which Bega used to use to smuggle out the small stelae. Had it not been for his innate caution, Shab would have been caught unawares. Two archers were standing guard, close to each other. It was clear from their behaviour that they belonged to a battle-hardened regiment.

The Twisted One crouched down and moved off, still bent low. Perhaps it was just certain places that were under such close guard. But he soon realized that this was not the case. There were soldiers everywhere. It was impossible to escape from Abydos through the desert.

Tense, he went back to his hiding-place. Almost at once he

heard someone coming. He pulled aside one of the concealing branches and peered out. It was Bega.

'Come inside,' said Shab.

Bega had difficulty bending his tall body and entering the little shrine.

'The army's watching the desert,' said Shab. 'I can't get away.'

'There are soldiers everywhere,' confirmed Bega. 'They have orders to fire without warning.'

'That must mean the pharaoh believes Iker's murderers are still in Abydos. But the Herald will get us out of this mess.'

'Don't move from here. I'll bring you food.'

'Why don't I mingle with the temporary workers? Iker isn't here any longer to identify me.'

'The guards will question them all. It would be difficult to justify your presence – you might be arrested. Just wait for your orders.'

Bega was as tense as Shab, but the feeling of victory reassured him. The king's reaction was laughable. Deploying the whole army would not bring Iker back to life!

Wearing an appropriately doleful expression, he lamented along with the permanent priests. They had been summoned by the Shaven-headed One, who they hoped would give them a clear explanation when he joined them.

'What a dreadful injustice,' said Bega mournfully. 'If the unfortunate Iker really is dead, death has struck him down just as he was reaching the zenith of his brilliant career. All of us had learnt to like him, for he was extremely respectful of our ways.'

The priests and priestesses nodded.

Bega noticed that the priest who watched over the Tomb of Osiris seemed particularly tired and grief-stricken.

'You look exhausted,' he said. 'Shouldn't you consult a doctor?'

'What's the use?'

'What do you mean?'

'I'm sorry, but I'm sworn to secrecy.'

'Not among ourselves, surely?'

'Even among ourselves. By order of the Shaven-headed One.'

Bega smiled inwardly. So the old man was trying to prevent the spread of the catastrophic news that would ruin the hopes of the inhabitants of the Great Land before spreading throughout the whole of Egypt.

'People are saying that Iker was murdered,' ventured the Servant of the *Ka*.

'That's nonsense!' exclaimed Bega. 'Don't listen to such mad rumours.'

'And wasn't an officer strangled?'

'Probably in a brawl.'

'And what about the increased number of soldiers, the extra security measures, the guards on all the buildings? It's obvious that terrible danger is threatening us.'

The Shaven-headed One's entrance put an end to the discussion. There were deep lines on his face, which had suddenly aged. His natural austerity was now accompanied by a poignant sadness. Even the most optimistic priests and priestesses could see the gravity of the situation.

'Iker the Royal Son is dead,' he declared. 'Nevertheless, we shall continue to prepare for the celebration of the Mysteries during Khoiak.'

'Was it a natural death or murder?' asked the Servant of the *Ka*.

'Murder.'

Absolute silence fell. Even Bega felt a sort of shock, as if a world had just crumbled. A crime sullying the sacred domain of Osiris, the worst violence at the heart of serenity!

'Has the murderer been caught?' asked the Servant of the *Ka*.

'Not yet.'

'Is his identity known?'

'Unfortunately not.'

'Can we be sure he's left Abydos?'

'No, we cannot.'

'Then we're in danger,' said the Servant of the *Ka* anxiously.

'And what about the commander of the security guards?' asked the priest who saw the secrets. 'He was murdered, too, wasn't he?'

'That is correct.'

'By another criminal or criminals?'

'We do not know; the investigation is just beginning. His Majesty has taken the measures necessary to ensure your protection. We must adhere to our Rule and devote ourselves to our ritual tasks. There is no better way of paying homage to Iker.'

'I have not seen poor Isis,' said Bega. 'Has she left Abydos?'

'She is so distressed that she no longer feels able to carry out her duties. Nephthys will lead the permanent priestesses.'

Bega was jubilant. Iker was dead, and Isis gone! A thousand soldiers were less dangerous than those two. For a long time he had wanted to kill Isis, for she was too beautiful, too intelligent, too radiant. Iker's death had destroyed her and taken away her power to harm the Herald. She would be prostrate with grief in some Memphis palace.

'The list of our misfortunes does not stop there,' said the Shaven-headed One. 'The tomb of Osiris has been desecrated and the precious *khetemet* stolen.'

'Neither Abydos nor Egypt can survive this disaster,' murmured the Servant of the *ka*, utterly devastated.

'I repeat,' said the old man, 'we must continue to live according to the Rule.'

'Even if there's no hope?'

'It is not necessary to hope in order to act. The rites are passed on through us and beyond us, whatever the circumstances may be.'

The distraught permanent priests attended to their usual duties, beginning with the assignment of tasks to the temporary workers, who were in a state of bafflement and anxiety. As the Shaven-headed One had not imposed silence, information would spread rapidly.

When evening fell, Bina massaged her lord's feet. In the darkness of their official house, he belonged to her and no longer thought of that accursed Nephthys, whom she would kill with her own hands. Gentle, considerate, submitting to the Herald's every whim, she would remain his chief wife, relegating the others to subsidiary tasks. And if one of them tried to take her place, she would slice her flesh to ribbons, put out her eyes and throw her remains to the dogs.

The Herald dined on a little salt; Bina fasted. She did not drink alcohol and ate nothing too fatty, for fear of getting putting on weight and displeasing her master. By continuing to be beautiful and desirable, she would defeat time's vicissitudes.

A shadowy figure slipped across the threshold. Snatching up a dagger, Bina barred the way.

'It is I, Bega!'

'One more step and I'd have run you through. Next time, announce yourself.'

'I didn't want to alert anyone. There are guards on duty near here, and soldiers and sentries keep watch on the site at all times. Nobody can enter or leave Abydos.'

'We still have our emergency route,' Bina reminded him.

'Shab says it's been cut, because there are archers patrolling in the desert.'

'Don't torment yourself,' advised the Herald in a tranquil voice. 'Has the Shaven-headed One revealed the truth?'

'He was too overwhelmed to keep silent. By tomorrow, everyone will know the full extent of the disaster. The permanent priests are devastated, and the beautiful Osiran structure is falling apart. Deprived of the god's protection, they feel doomed to nothingness. It's a total triumph, my lord! When Memphis is put to fire and the sword, the forces of order will scatter and we shall take power.'

'What news of Senusret?'

'He has left Abydos.'

'Where is he going?'

'I don't know. But Isis is so crushed by grief that she has also left.'

'Without attending her husband's burial rites?'

'They must have had to bury him in a hurry.'

'That is most un-Egyptian behaviour,' commented the Herald. 'Has the intoxication of victory stopped you thinking clearly?'

'The enemy is in full flight and behaving like a frightened animal.'

'Or at least that's what he wants us to think.'

'Why do you doubt it?'

'Because the king has re-established the protective barrier emanating from the four young acacias, reopened the eyes of the guardian lions and replaced the veiled post in the centre of the relic-holder.'

'It's just a diversion. He wants to make us think the head of Osiris has been saved.'

'Has the Shaven-headed One said as much?'

'No, but he admitted to the desecration of the Great God's tomb and the disappearance of the *khetemet*. Abydos no longer has any magical energy at all.'

'But the acacias' barrier is proving effective. Together with the soldiers' presence, it is preventing me from getting near the Tree of Life and hastening its destruction. Why are there all these precautions if the pharaoh is giving up the fight?'

'To create an illusion,' suggested Bega. 'He's concerned that there may be disturbances in Memphis, so he's hurrying back there.'

'Logic would indeed demand that. Nevertheless, this king knows how to fight a supernatural war. Death strikes his spiritual son, storms sweep through Abydos, and he leaves the place, contenting himself with a few makeshift measures . . . No, that is not like him.'

'He must defend Memphis,' disagreed Bega.

'Saving Osiris is even more important. A king of his stature neither retreats nor runs away. By recreating a magical barrier, however derisory it may seem to us, and by thus preserving the acacia, he betrays his desire to continue the fight with better weapons.' The Herald's red eyes flamed. 'Senusret is not going to Memphis,' he declared. 'I want to know his real intentions. Question the port officials and the sailors.'

'It will be risky – they may become suspicious.'

'Just go on proving your loyalty to me, my fine friend.'

The burning pain Bega felt in the palm of his hand dissuaded him from protesting.

'Doesn't Isis' departure worry you?' asked Bina.

The Herald stroked her hair. 'How could a mere woman possibly harm me?'

23

The provinces of Egypt were the earthly projection of the universe. Marrying the world beyond and the world below, correspondences and harmonies made the Two Lands the country beloved of the gods. It was like the body of Osiris, which was endangered by any lack of unity. By binding the South and the North firmly together, the pharaoh had celebrated the reality of resurrection.

Each province housed several relics, notably a part of the body of Osiris, carefully hidden and protected. Thanks to clues given in the *Book of Thoth*, Isis knew that fourteen of them were particularly important, since they were sufficient to assemble an enduring mummy, capable of receiving Iker's death.

However, formidable enemies stood in her way. First of all, there was time. Thanks to the 'Magic' sceptre, she would be able to contract it, if not control it, but she must not waste a single hour. Then there were the local governors. Although they had submitted to the royal will, of which she was the official emissary, they would not like her demands and might try to throw her off the scent. Lastly, the confederates of Set would certainly not leave her hands free throughout her quest. She would have the advantage of surprise for as long as they were unaware of her journey's goal, but sooner or later the secret would be betrayed.

Her first destination was Elephantine. When her boat berthed there, gentle sunlight bathed the capital of the first province of Upper Egypt, the southern border of the twin land, marked by the First Cataract. The canal Senusret had built had made river travel possible all year round, while the fortress and the brick wall had ensured the safety of communications and trade, facilitating the development of Nubia.

Isis went straight to the palace belonging to Sarenput, the province's governor. She was greeted there by Good Companion and Gazelle, a big, lean black dog and his inseparable companion, a small, plump bitch with pendulous teats. Despite their age, they were still excellent guards. Sarenput was wary of visitors if the dogs barked at them too much.

They greeted Isis with many signs of affection. Good Companion stood up on his hind legs and placed his paws on her shoulders, while Gazelle ran round and round her and licked her feet.

Their master soon appeared. He was a big man, with a square head, low brow, prominent cheekbones and chin, broad shoulders and a determined gaze.

'I am flattered to receive the High Priestess of Abydos,' he said solemnly and sincerely. 'To what do I owe the honour of your visit?'

Isis told him the whole story of the tragedy, witholding nothing.

Sarenput was aghast. He ordered strong wine, and said, 'Senusret's work is in danger of being destroyed, and the country of dying. How can we fight this demon enemy?'

'By recreating a new Osiris. I must begin with Elephantine's relic. Will you give it to me?'

Isis had feared his reaction, for he guarded his prerogatives fiercely and did not mince his words.

But he said, 'I'll take you to it immediately.'

He led her down to the Nile, and handed her into his favourite boat. He took the oars himself, and rowed hard.

The Great Secret

At the sight of the sacred island of Osiris, Isis remembered her terrifying adventure, when she had risked her life under the waters in the cave named 'Its Master's Shelter', in order to bring back the annual flood. Iker had saved her, carrying her up to the surface of the river. Now it was she who was trying to save him from death.

Sarenput moored the boat near the rock that protected the cave. Perched in the tops of an acacia and a jujube tree, a falcon and a vulture gazed down at the arrivals.

'There could be no better guards,' said Sarenput. 'One foolish fellow tried to discover the secret world within the cave, and the two birds gave him no chance. Anyone else who might have been curious was deterred by the sight of his dead body: there has been no trouble since then. What happens next is up to you, High Priestess. I shall wait for you outside.'

Isis set off along a narrow stone passageway, filled with the song of a spring. Although she did not recognize the place, she went forward unhesitatingly, ignoring the dampness and lack of air.

The corridor widened out, and a light shone up out of the depths. It was the dwelling of Hapy, the spirit of the Nile, the energy of the fertilizing flood. Reassured, Isis followed the rocky wall and came to the heart of a vast, bluish cave.

In front of her stood a fetish like the one in Abydos.

She took off the veil covering the top of the pole and found the feet of Osiris, made from gold, silver and precious stones.

'I am sorry to confirm your suspicions,' said Sarenput regretfully, 'but some provincial leaders and several High Priests will prove uncooperative. I don't deny the quality of your escort, but when faced with certain opinionated people their small numbers won't carry the day.'

'What do you suggest?' asked Isis.

'That I accompany you. A warship and a regiment of

soldiers will calm rebellious spirits and make them more conciliatory.'

She gladly accepted this valuable help.

'The problem,' said Sarenput, 'is that we shall be travelling into the northerly wind. We can use the river current, and the oarsmen will give of their best, but we shall make slow progress.'

'I hope to improve the conditions.'

Standing at the prow of her boat, with Sarenput's boat close behind, Isis pointed the 'Magic' sceptre at the First Cataract. A strong southerly wind began to blow and the two vessels sailed swiftly off towards Edfu, capital of the second province of Upper Egypt, the Throne of Horus.

A falcon was circling the prow of Isis' boat.

'We must follow it,' she ordered.

The bird drew them downriver, away from the main landing-stage; Sarenput fumed as he watched it.

After describing wide circles above a vineyard, the falcon perched in the top of an acacia tree.

'We must moor here,' said Isis.

Although not easy, the mooring was accomplished smoothly. The sailors put a gangplank in place, and the archers immediately went down it, alert and ready to fire. Everything seemed quiet.

'No chance of finding a relic of Osiris here,' commented Sarenput. 'On the other hand, they produce excellent wine. I'm one of its main purchasers and I've never had any cause for complaint.'

Enclosed by walls, the vineyard of the Throne of Horus comprised twelve varieties of plants as well as date-palms. In January and February, the old vine-stocks were carefully pruned and the earth turned over, where the new ones would grow. Many water-channels ensured controlled irrigation, and regular hoeing aerated the soil as well as getting rid of weeds. Pigeon-droppings were used as fertilizer, and diseases were kept at bay by watering with copper-based solutions, provided by the temple workshop.

The workers were finishing a late grape harvest. The result would be a robust, scented nectar, which was highly prized.

Isis and Sarenput approached a large wine-press.

Workers were bringing well-ripened bunches of grapes and putting them in an enormous vat; others were trampling them, singing as they did so. The juice trickled out through several openings, and would ferment for two or three days in open clay jars. Then the specialists would begin their work, transferring this first wine into other jars of a different shape.

Apprentices were gathering up the remains of the skins and pips, which would be placed inside a bag and squeezed tightly to extract a delicious liquid.

'Would you like some?' asked a somewhat tipsy fellow.

'I wouldn't say no,' replied Sarenput.

The master-winemaker intervened. 'What is the meaning of all these troops? I've paid all my taxes.'

'Don't worry, we aren't here to cause you any trouble.'

'Do you know the real name of the pressed grape?' asked Isis.

The craftsman was startled. 'Asking a question like that implies that you're a member of—'

'The priesthood of Abydos. Yes, I am.'

'The real name is Osiris, at once bread and wine, the divine power embodied in solid and liquid foods. By pressing the grape, we put him to death, and this ordeal separates the perishable from the immortal. Then, we drink Osiris. The wine reveals one of the paths of immortality to us. Today, we offer the dead an exceptional vintage. It will keep spectres and the evil dead away from us. The good dead, the Great Ones of Abydos, the beings of light, will continue to protect our vineyard. Forgetting to honour them would bring misfortune.'

Christian Jacq

'Apart from the wine, what other offerings will you make to them?'

'I'm waiting for the procession of the priests of Horus. They're bringing everything necessary.'

Sarenput did not have time to get drunk, for the priests soon arrived. They were led by an old man with the face of a falcon. Those behind him bore an impressive number of jars, pieces of fabric and flowers. In the centre of the procession was a ship.

Isis revealed to him who she was.

'The High Priestess of Abydos among us! What an honour! Will you grant us the joy of taking part in tonight's ritual? We shall light torches and feast to the memory of the dead by dedicating our finest wines to them.'

'Your ship is a special shape, isn't it?'

'It's a replica of Osiris's ship. As the symbol of the god's reconstituted body, it will receive the crown of justification and will keep our temple safe from death. Would you consent to lay it upon an altar and speak the words of protection?'

'My mission demands other rites. This is the Basket of Mysteries, which brings back together that which was scattered. Will you consent to give me the chest of Osiris, your province's sacred relic?'

During his long life, the High Priest of Edfu had heard many strange words and thought he could no longer be surprised. This time, though, he stood open-mouthed.

'The survival of Egypt is at stake,' she added in a low voice.

'The relic . . . the relic belongs to us.'

'Given the seriousness of the circumstances, it must return temporarily to Abydos.'

'I shall consult my fellow priests.'

One of the bearers of the sacred ship was a messenger by profession. He travelled on the fast boats used by Medes for disseminating royal decrees, and added to his salary by providing the captains with information concerning the province of Edfu. His fee varied according to the importance of the information.

Given the uproar in the vineyard, where a peaceful ceremony was supposed to be taking place, the informant scented profitable business. Avoiding the archers' malevolent gaze, he took a cup of grape-juice and mingled with the vineyard workers. They, who usually loved to laugh and joke, were looking none too pleased.

'Odd visitors, aren't they?' he observed.

'They're handpicked,' said one fellow knowingly, 'and they aren't joking, those fellows! Better not to get on the wrong side of them. My elder brother recognized Governor Sarenput. Usually he sends a trading-boat for us to load with jars of wine, but today he's commanding a warship. I have a bad feeling about this.'

'And what about that beautiful woman?'

'She's a priestess from Abydos – in fact a colleague with sharp ears says she's actually the High Priestess. Do you realize? We never ought to have caught a glimpse of her. Something serious must be going on.'

The informant was salivating. How much was information like this worth? Surely a fortune! He'd negotiate hard and get as much as possible, then he'd resign, buy a farm, take on several workers and enjoy a peaceful retirement. He was lucky to be in the right place at the right time.

A second conversation with some other vineyard workers confirmed what the first man had said. There was no point in waiting around any longer. Slipping discreetly away, he left the vineyard and ran towards the river. He followed it as far as the landing-stage, where one of Medes's boats was moored. The negotiations would take time, but he would stand firm. The messenger could already see himself lying in the shade of his pergola, watching his employees working.

The falcon took flight. Seer of the invisible, it detected its prey using the emissions of light, however tiny, from their urine or any other secretion.

A strange, alarming cry stopped the informant in his tracks. Panting, he looked up. Blinded by the sun, it seemed to him that a stone was falling towards him at incredible speed.

His skull perforated, he fell to the ground, stone dead.

Its duty as Isis' protector accomplished, the falcon of Horus returned to perch in the top of the acacia tree.

'The deliberations are leading nowhere,' said Sarenput. 'I'll shake up those praters and then you can take the relic.'

'Let us be patient,' advised Isis. 'The High Priest will understand the gravity of the situation.'

'You like human beings too much! They're just a collection of talkers, who mustn't on any account be given the chance to discuss anything.'

At last, the falcon-faced priest returned. 'Please follow me,' he said to Isis.

He led her to the ceremonial ship, and turned it round on itself to reach its plinth, a sycamore-wood box. The High Priest opened it and took out the chest of Osiris, made from precious stones.

'All the priests of Edfu consent to hand this priceless treasure over to you. Make best use of it and preserve the Two Lands from misfortune.'

24

Even the finest reader of faces would have passed Sekari close by without recognizing him. Unshaven, stooping, and with his hair and eyebrows dyed grey, he looked like a tired old man who was having great difficulty selling the second-rate pots carried by his slow, stubborn donkey, accompanied by a wheezing dog. Excellent actors, North Wind and Flesh-Eater were playing tormented animals at their last gasp.

Sekari had a simple notion: Curly-Head and Surly were hiding in their preferred district, where nobody would think to look for them. Unwariness or stupidity? Certainly not. The rebels had proved themselves efficient and painstaking. So these two and their comrades must have such a safe hiding-place that they feared neither raids nor searches, even unexpected ones.

No informant could infiltrate the network, and there had been no betrayals and no loose tongues. The separation of the groups was just about perfect. Sekari was beginning to formulate a theory. It was difficult to check, but there was a glimmer of hope: if he was not mistaken, sooner or later one of the Herald's men would emerge from his hole, simply to breathe and have a change of air. What risk was there, after all? The district was no longer being closely watched, and the lookouts would let the rebels know when a patrol was coming.

The residents were becoming accustomed to this harmless old man, who asked no questions and scraped a living from his poor trade. Passers-by willingly gave him bread and vegetables, which he shared with the donkey and the dog.

As night fell, Sekari dozed. He was almost asleep when Flesh-Eater laid a paw on his head.

'Let me get a bit of sleep.'

The dog persisted, and Sekari opened an eye. A few steps away, a man was buying dates from a travelling seller and eating them greedily.

It was Curly-Head.

This time, Sekari swore to himself, he wouldn't let him get away.

Still munching the fruit, Curly-Head walked away. Sekari got up and followed him. He had a major advantage: the donkey and the dog's acute sense of smell. So he could tail the rebel at a good distance without being spotted.

The trip was not a long one.

The donkey stopped in front of a neat two-storey house.

An irate housewife looked out and yelled at Sekari, 'Get away with you, you old flea-bag!'

'My pots aren't expensive. I'll sell you two for the price of one.'

'They're as ugly as they are flimsy! Be off with you, or I'll call the guards.'

Sekari moved off, grumbling loudly. He was now absolutely certain: Curly-Head was hiding in that house, even though it had been searched several times. His theory had been proved right.

As usual, Sekari slipped past the guards like a shadow, and made for the tjaty's office.

It was the middle of the night, but Sobek was still at his desk. Although he had known that his new office entailed an enormous amount of work, he had underestimated its scope.

There was only one solution: to toil unstintingly, make a close study of every case and learn in depth about all the problems, great and small, that threatened the prosperity of the Two Lands.

Contrary to his detractors' assumptions, Sobek was learning quickly. He frequently called on the valuable help of High Treasurer Senankh, so as not to leave any areas in doubt.

The safety of Memphis remained his obsession. Well aware of the terrible threat hanging over the city, he hoped his enemies would make a mistake or that one of his many current investigations would at last bear fruit.

As usual, he was surprised by the arrival of Sekari, who had clearly lost none of his talent for walking through walls.

The tjaty stood up, full of tension. 'I must inform you that—'

'Me first,' Sekari cut in. 'I've just located one of the rebels' hiding-places.'

The two men immediately pored over Sobek's map of Memphis. Sekari pointed out the place.

Sobek frowned. 'We've searched that group of houses at least ten times and found nothing.'

'It would be useless to do it again – you'd only fail again.'

'Then why are you so sure he's there?'

'Because we're foolish and blind. Curly-Head is indeed hiding here, and we haven't unearthed him because traditional methods don't work.'

'Don't talk to me about ghosts!'

'I think the reality's more solid than that.'

'Explain what you mean – I haven't the heart for riddles.'

'Not inside. Underneath.'

Sobek punched the map. 'Underground chambers – underground chambers have been dug out, and the rebels are lurking there like rats! You're right. That must be the answer.'

'If we act at once, we can destroy a whole section of their troops.'

'No, not yet. My official illness and Nesmontu's death are bound to provoke interesting reactions. As soon as the major part of the network reveals itself, we'll make our move. I want to strike very hard and crush the head.'

'That's a risky strategy.'

Suddenly, Sobek's expression became sombre. 'You've done excellent work, Sekari. I'd have liked to celebrate it with you, but I must tell you some terrible news.' The Protector's throat tightened. 'Iker is dead.'

'Dead . . . Are you absolutely sure?'

'I'm afraid so. This time, he was unable to avoid the fatal blow.'

Sekari sat down, devastated. To lose his friend, his brother, the companion with whom he had shared so many adventures, was unbearably painful. It was some time before he could ask, 'How did he die?'

'He was murdered.'

'What? In Abydos? That's unthinkable!'

'According to the king's message, he was murdered by the Herald.'

Now Sekari was not only distressed but stunned. 'You mean the Herald has succeeded in profaning the sacred domain of Osiris itself?'

'On the pharaoh's orders, you are to leave Memphis and join Isis in the South. She will explain the situation to you; your help will be vital to her.'

Sekari wanted to abandon everything and hand in his resignation. Defeating the Herald and his cohort of demons seemed impossible.

'Not you,' protested Sobek. 'You cannot give up. Iker would never forgive you.'

Filled with sorrow, Sekari got to his feet again. 'If we don't see each other again, Tjaty Sobek, don't grieve for me. By proving inferior to the enemy, I'll have deserved my fate.'

*

Sobek could not sleep. He kept thinking of Iker, whom he had so long suspected of collaborating with the enemy, of that young scribe with the never-ending courage and the brilliant career. How could anyone ever have imagined that the Royal Son would be in the slightest danger in Abydos, and that the Herald would dare strike at the heart of Osiris's kingdom?

Anger consumed him. He wanted to summon all the forces of order and raze to the ground the district where the rebels were hiding. He would strangle them himself, slowly – very slowly.

But that would dishonour his office and betray the king. Neither he nor the pharaoh's allies must give in to their rage and lose their heads. The Herald was counting on just such a weakness, so that he could drive home his advantage and make the structure fall apart more quickly.

For there was no doubt: Iker – the Royal Son, Friend of the King, and designated successor to Senusret – was irreplaceable. Since the very beginning of this war, sometimes underground and sometimes in plain sight, the Herald had been pursuing two main goals: the destruction of Abydos and the elimination of the young man who had been so patiently and harshly prepared for the highest offices. This terrifying crime perhaps marked the irrevocable defeat of Egypt, despite the will to fight evil.

Sobek would fight to the end. If the Herald's hordes invaded Memphis, they would come up against the Protector.

Nesmontu was pacing about like a caged lion. And yet there was no better hiding-place for a dead man whose funeral rites had just been conducted – discreetly, so as not to frighten the city's population. Who would think of looking for him in Sehotep's house when Sehotep himself was confined to the house and likely to face a terrible punishment?

At least the two brothers from the Golden Circle could talk

about Abydos and their initiations, forgetting the rigours of the moment.

'These delicious meals are rather a change from the usual fare at the barracks,' admitted the general, 'but comfort makes me soft. I can't wait to get back into the field, provided the rebels have been duly informed of my death.'

'Don't worry,' said Sehotep. 'We know how quickly and efficiently they pass on information.'

Nesmontu gave him a hard stare. 'You disappoint me. You've lost your appetite, and there's no joy in you. Do you miss women that much?'

'I'm going to be executed.'

'Don't talk nonsense!'

'My case is hopeless. You know Sobek the Protector: he'll apply the law rigorously – and I can't fault him for that.'

'The king won't authorize your execution.'

'The king is not above Ma'at. He is its representative on earth, and the tjaty is its instrument. Once found guilty, I shall be justly punished.'

'We haven't reached that stage yet.'

'The time is approaching, I can feel it. Dying doesn't frighten me, but such a downfall, such infamy, my name sullied and erased from all writings . . . I can't bear it. It would be better to die before being dragged through the mud.'

Nesmontu had never seen the brilliant Sehotep in the grip of despair. The old soldier took him by the shoulders and said, 'We must concentrate on the main fact: you are innocent. All right, proving it will be difficult, but we've faced other apparently insurmountable difficulties, haven't we? This is a battle and we're in a position of weakness, so we must turn the enemy's strength against him. I don't yet know how; we'll have to find a way. One thing is certain: the tjaty's court demands the truth, and we know that truth. Knowing the truth means we have the decisive weapon. We shan't fail.'

A pale smile lit up Sehotep's drawn face: Nesmontu could have given confidence to a regiment of wounded men surrounded on all sides. He said, 'You're almost convincing.'

'What do you mean, "almost"? I don't like being insulted! You can apologize by sharing this jar of wine.'

The wine was excellent and put a little colour back into Sehotep's face. 'Without you, Nesmontu—'

'Come, come! It isn't like you to lose heart.'

The guard in charge of security at the house announced the arrival of the High Treasurer.

Senankh had lost his usual joviality. Blank-eyed, he looked at his two brothers from the Golden Circle as if he did not know them. 'Sehotep, Nesmontu . . .' he murmured.

'Yes, that's us,' the general assured him. 'What's wrong?'

'I've just seen Tjaty Sobek.'

Sehotep stepped forward. 'Is there more evidence against me?'

'No, it's about Iker and Abydos. A disaster, a great disaster . . .'

'Explain yourself,' ordered Nesmontu.

'Iker has been murdered, and Abydos desecrated. The Herald has won.'

The trio wandered the streets of Memphis until dawn. An army of rebels armed to the teeth could have barred Sekari's way and he would not have noticed. Weighed down by grief, he walked without knowing where he was going, gazing into space. Flesh-Eater flanked him closely on his left, and North Wind on his right. They did not leave him for an instant. Both sensed his distress and, in their way, wanted an explanation.

Unable yet to face giving them one, Sekari looked back on all the adventures he had shared with Iker, from the worst moments to the inexpressable joys. He engraved upon his heart every small moment of brotherhood and every surge of spiritual exhilaration, on the way of Ma'at to which they had both devoted their lives. Now there was nothing but injustice and cruelty.

His legs gave way and he slumped down at the foot of some scaffolding.

The donkey and the dog came close to him.

'I owe you the truth,' he said, 'but it is so hard to tell. Do you understand?'

The tone of his voice was enough. Together, North Wind and Flesh-Eater gave a heart-rending cry, so loud that it awoke several householders.

One of them came out of his house and saw a strange sight: a man, his arms round a donkey and a dog, was weeping bitterly.

'Will you stop that racket? I have to go to work early, and I'd like some rest.'

'Shut up, idiot, and venerate the memory of a hero who gave his life to protect your sleep.'

25

The warship's arrival at the landing-stage in the capital of the Shrine, the third province of Upper Egypt, caused a sensation. The snake-goddess Wadjyt and the vulture-goddess Nekhbet protected this land, which was overlooked by the very ancient sacred city of Nekheb, guarantor of the royal tenure. Sarenput knew the province's governor.

The two men embraced, and then the governor asked, 'Is there a war in the offing?'

'The High Priestess of Abydos needs your help.'

Impressed by the beauty and nobility of his guest, he bowed low. 'You shall have it.'

Isis felt uneasy. Dark forces were prowling nearby. She asked, 'Governor, have there been any disturbances recently in the region?'

'The Red Mountain's colour has deepened, and many people think that's a bad omen. The priests are so worried about it that every morning and evening they speak the words of pacification of the Souls of Nekheb. Without their protection, this land would become sterile.'

'I have come to collect the relic of Osiris, his neck and jaws.'

The governor's expression became openly hostile. 'Tradition has entrusted that treasure to us, and no one's going to take it away.'

'If Abydos is to be saved, it is absolutely vital that I do,' explained Isis. 'Afterwards it will be returned to its place here.'

'Are you saying that Abydos is in danger?'

'It is a question of life or death.'

It was clear that this sad, proud woman was not lying.

'You promised to help,' Sarenput reminded him.

'I didn't know what you—'

'A promise is a promise. At the Judgment of Osiris, the hearts of liars bear witness against them.'

Shaken, the governor gave in. He said, 'Because of the Red Mountain's anger, the High Priest of Nekheb has removed the relic of Osiris from the temple. He, I and the master-blacksmith are the only people who know its hiding-place.'

'Then you must take us there,' said Sarenput.

'First, I must inform our High Priestess and—'

'No. There isn't time.'

Under the protection of the archers from Elephantine, the three went to the big forge where fifty or so men were working, using pipes made from reeds with a terracotta spout to maintain the roaring fire of a furnace on which they placed crucibles. Using their feeling for the right temperature, they smelted metals and knew instinctively the fusing-points of welds. Lifting the crucibles and pouring the molten metal into moulds of different sizes and shapes was a dangerous operation, which could performed only by brave and experienced men.

The master-blacksmith, a tall, strong, bald man, came out of the forge to meet the visitors. 'We don't permit strangers inside, because the secrets of our profession must be guarded. Not even the governor may enter.'

'What about the High Priestess of Abydos?' asked Isis.

The craftsman's lips clamped shut.

'Metals receive their purity from Osiris and would lose all quality if the Divine Light did not preserve their unity,' she reminded him.

'What do you want?'

'Give me the relic of Osiris that has been entrusted to you.'

'I thought—'

'I order you to do so,' confirmed the governor.

The master-blacksmith wore a strange expression. 'Only professionals can bear the heat of the forge and avoid the risks. I would not advise a young and fragile woman to try the adventure.'

'Guide me,' commanded Isis.

Sarenput had a bad premonition. 'I'm coming with you,' he decided.

'That's out of the question,' said the craftsman. 'Only an initiate into the Mysteries of Abydos may see and touch the relic.'

Isis nodded.

As soon as she entered this fearsome realm, she was attacked by burning gusts of air which ought to have made her flinch. But after the Way of Fire, this seemed almost calm.

As if she did not exist, the master-blacksmith stopped several times to examine the work in progress. He checked the moulds for ingots, the stones used for hammers and anvils, the pipes, the tongs, the thickness of the sheets of metal, and spoke to the man responsible for hammering, accusing him of carelessness. He himself cleaned the surfaces to be welded together using burnt wine-lees and finished off a mixture of gold, silver and copper, which would stand the test of time.

Isis displayed no sign of impatience.

'Oh,' he said, staring at her in astonishment, 'you're still here, are you? That's quite an achievement for a woman. Usually they chatter, complain or simper.'

'And what about their stupidity? On your own ground, you certainly rival them.'

The master-blacksmith seized a pair of tongs, whose pincers were glowing red.

'You'd like to strike me,' said Isis, 'but you haven't the courage. Since you left Abydos, you have sunk very low indeed.'

The tongs fell from his hand. 'How . . . how did you know?'

'From your way of working – you must have learnt it when you were a temporary worker at the Temple of Osiris. The alchemists of Abydos taught you everything you know. When you handle molten metal, the brother of the sun, you touch the flesh of the gods, the divine forms and the powers embodied by Sokar. Pieces of radiant eternity are born from the imperishable works in which your hands and those of your team take part. But you have forgotten the greatness of your profession and behave like a common petty tyrant.'

The craftsman hung his head. 'A priestess refused my proposal of marriage, even though my future looked extremely promising, so I chose to leave Abydos and return home. Here I'm held in high esteem. While women—'

'If evil destroys the domain of Osiris, your forge will be destroyed, too.'

'Aren't you exaggerating the danger?'

'The word of the High Priestess of Abydos should be enough for you.'

'Very well, I'll give you the relic. And then you must go away.'

He led her to the back of the forge, a low-roofed cave. Acrid smoke rose up out of its depths.

'The lake of flames,' he explained. 'This infernal cauldron was discovered centuries ago. Sometimes its jaws close, sometimes they open. It provides us with all the energy we need.'

Isis looked down; it was a truly terrifying spectacle. Bubbles were bursting at the surface, emitting angry gases.

'What better hiding-place for a relic?' asked the blacksmith with a smile. 'By burning it, the cauldron has mutilated the body of Osiris once and for all.'

208

'Why did you commit such a terrible crime?'

'Because I am a loyal follower of the Herald!'

Arms outstretched, he charged at Isis, with the intention of hurling her into the lake of flames. Less than a pace from her, his foot struck a jutting rock, and he lost his balance and fell into the cauldron. When his head touched the boiling surface, it caught fire instantly. In a few seconds, the whole body was roasting. A revolting smell filled the grotto.

Isis clutched the little ivory 'Magic' sceptre tightly to her breast. By warding off the attack, it had saved her life. But what was the use, since the vital relic had been destroyed?

It could not have possibly survived, but nevertheless she must be sure.

She began to descend the dangerous narrow path. Despite the heat, the rock was damp and slippery and, although she concentrated hard, she had to go slowly.

Then, though the smoke that blinded her, she caught sight of something. At the edge of the lake, licked by the flames, two stone blocks like jaws were preserving the relic. She tried and tried to get closer but it was impossible. Already her skin was being singed and her dress was starting to smoulder. She had to admit defeat and climb back up.

As she did she heard sounds of fierce fighting. She reached the top in time to witness the defeat of the Herald's supporters, a dozen of the blacksmiths. After attacking their colleagues, they had come up against Sarenput's soldiers, who had been summoned to the rescue.

'They're real demons,' he told her. 'Even mortally wounded, they kept on fighting.'

'Look out!' yelled an archer.

Armed with a freshly forged dagger, whose blade was still smoking, a young craftsman was about to stab Isis in the back.

Sarenput did not give him time. Head down like a ram, he butted him in the belly, so hard that the attacker was thrown a good ten paces backwards and was skewered on the point of a soldier's sword.

'Search everywhere,' he ordered furiously. 'There may still be other vermin like him about.'

'The relic looks intact but it's inaccessible,' Isis told him. 'Show me.'

When he saw the lake of fire, Sarenput grimaced. 'If we use a rope it'll simply burst into flame, and so would a long stick.'

The second suggestion made the Widow's eyes shine. 'It all depends on what kind of stick it is.'

'No wood can possibly withstand this furnace,' objected Sarenput.

'We must go back to the boat.'

The High Priestess must be deceiving herself. Still, he admired her tenacity, so he followed her.

As they emerged from the forge, Sarenput spotted a fugitive running full tilt towards the river, a torch in one hand. 'Stop him!' he shouted.

Two archers fired, but in vain: he was too far away.

'That madman wants to attack my boat!'

A cautious man, Sarenput had left on board several experienced soldiers, fully capable of fending off an attack and sounding the alert.

The rebel was not interested in the boat; he tried to set fire to the main mooring-stake. This time he was in easy range, and the archers on deck did not miss.

When Sarenput and Isis reached the scene, the torch was fizzling out on the damp earth of the riverbank.

'He'd lost his mind!' said Sarenput.

'Not at all,' replied Isis. 'He was hoping to destroy our sole means of saving the relic.' She knelt down by the mooring-stake. 'Weep for Osiris who suffers,' she prayed. 'I, the mourner, identify myself with you because I am searching for him. I push away the obstacles, I call out so that the master of

Abydos shall not know the exhaustion of death. Speak, drive away evil! Open the way to the lake and dispel the storm.'

She stood up and took hold of the heavy stake. To the astonishment of the soldiers, she lifted it without difficulty.

Warily, Sarenput and the archers escorted her back to the cave.

'Surely you aren't going to try to pacify that hell?' he asked.

Isis began to climb down the slippery path. Sarenput gave up uttering futile arguments.

Halfway down the path, she threw the mooring-stake into the lake. The stake was the bearer of the words of the Great Mourner, seeking the healing of her brother. It landed in the middle of the fiery lake, and enormous flames attacked it. But it remained intact, and absorbed them. One by one, the bubbles of gas burst, and the lake stopped boiling.

Isis went further down and soon reached the relic. She pushed away the two protecting rocks, and withdrew the neck and jaws of Osiris, perfectly intact.

Sarenput was so astounded that he hardly knew how to greet this feat. 'No evil forces can resist you,' he said.

Isis smiled faintly. 'The Herald is not defeated yet, and the dangers are likely to multiply.'

He shook his head. 'His followers here . . . Do you think other regional capitals are infected, too?'

'I'm sure they are.'

One worrying question remained: had Isis' arrival caught a dormant network unawares, or had it already been placed on alert by an informant? Perhaps the Herald's supporters were mobilizing all over the land, determined to kill the High Priestess of Abydos.

26

Thebes, or Waset, capital of the fourth province of Upper Egypt, the Power Sceptre, was the jewel of a broad, fertile plain whose inhabitants considered its charm and beauty second to none. It was said that the seed that came forth from the *nun*, the ocean of energy, coalesced here under the effect of the flame of the sun's eye. Out of the living earth rose up the primordial mound, surrounded by four pillars supporting the celestial vault.

Isis went to the principal temple at Karnak, 'the Iunu of the South'. There the fusion between Atum, the Creator, and Ra, the Divine Light, and Amon, the Hidden God, took place. Heavens and earth were united there, and the nine powers at the origin of all things were revealed to the East.

She meditated before the two huge statues of Senusret standing, the first wearing the Double Crown and the second the White Crown. Firmly grasping the Testament of the Gods, bequeathing the land of Egypt to him, the king was striding forward. He wore an expression of serene determination.

The High Priest of Karnak came to meet Isis, accompanied by Sarenput. The archers remained outside the temple.

'People will remember the splendours of this reign,' declared the priest. 'Thanks to his works, a pharaoh does not pass away. And the most radiant work of all is the eternity of which he is the guarantor. You are most welcome, High Priestess of Abydos.'

'Will you take me to the Shrine of Osiris?'

'The Great Way opens before you.'

As in Abydos, the god's tomb was surrounded by trees. A profound, almost oppressive silence filled it.

Inside the shrine was another, inner shrine, closed by a double door. Isis spoke the words of awakening in peace, and pulled aside the bolt, the finger of Set. When the door opened she saw an exquisite golden statuette of Amon-Ra, a cubit tall. But the little monument did not contain the symbol she had hoped for.

Containing her disappointment and anxiety, the priestess performed the required ritual, closed the door of the shrine again and backed out, brushing away her footprints with the Broom of Thoth.

The High Priest was waiting for her in the shadow of a colonnade.

'Have you been robbed?' she asked.

'No one would dare violate the peace of this shrine. Not even the worst criminal would even think of committing such a crime!'

'Do you know all the temporary priests, and can you answer for them?'

'Yes . . . at least, almost all. My assistants take on competent, trustworthy volunteers. No blame can be attached to the priests of Karnak.'

'Has anything unusual happened in recent months?'

'No, nothing.'

'Not even any minor disorder in the area?'

'Not even that. Or at least such a little thing—'

'I'd like to know the details.'

'They'll hardly be of use to you.'

'Tell me anyway.'

The High Priest hesitated, then yielded. 'The desert guards

213

said there were a few minor disturbances around the Hill of Thoth. The site is very isolated, so it is not often inspected. Some scoundrel thought he would find treasure there, but he ran off empty-handed.'

Armed with a detailed map provided by the High Priest, Isis crossed the Nile and reached the west bank. Protected by Sarenput and his soldiers, she crossed an arid area and made for a hill surrounded by ravines. The sun suddenly seemed to burn fiercely, and the burdensome heat slowed them down.

'Be on the alert,' ordered Sarenput, wary of an ambush.

As battle-hardened warriors, the archers identified the places where rebels might position themselves, ready to strike.

A metallic reflection alerted a soldier at the back of the procession. 'Get down on the ground! he shouted.

Everyone obeyed. Only Isis stayed standing, staring at the spot he had indicated.

'Get down,' begged Sarenput. 'You make an easy target.'

'We have nothing to fear.'

Since no arrows had been fired, everyone cautiously got up.

'We'll take this path,' said Isis.

'It's so narrow and steep that we shall have to climb in single file and very slowly,' warned Sarenput.

'I shall go first.'

'No, let one of my men run that risk.'

'The Hill of Thoth has a warm welcome for us.'

The governor did not persist. He knew the young woman's determination and that she was impervious to sensible advice.

The climb was difficult and tiring. The scree rolled underfoot and fell down the steep slope. Fortunately, nobody was afraid of heights. At the top they came out on to a sun-baked plateau, in the centre of which was a modest shrine whose walls bore the traces of fire. The parched soldiers stopped and drank some much-needed water.

Isis went into the shrine. Its walls were smoke-blackened;

all that remained was one depiction of Thoth in his ibis incarnation, and even that was damaged. However, the pointed beak was intact and it was touching the hieroglyph of the basket, which meant 'mastery'. Isis remembered one of the essential teachings of Abydos: the power of the gods is Thoth, who gives breadth of heart and unity. Despite the destruction the fire had wrought, the ibis's face was radiant.

Isis touched its beak. The basket moved back, revealing a cavity. Inside was a small gold sceptre, similar to the one used in the celebration of the Mysteries of Osiris and serving to provide the symbols with supernatural power. The rebels had burnt down the shrine of Thoth in vain.

Sarenput was relieved to see the High Priestess of Abydos emerge unharmed. He showed her a shortsword which had been found nearby.

'This is what caused the reflection we saw,' he said. 'A Syrian weapon by the look of it. I shall suggest that the governor has the area searched again.'

'I must pay homage to the pharaoh's *ka* and ask him if this province has another offering in store for us.'

The processional road that led to the temple of Deir el-Bahari was lined with statues of Senusret, hands resting against his kilt. While venerating her father, his daughter entered into contact with him; whatever the distance, their thoughts could communicate. She questioned him and obtained unambiguous answers. Yes, she must pursue her quest, fight off discouragement and not balk at any obstacle. Yes, Iker still lived; his soul was floating between earth and the heavens, fixed neither in death nor in the world beyond.

She thought of the beautiful Festival of the Valley celebrated in these parts, during which the dead and the living feasted together in the shrines of the tombs. For several days, the statue of Amon left Karnak aboard the royal ship to go to the western bank, the Land of Life, and endow its temples of a million years with new energy. At night, the burial-grounds were lit up and those of just voice were brought many offerings, notably the divine water of rejuvenation and bunches of flowers called 'life'. Songs rose up to the stars, the border between the world beyond and the earthly world disappeared, and each tomb became 'the dwelling of great celebration'.

The final stage of the procession was the arrival at Deir el-Bahari.* There stood the extraordinary monument of Mentuhotep,† who had reigned two hundred years before Senusret and inspired him as a re-unifier of Egypt, an initiate into the Mysteries of Osiris, and an alchemist.

From a greeting temple a roadway rose up, ending in a vast Osiran mound planted with acacias. At the foot of the ramp were fifty-five tamarisks and two rows of sycamores, housing seated statues of the pharaoh dressed in a white tunic, characteristic of the festival of regeneration.

An elegant priestess greeted Isis. 'What is your name and office?'

'Isis, High Priestess of Abydos and daughter of Pharaoh Senusret.'

Deeply impressed, the priestess bowed. 'Do you wish to prepare already for the Festival of the Valley?'

'No, I wish to know if the shrine of Osiris preserves a relic.'

'I do not know.'

'Do you never enter the Tomb of Osiris?'

'It has been closed for so long!'

'Open the door for me.'

'Would that not be . . . profanation?'

---

*In the New Kingdom, this is where the temple of the famous female pharaoh Hatshepsut was built.
†Nebhepetra Mentuhotep ('Mentu, the warrior bull, is at peace'), 2061–2010.

'My father protects this shrine, does he not?'

The priestess nodded. 'He has had many statues erected depicting him at worship facing Mentuhotep, his distant predecessor. Thanks to him, indeed, the peace of Osiris has been preserved.'

'Are you certain of that?'

'What do you mean?'

'Has anyone tried to disturb it recently?'

'The guards don't watch the site all the time. What can we have to fear?'

'Take me to the entrance to the tomb.' Despite her calmness and the gentleness of her voice, the young woman's authority brooked no argument.

The priestess led her to a cavern dug into the mountain. Its entrance was guarded by a gigantic statue of the pharaoh wearing the Red Crown and a white tunic. His face, hands and legs were black, his arms were crossed over his chest, and he held the sceptres of Osiris. Massive and keen-eyed, he kept away unbelievers.

'I can go no further,' said the priestess.

'I find that surprising,' said Isis.

'That giant is no laughing matter.'

'Should you not know the words of pacification of the *ka*?'

'Indeed, but this place is very special and—'

'The Herald has ordered you to discover the secret of the tomb of Mentuhotep and you don't know what to do.'

Unmasked, the false priestess shrank back towards the edge of a precipice. A flame sprang out of her left hand, making her scream in pain. Terrified, she toppled back into emptiness.

Isis went back to the giant statue. 'Rejoin your *ka*,' she told it. 'Close to your spirit, your son takes care of it, and you have become his own *ka*. The Light brings forth your vital power; you shall not perish. The creative principle and the earth-god offer you a temple and a house of eternity.'

The statue's face seemed less forbidding. Isis crossed the path that separated her from the entrance to the tomb, which was now open.

The corridor, whose false ceiling was covered in limestone tiles, served side chambers containing the funerary equipment. Running under the mountain, it led to the sarcophagus chamber where the royal *ka* communed with the Hidden God.

Isis meditated there for a long time, trying to perceive the great king's intentions. He, initiated into the Mysteries, must have preserved a major element of the Osiran cult. But the books of the House of Life did not mention a relic, so what could it be?

She walked seven times round the sarcophagus. At the end of this rite, the atmosphere in the chamber changed. The ceiling grew red, the walls white, and the ground black. A tongue of fire sprang up from the sarcophagus, ending at a small granite chamber.

Inside was a statue similar to the huge one outside, wrapped in a cloth and buried like a mummy of Osiris. Isis lifted it. It was resting on a ram-skin which, according to the hieroglyphic text, came from Abydos and had been used in the celebration of the Mysteries.

The priestess folded the ram-skin and went back out into the daylight. The door of the tomb closed behind her. The sun flooded the mound of Osiris.

When Isis emerged from the sacred enclosure, Sarenput ran up. 'I was beginning to worry. Did you have any problems?'

'We must return to the boat and continue our journey.'

27

As he entered the village of Madu, north-east of Karnak, Senusret knew that his daughter had found the ram-skin necessary for the celebration of the great Mysteries. This success marked an important stage in her quest, which had scarcely begun. Formidable dangers lay in wait for her, and the army of darkness would grant her no respite.

The communion of their thoughts gave them a strength like no other. Despite the distance separating them, Isis would never be alone. The pharaoh also remained in contact with the soul of Iker, fixed to his mummy, kept safe from the second death, but still a long way from resurrection. The words spoken each day by the Shaven-headed One and Nephthys prevented the process of decay and maintained intact the intermediary body, the basis for rebirth.

At the end of the month of Khoiak, if the ritual conditions had not been fulfilled, all these efforts would have been in vain. Therefore Isis must succeed in reunited the parts of Osiris's body, and the king must succeed in bringing back to Abydos a new *khetemet* containing the god's lymph.

Children ran about and shouted, housewives abandoned their brooms and their washing-up, and men left their fields and workshops to watch the astonishing sight of a procession of soldiers led by a gigantic man.

The pharaoh, here in Madu? Suddenly torn from his early

afternoon nap, the headman dressed hastily in his best tunic. As he left his house, he ran into an officer.

'Are you the village headman?'

'I wasn't warned. If I had been—'

'His Majesty wants to see you.'

Trembling, the headman followed the officer to the small village temple. The king was seated on a throne outside the door. Unable to bear Senusret's piercing gaze, the headman prostrated himself on the ground.

'Do you know the name of this place?' asked the king.

'Majesty, I . . . I don't often come here and—'

'It is called "the door where the requests of both the weak and the powerful are heard and where justice is given according to the Rule of Ma'at". Why is the temple so poorly maintained?'

'There hasn't been a priest here for a long time, because of the anger of the bull. And I don't have the means to take care of a building like this. You understand, I must think first of the well-being of the people I represent.'

'What caused the bull's anger?'

'I don't know, Majesty. Nobody can go near it any more, its festival is no longer celebrated and the priests have abandoned our village.'

'You yourself are the cause, aren't you?'

The headman spluttered. 'Me, Majesty? No, I swear I am not!'

'Four bulls magically protect this region. They dwell at Thebes, Iunu-Montu, Djerty and Madu, and form a fortress against the forces of evil, like a complete eye in the centre of which burns an indestructible light. You, by your wicked deeds, have placed the structure in peril and made the eye blind.'

'I'm just a poor man – I couldn't commit such a crime.'

'Have you forgotten? You sold young Iker to pirates when he was poor and had no family, then you robbed and

220

murdered the old scribe who was his master and protector. When Iker returned unexpectedly, instead of compensating him and begging his forgiveness you stole his inheritance, drove him out of his house and his village, and set a killer on him. It is the accumulation of these crimes that has unleashed the bull's anger.'

The headman, in a cold sweat, dared not deny it.

'Why have you done so many evil things?'

'Majesty, I . . . I was led astray for a moment, I—'

'By submitting to the Herald,' said Senusret, 'you have betrayed your country and sullied your soul for ever.'

The headman put his head in his hand and sobbed. 'I couldn't help it, he forced me. I curse him, I—'

Suddenly white-faced and breathless, the headman had the feeling that his heart was being torn out. He stiffened, vomited blood and bile, and then collapsed, stone dead.

'Burn the body,' ordered Senusret.

The king went to the Bull of Madu's enclosure. The forepart of its head was black, the back white, and it lived by its union with the sun. During the festival celebrated in its honour by musicians and singers, it healed many sicknesses, notably eye disorders.

The beast's eyes were burning with such fury that even the king himself could not appease it without understanding the true demands of the sacred animal.

'The headman's sins have been wiped away,' he told it, 'and he has been punished. The High Priestess of Abydos and I are doing everything we can to save Iker from oblivion. If other paths must be followed, I pray you to reveal them to me.'

The enormous bull stopped foaming at the mouth and pawing the ground, and fixed the king with its black eyes. Communication was established between the pharaoh and the animal incarnation of his *ka*.

Once its revelations were over, though, the bull grew angry again.

Together with the commander of his bodyguard, Senusret went into the temple and examined it. 'A messenger is to be sent to Thebes to summon builders, sculptors, artists and painters. The temple shall be restored and enlarged, a sacred lake created, and houses built for permanent priests. The work is to begin tomorrow, at dawn, and will continue day and night. Montu and the bull demand a domain worthy of them. A safety cordon shall be erected around the construction site.'

The messenger left immediately.

Senusret summoned the frightened village elders to the headman's house. They turned out to be self-seeking men, henchmen of the dead headman. He soon tired of their protestations of innocence and supplications, and summoned the Council of the Ancients, who had been excluded from the deliberations.

'You need a new headman. Whom do you suggest?'

'The owner of the best farming lands, Majesty,' replied a tall old man with a shock of white hair. 'He hated the dishonest headman you have rid us of, and managed to resist him, despite all the threats and dishonesty. His wealth will be used in the service of our village, and no one will ever go hungry again.'

The rest of the council agreed with him.

'Your temple is to become one of the jewels of the province,' announced the king. 'The best Theban craftsmen will provide Montu with a new dwelling.'

'Will that be enough to calm the bull?' asked the old man.

'No, for too many crimes have been committed and too many dangers threaten us. It is up to me to pacify your protecting spirit.'

'Can you help us?'

'Does anyone know where the ancient shrine of Osiris is?'

The villagers looked doubtful, but talked among themselves for a while.

'It's probably just a legend,' said the old man.

'The archives of the House of Life state that it exists.'

'As far back as the village's memory stretches, Madu has been the Mound of Geb, the earth-god. Victorious over the darkness, the Divine Light fertilized it and made it bear fruit.'

'Take me to this sacred place.'

'Majesty, the mound is lost amid a maze of impenetrable vegetation. In the old days, anyone mad enough to venture into it was smothered to death. Ever since childhood, I've wisely kept away from it, and none of us has tried to violate this fearsome domain.'

'Show it to me.'

Resignedly, the old man slowly set off, leaning on his cane.

Senusret gave him his arm. 'Did you know Iker?'

'The apprentice scribe? Of course. His teacher, who was a sage among sages, said he was particularly gifted and destined for great things. Iker was solitary, silent and worked to the point of exhaustion, because he was interested only in the sacred language. It was obvious that for him this world was a mere passage between the original universe and the invisible world. His kidnapping and the death of his master plunged Madu into sorrow and misery. Even the sun no longer warmed us. Today, Majesty, you have freed us from long unhappiness.'

'Iker's master would have known where Osiris's shrine is.'

The old man thought for a moment. 'If he did, he did not divulge the secret. Several times he warned us of terrible danger, but we thought he was being alarmist. And then the stranger with the turban and the woollen robe came, and took control of the headman's mind. After his brief stay, darkness covered Madu.'

Beyond the ruined temple lay a garden planted with many aromatic plants, which gave off sweet perfumes.

'This is the field of the ancestors, Majesty,' said the old

man. 'The silence weighs heavy here because there are no birds. Don't go near the tall jujube tree that marks the border of the forbidden domain. It gives off deadly waves of energy.'

'Thank you for your help.'

'Majesty, surely you aren't going to—'

'Have a banquet prepared to celebrate the appointment of the new headman.'

Senusret meditated for a short while. He thought of his spiritual son and of the bull's words. Iker's resurrection would come by way of the pharaoh's, which must take place at the heart of Osiris's most ancient mound. Meeting again in the other life required union in death.

The king walked towards the jujube tree. Yellow and white rays attacked him, but they were absorbed by his kilt, which bore the signs of stability. At the foot of the tree were two discs, one of gold and the other of silver, which had been defaced with magical figures of Canaanite origin.

Using acacia and sycamore leaves, the king wiped them away. A gentle wind began to blow, the fronds of foliage quivered and dozens of birds sang. The voices of the ancestors sounded once more, and the sun and moon would once again light up the garden at their proper times.

When the king pushed aside the heavy branches, they gave out heart-rending moans. He persevered and forced a way through. Fifty paces further on he reached a crumbling pillared gateway, the only opening in a partially collapsed brick curtain-wall. No birds lived in this sacred thicket, which had known absolute silence for several generations.

Senusret crossed the threshold of the little temple complex. There was a rectangular courtyard, overgrown with vegetation, then a second pillared gateway and a second courtyard, smaller and not so overgrown.

Suddenly, the undergrowth moved. Disturbed by the intruder, a long snake fled; it was red and white, the colours of the two crowns of Egypt. The king stamped his foot hard to warn any other snakes, and began exploring the place methodically.

There were no inscriptions or carvings, but to the west and the east he found two niches. From each a winding, vaulted corridor led to a rectangular room, with a floor of fine sand and covered by an egg-shaped mound. These were the two stellar matrices, the places where Osiris was recreated. Thus the bull's words revealed their full meaning, and the king's path was mapped out for him.

When the overseer of works arrived from Thebes, Senusret gave him detailed instructions: the major part of the temple of Madu was to be devoted to the pharaoh's festival of regeneration. Statues and carvings would celebrate this essential moment in which the king's power was renewed through his communion with the gods and ancestors.

Before knowing this joy, Senusret must undergo an ordeal which might mark the end of his earthly life. According to the bull's prophecy, the location of the *khetemet* would be revealed to him only during a sleep that was close to death, in the darkness of the burial chamber. There, the earth-god had passed on the throne of the living to his son Osiris. There, Senusret would become the repository of the *ka* of all his royal ancestors.

Would he succeed in traversing the darkness? There could be no question of indecision.

In the first Osiran matrix there was a throne. In the place of the king lay a bunch of flowers. In the second there was a makeshift bed. At its head was the seal of Ma'at, showing the goddess seated and holding the hieroglyph of life.

Senusret covered his scalp with an unguent enabling him to wear the Double Crown without fear of being struck dead. The uraeus, the female cobra equivalent to the eye of Ra, would not direct its flame against him. Round his neck, the king tied a fringed scarf of red linen, from the temple of Iunu.

Capable of lighting up the darkness, it guided thoughts beyond appearances.

Before lying down on his bed of death or rebirth, Senusret gazed for a long time at a lapis-lazuli star. In it were written the celestial laws to which he submitted himself, at the same time passing them on to his country and his people.

The king closed his eyes. Either he would celebrate his festival of regeneration and procure new help for Iker, or the Herald would win a decisive victory by killing his main adversary.

28

According to the *Book of Sacred Places* revealing the locations of the Osiran relics, Isis' next port of call must be Dendera, capital of the sixth province of Upper Egypt, the Crocodile. Thanks to unusually strong winds, the boat travelled extraordinarily fast.

When they reached Dendera, there was no one at the landing-stage. Worried, Sarenput ordered two of his men to explore the surrounding area. They reported that the villages were abandoned and the fields deserted.

'We must go to the temple,' said Isis.

The magnificent Temple of Hathor stood among verdant trees and wonderful gardens, which provided cooling shade. So much beauty and peace created the perfect place for meditation and contemplation. But Sarenput's archers were ready to fire at any moment.

There was nothing abnormal in the fact that the great double doors were shut. They were opened only in exceptional circumstances, notably when the goddess's ship was brought out: every year Hathor was taken upriver to Edfu, to be united with Horus and re-create the royal couple. All entrances to the temple, including the little porch where the temporary priests purified themselves, were sealed.

A priestess appeared at the top of one of the temple walls. She looked very frightened. 'Who are you?' she asked.

'The High Priestess of Abydos.'

'Why are all these soldiers with you?'

'They are my escort.'

'The bees . . . Didn't the bees attack you?'

'I didn't notice a single one.'

The priestess came down from her observation post, opened a side door a little way and invited Isis to enter.

Sarenput tried to follow, but the priestess stopped him. 'No armed men may enter the domain of Hathor.'

'What is happening here?' asked Isis.

'For several days the bees have been enraged. Usually they create plant-based gold, in harmony with the "Gold of the Gods", the name of our goddess, and provide us with an invaluable remedy. But now they're killing anyone who ventures outside this enclosure. We have housed the people in here and are begging the goddess to put an end to this calamity.'

'Have you found out what is causing it?' asked Isis.

'We have tried. We carry out the rites of pacification, play the sistrum and dance, but this horrible situation continues.'

'Where is the relic of Osiris?'

'In the sacred wood, which is inaccessible now because dozens of swarms have invaded it. Without help, we shall die. Since the bees do not sting you, perhaps you can save us.'

'Take me to the healing-rooms.'

Nervously, the priestess took Isis to Dendera's famous hospital. Sick priests and priestesses from all over Egypt came here to recover their health.

Hundreds of the province's frightened inhabitants – men, women and children – were praying to Hathor, begging her to drive away the misfortune and give them back a normal life. Seeing Isis calmed many of them. They were sure she was a messenger from the goddess, whose presence boded well.

The head doctor, a robust old woman, worked unstintingly and gave her assistants no respite. Between the serious cases and more minor ones, they had no time to waste.

'Open an incubation room for me, Doctor,' said Isis.

'There is not a single place free.'

'As High Priestess of Abydos, I am going to question the Invisible power and try to find out how to heal the province.'

The doctor found this argument persuasive. 'Wait for a moment,' she said. 'I'll transfer a patient who's recovering.'

When that had been done, she showed Isis into a small room with a low ceiling. There were magical words on the walls, and in the centre of the room was a bath full of scented hot water.

'Undress, and get into the bath,' said the doctor. 'Then lean your head back, close your eyes and try to sleep. The scented steam will fill the room. If the goddess sees fit, she will speak to you – but I warn you that since the start of this crisis, she has been silent.'

Isis followed the doctor's instructions. The bath produced a wave of delicious sensations. Relaxing, she let her spirit wander. The fragrances came one after the other, forming a whirlpool of intoxicating scents.

A monstrous bee attacked her. Clinging to the edge of the stone bath, Isis stayed absolutely still. She knew that mirages would try to frighten her into abandoning the experiment. Soon an entire swarm covered every part of her body.

Keeping her eyes closed, she thought of Iker, the aftermath of his journey and the vital reconstitution of the body of Osiris.

A sudden scent of lilies made her relax completely, and the face of the goddess appeared. In a peaceful voice, Hathor told Isis what to do.

The treasury of the temple of Dendera housed an impressive quantity of precious metals and gems. A priestess opened the boxes and gave Isis permission to take whatever was necessary. Her vision represented the last hope for overcoming the curse.

Calmly and accurately, Isis reconstructed the eye of Horus torn apart by Set: exceptionally pure rock crystal for the cornea, magnesium carbonate containing iron oxides in the form of little red veins for the white of the eye, obsidian for the pupil, brownish-black resin emphasizing the iris, asymmetry between the pupil and the cornea.* She faithfully represented the anatomical components, which became symbolic materials.

Carrying the symbol of perfect health, she left the temple and went towards the sacred wood. Clouds of bees surrounded her. Despite her fear, Isis kept her composure, for the eye's brilliance kept away the furious insects.

The sacred wood was a mass of infernal buzzing. In the centre was an earthen mound on which acacias were growing. When Isis placed the eye there, the queen bees reorganized their swarms, and each one became unified again. The bees went back to their hives, on the fringes of the desert.

At the foot of the tallest tree, a spring was flowing. Isis retrieved the relic, the legs of Osiris.

It did not take them long to reach Batiu, 'the Temple of the Power Sistrum', capital of the seventh province of Upper Egypt.

This time, there was a large, excitable crowd on the landing-stage and quays. The city guards were trying in vain to push back hundreds of curious people. Priests were chanting songs of lamentation as they gazed at the Nile.

'It might be wise not to berth yet,' observed Sarenput.

'We're going to find out the reason for this disturbance,' replied Isis, 'and collect the relic.'

A river guards' vessel blocked their way. On board was an

---

*See 'The Scribe's Intense Gaze', by Didier Dubrana (in *Science and Life: The Revealed Life of Works of Art*, 1998). It concludes: 'Behind the gaze of this statue from pharaonic Egypt [the Louvre's *Seated Scribe*], proton bombardment and radiography have revealed eyes whose anatomy is almost perfect.'

officer who had been trained by Sarenput. The prows of the two boats touched.

'Lord Sarenput, what a pleasure to see you again!'

'You've travelled a long way, my boy.'

'Ensuring the province's security is exciting work.'

'And not easy, by the looks of this.'

'The priests have done something terrible, and the people are afraid the gods will be angry.'

'The High Priestess of Abydos will restore calm. Let the people know she's here.'

As the news spread everyone calmed down – the magic of Osiris's emissary would dispel ill fortune. Sarenput's boat docked.

Although freed from the pressing crowd, the priests went on lamenting. Isis asked them what had happened.

'Our High Priest was leading a procession, carrying the province's relic, the penis of Osiris,' said one of them. 'He was taken ill and fell into the Nile, and we haven't been able to recover the relic. A fish swallowed it – we'll never find it again.'

'Why are you so pessimistic?'

'Even our most skilled fishermen have failed to catch the fish. It's a creature from the otherworld, and has evaded their nets.'

'Take me to your temple.'

The Herald could control not only people but the elements. He had used a denizen of the Nile's waters to interrupt Isis' quest and condemn Iker to destruction.

A glimmer of light, just a tiny glimmer, still illuminated the young woman's will. Refusing to accept the obvious, she clung to a slender hope: using the province's emblem, the Hathor-headed sistrum. Its vibrations might show her a new way.

Aware of how unforgivable their sin was, the priests remained prostrate.

Isis walked the pathways of a garden containing pools

covered with lotuses. Those with white flowers had leaves with elongated edges, rounded sepals and petals, and were almost scentless; they opened in the evening and closed at dawn. The blue ones, with their round leaves, opened in the morning and gave off a sweet scent. Their slender sepals and petals ended in a point. According to ancient writings, they evoked the creative sex of the venerable lotus, which had appeared in the first times.

The young woman picked a magnificent blue lotus and questioned it. No, the province's relic had not gone. A dark force was hiding it; the fish was merely a decoy.

When the priestess finally brought the 'Power' sistrum, its vibrations produced a succession of bright red rays of light, like flames, which travelled across the surface of the pools.

Isis gathered the priests together. 'Bestir yourselves,' she ordered. 'Do you not hear that song?'

A shrill music tore at their ears.

'Unless you tell me the truth, you will lose all your senses. What are you hiding?'

'The Tree of Set,' confessed an old man of eighty. 'We thought it better to forget the tree existed, for fear that it might trouble our peace and deprive us of the Osiran relic. We have committed an irreparable sin in underestimating the danger.'

'Tell me where the tree is.'

'I would advise you not to confront it, because it—'

'We must hurry. Take me there.'

To the north of the temple lay a desolate space: not one flower, not one blade of grass. The sun was burning hot.

'The heat comes from Set's nostrils,' explained the old priest.

From a rocky cleft a dried-up black tree with twisted branches grew. Lying down nearby was a strange four-legged beast with long ears and snout.

'May I . . . may I leave?' asked the priest.

Isis nodded, and the old man fled.

'I know you, Set,' she declared, 'and I offer you the blue lotus. You reign over the gold of the deserts and you give your strength to it. Through you runs the procreative fire that can vanquish death. Permit me to gather up the relic of your brother.'

The animal shook itself and stood up. It fixed its red eyes upon the intruder.

Isis took a step forward, and the beast did likewise. Slowly, they approached each other.

The priestess felt the burning breath of the tree's guardian. She dared to stroke the creature and found that its skin was covered with an unguent. Tearing off one of the sleeves of her tunic, she collected some of it and walked towards the cleft, heedless of the fact that with her back to the beast she was easy prey.

The branches cracked, and the black tree crumbled and fell into dust. Reddish smoke rose from the cleft, enveloping the young woman. The wind dispelled it, leaving behind the scent of the blue lotus.

At the edge of the cleft lay the phallus of Osiris, made from a mixture of gold and silver. Isis wrapped it in the tunic-sleeve. The beast of Set's unguent would restore strength and vigour to the divine member.

All around her grew soft green grass. The strange creature had disappeared.

They were in sight of the Great Land of Abydos, capital of the eighth province of Upper Egypt, place of all happiness and of the supreme misfortune. How Isis would have loved to live out a long and happy life there with Iker, far removed from the vicissitudes of the world.

An impressive number of soldiers were lined up on the landing-stage. With them were Sekari, North Wind and Flesh-Eater.

29

For a long time, Isis and Sekari could not say a word. He embraced her respectfully, while the donkey and the dog whined. Their eyes brimmed with tears, and she tried to console them. Her discoveries would ease their grief a little.

'All is not quite lost,' said Isis. 'I must collect together all the major Osiran relics and reassemble that which is scattered. If I succeed, if we can celebrate the rites and pass on the Mystery, perhaps Iker will be healed from death.'

Sekari had little faith in it, but he was careful not to express doubt. Egypt was the land beloved of the gods, and it had known many miracles. 'We'll continue the journey together,' he told her, 'and I'll protect you.'

'The Herald's creatures are everywhere,' warned Isis.

The donkey and the dog demanded her attention again. While she stroked them, Sekari and Sarenput embraced.

'She's extraordinary,' whispered Sarenput. 'Although she has no chance of success, she forges ahead like the finest of warriors and ignores the danger. No obstacle can stop her; she'd rather die than give up. But we've already had to extricate ourselves from some nasty situations, and the enemy won't weaken.'

'Your warship's too easily identified,' said Sekari. 'I'll take over from here, using a lighter boat.'

'Do you need my archers?'

'Tell them to stop looking like soldiers and behave like simple sailors, the crew of a trading-boat. They must hide their weapons and use them only if absolutely necessary. You, Sarenput, should return to Elephantine – and stay on your guard: the future may have some unpleasant surprises in store.'

'Do you mean an attack by the Nubians?'

'No, I've no fears on that score. But Memphis is still under threat. Obviously the Herald wants to destroy the throne of the living. All the governors have a vital role to play in maintaining the unity of their provinces.'

'Elephantine's loyalty will remain unshakeable,' promised Sarenput. 'And you, my friend, watch over Isis.'

The rugged old governor took an emotional leave of her. He wanted to say all the right things, to express his admiration and affection, but instead stammered out a host of dismally conventional platitudes. Fortunately, Isis' look reassured him that she perceived his true feelings.

'I know it's useless to tell you to be careful,' he added. 'But the enemy . . .'

'We shall defeat him, Sarenput.'

When Sarenput's boat had left, Isis, Sekari, North Wind and Flesh-Eater headed for the domain of Osiris. Now they were with Isis, the donkey and the dog were recovering their spirits somewhat.

'My father is in grave danger,' Isis told Sekari. 'Wouldn't you be more useful guarding him?'

'I've been ordered to help and protect you. The king's safe: he's surrounded by the best men from the personal bodyguard Sobek created.'

'Although he is staying motionless, his journey will be dangerous. If he does not return from the other side of life, and does not celebrate his regeneration using the sealed vase, we are lost.'

'Senusret will return.'

*

235

'A little more water? Bina asked the captain of the House of Life's guards.

'I've had enough, thank you.'

'When shall I bring you some more?'

The soldier was completely seduced by her charm and her sensuality. It took a valiant effort not to leave his post and take her off somewhere private. 'As soon as possible – I mean, at the proper time. We aren't supposed to talk to people.'

'So many men, day and night. You must be guarding something very precious.'

'We're just following orders.'

'You really know nothing?'

'Less than nothing.'

Bina placed a furtive kiss on the captain's cheek. 'You wouldn't lie to me, would you? Especially not if we were to meet again tonight, after the evening meal . . .'

'The guard's being changed tonight. I'm leaving Abydos, and a colleague will replace me. Now, be off with you.'

This sudden change of attitude was due to the arrival of the Shaven-headed One and Nephthys. Still playing the dedicated and discreet temporary worker, Bina vanished.

It was impossible to find out what was going on inside the mysterious building that the old priest and the accursed seductress entered several times a day. Bina had made her attempts at well-spaced intervals, so as not to attract attention, but she had come up against an impenetrable wall. Nobody, not even a permanent priest, could give her any information at all.

Armed soldiers in the domain of Osiris! This sad spectacle was shocking, but after all two murders had been committed. A simple explanation was circulating: the sacred archives must be protected, and the Shaven-headed One was using the strongest means possible.

Bina was not satisfied with this. The old man and Nephthys

236

might be consulting ancient books of magic, seeking new incantations to protect the site and prevent further crimes. Or they might be writing papyri of conjuration. Whatever it was, why such a strong military presence?

Disconsolately, she went to see the Herald. She still had nothing new to tell him.

As he carried out his daily duties – pouring the libation of fresh water on to the offering-tables, and scrupulously sharing out the food supplies – Bega hid his anger. Bile was eating away at him, and his legs were swelling up.

The Shaven-headed One still treated him as though he were nothing. It did not matter if that stubborn old man despised the temporary workers, but Bega was an experienced permanent priest, and the Shaven-headed One was refusing him access to the House of Life – and not even telling him why. It was intolerable.

Unfortunately, his fellow priests were like sheep and agreed with the Shaven-headed One, so Bega could not form an alliance to oppose this tyrannical behaviour. As soon as Senusret fell and the Herald took power, he would reduce the permanent priests to slavery. Condemned to wash soiled linen, the Shaven-headed One would die at the task. On that day Bega would at last burst out laughing.

Why had Senusret left Abydos? Had he gone back to Memphis, or had he gone elsewhere in accordance with some secret plan? There was an easy way to find out. Bega was well acquainted with a sailor from one of the escort warships. The sailor suffered from pains in his back, and liked to be given small amulets, which brought him relief.

The two men met at the main quay, where Bega was inspecting the delivery of fresh vegetables.

'How are you, my friend?' asked Bega.

'The pains have come back again.'

'A long journey to Memphis leaves its scars.'

'Memphis? I haven't been there recently.'

'Weren't you part of the royal escort?'

'Yes, but—' The sailor stopped himself. 'Memphis wasn't our destination. Sorry, I can't say any more – it's a military secret.'

'Oh, it's nothing to do with me, and I'm not interested, anyway.'

Bega took a tiny cornelian amulet from the pocket of his tunic. It was shaped like a little pillar. 'At night lay this symbol of greenery and growth on your back. It will ease the pain.'

'You're very generous. All these terrible things happening in Abydos! We all hope the king will be able to drive misfortune away. Why did he go to Madu, that village in the Theban province, instead of going back to the capital? Well, no doubt he has good reason; we must just trust him.'

'That's wise advice,' nodded Bega. 'Protected by a king like Senusret, what have we to fear? When this amulet's energy's exhausted, let me know and I'll give you another one.'

'That's kind of you – very kind indeed.'

'Madu,' repeated the Herald, with great interest. 'Is that information reliable?'

'It is from one of my best sources,' Bega assured him, 'a stupid, superstitious sailor who doesn't even realize he's told me.'

'Madu is Iker's native village, and the home of that old scribe who knew where the ancient shrine of Osiris is. Senusret hopes to find the shrine and discover a means of fighting me.'

'His defeat is a certainty,' said Bega. 'He's simply trying to delay it. His spiritual son murdered, the *khetemet* gone, the fetish of Abydos destroyed – he has no means of support left. Senusret is a broken man taking refuge in old beliefs.'

'You don't know that village's real importance, but the pharaoh senses it. And he will perceive its secret: the two stellar matrices where he and his *ka* will try to recharge themselves with energy.'

The Herald's knowledge amazed Bega. 'You seem to know everything about our rites!'

'And I shall therefore be able to ensure that not a single one survives.'

Fear tightened the priest's belly. Did the Herald's human appearance conceal a force of destruction that would outlive its fleshly covering? Repressing his conscience's warning, Bega convinced himself that he was doing the right thing. Only the Herald could make all his wishes come true.

'Even if he is regenerated, what can Senusret hope to do?'

The Herald looked upwards. 'I see Madu . . . I see the pharaoh . . . His soul is travelling.'

'Is he dead?'

'He is continuing to fight. I must take advantage of this moment of weakness to hurl him into oblivion.'

'My lord, leaving Abydos is impossible. Everyone's being questioned, and there are soldiers surrounding and watching the whole place – even the desert.'

'I shan't need to move from here. Thanks to Bina's abilities as a medium, I shall put a curse on the name of Senusret. His soul won't rejoin his body; it will wander through desolate landscapes and die of starvation.'

Bina came into the room and prostrated herself before her master. 'Lord, Isis has returned.'

Isis lifted the covering that concealed Abydos's priceless relic, the head of Osiris. The god's serene face still bore Iker's features: the Herald had not succeeded in removing them. Yet the atmosphere was gloomy.

The Shaven-headed One did not try to conceal his failure. 'Dozens of people have been questioned and re-questioned, detailed investigations have been carried out, vigilance has been increased . . . And we still have not the smallest clue, not one serious lead. The permanent priests and temporary workers are carrying out their duties zealously, as if Abydos knew nothing of crime and despair.'

'Has anyone tried to penetrate the secret of the House of Life?' asked Isis.

'No, our security measures are working. I deeply regret the presence of all these soldiers, but there is no other way of protecting Iker.'

'Has anyone asked you why they're here?'

'Of course – I'd have thought it suspicious if no one had been surprised. It's only normal that the permanent priests and long-term temporary workers should ask me. Nephthys and I have let people believe that we are making a frantic search for ancient incantations capable of protecting Abydos.'

Nephthys took Isis' hands. 'The ship of Osiris is preserving Iker's mummy,' she said. 'I magnetize it several times a day, and the Shaven-headed One speaks the words of power. There's no trace of decay: your husband still survives between two worlds. We water the garden where Iker's soul-bird comes to drink, and the plants are still growing. Bring the relics back together, Isis. Don't give up your quest for any reason whatever.'

The Widow's faint smile showed how slender she thought her chances of success were.

'Do you wish to see him?' asked Nephthys.

'The House of Life is undoubtedly being watched by the criminals. If I go in, they'll realize that we're attempting the impossible. We must try to keep this secret for as long as we can. The moment it's divulged, the Herald will use new destructive forces to murder Iker a second time.'

'Neither I nor the Shaven-headed One would ever betray you.'

'I should dearly like to speak to Iker, but it would put him in danger. You must explain it to him, my sister.'

From the Basket of Mysteries, Isis took the relics she had gathered during the first stages of her journey. 'Place these inside the House of Life. I'm leaving again immediately.'

As she accompanied her sister to the landing-stage, Nephthys said confidentially, 'There is one of the permanent priests I don't trust.'

'Bega?' asked Isis.

'Do you suspect him, too?'

'"Suspect" is too strong a word. I can't detect the reality of his being. Have you anything specific to accuse him of?'

'Not yet.'

'Do you believe he's linked to Iker's murder?'

'It is impossible to say so without absolute proof.'

'Be careful,' warned Isis. 'The enemy won't hesitate to kill.'

Nephthys did not mention her relationship with the enigmatic and seductive Asher. She did not wish to sadden Isis, or perhaps anger her, by speaking of the world of feelings at a moment when Abydos's fate and Iker's survival hung in the balance.

30

Memphis was sleeping, but General Nesmontu was not. After a delicious evening meal, he was pacing up and down the terrace of Sehotep's house – he ignored the beautiful view of the capital. The old general hated being idle. Away from the barracks and the ordinary soldiers, he felt useless.

Sehotep joined him. Deprived of the society gatherings during which he probed dignitaries' minds and intentions, and of his work on renovating and building temples, the scribe with the lively eyes and the boundless intelligence was withering away.

'I'm getting fat,' grumbled Nesmontu. 'Your cook's so talented that I can't resist any of his dishes. As I'm not getting any exercise, obesity awaits me.'

'Would you like to hear a few of Ptah-Hotep's maxims on the subject of self-control?'

'I know them by heart and I go to sleep repeating them. But never mind that. Why is Sobek making us wait so long?'

'Because he doesn't want to strike until he's certain the time is right.'

'Sekari found a nest of rebels. I could flush them out and interrogate them. They'd give me the names of their leaders, and we could cut off the head of the army of darkness.'

'We aren't fighting an ordinary enemy,' Sehotep reminded him. 'Remember Thirteen-Years and the other fanatics like him. Their fanaticism increases their hatred tenfold. They don't surrender and they don't talk – they'd rather die. Sobek's adopting the same tactics: make the rebels believe they have free rein.'

'There's no sign of any of that.'

'We must allow time for information to circulate and be believed, particularly the news of your death and Sobek's mortal illness. No more commander of the guards, no more tjaty, squabbles between the claimants to vital offices: what a superb opportunity to attack. But the Herald's men are cautious: they won't commit him to attacking until they're sure of winning.'

'Understood, understood. So let them stick their noses out!'

'It won't be long,' predicted Sehotep.

'I wish I shared your optimism.'

'Actually, that isn't my dominant feeling.'

'Stop tormenting yourself. Your innocence will be proven.'

'Time is against me. But that doesn't matter if the pharaoh saves the Two Lands and preserves Abydos.'

Hands folded behind his back, Nesmontu started pacing up and down again. Sehotep gazed out over Memphis: it was an easy target for the Herald's fearsome predators.

The Herald's spy in Madu, the former assistant to the village headman, was furious at his dismissal from office, though he had in fact come out of it rather well.

He had been astonished by Senusret's arrival, and even more astonished when it turned out that the pharaoh had not come just to punish the headman. In asking questions about the village's Temple of Osiris, he had given away his true goal: to find a forgotten shrine, which had probably been destroyed long ago.

Once more merely one of the villagers, the rebel shaved off

his moustache, put on a peasant's kilt and hung around the site where the craftsmen from Thebes were working. They were very well-organized, and worked day and night, divided into teams. This was unusual, too. Why did the king want the rebuilding work done so quickly? Why were handpicked guards watching the site? It was clear that the king attached major importance to Madu.

If the rebel could find out the reasons for this strange behaviour, the Herald would promote him. He'd be able to leave this dreary village and live in a fine house in Memphis, and senior courtiers, reduced to the status of servants, would satisfy his smallest desires. Such a future was worth a few risks.

Head bowed respectfully, he presented warm flat-cakes to the captain of the guards. 'A gift from the new headman,' he said. 'Would you like me to bring you some more?'

'I wouldn't say no.'

'This evening I'll bring you some spiced bean paste. The king, though, must prefer refined dishes. What should I order from the headman's cook?'

'Don't worry about that.'

'Is His Majesty ill?'

'Go and fetch the rest of the flat-cakes.'

The captain's silence spoke volumes. Senusret was having to stay here because of some major stumbling-block, unless he was carrying out a rite connected with the Osiran shrine. Could the rebel get past the encircling soldiers? No, that was impossible. But he managed to sneak past the temple and, to his great surprise, saw that the sacred wood, which had been inaccessible for generations, was also being closely watched.

The king had broken through the wood's magical barrier! Only he could drive away the demons that suffocated the over-curious. During the restoration and enlargement of the temple, Senusret was living in the heart of this forbidden garden. How could the rebel get in there and find out what the king planned to do?

Willingly or by force, one man would help him: the eighty-year-old who led the Council of the Ancients.

Sitting on a straw-seated chair, the old man gave the rebel a black look. 'The shrine of Osiris doesn't exist. It's only a legend.'

'Stop lying. You have persuaded the entire population to keep a secret, and I want to know it.'

'You're talking nonsense. Get out of my house.'

'Even at your age, one values one's life – and even more the lives of one's children and grandchildren. Answer me or you'll regret it.'

'You'd dare to—'

'I have a great deal at stake, so I'll do whatever I must.'

The old man did not take the warning lightly. 'The shrine does indeed exist, but it lies in ruins.'

'Does it include underground chambers containing treasure?'

'It may do.'

'Hurry up – I'm getting impatient.'

'Very well. Yes, there are two underground shrines.'

'What's in them?'

The old man smiled. 'They're empty.'

'You're joking!'

'Check for yourself.'

'Give me a detailed description of the area.'

The old man did so.

Convinced that his informant was telling the truth, the Herald's disciple strangled him. In view of his great age, his family would think he had died a natural death.

The rebel still had to find out how to get into the sacred wood, steal the treasure and discover what Senusret was up to. With a little luck, he might even be able to kill the king! Imagining the reward for that made the murderer's head spin.

He laid his victim on his bed, left the modest house and went to get something to eat.

Admiringly, Sekari examined the small ivory sceptre. Isis had used it to summon a strong southerly wind, enabling the boat to travel at great speed.

'It belonged to the Scorpion King, one of the first kings buried in Abydos,' she explained. 'My father entrusted it to me to alter destiny. This sceptre and the Blade of Thoth are my only weapons.'

'You're forgetting your love for Iker, which is unique and indestructible. What you forged on this earth will endure.'

Ipu, capital of the ninth province of Upper Egypt, was proud of its temple. It housed an extraordinary manifestation of its protecting god, which had given its name to the region: the star-born Stone of Min. It had fallen from the sky in the time of the earliest pharaohs, and guaranteed prosperity and fertility.

Despite his ritual garment, a white shroud recalling the passage through death, Min declared the triumph of life in the most obvious manner: with his permanently erect penis, he rendered fertile the cosmos and all forms of matter.

When they reached Ipu, Isis went straight to the temple. A priest was guarding the door of purifications.

'I would like to see your High Priest.'

'For what purpose?'

'Would you deny me entrance to the Citadel of the Moon? Here the universe is heard and its message transcribed.'

The priest was taken aback. In those few words the young woman had revealed that she was no ordinary visitor, for she knew one of the secret names of the temple and the virtues of the Osiran relic.

After she had undergone purification, the priest invited her to meditate in the great open-air courtyard while he went to fetch his superior.

The High Priest, an imposing man of around forty, was not long in coming. He did not bother with polite niceties. 'When did you see the Citadel of the Moon?'

'During my initiation into the Two Ways.'

'But then . . .'

'I am Isis, High Priestess of Abydos, and I wish to collect this temple's relic.'

The High Priest needed no further explanations. Since the body of Osiris must be put back together again, a resurrection similar to that of Master-builder Imhotep was being prepared.

He therefore entrusted to the young initiate the ears of Osiris.

Swiftly, the boat continued its journey northwards. Isis' magic stretched time, contracted the hours, eased the crew's tiredness and maintained their vigour.

They passed through several provinces without incident, until they reached Khmun, the great city of Thoth and of the Eight Deities.

Sekari saw that Isis was nervous. 'Are we to stop here?' he asked.

'In principle, no – our next stop is the shrine of the cheetah-goddess Pakhet – but I sense danger.'

Above them a strange falcon was wheeling. It lacked the majesty of the bird of Horus; it seemed covered in blood and moved in an uncoordinated way. In place of talons, it had enormous claws.

Isis paled. 'It's the man-falcon, come from the cauldron of hell! A ghost that slashes its enemies' flesh, destroys their possessions and their descendants.'

'A creature of the Herald,' said Sekari.

He hurled a throwing-stick, but the falcon easily avoided it. Furious, it let out cries no human ear had heard before.

247

Only the presence of the ears of Osiris stopped the crew going mad with fear.

'Look ahead!' shouted the captain. 'The island's on fire!'

It blocked the Nile, forming an impassable barrier.

'It's the man-falcon's nest,' said Isis. 'We must remember the words of the king, during the harvest ritual: "Osiris came from the island of flame to become incarnate in the grain." By stealing the fire, and perverting the falcon's nature, the Herald is trying to make Egypt sterile and to imprint her with the seal of death. We must fight him.'

Despite their courage and determination, Sarenput's archers could not help trembling.

'Take up the oars,' commanded Isis.

'The river's boiling, my lady,' said the captain. 'We'll never be able to get past.'

'Thanks to the "Magic" sceptre, the fire won't burn our oars and the water won't wet them.'

Sekari seized an oar, and the other men soon followed his example.

On the island tortured shapes were writhing. Trying to become incarnate by feeding on the flames, they cracked apart, fell into pieces, reformed in an anarchic way and screamed their hatred.

Only Isis, North Wind and Flesh-Eater dared look at the convulsions of *isefet*. Living entirely within the harmony of their being, the donkey and the dog were not afraid of the enemy of Ma'at.

Using all their strength, the sailors fought to get clear of the nightmare. Their oars were indeed unharmed.

'We must moor here,' ordered Isis.

The captain thought he had misheard. 'You mean we should moor at the riverbank and disembark?'

'No, moor at the island.'

'But we'll all be killed.'

Seizing a bow, the High Priestess of Abydos fired an arrow

into the top of the highest flame, where the man-falcon was hiding. Pierced by the arrow, the foul creature exploded in a shower of sparks, spreading a vile stench.

'Moor here,' repeated Isis.

The fire's intensity diminished, the flames devoured each other, and the enemies of the Light tore each other apart. The captain nerved himself to moor at the island.

When Isis disembarked, she walked across a bed of embers without burning herself. At once a tempestuous gust of wind put out the fire and dispersed the smoke.

Flesh-Eater leapt ashore and devoured a tardy spectre. Ears erect, nose to the wind, moving unhurriedly, the donkey disembarked in turn.

The sailors waved their oars and cheered Isis. Then they followed Sekari ashore.

'No man could have done what you've just done,' said Sekari.

'The island's fire didn't belong to the Herald. I gave the flame back to Ra and the water back to Osiris. Let us fill ourselves with magic, and transform this domain of *isefet* into a land of the living.'

For the first time since he had learnt of Iker's murder, Sekari began to think that Isis might just succeed, though it still seemed almost impossible.

31

Bina was woken by a terrible howl from the Herald. Frightened, she kissed his brow, which was bathed in sweat. His eyes were staring, and he seemed lost in an inaccessible world.

'Come back, I conjure you!' she cried. 'Without you, we are lost.'

The Herald's condition horrified her. He half-opened his mouth, and spittle covered his lips. Seized by convulsions, he muttered incomprehensible words. Bina massaged him from head to foot, lay down on top of him, begged the evil to leave her lord and to transfer itself into her.

Suddenly, his great body came to life, and a red glow once again lit up the Herald's eyes.

'Isis has destroyed the man-falcon's nest,' he groaned.

Bina burst into tears, and flung her arms round him. 'Oh my lord, you're saved! You'll destroy that Godless woman – no one can resist your power.'

He sat up and stroked her hair. 'You must teach other women that they must submit to men, as you do. You are inferior creatures, and your sex prevents you from emerging from childhood. You must obey men if you wish to save your souls. By permitting women to hold high office, Egypt is refusing to observe God's commandments. In future there will be no priestesses.'

250

'That woman Nephthys . . .'

'She shall give me pleasure before being stoned to death. That is the fate reserved for those who have no shame.'

'Permit me to dry you and to perfume you.'

Even as he enjoyed Bina's gentleness the Herald felt pain, for he experienced again the death of the man-falcon and the disappearance of the nest of the ghosts that had come back from hell to persecute humans. Isis had won a great victory by destroying an obstacle he had believed impregnable.

Why did she fight on so eagerly? With Iker dead, the *khetemet* destroyed and the pharaoh powerless, the High Priestess of Abydos ought to have given way to despair. His well-trained and disciplined followers would do well to kill that madwoman while she was drunk with the pain of her losses. Her senseless fight was leading nowhere.

In the meantime, an urgent need beckoned. 'Undress, Bina, and lie down.'

The pretty brunette hastened to obey. Offering herself to her lord was the most beautiful of all rewards.

To her surprise, instead of enjoying her body the Herald placed a lamp on her navel and traced signs on her forehead.

'Close your eyes,' he said, 'concentrate, think of our enemy Senusret, whose name I have just written. Your flesh thus bears the mark of the enemy. May it curse him and drive him back!'

The Herald repeated again and again the words he taught his followers. In the future, these words would constitute the only valid form of knowledge, and the faithful would repeat them every day.

Bina drank them in and went into a trance. The hieroglyphs forming the name of the pharaoh grew larger until they became illegible, then liquefied. Black blood covered her face.

The Herald gloated. Senusret would not awake from his sleep. The bed of resurrection would support only a corpse,

251

and the father would rejoin his son in the very depths of oblivion.

As they approached the cave of Pakhet, the cheetah-goddess of the sixth province of Upper Egypt, Flesh-Eater growled and North Wind pawed the deck with a nervous hoof.

'Don't worry,' Isis told them. 'I know this place.'

During the celebration of a ritual there, the young priestess had embodied the south wind bringing the flood. Among those privileged to watch the ceremony had been Iker. Perturbed, Isis had acted her part as if he did not exist, yet since that moment she had been unable to forget him, though she had not then realized that he was the only man she would ever love.

'Be careful,' said Sekari. 'The way North Wind and Flesh-Eater are behaving is a warning of danger.'

Isis did not ignore the warning. However, Pakhet was a faithful ally. 'Great in magic', she offered the initiates of Abydos the ability to confront their destiny and to bring it into harmony with Ma'at. Better still, she guaranteed the unity of the body of Osiris, which she defended against all attacks.

The wild cat ought to have come out of her cave. Puzzled, Isis went forward.

Suddenly, out of the darkness sprang an enormous cobra. The archers instantly drew their bows and aimed at the monster.

'Don't fire!' ordered Isis.

Pakhet, 'She who Claws', could control the destructive fires and transform herself into a reptile, able to fight the enemies of the sun.

Isis prostrated herself. 'Here I am, once more before you. The survival of Osiris is in peril. I have come to ask you for the relic you protect.'

The cobra spread its hood and prepared to strike.

'I'm going to kill it,' declared Sekari.

'Don't move!'

On the bank, Isis drew nine circles and, in the centre, a coiled snake. She said, 'You embody the spiral of fire rising up towards the light, the road to follow to emerge from the darkness. In you the transformations of rebirth are accomplished. Examine my heart and see the purity of my intentions.'

When the cobra's forked tongue brushed the priestess's forehead, Sekari almost let fly a fatal arrow. But he obeyed the will of the High Priestess of Abydos.

Isis replaced the drawing of a snake with one of a cheetah. Immediately, the huge cobra slithered to the drawing, followed the outline of the nine circles and swallowed its own body.

The cheetah's roar stunned everybody except Isis. Meekly, the great cat accepted her caresses and accompanied her into the cave. Despite Isis' calm, North Wind and Flesh-Eater were uneasy, and Sekari and the archers remained ready to fire.

When Isis re-emerged from Pakhet's lair, she was carrying the precious relic, the eyes of Osiris.

The twentieth province of Upper Egypt was the Upper Oleander. Innumerable reed thickets adorned the banks and the area around the capital, Henen-nesut, whose name meant 'Child of the Reed'. The reed was one of the symbols of royalty; in the image of this simple plant, used for so many things, the pharaoh served his people at all times.

Near the temple was a great lake protected by a ram-god.

'It's too quiet here,' muttered Sekari.

A small boy came up to the visitors. 'Welcome. Would you like something to drink?'

'Who are you?' asked Sekari suspiciously.

'The youngest temporary priest in the temple.'

'Take us to your superiors.'

'The permanent priests are ill.'

'Is the illness affecting the whole province?'

'No, only them. They ate a bad meal, and it's made them feverish and delirious.'

'Who prepared the meal?'

'The replacement for the usual cook. The guards wanted to question him, but he ran away. Would you like to see the man in charge of the temporary priests?'

He was a forbidding man, who gave Isis and Sekari a chilly welcome. 'In the absence of the permanent priests, I am overloaded with work and have no time for idle chatter, so be brief.'

'Show us the relic of Osiris,' demanded Sekari.

The priest choked. 'Who do you think you are?'

'Bow before the High Priestess of Abydos and obey her,' snapped Sekari.

From Isis' bearing, the priest sensed that he was not exaggerating. 'I am not qualified, I—'

'We are in a hurry.'

'Very well. Follow me.'

The priest guided them to the shrine of the relic, a small room whose walls were covered with texts relating to the birth of 'the Great One of Shapes and Seven Faces', the child of the Divine Light who had appeared on the primordial lotus.

'I am not permitted to enter,' he said, 'still less to open the innermost shrine.'

'We'll let the High Priestess do so,' said Sekari, leading the priest outside.

Isis read out loud the ritual engraved in the stone. Becoming herself the living Word, she pacified the guardian spirits that forbade access to the relic-holder and unlocked its door.

When Isis emerged from the temple, her hands were empty. 'The relic has gone.'

'That's impossible,' protested the priest. 'The invisible

guardians would have killed the thief.' In view of the magical protection surrounding the relic-holder, this was a powerful argument.

Isis and Sekari had the same thought: the Herald was able to break down even the best defences.

'Describe the replacement cook,' said Sekari.

'He was a proper professional cook, from a neighbouring village. There was no reason to be suspicious of him.'

'And no one's been showing curiosity about the temple recently?'

'Nothing unusual.'

Isis sank down on the base of a pillar. The Herald, or one of his demons, had stolen the relic, which was now impossible to find, and had thus put an end to her quest. There was nothing left for her but to return to Abydos and see Iker one last time.

'Come with me, whispered a child's voice.

She turned and saw the young temporary priest, his face lit up with a kindly smile.

'Forgive me, but I'm tired, so tired . . .'

'Please come.'

Isis gave in.

The little boy led her inside the covered temple. Together, they entered the shrine of Ra. On an altar lay the gilded wooden ship of the God of Light.

'For several days,' said the boy, 'I'd been having bad feelings. Evil forces were prowling around, but my superiors did not take the threat seriously, so I decided to act alone and hide the relic. It is written that the arms of Osiris are like the oars of the ship of Ra. I can entrust my secret to you, and only you.'

Isis went up to the altar. The ends of the two great oars unscrewed. They contained the upper limbs of the Lord of Abydos.

She turned to thank her benefactor, but he had gone.

From Isis' smile, Sekari realized at once that something good had happened.

'We are continuing our journey,' she announced. 'From now on, our oars will have the power of the arms of Osiris.'

'Your magic—'

'No, the help of the little boy. What is his name?' she asked the priest.

'A boy, here in the temple?'

'The youngest of your temporary priests.'

'With respect, High Priestess, you're mistaken. The youngest is twenty years old.'

Isis looked at the sun. The child of the Light, born of the lotus, had intervened to help her.

In the middle of the night, Medes arrived at the Phoenician's house and demanded to see him.

'Help me down the stairs,' the Phoenician ordered his steward. He was so fat that moving was becoming difficult, but he found it impossible to eat fewer cakes. So many cares and uncertainties kept gnawing away at him, and eating sweet things helped to keep his brain working and meant he could keep calm.

Medes was nervous and agitated. 'Sobek's jackals seem to have relaxed their vigilance,' he said, 'but I'm still wary.'

'A recipe for a long life,' commented the Phoenician. 'Any news of the tjaty?'

'He doesn't leave his bedchamber, and his private secretary is dealing with all current matters. It's a sickness that even Doctor Gua himself cannot cure. His death is expected any day.'

'And Nesmontu's dead, and Sobek's dying. Excellent!'

'Better still, I have no royal decrees to write.'

The Phoenician nibbled a soft date soaked in wine. 'How do you read the situation?'

'My view may seem miraculous, but it's credible: either

Senusret's dead or he's incapable of acting and commanding. Without his leadership Egypt's falling apart.'

'What about the queen?'

'She's prostrate in her apartments.'

'And Senankh?'

'He hasn't recovered from the death of his friend Nesmontu. He's deeply depressed and is neglecting his work more and more.'

The Phoenician scratched his chin. 'An admirable conjunction of circumstances. In my place, nobody would hesitate to launch the attack.'

'Why do you have reservations?'

'Instinct, just instinct . . .'

'Sometimes one can be too cautious. Memphis is there for the taking, so let's take it.'

'We must carry out one more check,' decided the Phoenician. 'We'll arrange a few isolated operations. If the enemy doesn't react effectively, I'll order all our men to take action.'

32

At dawn, Curly-Head left his hideout. Memphis was waking up. Swallows were dancing high in the sky, warm bread and fresh milk were being delivered, and the first conversations being struck up.

A seller of flat-cakes offered him one.

Curly-Head took it and murmured, 'Immediate action.'

'Where did the order come from?'

'From the Phoenician himself.'

'What's the password?'

'Glory to the Herald!'

'And the second password?'

'Death to Senusret,' said Curly-Head, nibbling his flat-cake.

Glad to be taking action at last, they separated. Each man knew what he had to do.

The officer commanding the city guards who were watching the suspect area reported to the tjaty. 'Things are moving, sir. The lookouts saw Curly-Head and Surly leave the house and go off in opposite directions. My men are taking turns at following them.'

'Whatever happens,' ordered Sobek, 'don't lose them.'

'There's no risk of that. When should we intercept them?'

'You don't.'

'But, sir, if they attack innocent people or—'

'That's a direct order: under no circumstances are you to intervene. Any man who disobeys will be accused of treason and severely punished. Do I make myself clear?'

The officer swallowed hard. 'Absolutely clear, Tjaty Sobek.'

Curly-Head alerted the undercover rebels. Itinerant traders, shopkeepers and craftsmen, they had melted into the general population. Some had even become guards' informants, providing them with reassuring information and contributing to the arrest of petty criminals, thus strengthening their credibility.

The thought of causing chaos delighted the Herald's men. The people of Memphis thought they were safe from new murders, but they were going to learn the truth. Insecurity would breed panic, which would favour the army of darkness when it attacked.

The first operation took place in the port at night.

After the dock-workers had left, Curly-Head and five of his men set fire to an unguarded storehouse where bales of linen were stored. The smoke rose up into the Memphis sky, and shouts of alarm rang out.

Rigid with anger, the guards who responded to the alarm cursed their orders.

The young married couple were strolling along the banks of the Nile. Enjoying their quiet happiness, they liked to take the air at the end of a day's work, far from the city's bustle.

Ahead of them, they suddenly saw a man armed with a knife.

'We'd better turn back,' said the husband.

But behind them stood Surly and three henchmen, all armed with clubs.

'Give us your jewels and your clothes or we'll beat you to death,' growled Surly.

'We must do as they say,' said the wife.

'I'm not letting myself be robbed!'

A blow from a club knocked his legs from under him. The poor man roared with pain.

His wife took off her necklace, bracelets and rings. 'Take everything,' she begged, 'but don't kill us!'

'Your dress, his tunic, and your sandals – quickly!' demanded Surly.

Naked, humiliated and weeping, the victims tried to comfort each other, not even daring to watch the attackers as they left.

The guard shadowing the rebels clenched his teeth.

The scribe counted the weights used in the market. Always meticulous, he kept a register which his superior checked every week. In twenty years of good and loyal service, there had not been a single error. Knowing they would not be cheated, customers could buy goods with confidence.

Petty crooks had more than once tried to bribe him or give him false weights at the end of suspect transactions. All had ended up in prison, for the Double White House took such things very seriously.

Once his check was done, the scribe prepared to close the door of his office. He was thinking about the delicious meal he would have later: roasted quails, haricot beans, soft cheese and round cakes with honey. It was his wife's birthday and there would be a real celebration.

He was utterly stunned when Curly-Head and two men armed with knives burst in.

'Get out of here at once,' he ordered.

Curly-Head silenced him with a punch in the belly. Winded, the unfortunate man fell heavily. His head struck a wall and he passed out.

'Wreck the place,' Curly-Head ordered his men.

They tore up the records and threw the remains on their victim's body.

Outside, invisible, the guards stood motionless.

Nesmontu and Sehotep listened attentively to the tjaty's detailed report. Fires, attacks on civilians, thefts, the wrecking of offices . . . All Memphis was talking about these crimes and criticizing the guards' incompetence.

'Only Curly-Head and Surly left their lair,' said Sobek, 'and theirs was the only group involved. After committing their crimes, they went back to their hiding-place. As I thought, their leader is being particularly cautious and is testing our ability to react. So I've sent out patrols all over the place. They'll find nothing, thus proving how disorganized we are.'

'After such serious incidents,' protested Nesmontu, 'are you still refusing to make your move?'

'Sekari has pinpointed only one nest of rebels; there must be several others. The Herald has spread his net over the whole city, and the success of his offensive will depend on how quickly his troops act.'

'How will you counter them?'

Sobek gave a half-smile. 'That's where you come in, General. I have here a detailed map of the city, and you're going to show me where best to position our soldiers so they won't be seen.'

'Now there's a task to rouse a man from the dead!' declared Nesmontu with enthusiasm.

'Of course, you will take command the moment the attack begins.'

'What will my successors do?'

'All is going according to plan. The senior officers are fighting among themselves; everyone wants to be made commander-in-chief. With the king away and the tjaty so ill, no decision can be made. The army and the city guards are paralysed, and no decrees can be promulgated.'

'Have you taken Medes into your confidence?' asked Sehotep.

'I think it preferable that he knows nothing. That way, he'll go on behaving normally. If the Herald's spies are watching him, they'll see the progressive disintegration of the state secretariats.'

'And what about Sehotep?' asked the general anxiously.

'Justice must follow its course,' declared the tjaty.

The crew looked admiringly at Isis. She had overcome the island of flame, caused the south wind to blow, and made their oars light, easy to handle and incredibly effective . . . This priestess worked miracles.

The boat entered the twenty-first province of Upper Egypt, the Lower Oleander; it was one of the country's most fertile areas, thanks to the canal serving Faiyum.

Sekari knew the region well and remembered his many adventures there with Iker. Despite all the snares and ambushes, he had succeeded in saving the Royal Son from his attackers. How could he ever have imagined that the most dangerous place of all would be Abydos?

'Don't blame yourself,' Isis urged him.

'I wasn't there at the moment chosen by the Herald, so I didn't do my job properly. When the king convenes the Golden Circle again, I shall hand him my resignation.'

'You'd be making a grave mistake, Sekari.'

'I've made it already.'

'I don't think so.'

'Only the pharaoh and you are capable of defeating the Herald,' said Sekari. 'The Golden Circle will help you unstintingly.'

'In that case you mustn't resign. If you do, you'll be betraying Iker.'

262

The boat approached Shedyet, the City of the Crocodile, capital of the province, which was criss-crossed by canals. Standing atop a vast mound, the little town dozed in the sunshine. Here an enormous crocodile, incarnation of the god Sobek, was fed. Its mate was scarcely less enormous, and wore earrings of gold and glass.

'What relic are we to collect here?' asked Sekari.

'I now have all those described in Abydos's *Book of Sacred Places*. Every year this city's temple celebrates the reconstruction of the divine body. By regenerating the old sun at the heart of the great lake, the crocodile of Sobek triumphs over the darkness and proclaims the royalty of the reborn Osiris.'

Activity around the landing-stage was normal. Dock-workers were unloading cargo vessels, while scribes noted down the nature of the goods and their quantity.

'Wait here for me,' said Sekari. 'I'm going to look around.'

'What are you concerned about?'

'In the present situation, I'm suspicious of peaceful places.'

During Sekari's absence, the crew ate and drank, North Wind and Flesh-Eater included. The giant hound deterred any onlookers from taking too close an interest in the boat.

When he returned, Sekari looked worried. 'The temple's closed,' he said. 'We must investigate without attracting too much attention, because I sensed hostility among the people here.'

Accompanied by North Wind, Isis strolled towards the temple. A few paces behind her walked Flesh-Eater, all his senses on the alert.

Isis said to a fish-seller, 'I should like to make an offering to the temple.'

'You'll have to wait, my beauty. Because of a curse, the priests have abandoned the place. If they don't come back, the crocodile will eat us all.'

'Where have they gone?'

'To the Realm of the Flame, a hidden island at the northern end of the great lake. Unless there's a miracle, they'll be drowned.'

'Who can take me there?'

'The ferryman knows where it is, but he loathes pretty women and charges them exorbitant rates. Forget it, my beauty, and leave this province. It'll soon be laid waste by demons.'

The calmness of the dog and the donkey reassured Isis that nobody was following her, and Sekari had not spotted anyone threatening.

'The Herald got here first,' he commented when Isis told him what the fish-seller had said.

'I must change my appearance and persuade the ferryman to take me to the island.'

'No, Isis – it's a trap.'

'We'll see.'

With her hair coloured grey and her complexion darkened, and wearing a threadbare dress, Isis was transformed into an old woman. When she stepped aboard the ferryman's boat, he stayed seated and did not even look at her.

'Will you take me to the Realm of the Flame?' she asked.

'It's a long way and it costs a lot. You can't afford it.'

'How much is it?'

'I won't be content with a scrap of bread and a goatskin of fresh water. Have you got a gold ring?'

'Yes. Here it is.'

The ferryman took a long time examining the ring. 'And I must also have some finest-quality fabric, to the value of one hundred and fifty measures of spelt and a bronze vase.'

'Here you are.'

He felt it and folded it up. 'Do you know the Numbers?'

'The sky is One. Two expresses the creative fire and the

radiant air. Three is all the gods. Four is the directions of space. Five opens the spirit.'

'Well, you do know how to assemble the ferry, so it will take you where you want to go. But avoid the slaughtering-place, because Set's supporters will be waiting for you there.'

The ferryman got out of the boat, which moved off of its own accord towards the great lake. Caught unawares, Sekari was left standing on the quay.

A thick mist covered the Realm of the Flame. The ferry made its way through a maze of watercourses and came to a halt near a grassy islet. The priests of the Temple of Sobek were standing on the shore, waving their arms and calling to her for help. Behind the priests, and shielded by them, the followers of Set brandished their spears.

Using the steering-oar, Isis rowed closer. In spite of the danger, she must save the priests.

A pelican flew over the islet. From its beak shone a ray of sunlight so intense that it dispelled the mist and burnt away the slaughtering-place and its torturers.

Safe and sound, the priests hailed their rescuer.

'May the pelican's beak open once again for you,' Isis told the High Priest, 'and permit the Reborn One to emerge into the light of day. Giving its blood to feed its young, it embodies the generosity of Osiris. Thus the relics of Upper Egypt are regenerated. By coming here, they have been rendered fully effective.'

33

Medes and Senankh ate their midday meal together. Medes noted that the High Treasurer, usually so fond of his food, did no more than nibble, and drank more than usual.

'The people of Memphis are afraid,' said Senankh, 'and we cannot reassure them.'

'Shouldn't His Majesty intervene?'

'We don't know where he is,' confessed Senankh. 'The King's House is receiving no instructions.'

'Can the queen not help?'

'She remains in seclusion, the tjaty is on his deathbed, and Sehotep awaits the court's sentence. It falls to me to deal with current matters, but my hands are tied in matters of security. Neither the city guards nor the army will listen to me.'

Medes assumed a look of fear. 'You mean Senusret is . . . ?'

'No one dares utter the fatal word. It's possible that he's simply withdrawn into a temple. Whatever the case, Iker's death has destroyed him, and the state is deprived of its leader.'

'A successor to Nesmontu must be appointed, and the army deployed,' exclaimed Medes.

'Each senior officer heads his own group, and they're all at loggerheads with one another. We're on the verge of civil war, and I can see no way of preventing it. Fortunately, the rebels have so far mounted only isolated minor actions. If

266

they were better informed, they'd launch a major offensive and take Memphis with ease.'

'That's unthinkable!' cried Medes. 'You and I must try to coordinate our forces.'

'The guards obeyed Sobek, and the army obeyed Nesmontu. In their eyes we're nothing – or even obstacles.'

'I don't dare understand you.'

'It would be madness to stay in Memphis – we'd escape neither the rebel attack nor the mobs. The regime's going to collapse, and we must leave.'

'I refuse to do so. Senusret will reappear; order will return!'

'I admire courage, but in certain circumstances it becomes stupidity. It's pointless to deny the facts.'

Medes stopped eating and drank two cups of wine, one after the other, without pausing for breath.

'There must surely be a solution,' he ventured in a trembling voice. 'We cannot simply abandon everything.'

'It is Ma'at who has abandoned us,' said Senankh mournfully.

'But what if the rebels aren't as powerful as we think? What if their crimes are limited to minor attacks?'

'Their leader, the Herald, is determined to cause the death of Osiris, the downfall of the pharaoh and the destruction of our whole civilization. Soon all those wishes will come true.'

'No!' roared Medes. 'Running away would be unworthy of us. Anyway, where would we go? Let us fight here, gather together all those loyal to Senusret, and proclaim our determination loud and long!'

Senankh was greatly surprised by this reaction. He regarded Medes as a conscientious official and a skilful courtier, but had believed he was attached to his own comfort and had little inclination to self-sacrifice.

'Even in reduced form,' Medes went on, 'our central institution still exists. It may be impossible to distribute a decree, but there's nothing to stop us declaring the continuance of power. The pharaoh has often left Memphis before, and the queen has ensured the state's continuity. Speak to her, I beg you, and convince her that she must hold fast. The enemy hasn't won yet.'

'Are we really capable of withstanding him?'

'I'm certain of it. But the soldiers and guards need to feel that they have a leader.'

'I'll try,' promised Senankh.

'For my part,' Medes assured him, 'I shall spread reassuring news. Our confidence in the future will play a vital role in ensuring Egypt's survival.'

Senankh was even more taken aback. Perhaps he ought to reveal Sobek's plan to Medes? No: he must be faithful to his word and keep silent. But he revised his judgment, and was now glad to count the secretary of the King's House among Senusret's most ardent supporters.

At the secondary port of Memphis, Sekari ordered a change of crew. Although Sarenput's archers were glad to be going home, they would never forget the priestess's courage. One after another, they thanked her for her protection. The new sailors belonged to the special forces set up by Nesmontu.

The new captain, a rather rough-and-ready man but a good fighter, knew every corner of the often inhospitable areas of the North for which they were bound, and could sail just as well by night as by day – he never needed to use a map. And, coming from a village in the coastal marshes, he was unworried by snakes and insects.

'A woman?' he exclaimed when he saw Isis. 'She's not thinking of travelling on my boat, I hope.'

'It is *her* boat,' replied Sekari, 'and you will obey her.'

'Are you joking?'

'I never joke when I'm in the service of the High Priestess of Abydos.'

The captain regarded Isis suspiciously. 'I don't like being made a fool of. What's this all about?'

'Our country is in grave danger,' she said. 'There are relics dispersed throughout Lower Egypt, and I must reassemble them as soon as possible. Without your help, I shan't be able to do it.'

'Then you really are . . . '

'Are you ready to leave, Captain?'

'My friend Sekari chose the crew, and I trust him. All the same . . .'

'I'll tell you the destinations, but you are in command of your boat. The oars have been blessed by the magic of Ra, and the winds will favour us. On the other hand, many enemies will try to kill us.'

The captain scratched his head. 'I've carried out plenty of insane missions in my damned life, but this one beats them all. No more talk – we're leaving. If I understand you rightly, time is at a premium. First stop?'

'Kom Ausim, capital of the Thigh, the second province of Lower Egypt.'

As the boat sailed north, they entered another world, the world of Lower Egypt. After winding between two deserts, the Nile took its ease and eventually spread out into a vast delta. The river gave birth to seven branches, supplying countless canals which irrigated a verdant region filled with palm-groves. Kom Ausim lay on one of the left-hand branches.

The city's High Priest was a gentle, affable man who gave the High Priestess of Abydos an enthusiastic welcome. She had come to seek not a part of Osiris's body but one of his sceptres.

'Are you doing this because grave dangers face us all?' he asked.

'I'm afraid so.'

'Is the domain of Osiris itself threatened?'

'My mission is to protect it. By handing me the *nekhakha*, the symbol of the threefold birth, you will give me invaluable help.'

'It is an honour to assist you.'

Together, Isis and the High Priest evoked the mysteries of the Light, of the stars' matrix and of the earth. Then he opened the doors of a shrine and took out the sceptre with its three leather thongs.

Isis felt the first one. The leather remained inert.

'Try again,' urged the High Priest.

She touched the second, with no better result.

'Perhaps you must begin with the third.'

Failure again.

The priest swayed. 'No,' he gasped, 'I don't believe it!'

'This is a forgery,' concluded Isis. 'Apart from you, who has access to the shrine?'

'My two assistants, a ninety-year-old who was born here in Kom Ausim, and a young temporary priest. I have total confidence in them both.'

'Should you not open your eyes?'

'You think that . . . ?'

'One of them has stolen the real sceptre and substituted a useless copy.'

'Such a wicked crime, here, in my temple!' The priest felt suddenly faint, and Isis had to prevent him from falling.

'The dishonour,' he groaned, 'the shame, the—'

'Where do your assistants live?'

'Beside the sacred lake.'

'We must question them.'

Although still unsteady on his feet, the High Priest agreed. His distress and grief gave way to muffled anger. The insult to his dignity made him eager to find the culprit and bring him to justice.

Although they roused him from his afternoon nap, the

ninety-year-old had all his wits about him. He told them his duty times and thanked the gods for granting him such happiness. As far as he was concerned there was nothing untoward to report. Kom Ausim's days were peaceful and his old age happy.

The High Priest knocked at the door of the second assistant. There was no answer.

'That's strange. He ought to be here.'

'Let's go in.'

'That would be violating his privacy.'

'We have no alternative.'

The little house was empty, as were the clothing storage chests.

'He's run away,' admitted the High Priest, bitterly disappointed. 'A thief – it's beyond belief!'

'Let us try to find one of his personal effects.'

All they found was one worn-out mat.

'It will be enough,' said Isis.

She rolled up the mat and raised it to her eyes. Little by little, she entered into contact with its owner: she saw him clearly and was able to tell where he was.

The thief gazed at the stolen sceptre. He was a follower of the Herald, and hoped his master would reward him generously for breaking this symbol of Osiris's power.

So far his assignment had been easy. His superior's naivety, the lack of guards at the shrine, a new house outside the town . . . Soon his fellow rebels would come and fetch him, and take him far away from Kom Ausim to swell the ranks of the future masters of Egypt.

Although this fine future beckoned, he hesitated to destroy the sceptre. In his time as a temporary priest he had been presented with so many revelations that he was having great difficulty in profaning the precious relic. The new religion certainly attracted him, especially because of the advantages accorded to men and the absolute subjection of women, who were perverse creatures too quick to display their charms. He had thought that his conversion to the new faith would enable him to forget his duties and his past life, and easily destroy this simple acacia-wood sceptre with its three leather thongs.

For the tenth time his knife-blade touched them. And for the tenth time he gave up.

Furious with himself, he slashed his arms and chest. The smell of the blood calmed him. Before long the unbelievers' blood would flow in great tides.

This certainty gave him back his zeal. He was overcoming Osiris's magic. Snatching up his knife again, he prepared to rid himself at last of his inconvenient booty.

The door burst open. Caught in the act, the priest stopped dead. A stocky man charged at him, seized him by the legs and toppled him over. Stunned, the thief dropped his knife and Sekari slipped a rope round his neck.

Isis reclaimed the sceptre.

Losing his self-control, the thief praised the Herald and cursed his enemies until Sekari got tired of his diatribe and knocked him out.

When Isis touched the first thong, the thong of radiant birth, the blue of the sky became more intense, under the effect of a dazzling sun. Golden rays enveloped the temple, and the statues' eyes filled with supernatural life.

Touching the second thong caused a host of stars to shine, in broad daylight. From the stars' matrix that surrounded the heavens and the earth, the innumerable forms of creation were continually born.

When she touched the third thong, flowers emerged from the ground, and the garden in front of the shrine blossomed into a multitude of colours.

She laid the sceptre in the Basket of Mysteries and returned to the boat.

34

In Madu, the former assistant headman was trying hard to prove his loyalty to the king. Besides ostentatiously criticizing the former headman, regretting his own misdeeds and praising the new village council, he took food and drink to the soldiers who were guarding the building works at the temple and preventing anyone from entering the sacred wood.

The rebel was hoping to find someone with a loose tongue. In accordance with their orders, the soldiers hardly spoke to anyone, confining themselves to brief words of thanks. But he was sure of one thing: the king had not reappeared since entering the forbidden domain where the shrine of Osiris was hidden.

The old man the rebel had murdered had been well liked by the villagers, and his funeral rites had been performed with great reverence. During them his murderer had delivered an eloquent elegy to the deceased.

'We have lost the village's memory,' mourned the dead man's closest friend, who was almost as old. 'Many secrets have died with him.'

'How he would have loved to see the new temple,' said the murderer. 'His last joy was meeting the pharaoh. It's such a pity the king left so soon. His presence at the inaugural ceremony would have made it truly memorable.'

The old man's hands tightened on his stick. 'The pharaoh hasn't left,' he whispered.

'Is he directing the building works in person?'

'I believe he is experiencing the ordeal of Osiris in the sacred wood.'

'What does that consist of?'

'I don't know. Only the king can attempt it, and even he runs great risks in doing so. The country's prosperity depends on the outcome.'

'Let us pray that he succeeds.'

The old man agreed.

The murderer was jubilant. So the king was in a vulnerable position! If the rebel could penetrate the domain of Osiris, he might succeed in killing Senusret. Then he would be a hero in the eyes of the Herald and his followers, and would receive an unimaginable reward. He could already see himself as mayor of Thebes, receiving the citizens' adulation. All opponents would be mercilessly slaughtered and terror would strike all unbelievers.

But he had yet to get past the soldiers. He could not rely on any allies, so he had no chance of stabbing one of the well-trained soldiers without attracting the others' attention.

He would use subtler means: drugging their food.

Medes was putting on weight. As the fatal day approached, he found that eating was the only thing calmed him down.

Ravenously hungry, he ate greedily of the Phoenician's lavish evening meal. The duck in sauce was worthy of a royal table. As for the wines, they would have enchanted the souls of the ancestors on the day of the wine festival.

'Senankh confided in me,' he said. 'He doesn't much like me and has always been suspicious, but I changed his mind by demonstrating my absolute loyalty to the king in this time of grave crisis. Our good High Treasurer's in despair; he wanted to run away and advised me to do the same. Instead of agreeing with him, I shook him by declaring that it was our common duty to fight the enemy, while declaring to the people of Memphis that they were in no danger.'

Medes burst out laughing, but the Phoenician was icily unmoved.

'We must launch the attack,' advised Medes. 'We'll meet only disorganized resistance. Once Memphis is in our hands, the rest of the country will collapse.'

'Is there still no news of Senusret?'

'I'll be the first person to get it, because I'll have to draw up a decree as soon as he returns. Whether he's ill or powerless, the pharaoh isn't governing the country, and the cracks caused by his absence are getting wider by the day.'

'What about the tjaty?'

'He's on his deathbed. Senankh doesn't even visit him.'

'And the queen?'

'On my advice, Senankh will try to persuade her ostensibly to resume her public position, in order to affirm the continuity of power. But he's bound to fail. The Great Royal Wife's depression will be Senusret's downfall. He certainly can't hold the tiller of ship of state, and may even be dead.'

'There's still the army.'

Medes shook his head. 'It's broken into rival groups, which are at one another's throats. Without a supreme commander, it's falling apart. And the city guards are no better. Egypt's sick – very sick. Let's finish her off before an unlikely sorceress of the corpse leads to hopes of a cure.'

The Phoenician sampled several different kinds of cream cheese, accompanied by a fine red wine from Imau. 'Why has there been no word from the Herald?' he asked worriedly.

'Because Abydos is completely encircled by soldiers,' replied Medes, 'and no one is allowed in or out. Trying to send us a message would be suicidal.'

'I can't launch the final attack without a specific order,' said the Phoenician.

'Do you still doubt the enemy's weakness?'

'Suppose Senankh was playing a part?'

'I thought of that, too. The fellow is sly, suspicious and a skilful tactician. But he's lost all his points of reference. I'm a good judge of people: and this one is falling apart.'

'It's too good,' said the Phoenician.

Medes exploded. 'You wanted to see the reaction to our small, isolated operations – the fires, thefts and so on – and you've seen it: ineffective patrols and futile investigations, as usual! Me, I've got you first-hand information and am at the very heart of the false resistance of a state in its death throes. Assume your responsibilities, and the Herald will reward you.'

'My instinct tells me to be cautious.'

Medes raised his arms to the heavens. 'And because of your instinct we're to give up trying to take Memphis!'

'It's always spared me a lot of problems.'

'Are you afraid? At the very moment of seizing power?'

The Phoenician's small black eyes fixed on Medes. 'I've worked for the Herald for a lot longer than you have, and I don't permit anyone to accuse me of cowardice. Remember that, and never do it again.'

'What have you decided to do?'

'There must be one last check, in the form of a spectacular crime and the denunciation of one of our groups. We'll see if the authorities react in accordance with your optimistic forecasts.'

After Medes had left, the Phoenician finished off the dish of sweetmeats. As soon as he was head of the political and religious guards, he would kill the arrogant secretary of the King's House.

'Which direction now, my lady?' the boat's captain asked Isis.

'To the West, the third province of Lower Egypt.'

The voyage had changed in nature and was nothing like the

descent of the Nile Valley from Elephantine to Memphis. Isis would try to gather the Osiran relics from the Delta by heading first west and then diagonally east, before taking a southerly direction and reaching the province of Iunu, called 'the Master Is in Good Health'. If the gods permitted her to succeed, she would then possess all the elements enabling the body of Osiris to be reassembled, providing a vital basis for Iker's resurrection.

The captain was thoroughly enjoying himself. The weather was perfect, the wind in the right quarter, the sailing conditions idyllic, and the crew made up of sturdy fellows who did not mind hard work. Should he revise his opinion of women on boats? No, because this one was unlike any other.

As they approached the Citadel of the Thigh, the province's main temple, Isis thought of the 'Beautiful West', the wondrous goddess with the sweet smile who welcomed those of just voice into the afterlife. There they rested in peace, their lives transfigured, nourished by Ma'at. But it was too soon for Iker to meet the goddess. He had not exhausted his potential; he must continue on his earthly path and ensure that Senusret's work continued.

When the boat touched land, North Wind brayed so loudly that all the dock-workers and passers-by stopped in their tracks.

'There are going to be problems,' commented Sekari.

Flesh-Eater's aggressive stance confirmed this.

A delegation of priests and soldiers asked to come aboard, but Isis preferred to descend the gangplank.

A forty-year-old priest with hollow cheeks addressed her. 'You must leave immediately: this place is cursed.'

'I must go to the shrine.'

'You can't – nobody can cross the field of scorpions. Monsters have awoken, and they've killed most of my colleagues. An enormous crocodile is now living in the sacred lake, preventing all purification.'

'I shall try to conjure fate.'

The survivor grew angry. 'Leave at once, I order you!'

Isis walked forward. A soldier tried to seize her, but Flesh-Eater leapt forward and knocked him to the ground. At a signal from Sekari, the archers aimed at the procession.

'That is no way to treat the High Priestess of Abydos,' said Sekari.

'I didn't know. I—'

'Go away, all of you. We shall deal with the situation.'

Although he doubted the outcome, Sekari certainly did not lack flair.

When he saw the number of yellow and black scorpions seething in the garden, and on the forecourt of the temple, his doubts grew, but Isis did not flinch.

'Thoth spoke the great words giving plenitude to the gods,' she chanted. 'It unites Osiris so that he may live. You, the children of Serket, goddess of the narrow pathway to the Light of resurrection, regent of the height of the sky and the elevation of the earth, do not oppose the Widow. Let your venom enter the heart of impurity, burn the perishable, sting the enemy. May your flame halt my opponents and clear my path.'

The dangerous creatures halted. One by one, they slid under stones. Sekari thought the magic words had been effective, until a black scorpion climbed up Isis' tunic.

She held out her hand. The venomous sting seemed ready to strike.

'Show me where the relic is,' she said quietly.

The sting withdrew. Isis put the scorpion down and followed it. It led her to the sacred lake. As she descended the first few of the steps that led down into the lake, a gigantic crocodile rose up from its depths.

On its back lay the thighs of Osiris.

Sekari held her back. 'Be careful, please! That monster doesn't look very friendly.'

'Remember the mysteries of the month of Khoiak, my brother from the Golden Circle. Remember, too, that Osiris takes on the form of the animal of Set in order to cross the primordial ocean.'

Sekari remembered the exploration of Faiyum, during which Iker had been saved from drowning by the master of the waters, a giant crocodile. He said no more.

The spirit of the lake approached Isis, who went further down the steps until she was submerged up to the chest. Its mouth opened, baring menacing teeth.

'You handsome seducer,' she said, 'you ravisher of women, continue your work of reassembly.'

A sort of tenderness appeared in the crocodile's eyes. Isis reached out and took the relics.

The captain much enjoyed demonstrating his skill at navigation by choosing the best route to the seventeenth province of Lower Egypt, the Throne. Any other sailor, even an experienced one, would have lost his way in the watery maze near the coast of the Great Sea. But the captain was constantly alert to every trick of these dangerous waters, where many unseen snares could trap the unwary.

The current was capricious, sometimes fast, sometimes non-existent. It demanded extreme vigilance and quick reactions.

'What is our destination?' the captain asked Isis.

'The Isle of Amon.'

'I've always avoided it. According to local legend, ghosts bar access to it. I don't believe that, but some curious people have been shipwrecked for their pains.'

'We'll land at the northernmost point, which is exposed to the sea winds.'

The captain did not argue.

Sekari looked hard at the island, trying to spot any aggressors, but the place seemed deserted. 'I'll go ashore first,' he decided.

Isis agreed.

Accompanied by a playful Flesh-Eater, Sekari explored that part of the deserted land. The only signs of life were mosquitoes. There was no shrine, let alone a shrine likely to contain a relic.

North Wind explored the area in search of food. He stopped before a plant with a red stem and white flowers.

Isis knelt and dug in the soft earth. She unearthed the fists of Osiris.

35

In his great anxiety, Gergu was drinking too much. The approach of the final attack was making him nervous. And yet the situation was becoming brighter by the day, and Memphis would fall like a ripe fruit into the hands of the Herald's supporters. He could therefore look forward to a senior post, a luxurious house and all the women he wanted.

Women: that was precisely the main problem at the moment. Because of his violence, the best brothels would no longer accept him or provide him with even foreign women. He had to resort to a third-rate establishment, near the house Medes had given to the dancer Olivia, an ambitious creature he had used to trap Sehotep. The attempt had been a complete failure, with the result that the foolish trollop had been brutally killed.

The tavern really wasn't much to look at.

'I want a girl,' demanded Gergu.

'You'll have to pay first,' said the owner.

'Will this cornelian bracelet do?'

'Oh, my prince! I have two little foreign girls available, totally dedicated to their work. Take them where you like.'

Accompanied by the sluts, Gergu asked the doorkeeper who lived opposite for the key to the house belonging to a certain Bel-Tran. Under this name, Medes owned several premises where he stored large quantities of valuables derived from his smuggling operations.

Although cooperative at first, as soon as Gergu hit them the girls protested. Frightened, they started to cry, and one of them managed to run away. In fury, Gergu drove out the other one with kicks, handed the key back to the doorkeeper and went to try his luck elsewhere.

The brothel-keeper, who was a guards informant, was angry at the treatment meted out to his girls. He contacted the officer to whom he reported and told him about the incident.

The officer spoke to the doorkeeper of the house. 'Do you know this fellow?'

'Yes and no. I don't know his name – he's not from round here – but I think I've seen him before, when a pretty dancing-girl was planning to come and live here.'

'Who does it belong to?''

'To a trader, Bel-Tran.'

'And you gave the key to that brute?'

'Yes, seeing as he'd come on behalf of the owner.'

In ordinary times, the officer would have put the matter on file. Given the current climate, he had been ordered, like his colleagues, to follow up the smallest clue that might lead to the rebels. He asked the doorkeeper for a detailed description of 'that brute', made a drawing from it, and promised himself that he would discreetly search Bel-Tran's house when night fell.

Furious that his victims had got away, Gergu went in search of another. He found one at the village of Mount of Flowers, where, using his high position, he had forced the man responsible for the granaries to pay him in order to avoid heavy fines for imaginary errors and the loss of his job. The unfortunate villager was afraid that Gergu would send in a signed report – and of course no one would doubt the principal inspector's word.

The sight of Gergu turned his blood to ice. 'I . . . Everything's in order.'

'You think so? The list of your oversights seems unending. Fortunately, I like you.'

'But I paid you less than a month ago!'

'This is a supplementary tax.'

The man's wife spoke up. 'Please understand, we can't—'

Gergu slapped her. 'Silence, woman! Go back to your kitchen.'

The villager was frightened, but he would not tolerate anyone touching his wife: this time Gergu had gone too far. It was impossible to confront him openly, so he must pretend to submit.

'Very well, I'll do as you say.'

Medes's wife burst into tears.

Dr Gua awaited the end of this new outburst, listened to the voice of her heart and drew up a prescription. 'You're in excellent physical health,' he said, 'but I cannot say the same for your state of mind.'

The doctor was unusually gentle, because he wanted to understand why this wealthy woman, who had everything she could possibly want, suffered such serious illnesses. 'Did anything bad happen to you during your childhood?'

'No, Doctor.'

'How would you describe your relations with your husband?'

'Wonderful! Medes is a perfect husband.'

'Is something worrying you?'

'I wish I could get thinner without giving up . . . I just can't!'

This deception irritated Doctor Gua. He would not be content with the formula 'a sickness I do not know and cannot heal'. Sensing that he was close to the truth, he planned a different method, which was sometimes very effective.

'Take your remedies scrupulously,' he advised. 'But on their own they won't be enough, so I am planning a new kind of treatment.'

'Will I stop crying and feel well?'

'I hope so.'

'Oh, Doctor, you're so kind to me! Will it be . . . painful?'

'Not at all.'

'When will you begin?'

'Soon. But first, the medicines.'

They were preparing Medes's wife to undergo a delicate experiment: hypnosis. It might reveal the terrible anxieties that this patient was hiding deep within her.

As they headed towards the fifteenth province of Lower Egypt, the Ibis, the captain's skill became even clearer. Very much at ease in this watery world, he instinctively took the right decisions.

'Where shall I drop anchor?' he asked Isis.

'I'm waiting for a sign.'

Here, Thoth had separated Horus and Set during the terrifying battle on which the balance of the world had depended. By pacifying the two warriors, enemies for ever, and by recognizing the supreme legitimacy of Horus as Osiris's successor, the god of knowledge had become the interpreter of Ma'at.

Sekari scrutinized the fishing-boats that were making signs of welcome to the travellers.

Suddenly, the donkey and the dog woke up and looked at the sky. A huge ibis was descending from above and heading for the boat. Majestically it alighted on the prow, gazed for a long time at the priestess and then took flight again.

The great bird had left behind two vases made of alabaster, the excellently hard stone placed under the protection of Hathor.

'They contained the water of the *nun*,' said Isis. 'It will facilitate the regeneration of the body of Osiris.'

No longer surprised by anything, the captain took the heading given to him by the High Priestess of Abydos: southeast, to the twentieth province of Lower Egypt, the Mummified Falcon.

The further they got from the shore of the Great Sea, the better the crew felt. Fewer marshes, fewer biting or stinging insects, more cultivated fields and palm-groves. The boat set off along one of the broad branches of the Nile. A steady north wind enabled it to make good progress.

'What is our exact destination?' asked the captain.

'The Isle of Soped.'

'That's forbidden! Well, it's forbidden to outsiders, but I don't suppose that concerns us.'

Isis' faint smile reassured him, and he made it a point of honour to manoeuvre the boat smoothly.

On the island lived a small community of priests and priestesses, who maintained the shrine of Soped, the mummified falcon who wore the beard of Osiris. Two feathers of Ma'at adorned its head.

The High Priestess, a slender brunette with a solemn face, welcomed Isis. 'Who is the mistress of life?'

'Sekhmet.'

'Where does she hide?'

'In the venerable stone.'

'How do you obtain it?'

'By penetrating its secrecy with the sharp, accurate acacia thorn,* which is dedicated to Soped.'

The priestess led Isis to the shrine. At the feet of the mummified falcon lay the thorn, made of turquoise.

Isis took it up. 'From Ra, the being of metal, was born a stone destined to make Osiris grow,' she declared. 'This

*The *sepedet* thorn, linked to Soped.

285

hidden work transformed that which is inert into gold. I need it today in order to accomplish resurrection.'

The falcon's eyes flamed.

With the point of the thorn, Isis touched the two feathers. The bird's body opened up, revealing a cube of gold.

Bubastis, capital of the eighteenth province of Lower Egypt, the Royal Child, was a bustling city, and obviously prosperous. Here a great festival was celebrated in honour of the cat-goddess Bastet, during which the participants cast off all their inhibitions.

'It's strange,' commented Sekari. 'Why don't the Herald's creatures show themselves? He never gives up, so he must have planned a trap that's even more cunning than the previous ones. Here, perhaps. We must not lower our guard on any account.'

North Wind and Flesh-Eater were on the alert. At the sight of the giant hound, many cats scrambled for high positions, out of his reach.

In front of the main temple stood a huge statue embodying the *ka* of Senusret. The little band paid homage to it, and Isis asked it to give her the strength to pursue her quest to the end.

The pretty High Priestess, who had almond-shaped eyes, received her counterpart from Abydos in a garden where a hundred different species of medicinal plants grew. There the doctors, followers of the fearsome Sekhmet, gathered the gifts of the gentle Bastet, necessary for the preparation of remedies.

Under its mistress's chair, an enormous black cat stared at Isis, then settled comfortably and began to purr contentedly. It had accepted this unexpected visit.

'Does the garden perceive the brightness of the sky's window?' asked Isis.

'The window has closed,' lamented the High Priestess, 'and the radiance of the world beyond no longer illuminates the mysterious chest. Henceforth, it will remain sealed.'

'Its contents are vital to the celebration of the Mysteries,' revealed Isis. 'Have you spoken the words of conjuration?'

'Yes, but without success.'

Sekari was right: the Herald was not giving up. By obscuring the window of Bubastis, he had barred a major pathway between the visible and the invisible, and was preventing the Widow from collecting a treasure necessary for reconstructing the body of Osiris.

'Have any of your colleagues been behaving strangely?'

'One of the permanent priests has disappeared, taking with him the *Book of Celestial Windows*,' admitted the High Priestess.

Isis went out into the garden and began to walk around it. As she approached a patch of camomile, an enormous cat leapt out. Spotting a viper that was about to attack the priestess, it pounced with remarkable speed and killed the viper with a single quick bite.

The High Priestess of Bubastis was shocked and alarmed when Isis told her. Never before had a snake violated the shrine.

'The cat of the sun triumphs over the killer of the darkness,' said Isis calmly. 'Take me to the goddess's shrine.'

Seven arrows protected it. One by one, the Widow fired them into the sky. Falling in behind each other, they formed a long streak of light. It tore through the azure sky as though it were fabric, and fell on to the threshold of the shrine, whose bronze door Isis opened.

Inside was a chest.

'I see the energy you enclose,' chanted Iris, 'I bind the strength of Set and that of the enemy, so that they do not damage the parts of the body of Osiris.'

With the aid of the arrowhead, at once one and sevenfold, Isis opened the lock. She took four ritual pieces of fabric from the chest. Corresponding to the four cardinal points, they symbolized Egypt reunited to the glory of the Reborn One, and would be used to wrap the Osiran mummy.

'They will be returned to you at the end of the ritual of Abydos,' Isis promised the High Priestess.

'Have a care. The thief will use the *Book of Celestial Windows* against you.'

'Don't worry, he will not get far. And I shall provide you with a new copy of the book.'

The big cat enjoyed the Widow's caresses before she rejoined her boat.

Perched at the top of the mast, the lookout signalled that something was amiss. Floating in the water nearby was the body of the priest who had sold his soul to the Herald. His right hand clasped a papyrus, soaked through and unreadable.

36

High Treasurer Senankh had a profound respect for order and method, so the offices of the Double White House were models of neatness and tidiness. Each scribe knew exactly what his duties were, and those duties took precedence over his rights. Nothing exasperated Senankh more than petty officials who tried to abuse their position to the detriment of others and, notably, the taxpayers. He always ended up detecting them and putting a sudden end to their careers. No job was guaranteed for life, so nobody was lazy. And everyone in the secretariat knew that he was responsible for a vital aspect of the prosperity of the Two Lands.

When five armed men burst into one of the archive rooms, the scribe in charge couldn't believe his eyes. After knocking out a guard and two scribes, they flattened the unfortunate man against the wall and threatened him with a knife, tore up dozens of accounting papyri, started a fire and fled.

With no thought for his own safety, the scribe took off his tunic, tried to beat out the flames with it, and shouted for help. Frantic at the sight of his precious documents being destroyed, he fought on until his hands and arms were badly burnt, and he would have died if help had not arrived quickly.

Still officially on his deathbed, Tjaty Sobek was working with only a select few colleagues, loyal men whom he had trained in the days when he reorganized the guards force. Skilled, efficient and silent, they admired their leader.

'A particularly spectacular rebel action,' remarked one of them, at the end of his detailed report on the attack. 'Fortunately, the injured scribe's life isn't in danger. This wicked deed must have frightened one member of the network, because he's sent us a letter of denunciation. We know the culprits and where they live.'

'Is this plausible?' asked Sobek.

'Yes, sir. Checks have been made. I assume we shall continue to follow our strategy and not intervene?'

The tjaty thought for a while. 'Usually they organize a series of crimes, but this time we have an isolated incident and a denunciation. That's unheard-of. A test . . . Yes, that's what it is. The leader of the network is testing our real ability to act. If we stay inert in the face of such a godsend, he'll think our behaviour abnormal, will detect the trap, and won't launch the great offensive. So, since we're only too happy to have a good lead at last, we're going to try to arrest some criminals. And note that I said "try".'

The Phoenician chewed a leg of duck while he listened to his door-keeper's report.

Making use of the letter, three detachments of guards had surrounded the home of the rebels, who had not been warned. The Phoenician wanted a real check.

The raid was badly coordinated, because of disagreements among the guards' commanders, who advocated incompatible tactics, and it had ended in a fiasco. Alerted by the guards' overt approach, the lookouts had immediately warned their comrades. They had cut the throat of one of their number, who was sick and unable to move, and then fled. Despite their haste, all the rebels had got away.

The conclusions were obvious. First, the guards had no serious leads, and had pounced on the first piece of information that came along. Second, Sobek the Protector no longer commanded his troops, who were visibly disorganized, self-absorbed and without a true leader.

The Phoenician began to come round to Medes's way of thinking. The moment was approaching when they must seize Memphis, preparing all the rebel groups to launch a furious attack which neither the main barracks nor the royal palace would be able to withstand. They must strike hard and fast, spreading such terror that the capital's last defences would collapse without a real fight.

There was a lot of work in prospect, but also the possibility of dazzling success. Here in Memphis the future of Egypt would be played out. After his triumph, the Phoenician would become its absolute master. The Herald's new religion would scarcely hinder him, and he would provide his master with enough executions of unbelievers to satisfy him.

Two statues of Senusret protected the main temple of the eleventh province of Lower Egypt, the Heseb Bull. The High Priest greeted Isis cordially and entrusted to her the province's precious relic, the fingers of Osiris, whose thumbs corresponded to the pillars of the sky-goddess Nut.

Sekari was surprised by such easy success, and wondered if things would be so easy at their next ports of call. The first was Djedu, capital of the ninth province, the Walker. They hoped for a favourable reception here, since it was *Per-Usir-neb-djed*, 'the Dwelling of Osiris, Master of the Pillar', the god's cult centre, where a annual festival was held in his honour. Linked to Abydos, Djedu was imbued with a calm, reflective atmosphere. Already the preparations for the ceremonies of Khoiak were beginning.

On the forecourt of the temple stood a strange individual. With a headdress decorated with two feathers of Ma'at, a shepherd's kilt, rustic sandals, and a long staff in his hand, he embodied the tireless pilgrim in search of the secrets of Osiris.

'I am the guardian of the divine words,' he declared. 'He who knows them will reach the heavens in the company of Ra. Can you pass them on, from the prow to the deck of the sacred ship?'

'This temple's ship is called *She Who Illuminates the Two Lands*,' replied Isis. 'It carries these great words to the mound of Osiris.'

The Walker pointed his staff at Sekari. 'This outsider must leave.'

'The Golden Circle purifies and reunites,' said Sekari.

Asonished, the Walker bowed. He had never imagined that someone initiated into the Great Mysteries, and who knew the words that opened up the paths, could look like Sekari.

'We are burdened by great misfortune,' he said. 'The golden plant* of Osiris has disappeared, and the bird of light no longer flies above the mound planted with acacias. Set now has a free hand, for Osiris will remain inert.'

Goats had invaded the temple garden and were beginning to eat the leaves of the acacia trees.

'They are not afraid of my staff,' said the Walker, 'and I cannot drive them out.'

'Let us use a different weapon,' suggested Sekari, and he took out his flute and began to play a calm, solemn melody.

As soon as they heard the first notes, the animals stopped destroying the garden, seemed to dance, and left the sacred place.

At the foot of a centuries-old acacia, the golden plant of Osiris emerged from the ground. But, alas, there was no bird of light.

'Has the shrine been profaned?' asked Isis.

'May the High Priestess of Abydos walk through it and re-establish harmony.'

By attacking Djedu, the Osiran city of the Delta, the Herald

---

*The *nebeh* plant, with a play of sounds on '*nub*', 'gold'.

had weakened Abydos. Had he succeeded in damaging the relic?

Isis passed through the great doorway, entered the domain of silence and descended the staircase leading to an under ground chamber whose threshold was guarded by Anubis. The jackal allowed her to pass, and she found a sarcophagus housing the glorious body of the god of resurrection.

The flowers making up the crown of the Lord of the West had been scattered.

Isis gathered them up, re-created the crown and placed it on the brow of the sarcophagus.

When she emerged from the shrine, a splendid ibis *comata*, with red beak and legs and dazzling green plumage, was flying over the holy mound.

'The souls of Ra and Osiris are once again in communion,' declared the Walker.

The *akh* bird knew the gods' designs and revealed a light which was not given naturally to humans but which they must conquer. Without it, Iker would not emerge from death.

The beautiful ibis landed on the top of the mound. There Isis found the province's relic, the spine of Osiris.

The Walker gave her the two feathers of Ma'at that had decorated his headdress. 'You alone can wield them and use their energy.'

The Phoenician's door-keeper looked pleased with himself. 'Three-quarters of our groups have been contacted. They're all delighted at the thought of taking action at last.'

'Are they following orders as regards security?

'They're being extremely careful.'

'No alarming signs?'

'None at all. Patrols, searches, interrogations, a few parades of soldiers . . . The authorities are still making no headway.'

'Make sure our men don't move too soon. One false step could endanger the entire operation.'

'Everyone knows your orders and will obey them. May I send in your visitor?'

'Has he been searched?'

'He's unarmed and gave the correct password.'

The visitor was young, athletic and bright-eyed, a fellow Phoenician who had worked for him for a long time.

'Have you brought good news?' asked the trader.

'Unfortunately, no.'

'Is that priestess still continuing her journey?'

'She'll soon be in sight of Hwt-Heryib, capital of the Black Bull province, and Iunu, the ancient and sacred city of the divine sun. There she will be able to acquire formidable powers.'

'"Formidable"? Let's not exaggerate. Isis is only a woman, and her wanderings are like those of a crazed woman who can't recover from the death of her husband.'

'According to what I've heard,' insisted the informant, 'her arrival is arousing great enthusiasm among the temple priests. She seems able to destroy curses and spring traps. I don't know any more because she's being escorted by soldiers and I daren't go too near.'

This interested the Phoenician. So Isis was fulfilling a specific mission, under close watch. Was she trying to raise the morale of the High Priests and Priestesses? Was she taking them a confidential message from the king? Was she telling them to be on their guard against attacks by the Herald's supporters?

Even if she had not lapsed into madness, the Widow's scope for action was limited. Nevertheless, the Phoenician wanted to be absolutely sure he would not be running any risks.

'We must have a little surprise in store for her,' he decided. 'We have an agent in Iunu, have we not?'

'Our best man in Lower Egypt.'

'The priestess apparently likes travelling, so I'm going to give her an opportunity to go on a long journey – with no return.'

Nesmontu could not keep still. Never, in his long career, had he been kept away from the field of battle for so long. Away from his headquarters, the barracks, the rank and file soldiers, he felt useless; even the comfort of Sehotep's home was becoming unbearable. His only distraction was several daily sessions of punishing exercise, which even a fit young soldier would have found it hard to emulate.

For his part, Sehotep spent much of his time reading and rereading the words of the sages. The two brothers of the Golden Circle of Abydos were united by a firm friendship, the only thing that enabled them to endure this painful waiting.

At last, in the greatest secrecy Sobek paid them a visit.

'The rebels' leader is an exceedingly skilful player,' said the tjaty. 'He's cunning and suspicious, and he thinks the situation looks too favourable to be true.'

'Our failure to react has intrigued him,' said Nesmontu, 'and he doesn't believe that the state is falling apart. And that means our plan isn't working.'

'On the contrary,' disagreed the Protector, and he related the latest events.

'You're an exceedingly skilful player yourself,' commented Sehotep. 'Do you think you've won this round?'

'I don't know. I don't think I've made any mistakes, but will the enemy take the bait?'

'Are the defensive measures in place?' asked Nesmontu anxiously.

'Yes, they are,' the tjaty assured him. 'Here are the details.'

The explanation lasted a good hour, and the general memorized the various positions.

'There are still ten weak points I'd like to improve,' he said. 'We must have full control of every single district of the city, so that when the rebels emerge from their rat-holes either they'll be caught in a pincer movement or else they'll come up against solid walls.'

Sobek noted down the improvements on his map. 'General, your forced withdrawal hasn't dulled the sharpness of your mind.'

'It would take more than that. If you only knew how much I'm longing for this attack. At last we're going to see the faces of those murderers and fight the army of darkness in the open.'

'The risk are still high,' said the tjaty. 'We don't know the exact number of the Herald's supporters, or their objectives.'

'The royal palace, the tjaty's offices and the main barracks,' said Nesmontu. 'If they take those strategic points, they'll cause utter disarray. For that reason, my regiments will guard those buildings from concealed positions nearby. What we must not do is strengthen the overt guard on them.'

The tjaty turned to Sehotep. 'The court case is moving ahead.'

'Not in my favour, I assume?'

'I have not intervened in any way,' Sobek assured him. 'The court will soon summon you and pronounce its judgment.'

37

The voyage to the port of Hwt-Heryib, capital of the tenth province of Lower Egypt, the Black Bull, presented the captain with no problems. However, heavy clouds were coming in from the west and gathering above the region, the wind was growing stronger by the minute, and steep waves were making the Nile dangerous. He was glad to reach land before the storm burst.

'Here rests the heart of Osiris,' Isis told Sekari. 'It's the last part of his body that I must collect.'

Bolts of lightning zig-zagged across the sky, and thunder rumbled.

'The voice of Set,' said Sekari. 'He doesn't seem disposed to make your task easy.'

Although the crewmen were sturdy fellows accustomed to danger, they were alarmed by the violence of the storm.

'Moor the boat securely,' ordered Isis, 'and take shelter.'

Despite the first drops of rain, North Wind and Flesh-Eater accompanied Isis as she set off. As usual, Sekari followed her at a distance, ready to intervene in the event of an attack.

The town was deserted. Not a single house was open.

Isis took the processional road leading to the temple, 'the Shrine of the Centre'.

The two animals halted, and Flesh-Eater growled. Then she saw the temple's guardian: a gigantic black bull, taller than a man at the shoulder, more powerful than a lion. It feared nothing, not even fire, knew how to hide to catch its enemies unawares, and became enraged at the slightest provocation. Even the best hunters dared not confront it; they left that task to the pharaoh, for the fearsome beast bore the name of *Ka*, the creative and indestructible power passed from king to king.

'Be calm,' urged Isis, stroking the donkey and the dog.

Sekari stepped in front of her. 'We must back away slowly,' he said.

'You three go back,' said Isis. 'I must go on.'

'That's crazy!'

'I have no choice. Iker is waiting for me.'

An excellent father and good teacher, and the protector of its wounded fellows, the wild bull was sociable and peaceable at the heart of its herd. But reduced to a solitary condition, it could explode into fearsome violence.

Isis walked towards it calmly: the only death she feared was the death of Iker.

The donkey, the dog, and Sekari stood their ground. If the bull showed any signs of attacking, they would fly to the young woman's aid.

The bull scraped the ground with its hooves, and foam covered its stiff beard. Isis managed to capture its gaze and realized why the inhabitants and priests of Hwt-Heryib had fled their city.

'You're suffering, aren't you?' she said. 'Please allow me to help you.'

The answer was a bellow of pain. She went closer and was able to touch the weakened giant.

'Eyes filled with pus, a high fever, the roots of the teeth inflamed . . . This is a sickness I know and can heal. Lie down on your side.'

At the priestess's request, Sekari hurried off to fetch the necessary remedies from the boat. When he returned, North

Wind and Flesh-Eater also rejoined Isis, who dripped cleansing drops into the bull's eyes, and rubbed first its gums and then its entire body with wads of medicinal herbs. The rain stopped, and the storm moved away.

The bull was sweating profusely.

'That's a very good sign,' said Isis. 'The sickness is leaving your body, the fever is being smothered and your strength is returning.'

'Wouldn't it be sensible to move further away?' suggested Sekari.

'We have nothing to fear from this valuable ally.'

The bull got to its feet again and stared at its saviours one by one. A sudden movement of its head did not reassure Sekari, for the sharp horns brushed his chest.

Isis stroked the bull's broad forehead. 'I'm going to the Temple of the Centre,' she said.

Although accepting the presence of the donkey and the dog, the black bull reserved a more suspicious look for Sekari. Forcing himself to smile, he decided it was best to sit down and stay still, while hoping that Isis would return soon.

The great door of the temple was ajar. Terrified by the curse that had struck down their protecting spirit and rendered the city uninhabitable, the priests had completely abandoned the place. Immediately, seventy-one guardian spirits had hastened to stand guard around the shrine containing the heart of Osiris. Hybrid beings, wild beasts, flames, soul-eaters, they formed an indestructible and merciless army.

Isis brandished the solid silver Blade of Thoth. 'Here is the Great Word,' she chanted. 'It cuts through reality and makes out the right way. I have come not as a thief but as a servant of Osiris. May his heart bring life to the heart of Egypt and preserve the Great Secret.'

Granting free access to the Widow, the guardian spirits returned into the stone and once more became carved figures or hieroglyphs.

Before the vase containing the precious relic lay a scarab beetle made of jasper.

'You, the master potter, who fashion the new sun, live for ever and be stable as the pillar of resurrection. Reveal to me the celestial gold, the path of eternal life. Yesterday, today and tomorrow, let the time of Osiris be accomplished and transformations beyond death be effected.'

When Isis emerged from the temple, the sun was at its height. Returning from the surrounding areas and the countryside, the inhabitants of Hwt-Heryib saw her lay the relic on the back of the enormous black bull, which was now clearly in perfect health.

The bull led an improvised procession to the port, where the sight of it made the captain's blood run cold: one fit of anger, and the gigantic animal's horns might cause serious damage to his boat.

Isis' calm demeanour reassured him. Nevertheless, he was not sorry to cast off and head for the city of the sun, Iunu, the illustrious capital of the thirteenth province of Lower Egypt, which lay at the southern tip of the Delta, to the north of Memphis.

Sekari gazed at Isis with deep emotion and admiration. 'All the parts of the body of Osiris have been brought back together. You have reached the end of your quest.'

'There is still one more step.'

'It should be no more than a formality.'

'Do you think Iunu's reputation will deter the Herald?'

'Probably not. But he's failed. Despite all his traps and attacks, he hasn't interrupted your journey.'

'Underestimating him would be a fatal mistake.'

Sekari inspected the boat from top to bottom. Was one of the members of the crew in league with the Herald? He knew them all, but one of them might have succumbed to promises of a brilliant future or the attraction of a fortune easily won.

300

However, neither the dog nor the donkey showed any suspicion of these men, all of whom had been trained by Sobek himself.

What type of danger did Iunu hold in store for them?

A river tributary sparkling in the sunshine, a verdant landscape, vast palm-groves, a peaceful and austere temple-city . . . Here stood the sole obelisk, the ray of petrified light. Here reigned Atum, the Creator, and Ra, the Light in action. Here the *Pyramid Texts* had been devised, containing the words that enabled the pharaoh's soul to vanquish death and accomplish multiple transmutations in the otherworld. Resulting from the spiritual perceptions of the initiates of Iunu, the great pyramids of the Old Kingdom translated the eternity of Osiris in a colossal way.

The centre of the city was made up of shrines that were both independent and complementary, in which a small number of experts worked. No disturbance seemed to have troubled this sacred land.

At the landing-stage, several shaven-headed priests welcomed Isis.

'High Priestess of Abydos,' said their spokesman, 'we rejoice at your visit. The echoes of your journey are spreading, and you are assured of our help.'

Such declarations ought to have reassured Sekari but, curiously, they made him more anxious. This was too simple, too easy, too obvious . . . What was this ingratiating behaviour hiding?

'I should like to see the High Priest,' said Isis.

'That is impossible, unfortunately. He has suffered a seizure and has lost the power of speech.'

'Who has replaced him?'

'For the present, one of his assistants. If the High Priest should die, the permanent priests will propose to His Majesty the name of a successor.'

'I wish to speak with his assistant.'

'We shall inform him of your arrival immediately. In the meantime, pray take some refreshment and rest.'

A temporary priest took Isis, Sekari, North Wind and Flesh-Eater to the palace set aside for notable guests. The donkey and the dog enjoyed a copious meal and fell asleep, leaning against each other.

Still on edge, Sekari drank only water, and he went through all the rooms, which were decorated with pictures of flowers, animals and shrines. He found nothing abnormal.

When the acting High Priest arrived, Sekari hid behind a door and hung on to every word of the conversation.

'Your presence honours us,' said the priest.

'This province is called "the Master Is in Good Health",' Isis reminded him. 'Here, you preserve the magic sceptre of Osiris, which enables him to maintain his unity by linking together the parts of his body. Will you consent to give it to me?'

'Will you use it for the celebration of the Mysteries of the month of Khoiak?'

'Indeed.'

'The High Priest would have agreed, I assume?'

'I am certain of it.'

'Permit me to consult the principal permanent priests.'

Their deliberations were brief. He returned with the sceptre, wrapped in a white cloth, and handed it to Isis.

His sombre expression revealed deep concern. 'The success of your quest,' he said, 'permits us to believe that Abydos will endure for ever. Unfortunately, your journey is not at an end.'

'What do you mean?'

'Iunu held not only this sceptre but also the sarcophagus in which the relics must be reassembled. Without it, they will remain lifeless.'

'Has it disappeared?'

The priest looked shocked. 'No, indeed not! But some of the wood had begun to rot, so the High Priest decided to send it to Byblos, capital of Phoenicia. One of their most skilled craftsmen will replace the damaged parts with the highest-quality wood.'

'When will the restoration be finished?'

'I do not know.'

'Khoiak is approaching, and I cannot wait.'

'I understand, I understand . . . If you wish to go to Byblos and bring back the sarcophagus, we have a ship which often makes trips between Egypt and Phoenicia.'

'Are the crew aboard and ready to leave?'

'It will not take long to assemble them. Do you wish me to do so immediately?'

'As quickly as possible.'

The priest bowed and hurried away.

Fuming, Sekari emerged from his hiding-place. 'That man has the voice of a hypocritical hyena. I've never heard anyone so oily and unctuous.'

'I don't care much for him,' conceded Isis, 'but he's given me valuable information.'

'He's lying – and this is a trap.'

'Possibly.'

'Definitely! Don't listen to him, Isis. The priests of Iunu have committed a crime, the sarcophagus has been destroyed, and they've made up some nonsense to keep the matter quiet. By sending you to Phoenicia they hope to get you out of the way – and they'll probably try to kill you.'

'Yes, probably.'

'Then don't take that ship.'

'If there's one chance – one single chance – of success, I must try.'

'Isis . . .'

'I must.'

38

Senusret's spirit was on a journey. It travelled the universe, danced with the constellations, accompanied the tireless planets in their never-ending movements and fed on the light from the indestructible stars. Beyond sleep, day and night, and the passing of time, his *ka* met the *ka*s of the ancestors. Apparently asleep, exposed to physical attack, from which his personal bodyguard was protecting him, the king was deriving the greatest possible amount of energy from outside the earthly sphere.

It was vital to him in order to regenerate, experience the festival of rebirth at the Temple of Osiris and confront the Herald.

Soon, his eyes would reopen.

The Herald's man in Madu served the guards a tasty stew into which he had mixed a powerful sleeping-draught, went away and did not go anywhere near the sacred wood until two hours later.

The soldiers had collapsed at their posts and were deeply asleep. Two were still fighting sleep, but they were unable to move.

Cautiously, the rebel waited until he was sure all was clear. Then, at last, he entered the sacred wood. The silence frightened him and he almost gave up, but the opportunity was too good.

Pushing aside some heavy branches, he saw the ancient Temple of Osiris and the entrance to an underground chamber. Did it contain treasure? Yes, obviously it did if the king had imposed such strict security. And what about the king? Where was he hiding?

The rebel summoned the courage to explore the narrow tunnel. It led to the funerary chamber, from whose walls a soft light emanated. Lying motionless on a bed in the centre of the chamber was a huge man.

It was the pharaoh!

At first, the rebel thought the king was dead. No, he was breathing. Senusret was two paces away and defenceless. Should he strangle him or cut his throat? One violent, accurate stroke would suffice. The king would bleed to death, and the murderer would be able to boast of a fabulous exploit. The knife rose.

The pharaoh's eyes opened.

Panic-stricken, the criminal dropped his knife and fled out of the underground chamber and back through the sacred wood. As he emerged into the open, he bumped into the soldiers' relief guard. Arms flailing, he knocked one soldier down and tried to escape, but a spear soon felled him.

Ignoring the victim, the commander of the relief guard shook the sleeping men vigorously: they faced severe punishment.

'The king,' he shouted. 'Has anyone seen the king?'

'I am here,' came Senusret's deep voice.

The acting High Priest of Iunu came to fetch Isis. Ingratiating and reverent, he led her to the quayside, where an imposing ship, built in Phoenicia, was moored.

'Here is a letter to Abi-Shemu, Prince of Byblos, a trusted ally of Egypt. He will offer you a warm welcome and hand over the precious sarcophagus to you. May the winds favour you.'

Flesh-Eater and North Wind hurried up the gangplank and settled on the deck, provoking an indignant reaction from the captain, a tall fellow with an emaciated face.

'No animals on board!' he snapped. 'Either they get off or I kill them.'

'Don't go near them.' advised Isis. 'They travel with me and protect me.'

The hound's menacing growl dissuaded the captain from putting his threats into action. With a shrug of his shoulders, he assembled his eighteen sailors and gave them instructions for departure.

'Don't touch the steering-oar,' Isis told him.

'Are you making fun of me?'

'Don't you know that only Hathor may guide us?'

'I respect her and know her powers, but I'm choosing our route.'

'As time is short, we shall avoid the coastal route and take the open sea.'

'You . . . you can't even think of doing that! It's too dangerous!'

'Let Hathor command.'

'Out of the question.'

A sailor gave a shout. 'The ship! She's moving all on her own!'

The captain seized the heavy wooden steering-oar. Obeying a superior power, it did not respond to him.

'Don't persist,' Isis warned him, 'or the goddess's fire will destroy you.'

The captain's hands began to burn, and he roared with pain.

'That woman's casting a spell on us,' said one of the crew. 'We'd better throw her into the sea.'

He raised a threatening arm, but before he could do any more Flesh-Eater sprang at him and knocked him over, while North Wind bared his teeth and stood in front of Isis.

'These aren't mere animals,' said a clear-thinking crew-man. 'We'd better not try to attack the sorceress, or they'll kill us.'

'Tend to your captain,' said Isis, 'remain at your posts, and all will be well with the journey. Hathor will grant us favourable winds and a calm sea. She is venerated in Byblos, and will be happy to see her temple again.'

The High Priestess's predictions came true. The ship sailed at a speed which astounded the sailors.

Despite his pain, the captain would not accept humiliation. An employee of the Phoenician, he must honour his contract if he was to receive his enormous reward, and he was not going to let an opportunity like this slip by. Because of Hathor's magic, the journey was going to be fast and Byblos would soon be in sight. He had little time to act, and he could not get near his victim because she was was still flanked by her two guardians.

There was only one solution: climb up the mainmast and kill the sorceress by stabbing her in the back with a harpoon. The captain was particularly skilled with the harpoon, and in spite of his bandages he would not miss his target.

Isis was gazing at the sea and thinking about Iker and the terrible fear he must have known, first of all when he knew he was destined to drown, and then when the *Swift One* was shipwrecked.

Her husband was still alive. She could sense it; she knew it.

Flesh-Eater growled. She stroked him but it did not calm him. The giant hound looked all around for the source of the danger. As he lifted his head, the captain overbalanced, fell from the top of the mast, struck the rail hard and crashed into the sea.

'We must help him!' shouted a sailor.

'It's no use,' said another. 'We'd have no chance of finding him. Hathor's protecting us, so let's forget him – he overworked us and paid us a pittance.'

The rest of the crew agreed, and the ship sailed on.

What they did not know was that the captain's fall was due neither to clumsiness nor to an accident. Isis had seen a dagger protruding from his chest, and recognized it as yet another proof of Sekari's skill. Adept at keeping out of sight, he had stowed away and was watching over her safety.

'Byblos in sight!' called the man at the prow. 'We're there.'

The arrival of such a large ship prompted a celebration, which was only slightly dampened by the first mate's explanation of the captain's regrettable demise.

The port overseer greeted Isis.

'I am the High Priestess of Abydos and I have an important letter for Prince Abi-Shemu.'

'An escort will take you to him immediately.'

They led her to the palace in the ancient city, which was surrounded by ramparts.

The official in charge of ceremonial matters showed her every respect. He told her that the prince was at the main temple, celebrating a ritual dedicated to Hathor, and suggested that she should join him there.

Inspired by Egyptian architecture, the building was certainly grand. Two ramps, one on the east and the other on the west, led up to the entrance. Among the five huge statues that backed on to the east wall was one of a pharaoh.

A priest purified Isis with water from a large basin. Then she prostrated herself before the altars covered with offerings, crossed a courtyard bordered by shrines and entered the principal shrine, where a majestic statue of Hathor stood, wearing the solar disc upon its head.

A short, round man, dressed in a many-coloured tunic, greeted her warmly. 'I have just been informed of your arrival, great priestess. Did you have a good journey?'

'Excellent, thank you.'

'Each morning, I thank Hathor for the prosperity she grants

to my little country. Egypt's unfailing friendship guarantees us a happy future, and we rejoice at the strengthening of our ties. What do you think of this shrine?'

'It is magnificent.'

'Of course, it cannot compare with your temples, but our local craftsmen, directed by Egyptian masters, have rendered vibrant homage to Hathor. When the new work was dedicated to the goddess, the pharaoh gave me a golden diadem adorned with magical symbols, the signs of life, prosperity and duration. I never fail to wear it on great occasions. My subjects adore the Egyptian style.'

The prince and Isis went out onto the temple's vast forecourt.

'The view is superb, isn't it?' he said. 'The ramparts, the old city, the sea – I never tire of it. My lady, please forgive my curiosity, but does Abydos not house Egypt's greatest secrets?'

'I have come here to seek one of them.'

Abi-Shemu looked astonished. 'A secret of Osiris, in Byblos?'

'A sarcophagus.'

'A sar-co-pha-gus,' repeated the prince, accentuating each syllable. 'Are you referring to the legend that says it floated to the garden of this palace, where a tamarisk hid it from unworthy eyes in a miraculous manner, as it grew? That is only a fable.'

'Nevertheless, will you show me the place?'

'Of course, but you will be disappointed.'

'Here is a message for you, from a priest of Iunu.'

In fact, the letter was from the Phoenician trader. After a series of polite formalities came a clear order:

'*Discreetly kill Isis, the High Priestess of Abydos. Make her death look like an accident. The Herald will not attack your country and will reward you. Our trading operations will recommence.*'

The word 'trading' filled Abi-Shemu with delight. He had provided the goods smuggled to Egypt in the Phoenician's ships, and he had been greatly upset by the interruption of this traffic. As this frail young woman seemed to be responsible for it, she would die.

'Would you like to rest and—'

'I should like to see the garden.'

'As you wish. Urgent matters call me to the palace, but my head steward will take you there.'

Cedars, pines, tamarisks, olive trees . . . Isis walked slowly along the pathways, searching for old tamarisks sufficiently well grown to hide a sarcophagus. She missed her guardians, who had remained on board the ship.

A group of stern-faced women suddenly appeared in front of her. Behind her was another group – and two more, at the sides. There was no chance of escape. Elegantly dressed and with their faces beautifully painted, they were clearly from the highest levels of Phoenician society. Slowly, they closed in.

'You thief and profaner!' one of them said accusingly. 'You thought you could cast a spell on us and make us barren. But our prince found you out and we shall stop you.'

'You're mistaken.'

'Are you accusing our prince of lying? You're a foreign criminal, known to practise evil magic in Egypt. Together, we shall trample you into the dust and throw your body into the sea.'

The mob came closer still.

'I am Isis, High Priestess of Abydos, and—'

'Your nonsense doesn't interest us. We have no mercy on criminals.'

Faced with her would-be killers, Isis held her head high and she untied her hair as a sign of mourning. Sekari had not been wrong. It was the perfect trap: an accidental drowning.

The leader was on the point of giving the signal to strike.

'Wait!' ordered a beautiful, mature woman with natural authority. 'The delicate perfume of this woman's hair is not that of a slut.'

The women had to agree that this was true.

'Would you dare lie to the Princess of Byblos and lay claim to a title you have usurped?'

'My father, Pharaoh Senusret, did indeed raise me to the rank of High Priestess of the sacred city of Osiris.'

'What are you doing here?'

'I must take to Abydos the sarcophagus of Osiris, which is hidden in this garden. The prince, your husband, gave me permission.'

There were exclamations, murmurs and varied comments, and gradually the women's wrath was dispelled. At a gesture from the princess they dispersed.

'Follow me,' she told Isis. 'I want an explanation.'

39

Dressed in the white Osiran tunic, Senusret united the heavens to the earth four times, facing each cardinal point in turn. His neck protected by a scarf of red linen, the symbol of the Light of Ra dispersing the darkness, he inaugurated the new temple dedicated to Osiris. Six underground storerooms contained vases, terracotta cups, sandstone polishing-stones, miniature bronze tools, bracelets of cornelian beads, bricks of sun-baked earth, green and black face-paint, and the head and shoulder of a bull, made of diorite. The floor was covered with silver, automatically purifying the priests' steps.

The king lit up the innermost shrine for the first time, and burnt incense there.

'I give you all strength and all joy like the sun,' he told Montu, lord of the shrine.

His earthly representative, the wild bull, would maintain the vitality of the *ka* belonging to the building, in which scenes from the pharaoh's festival of regeneration were depicted. On the lintel of the monumental doorway, Horus and Set were shown presenting him with the stem of millions of years, the sign of life perpetually renewed and the sign of power.

Statues featured the king as an old man, back to back with the king as young man. In his symbolic being, beginning and end, dynamism and serenity were linked together. A courtyard was adorned with Osiran pillars, declaring the triumph of resurrection.

A small street separated the temple from the residential district set aside for the permanent priests, who would purify themselves with water from the sacred lake. Among them were experts from the temple workshops where unguents, aromatics and gold from Punt would be stored.

By re-establishing the Osiran tradition in Madu, Senusret had provided himself with a weapon of the greatest importance against the Herald. But it had still to be made effective.

The king went to the bull's enclosure. At his approach, the beast flew into a fierce rage.

'Be at peace,' ordered the pharaoh. 'You are suffering from blindness because of the lack of a feminine sun. The construction of the new temple will bring it back to light.'

During the night, songs and dances delighted the heart of the golden goddess. Nourished by music, she consented to reappear and drive away the darkness.

Pacified, the bull allowed the pharaoh to enter its enclosure. At the centre was a small shrine, in the shade of an old acacia tree.

Inside was the *khetemet*, the sealed vase containing the lymph of Osiris, source of life and mystery of the divine work.

The Princess of Byblos was astounded. 'And so,' she concluded at the end of Isis' explanation, 'you say that my husband decided to kill you by setting a wicked trap for you. Are you aware of the gravity of such accusations?'

'Had you not intervened, the ladies of your court would have murdered me. Do you need any additional proof?'

Furiously, the princess raised her eyes to the heavens.

'Is your country betraying Egypt?' asked the Widow.

'Our trading interests are paramount, and the prince is

gaining many trading partners, sometimes to the detriment of his promises.'

'Other cares are troubling you, Princess, are they not?'

'My son is ill. Heal him, and I will tell you where the sarcophagus really is.'

The child was in the grip of a high fever, and was delirious. Isis arranged seventy-seven torches around him in order to attract the guardian spirits capable of driving back the forces of destruction.

When she placed her index finger on his lips, the sick child grew calm and smiled at her.

'The sickness is being dispelled,' she told him, 'and the pain is already easing. Your vitality is returning.'

One by one, the lamps went out. Colour returned to the little boy's cheeks.

'The sarcophagus is usually protected by a tamarisk-tree,' said the princess, 'but the prince received a message telling him to remove it and hide it in one of the pillars in his audience chamber. You must leave at once, Isis, or you will die.'

'Has the Herald taken control of your land?'

The princess blanched. 'How . . . how do you know?'

'Take me to the palace.'

'Isis, that would be madness!'

'Do you not wish to save Byblos?'

The prince's plan required finesse and diplomacy. Without upsetting Egypt, he was garnering enormous profits by backing the Phoenician's smuggling operations. The Herald's doctrine was of scant interest to him, but certain concessions were sometimes necessary.

The prince was very fond of his pillared audience chamber, which was decorated with magnificent paintings of the Phoenician countryside. He was seated there, his back to a window which looked out over the sea. When it was rough,

the waves' crests reached up to there, and then the prince felt
as if he was dominating nature, safe from its fury.

His wife entered.

'What do you want?' he asked.

'To introduce you to a healer – she has cured our son. It's
a miracle! The fever has at last broken, he is eating normally
and has begun to play again.'

'I shall give her a wonderful reward.'

'Will you grant her whatever she asks of you?'

'You have the word of Abi-Shemu.'

The princess gave her husband a sarcastic look. 'Beware of
Hathor. She punishes those who lie.'

'Do you doubt my word?'

'Not this time, dear husband. No one would play games
with his own child's life. Here, then, is our healer.' The
princess showed Isis in.

Horrified, Abi-Shemu got to his feet. 'You! But—'

'I should be dead, the victim of an accident. According to
one of our sages, falsehood never arrives safe and sound. Can
you imagine what Pharaoh Senusret's reaction would have
been when he heard of the death of his daughter?'

The prince lowered his gaze. 'What are your demands?'

'The sarcophagus.'

'It has been destroyed.'

'No. Your wife has told me the truth.' Isis touched each of
the pillars in the chamber and halted at the seventh. 'Keep
your promise, Prince.'

'I am not going to destroy that pillar to prove that it doesn't
contain what you seek.'

'Hathor, protector of Byblos, can transform herself into
Sekhmet – the venom of the cobra is added to the ferocity of
the lioness. To break your promise would be an unforgivable
sin.'

Abi-Shemu's fingers tightened on the handle of his dagger.
Might the best solution be just to kill this meddling priestess?

Gripping the windowsill, Sekari observed the Prince of Byblos. Having left the formidable Flesh-Eater and North Wind guarding the boat, he had followed Isis' trail.

The dagger slipped slowly out of its sheath. Sekari prepared to leap forward and prevent Abi-Shemu from committing murder.

The princess spoke again. 'The High Priestess of Abydos has saved our son. Do not insult either the gods or the pharaoh. Show your gratitude.'

The prince capitulated.

A carpenter delicately freed the sarcophagus from its prison. It was made from acacia-wood which would never decay, and was decorated with two complete eyes, enabling it to see the Invisible.

When Isis came out of the chamber with the princess, Sekari left his post and swam out to the ship.

'Please don't let the pharaoh punish Abi-Shemu too harshly,' begged the princess. 'My husband is so concerned to maintain his city's prosperity that he makes regrettable mistakes.'

'Have him expel the Herald's supporters. If he does not, they will kill him and transform Byblos into hell.'

'I will be very persuasive, Isis.'

The donkey and the dog gave Isis a noisy welcome, and Flesh-Eater jumped up and placed his paws on her shoulders.

Carefully wrapped in thick cloths, and roped firmly to the inside of the central cabin, the precious sarcophagus was in no danger of being damaged.

'We still have one small problem,' said Sekari. 'Since the captain's death, all the sailors here believe the ship to be haunted. It's impossible to raise a crew.'

'Hathor will replace them and guide us. Hoist the mainsail; I shall handle the steering-oar.'

Isis spoke the words of good sailing, which was under the

protection of the queen of the stars.

A wind arose, and the ship sailed out of Byblos and set course for Egypt.

North Wind and Flesh-Eater slept through the entire return journey, which was even faster than the outgoing one. As soon as they reached the river port of Iunu, Isis presented Hathor with an offering of flowers and wine.

'Don't take your eyes off the sarcophagus,' she told Sekari and his two men.

'Shouldn't I accompany you to the temple?'

'I'm not in any danger,' she declared.

On the threshold of the sacred domain stood the High Priest's substitute. Completely disconcerted, he stammered out greetings. 'You . . . you have returned!'

'Do you take me for a ghost?'

'Your journey . . .'

'Was uneventful.'

'It was so quick, so—'

'The queen of the stars contracted time. How is the High Priest?'

'No better, alas. We fear that he may die. Did you find the sarcophagus?'

'The Prince of Byblos gave it to me. It is now under close protection.'

'Perfect, perfect! Would you like something to eat, something—'

'I am leaving immediately. Kindly give me back the Basket of Mysteries, containing the relics of Osiris, which I entrusted to you.'

The substitute priest almost burst into tears. 'It is terrible, horrible! Nothing like that should have happened, especially not here in Iunu!'

'Explain yourself.'

'I can't find the words, I—'

'Make an effort.'

'The basket has been stolen,' confessed the priest in a strangled voice.

'Have you conducted an enquiry?'

'Yes, but with no success.'

'That is not what I think,' declared a sonorous voice.

The priest was stunned. After Isis, a second ghost! 'High Priest, but . . . you were dying!'

'I had to make everyone think so in order to unmask the Herald's creature, who was lurking among us. I needed definite proof. You have provided me with it by stealing the Basket of Mysteries.'

'You are mistaken, you—'

'Denial is pointless.'

The guards who watched over the temple surrounded the accused.

His attitude changed abruptly. 'Yes, I am in the service of the future master of Egypt, and he will destroy your shrines and impose the new belief everywhere! Your defeat is certain, for Osiris will not come back to life. The man to whom I gave the Basket of Mysteries has burnt it.'

'Here it is,' said the High Priest, handing it to Isis. 'Your accomplice was arrested before he could commit that abominable crime. As you are both guilty of high treason, you will be executed together. He has talked freely, and we know the Herald has no other spies in Iunu.'

Isis' quest was at an end. The Basket of Mysteries contained all the parts of the body of Osiris that she would try to put back together in Abydos, though with no certainty that she would succeed.

Iker was waiting for her. And her love for him grew stronger with every moment that passed.

Part III

The Mysteries of the Month of Khoiak

First Day of Khoiak,*
Abydos

At the end of the dawn ritual, the Shaven-headed One and Nephthys went to the House of Life. The priest recited the words of preservation over Iker's mummy, and the priestess magnetized it.† The absence of any sign of decomposition proved that Iker continued to live an intermediate form of life, between nothingness and rebirth.

At noon, more interrogations began.

Asher's turn came.

'According to your superiors,' said the Shaven-headed One, 'you know how to make vases and ritual vessels, and you clean and restore the cult objects meticulously.'

'I am very moved by that judgment. I try to make myself useful.'

'What are your ambitions, Asher?'

*20 October.
†The process of resurrection depicted in the pages that follow is revealed in crucial Egyptian texts such as the Pyramid Texts, the Sarcophagus Texts, the *Book of Going Forth by Day*, Osiran texts from the Ptolemaic temples, notably Dendera (see the translations by Emile Chassinat and Sylvie Cauville), and several other sources such as the Salt Papyrus 825.

'To start a family and work in Abydos for as long as possible.'

'Would you like to rise to the rank of permanent priest?'

'That is a mere dream!'

'And if it were to become reality?'

'Egypt would really be the land of miracles! I dare not believe it, but I would gladly abandon my worldly activities to serve Osiris.'

'The demands of our Rule do not frighten you?'

'On the contrary, they strengthen me in my beliefs. Abydos is still the foundation of Egyptian spirituality.'

'Answer me clearly: have you noticed anything unusual or any suspicious behaviour?'

The Herald reflected. 'I detect a harmony that unites the world beyond and the world here below. Here, each second of our existence takes on meaning. Temporary and permanent priests carry out specific tasks, at the appropriate time and according to their abilities. The spirit of Osiris carries us beyond ourselves.'

He voiced no accusations and no suspicions. According to what he had said, Abydos was like paradise.

Nephthys merely picked at her food.

'Aren't you hungry?' asked the Herald, surprised.

'This is the first day of Khoiak, the month of the celebration of the Mysteries, on which the survival of the Two Lands depends.'

'Are you worried?'

'The process of the resurrection of Osiris remains a perilous adventure, and we await our High Priestess with impatience. Without her, we cannot begin the ritual.'

'Does she play such a vital role?'

'She is the holder of the Great Secret.'

'Is that not too important a role to grant to a woman?'

Abruptly brought to her senses, Nephthys made herself

ignore Asher's charm. She managed to control herself, and did not alter her behaviour – she seemed still to be a woman in love and under a spell.

'Too important? Well, perhaps you're right.'

'Egypt is wrong and weakens herself by granting too many privileges to your sex.'

Nephthys took a sip of wine, and changed the subject. 'In the interview with the Shaven-headed One, who is so harsh, you did extremely well.'

'Why didn't you say anything?'

'There was no need – your promotion seemed certain.'

The Herald took Nephthys's hands tenderly. 'I spoke of my wish to start a family. Will you become my wife?'

'It's a serious decision,' she murmured. 'I'm very young and—'

'Obey me and I'll make you happy. A woman should submit to her husband and satisfy his every desire, shouldn't she?'

'But what about my duties as a priestess?'

'They're merely illusions: the realm of the spirit is inaccessible to women. You have enough intelligence to understand that. And you will also agree that a single wife is not enough for a man. Women's impulses are limited by nature, but men's are not. We must respect God's law, which dictates the superiority of the man.'

Nephthys pretended to be docile, and too modest to look her seducer in the face. 'This way of speaking is so new, so unexpected . . .'

The Herald took her in his arms. 'Soon we shall seal our union. You shall share my bed and become my first wife, the mother of my sons. And you cannot imagine the radiant future you will enjoy.'

The commander of Abydos's guards paced up and down the quay. Although he was a soldier, he understood the vital importance of Khoiak. In the absence of the High Priestess, the rites would be ineffective.

'Boat coming,' a sentinel informed him.

Immediately, the soldiers took up their positions.

At the sight of the tall man standing at the prow, the commander's anxieties were dispelled. The pharaoah's return would enable all in Abydos to breathe more easily.

Bearing the *khetemet*, Senusret strode to the House of Life, where he was greeted by the Shaven-headed One and Nephthys.

'This is the source of Osiran energy,' he said. 'Place it at Iker's head.'

While they were doing so, the king ordered the guard to be trebled. Archers would occupy the roof of the House of Life, transforming it into an impregnable fortress. Each soldier was handed an obsidian knife, charged with magic.

'The king has returned!' exclaimed Bina.

'So,' said the Herald in surprise, 'his soul has journeyed to the other side of life, re-entered his body and celebrated his festival of regeneration at Madu. New strength dwells in him, and he wants to take advantage of it in Abydos.'

'Is he becoming a threat?'

'He has always been one. We must discover his plans.'

'Lord . . . you dined again with that woman Nephthys.'

The Herald stroked Bina's hair. 'She's a submissive and understanding young woman. She will rally to the true faith.'

'Are you going to marry her?'

'You will both obey me and serve me, for such is God's law. There is no point in talking of it again, my sweet one.'

Bega burst into the Herald's house in terror. 'The pharaoh has just arrived, carrying a sealed vase! And another boat's docking – Isis is back!'

*

At the inner corners of the House of Life, the Shaven-headed One had placed four lions' heads spitting fire, four uraei, four baboons and four braziers. This would prevent any negative force from entering the stone-walled building, which was reached by a monumental doorway of white limestone.

The ceiling of the principal courtyard represented the celestial vault of the sky-goddess Nut, its sandy floor the realm of the earth-god Geb. In the centre, a shrine housed the ship of Osiris, where Iker's body lay.

At last Isis saw him again! She could not hold back her tears, but scolded herself for her weakness and immediately set to work, in the presence of the pharaoh, the Shaven-headed One and Nephthys. What Iker needed was not displays of mourning but the success of a transmutation which would bring him back to the light.

Resurrection required a transfer of death. Iker's death must pass into the body of the Reborn One,* Osiris, vanquisher of oblivion. Only it could absorb all forms of death and transform them into life. Also, three Osirises must be recreated and a ritual process followed with absolute precision, free from all errors. And the priests had only the thirty days of the month of Khoiak.

Isis assembled the stone body of Osiris by reuniting the relics she had collected during her quest: the head, the eyes, the ears, the neck and jaw, the spine, the chest, the heart, the legs, the fists, the fingers, the phallus, the legs, the thighs and the feet. Using the sceptre of Iunu, she ensured the unity of the parts of this body of resurrection; and the golden sceptre from the hill of Thoth provided them with supernatural strength.

Then the king opened the sealed vase containing the god's lymph, the Mystery of the alchemical word and the source of life. The Osiran fluid, like the tide of the annual flood, solidly

---

*Unen-nefer, one of the commonest names for Osiris.

bound together the assembled parts of the statuette. The perfume of Punt radiated out from it.

Isis touched the mummy with the venerable stone collected on the Isle of Soped, to give life to that which seemed lifeless and to make the mineral heart beat. She then applied three layers of unguent to it, wrapped it in four cloths symbolizing four states of light revealed during the opening of the sky's window, and slipped it inside the ram-skin she had brought from Thebes.

'Your name is Life,' chanted the king. 'Our mother, the sky-goddess, will give birth to you again and reveal to you your secret nature by passing it on to your son, the Osiris Iker.'

Senusret placed the first Osiris, composed of metal and minerals, in the belly of the cosmic cow made of gilded wood covered with stars and constellations, the true origin of living beings. Here there would take place a resurrection which was invisible to human eyes but without which the trans-formations could not take place.

'From Ra, the creative Light,' the pharaoh continued, 'a metallic stone is born. Through it, the hidden work is carried out. Made of metals and precious stones, it transforms Osiris into a golden tree. My sister Isis, continue the alchemical work.'

Isis stretched a piece of linen over a wooden frame. In its centre, she drew the shape of Osiris, then she fashioned it with moist and fertile silt, barley and wheat grains, aromatic herbs and powdered precious stones.

'You are present among us; your death does not make you decay. May the barley become gold, may your rebirth take on the aspect of green stems that grow out of your radiant body. You are the gods and the goddesses, you are the fertilizing tide, you are the entire country, you are life.'*

*S. Cauville, *Le Zodiaque d'Osiris* ('The Zodiac of Osiris'), 1997, p. 57.

The second Osiris had taken form. Intimately linked to the first, the second process of resurrection was beginning.

The third ought to have been the god's mummy resting in his house of eternity in Abydos and brought back to life at the ninth hour of night, on the last day of Khoiak the previous year: thus immortality passed from god to god. By violating the tomb and destroying the mummy of Osiris, the Herald thought he could prevent this rebirth.

Now a Royal Son and Friend of the King would serve as the basis for the ritual. But would he be strong enough to survive the ordeal?

The Widow gazed at her husband. 'Be the third Osiris,' she implored him, 'and accomplish the final resurrection.'

There were only twenty-nine days left.

Second Day of Khoiak
Abydos

'The guard has been trebled,' said Bega, 'and in addition to their usual weapons, all the soldiers have been given obsidian knives capable of piercing ghosts' outer shells. Isis, Nephthys and the Shaven-headed One are still in the House of Life.'

'Have you consulted the other permanent priests?' asked the Herald.

'They all agree that the rites of resurrection have begun.'

'Using what basis?'

'Iker,' replied Bina, her eyes wild.

The Herald took her by the shoulders. 'Iker is dead, my sweet one. I have destroyed the mummy of Osiris and the vase containing the source of life. Abydos is an empty shell; the rites will not succeed.'

'Iker is travelling between life and death,' she declared. 'His eyes are still open. Isis and the king are trying to bring him back to life.'

'They must be stopped!' said Bega furiously.

'Tell Shab to study the security arrangements. If there's a way to get into the House of Life, he'll find it.'

Glad of a chance to stretch his legs, the Twisted One took endless precautions so as not to attract the guards' attention.

Contrary to his hopes, night-time did not offer any extra opportunities, for hundreds of lamps lit up the House of Life and its surroundings. The archers were relieved frequently, so they did not suffer from tiredness or lack of sleep, and were constantly watchful. He soon concluded that the area was inaccessible.

The Herald calmed Bina, who was suffering convulsions. Since her vision, she could not stop shaking.

'I fear the powers of the pharaoh and that cursed High Priestess,' admitted Bega. 'You should leave Abydos, my lord. Sooner or later, the authorities will learn the truth.'

'You have taken part in the ritual of the Great Mysteries. What does the king do?'

'He uses the past year's Osiris, whose energy is exhausted, fashions a new one and creates a threefold resurrection – mineral, metallic and plant-based. The lymphatic fluids in the *khetemet* are vital. The archives of the House of Life, "the Souls of Light", teach the method to be followed.'

'So, from being a victim Iker has become the basis for an Osiris,' said the Herald thoughtfully. 'Only one person can give me first-hand information: Nephthys. Tell me as soon as she reappears.'

Isis and Nephthys arranged the four vases making up the reconstituted soul around Iker. To the west, the first, which bore a falcon's head, contained Osiris's intestines, vessels and conduits; to the east, the second had the head of a jackal,* and held the stomach and the spleen; to the south, the third, with the head of a man,† contained the liver; while to the north, the fourth vase bore the head of a baboon,‡ and contained the lungs.

Dua-mutef, 'he who venerates his mother'.
†*Imseti*, 'he who makes fertile (?)'.
‡*Hepy*, 'the swift one'.

Brought together, the four sons of Horus, Osiris's successor, strengthened their father's *ka* and heart.

The two sister-priestesses lifted the lids and spoke the words of veneration to the falcon, the jackal, the man and the baboon. New organs, which were at present still embryonic, gave life to Iker's mummy. At that moment, the three Osirises – mineral, metallic, vegetable – and the human being functioned in symbiosis. Henceforth indissoluble, they would be reborn or die together.

Only the pharaoh and the Shaven-headed One left the House of Life when night fell. The latter assembled the permanent priests and priestesses, and told them of the start of the celebration of the Great Mysteries of Khoiak.

'But hasn't the *khetemet* disappeared?' asked Bega in astonishment.

'The king found another at the temple in Madu. The correct conditions for Osiris's rebirth have been created.'

Third Day of Khoiak
Abydos

The seven priestesses of Hathor selected the finest dates. They laid some of them on a silver platter and pressed others to extract their juice, producing a liquor symbolizing Osiris's regenerative lymph.

When their work was done, they gave the fruit and the alcohol to the pharaoh. He celebrated the dawn ritual at his Temple of a Million Years, then returned to the House of Life and presented the offering to the three Osirises.

'This is the incarnation of the beneficent fire. May it help you to be reborn with the new year, at the heart of the Great Mystery.'

'Here we carry out the secret work that is concealed for ever,' added Isis. 'In your body of light, Osiris, the sun shall rise.'

The three Osirises now had their first solid and liquid food. The Shaven-headed One's next task was to prepare for the procession of fat oxen and their slaughter, which was planned for the sixth day of the month.

Isis stayed with Iker, but the other ritualists left the chamber.

'One of the temporary priests worries me,' Nephthys confided to the Shaven-headed One. 'I admit I am attracted to him, and he has asked me to marry him. He's an excellent worker, liked by all, and you're even considering accepting him as a permanent priest.'

'Who is this man?'

'Asher, the tall, handsome maker and restorer of vases. In a gentle, amiable, almost tender voice, he gave me a dreadful lecture about women. According to him, not one woman in the world is worthy of being a priestess, and men have absolute authority over women because they are infinitely superior. I pretended to agree with him.'

'Was he joking or was he serious?'

'I don't think it was a joke, but I need to be sure.'

'Be careful. If he is a follower of the Herald, you are in danger.'

'If he is, he will lead me to his master.'

'Why would he do that?'

'Because I can reveal the secrets of the House of Life to him.'

'We must ensure that you are well protected.'

'Then be very sure that the protection is invisible, or Asher will be suspicious and I shall fail.'

'Are you truly aware of the risks?'

'We must at all costs eradicate the evil that has taken root in Abydos. At last, we may have a chance of doing so.'

'There is a less dangerous way,' said the Shaven-headed One. 'I shall re-examine the details of this man Asher's admission. Await my conclusions before you sound out your suitor.'

Nephthys thought of the sufferings and bravery of her sister Isis. Even at the risk of losing her life, she must try to drive away the threat to the house of resurrection.

Fourth Day of Khoiak
Memphis

General Nesmontu sensed that something terrible had happened the moment he saw Tjaty Sobek's sombre expression.

'Have the rebels attacked?' he asked.

'No. The court has delivered its judgment.'

'You don't mean . . . ?'

'The maximum penalty,' said Sobek.

'But Sehotep hasn't killed anybody!'

'According to the court, intention is the same as action. And there were aggravating circumstances, because he was a member of the King's House.'

'We must appeal against the decision.'

'It is final, Nesmontu. In these troubled times, justice must show an example. Even the pharaoh can do no more for Sehotep.'

'A member of the Golden Circle of Abydos sentenced to death because of falsified evidence!' The old soldier was so distraught that for a moment he thought the Herald was going to win. But his warrior instinct regained the upper hand, and he thought of gathering together those loyal to him, attacking the prison and freeing his brother.

'Don't do anything foolish,' warned the tjaty. 'Where would violent action get you? The rebels may begin their offensive any day now, and you will have to coordinate our response – Memphis's survival will depend on you.'

Reluctantly, the general admitted to himself that the Protector was right to remind him of his duty.

'Above all,' Sobek went on, 'stay hidden here. If you were to make an appearance, the rebels' leader would realize that we have set a trap for them. Soldiers will guard this house, which will be requisitioned following its owner's execution.' His voice shook a little, but that was all. Neither he nor the general was the sort of man to express his profound grief openly.

Sleeping only two hours per night, Sobek continued to examine every tiny piece of information resulting from the guards' enquiries. He was hoping against hope that he would find a clue which might enable him to defer the execution.

One drawing of a suspect caught his attention: it bore a vague resemblance to Gergu, the principal inspector of granaries. According to the accompanying report, the man pictured might have been involved, directly or indirectly, in the Olivia affair. A discreet search of a house owned by a certain Bel-Tran had produced a curious result: large quantities of valuable goods which were either stolen or undeclared.

The Protector remembered that Iker had requested an investigation into Gergu. It had come up with nothing.

There was a second collection of documents about Gergu. This time, they concerned not mere suspicions but a properly formulated complaint. The granaries official at the village of Mount of Flowers accused Gergu of aggression, extortion and abuse of power. Sobek knew that too many officials behaved like that, and it was up to the tjaty to punish them severely. If the facts were proven, Gergu would go to prison.

Before arresting him, though, perhaps it would be a good idea to follow him and find out whether or not he was linked to the rebels.

Fifth Day of Khoiak
Memphis

'Can you guarantee that this remedy will work?' asked Dr Gua.

'In the name of Imhotep the healer, I swear it!' Renseneb the remedy-maker assured him.

'And there won't be any harmful consequences or side-effects?'

'I've tested it on myself. It is a subtle blend of essences of lotus, poppy and a dozen rare flowers, in small quantities. Your patient won't suffer and won't feel troubled when she wakes from her trance. I have just a few words of advice: don't ask her too many questions, speak in a calm, firm voice, and don't be impatient.'

Gua took the packet of pills and went to Medes's house, where his patient greeted him with enthusiasm.

'At last, Doctor! In spite of your remedies, I can't stop weeping. My life is becoming a living hell.'

'I did tell you we'd have to try a new treatment.'

'I'm ready.'

'May I speak to your husband?'

'Because of all that's happened, he won't be home until late. Do you realize that we have no pharaoh, no tjaty, and no overall commander of the army or the city guards? Memphis is heading for disaster.'

'Let us attend to your health.'

'Oh yes, Doctor, yes!'

'Take these four pills.'

Medes's wife hastened to obey.

Gua checked her pulse. 'You'll soon have a marvellous feeling of wellbeing. Don't resist the desire to sleep. I shall be close by.'

The drug acted fast. The doctor gave her another two pills to swallow. Completely relaxed, she lost all traces of her hysteria.

'It is I, Doctor Gua. Can you hear me?'

'I hear you,' she replied in a strange, hoarse voice.

'Don't worry, I'm going to free you from the sickness that afflicts you. Will you tell me the truth – the whole truth?'

'I . . . I will.'

'The truth will cure you. Do you understand?'

'Yes.'

'Are you the wife of Medes, secretary of the King's House?'

'I am.'

'Do you live in Memphis?'

'Yes, I do.'

'Are you happy?'

'Yes . . . No . . . Yes . . . No, *no*!'

'Does your husband beat you?'

'Never! . . . Yes, sometimes.'

'Do you love him?'

'Very much. He's a wonderful husband, so wonderful!'

'So you obey him?'

'Always.'

'Did he order you to do something you regret?'

'No, oh no! . . . That is, yes. I regret it . . . but it was for him. No, I don't regret anything.'

'We are reaching the cause of your illness. By tearing it out at the root, I can heal you. Trust me, and you won't suffer any more. What did your husband ask you to do?'

The patient's belly heaved, her limbs shook, and her eyes rolled up in her head.

'I am Doctor Gua, I am treating you, and we are close to our goal. Speak to me: free yourself from your torment.'

The spasms grew less frequent, and the sick woman became calmer. 'A letter . . . I wrote a letter in High Treasurer Senankh's handwriting, so as to discredit him. I have a gift, a very unusual gift, and Medes was pleased, so pleased . . . But we failed. And then . . .'

'Then?'

She went into spasm again.

'I am Doctor Gua, and I am treating you. The cure is very close now. Speak to me. Tell me the truth.'

'I wrote a second letter in Sehotep's writing so that he would be accused of treason and murder. This time we succeeded. Medes was happy, so happy . . . How good I feel now. I'm cured!'

Medes's liver was telling the truth, too. Deprived of Ma'at, it revealed the character of a man full of envy and hatred.

Dr Gua had uncovered one of the rebels' main allies, no doubt a key figure in their network, and he could prove Sehotep's innocence. To whom should he give this vital information? The tjaty was dying, General Nesmontu was dead, and the queen was not receiving anyone. That left only Senankh, the High Treasurer, who was deeply depressed. Would he listen, and was he in a position to act?

A horrible thought flashed through Dr Gua's mind: what if Senankh was working with Medes?

Sixth Day of Khoiak

Abydos

The animal-doctor examined the fat oxen, which had been adorned with necklaces of flowers, ostrich feathers and coloured fabrics. Each ox considered pure walked slowly towards the temple slaughterhouse. The master-butcher would carry out a further examination to confirm the quality of the meat. It must contain the maximum amount of *ka*.

Preceded by North Wind, Flesh-Eater followed the enormous animals. Their arrival usually caused joy among the temporary priests, who were certain to share in several banquets celebrating the rebirth of Osiris. But the dramatic events that had struck Abydos were still uppermost in everyone's mind, and nobody was thinking of the celebration.

Once again, Bina tried to take food to the soldiers guarding the House of Life.

An officer barred her way. 'Are you authorized to be here?'

'I usually—'

'New orders. Go back where you came from.'

Bina gave him her most seductive smile. 'I can't throw these loaves away and—'

'Do you want to be arrested?'

She left at once and went and laid her burden on one of the

altars at Senusret's Temple of a Million Years, where Bega was officiating.

He made sure that no one could overhear them, then said, 'The Shaven-headed One called a meeting of the permanent priests. Judging by the rites we are to conduct here and the words to be chanted, I am certain that a transmutation is taking place in the House of Life.'

'Using what basis?'

'The parts of Osiris's body and the barley that is to be transformed into gold. And perhaps . . . No, it can't be! You can't be right. Iker is dead, well and truly dead – nobody could bring him back to life. And yet, in the case of Imhotep . . . But the Royal Son can't be compared to him. Besides, any such attempt is doomed to fail.'

'But didn't Senusret return from Madu with a new *khetemet*?'

Bega was troubled; he could not answer.

'Do you have access to the House of Life?' asked Bina.

'Unfortunately not. The only ones who may enter are the pharaoh, the Shaven-headed One, Isis and Nephthys.'

That cursed woman again! thought Bina furiously. Nephthys would either talk or die.

Seventh Day of Khoiak
Abydos

The first quarter of the waxing moon shone in the sky, opening up the way of Ra, the Divine Light that was more powerful than the darkness, and that was hidden at the heart of both spirit and matter.

Isis had awaited this moment with terrible anxiety. With the aid of the two light sources, the sun of day and the sun of night, would the three Osirises grow in harmony?

The mineral and metallic Osiris was being strengthened away from human eyes, inside the athanor, the celestial cow. Fed by the stars' radiance, the parts of Osiris's body were becoming solidly bound together. The plant-based Osiris served as a witness and a proof of this secret evolution: the first grain sprouted.

'Don't be afraid,' Isis whispered to Iker. 'All the conditions for a new life have been brought together. Already you are linked to the two forms of eternity: the moment of transmutation and the cycles of nature. The House of Life has truly become the House of Gold.'

Outside, in front of the building, the pharaoh celebrated a banquet in company with the souls of the dead and the reborn kings. The Shaven-headed One and the permanent priests and priestesses also took part. They shared the *ka* of the fat oxen and bread made with acacia-flowers, from the happy land where the gods feasted.

Senusret then brought food to the three Osirises, which absorbed the subtle essence of these sanctified foods.

Linked to the other Osirises, the Osiris Iker was gradually emerging from the intermediate world. The process had not been delayed at all, but the most important stages and greatest dangers were still to come.

'Iker's death is giving ground and is beginning to be transferred,' said Senusret. 'Nevertheless, this first phase is not decisive. The metallic Osiris still lacks unity and power. Now, there must be no gap between the three forms of the Great Work. Like a fire, your love gives it life, Isis; without it, the vital elements would fall apart. And only it can overcome the destiny imposed by the Herald, because it is not of this world.'

Tirelessly, the Widow recited the words of transformation into Light.

Wearing the mask of Anubis, the king unlocked the gate of the heavens, which was carved into dazzlingly white limestone. From now on, the forces of the cosmos would fill the House of Gold.

Although vital to the continuance of the transmutation, they were extremely dangerous. Could the Osiris Iker bear their impact?

Eighth Day of Khoiak
Abydos

Bina was full of rage. Why did Nephthys not visit her betrothed, the Herald? She, Bina, would make her talk by torturing her as nobody had ever been tortured before. The priestess would reveal the secret of the rites and describe how Isis and the pharaoh were managing to stop Iker being consigned to oblivion.

For there was no doubt: the Royal Son was being used as the basis for the resurrection of Osiris. And there were only twenty-two days left in which to achieve the impossible.

'They'll fail!' she snarled.

'Of course they will, my sweet one,' whispered the Herald, stroking her hair.

'It's impossible to get into that accursed building, my lord. Shab has examined it from every angle, and there are no weak points. And Bega is not authorized to enter.'

'Through Nephthys, we shall find out how to destroy the House of Life and prevent it from harming us.'

'She should be here, at our feet!'

'Don't worry, she'll come.'

'Our records contain references to Asher going back several years,' the Shaven-headed One told Nephthys. 'The information he gave was correct and he has not changed his story at any time. He does indeed come from a hamlet near Abydos and is a modest craftsman, a maker and restorer of stone vases. It seems that he gives satisfaction, performs his duties as a temporary priest diligently for the two or three months a year that he is here, and has never attracted any criticism.'

'Modest, you say? That does not match his character at all. Who engaged him?'

'Just a moment, I'll check . . . Permanent priest Bega. And Bega has just spoken on his behalf to the investigators. Like his colleagues, he thinks very highly of Asher.'

'Bega . . .'

'Don't let your imagination run away with you,' advised the Shaven-headed One. 'Bega may be unbending and unfriendly, but he is above suspicion – he is the embodiment of thoroughness and honesty.'

'As soon as possible, I shall talk to Asher again,' decided Nephthys. 'This time, things will be clarified.'

Iker's head touched the firmament. Isis passed on to him what she had experienced during her initiation into the Golden Circle.

At the same moment, cranes, pelicans, pink flamingos, wild ducks, white spoonbills and black ibis flew in wide circles above the House of Gold. Rising up from the *nun*, the ocean of energy in which all forms of life were born, they spoke the language of the world beyond and taught it to the Widow so that she might continue to carry out the Great Work.

A human-headed bird perched on Iker's mummy. In its claws it held two rings, symbols of the two eternities. The soul had returned from the cosmos, and was giving life to the body of Osiris.

Until the twelfth day of Khoiak, the Widow must maintain absolute silence.

Ninth Day of Khoiak
Memphis

Gergu had been drinking wine all evening, and was thoroughly inebriated. He wanted to treat himself to an understanding but demanding Syrian girl. But she insisted on being paid in advance, his pockets were empty, and Medes could not be reached because he was busy with the preparations for the final attack.

So Gergu went to the workshop owned by the sculptor who made false stelae for him. They were sold to wealthy customers who believed they were buying priceless works of art from Abydos, for the stelae bore the words of Osiris, guaranteeing their authenticity.

The sculptor took him to the back of the workshop.

'I want copper ingots, amulets and fabrics, and I want them now,' demanded Gergu.

'Calm down, and let's see what there is.'

In fury, Gergu hit the man hard, knocked him down and stamped on him. 'My share – give me my share!'

A powerful fist seized the attacker by the hair and flattened him against the wall.

Gergu could not believe his eyes. 'Tjaty Sobek! But . . . but you're dying!'

'At the thought of interrogating you, my health suddenly

improved. The dancing-girl Olivia, the house belonging to the trader Bel-Tran – do they mean anything to you?'

'No, nothing.'

'And what about the complaint made by the granaries' official at Mount of Flowers?'

'An error, just an administrative error.'

'You're going to talk, my lad!'

'I can't – they'd kill me!'

'Well, I'll talk,' said the sculptor, clutching his swollen face. He was afraid of Sobek and his guards, some of whom were searching the workshop. His best course of action was to confess and beg the tjaty for mercy, laying most of the blame on the dangerous drunkard who had attacked him.

Faced with the sculptor's revelations, Gergu broke down. He confessed to his extortion, begged the authorities for forgiveness, and wept copiously.

'The real criminal is Medes,' he snivelled.

'The secretary of the King's House?' Sobek was astonished.

'Yes, he entrapped me and forced me to work for him.'

'Stealing, smuggling and receiving goods under the name of Bel-Tran?'

'He wanted to make his fortune.'

'Was he involved in the Olivia affair?'

'Of course.'

'Are you and he linked to the Herald's network?'

Gergu hesitated. 'He may be, but I'm not.'

'Haven't you sold your soul to the Herald?'

'No, oh no! Like you, I hate him and—'

Gergu's right hand caught fire, and he screamed with pain. Then his arm, his shoulder and his head burst into flame. Before the appalled Sobek and his men could do anything, Gergu collapsed and fell to the ground, burnt alive.

Dr Gua decided to pass on his discoveries to Senankh.

Senankh listened intently, then said they must go at once to see the tjaty.

'But Sobek's on his deathbed,' the doctor said. 'Even I have been forbidden to see him.'

'His recovery is a state secret.'

Once he was face to face with the tjaty, Gua outlined the facts quickly and concisely.

'So,' concluded Senankh, 'using his wife's talents as a forger, Medes tried to discredit me and have Sehotep murdered under form of law. And he was planning to destroy the King's House.'

'He is also a thief,' added Sobek, 'and probably an ally of the rebels. You, Doctor, must maintain absolute silence. You, Senankh, must present Gua's statement to the court immediately. Here is the order to free Sehotep, marked with the tjaty's seal.'

Sobek was frustrated over how little information he had obtained from questioning Gergu and from closely interrogating the sculptor. He hoped to learn more from Medes, concerning both the Memphis network and his accomplices in Abydos.

Tenth Day of Khoiak
Memphis

Soon Medes would rule over Memphis. The rebel groups would launch an all-out attack on the royal palace, the tjaty's offices and the main barracks. They would have only one order: to spread terror. No prisoners were to be taken, women and children were to be slaughtered, and there would be summary executions. Deprived of their usual leaders, the forces of order would soon disintegrate and offer only feeble resistance.

When he went to congratulate the Phoenician, Medes would strangle him with his own hands. Officially, the trader would have succumbed to the emotion of the victory, which he had celebrated with an orgy of gluttony.

After killing the queen, the tjaty, Sehotep and Senankh, Medes would have himself crowned pharaoh and impose his law on the whole of Egypt, wherever the Herald spread his beliefs. He would also have to get rid of that drunkard Gergu. Then he'd deal with his hysterical wife, though at least she'd done nothing but sleep since Doctor Gua's last visit – the house was quiet at last!

Sudden noises shattered this idyll: a muffled shout, the slamming of a door, running footsteps. And then silence again.

Medes called for his steward. There was no response.

He looked out of the window at his garden and his lake, which was surrounded by sycamores. There were guards swarming everywhere! And others had got the better of the servants and were climbing the stairs.

He must escape. But how? There was only one way: across the roof. Although frightened and lacking a good sense of balance, he managed to reach it. Teetering unsteadily on the roof of his luxurious house, Medes hesitated to jump to the other side of the street.

'Surrender,' ordered an imperious voice. 'You will not escape us.'

'Sobek? But . . . you're dying!'

'It is finished, Medes. You have failed, and the Herald cannot save you.'

'I'm innocent! I do not know the Herald, and I—' Terrified, Medes saw his hand burst into flame. He lost his balance, fell off the roof, and was impaled on the metal spikes that topped the wall surrounding his estate.

'The greedy man shall have no tomb,' decreed the tjaty, quoting sage Ptah-Hotep.

Fortunately, Medes was in the habit of writing everything down, and his records spoke for him. Sobek learnt that Medes had hired the *Swift One* by forging official documents, bribed trade-control officials, trafficked with the Phoenician, stored illicit goods under the name of Bel-Tran, used state vessels in order to pass on instructions to the rebels, ordered a bogus desert guard to kill Iker . . . The list of his crimes seemed never-ending.

The last words he had written were undoubtedly the worst: '*Eleventh day of Khoiak: the final assault.*'

Eleventh Day of Khoiak
Memphis

There were three knocks on the trapdoor that gave access to the rebels' underground hideout.

'We're going into action,' Curly-Head told his men.

Like every other group-leader, he had received the order from the Phoenician to attack before dawn. The woman who owned the house had just given the signal. At many places in the city, at this very moment, the Herald's troops would be coming out of hiding and charging towards their objectives. The conquest of Memphis had begun. Curly-Head rejoiced at this dash to attack, because he loved killing.

He raised the trapdoor, but had no time to haul himself up to ground level, for a powerful fist dragged him out of his hole and threw him against a wall.

'Glad to see you, you piece of filth,' said General Nesmontu.

'It's you!'

'Well spotted.'

Only semi-conscious, Curly-Head tried to run away, but Nesmontu struck him so hard from behind that he broke his neck.

'Smoke them out,' the general told his soldiers. 'These rats seem to like being underground, so that's where they'll end their sinister career.' Eyes sparkling, he went off to another strategic point.

Galvanized by his return, both officers and soldiers followed his orders to the letter. Not one rebel group had the chance to commit a single crime.

On this, the eleventh day of Khoiak, in Memphis, the evil was warded off.

The Phoenician was guzzling cakes. The sun was starting to rise, and still there was no news. The Herald's men must have met a little resistance, a few madmen playing at being heroes and delaying the moment of their defeat.

'A visitor has arrived, my lord,' his door-keeper informed him. 'He showed me his pass, the little piece of cedarwood with the tree hieroglyph on it.'

The Phoenician swallowed half an enormous cream-filled cake. Medes, at last! He was only to come when the fighting was over, when victory was won, so Memphis must have been taken more quickly than expected.

'Send him up.'

The Phoenician greedily quaffed a cup of white wine. He would take particular pleasure in killing Medes, selecting a form of very slow torture. This would be the first execution of an unbeliever in the centre of Memphis. Many conversions would follow, and the Herald would be pleased with the head of his religious guards.

The little piece of cedarwood hit the Phoenician full in the face. He dropped his cup in amazement.

A big man was standing before him. 'I am Tjaty Sobek. And you are the leader of the rebel network that has been lurking in Memphis for so long. You are the man behind all the murders and unforgivable atrocities.'

'You're mistaken, I am just an honest trader! My respectability—'

'Medes is dead. He kept detailed private records, and

through them I have at last traced the poison back to its source. Your raiding-parties have been destroyed, and Nesmontu's men have suffered only a few slight wounds.'

'Nesmontu? But—'

'The general is very much alive.'

Unable to stand, let alone try to escape, the Phoenician did not bother to babble useless protestations of innocence.

'You were in charge of the Memphis network,' Sobek went on. 'Above you is the supreme leader, the Herald. Where is he hiding?'

The fat man turned purple with rage. 'The Herald, that madman who ruined my life! Instead of bringing me power and fortune, he's ruined me. I hate him, I curse him, I—'

The long scar across the Phoenician's body suddenly deepened and split his body in two. In such agony that he could not even cry out, he saw his lifeblood pour down over his tunic and his heart explode from his chest.

The queen, the tjaty and General Nesmontu walked out to meet the people of Memphis, who were wild with joy. Each district organized a feast to the glory of Pharaoh, protector of his people.

Despite their undeniable success, neither the tjaty nor the members of the Golden Circle shared the citizens' relief. The Herald was still at large, and the king was still absent. And what was really happening in Abydos?

They had one good reason for satisfaction, though: Sehotep was free. It was therefore possible to reunite the members of the Golden Circle and to fight the forces of darkness more effectively. But first they must make sure that Memphis was once and for all at peace. General Nesmontu would not leave the city before he was certain of that.

'It's already the eleventh day of Khoiak,' observed Senankh. 'Will Osiris come back to life on the thirtieth?'

'The pharaoh and Isis are conducting the ritual of the Great

Secret,' Sehotep reminded him, 'and they are fighting without respite.'

'The twelfth is a worrying date. If there is even one mistake, the process of resurrection will be interrupted, and in the place of the Tree of Life the Herald will have planted the Tree of Death.'

Twelfth Day of Khoiak
Abydos

Night was still reigning over the Great Land when the Herald awoke with a start, his eyes fiery red. 'Bina, a wet cloth, quickly!'

Torn from sleep, the young woman did not waste a second.

Several times the Herald had to put out the flame that leapt from the palm of his right hand and ate away at his flesh.

The wound horrified Bina. 'Lord, you must have treatment immediately!'

'Salt will suffice. By this evening, the wound will have disappeared. Those worms have betrayed me: Medes the greedy and the disgusting Gergu are dead.'

'But weren't you planning to kill them anyway?'

'They were indeed pawns, destined to die. As for the fat man, he was torn apart like a worn-out rag.'

'Do you mean the Phoenician?'

'Instead of praising me and proclaiming the greatness of my name, he insulted me. His punishment will serve as a lesson to the impious.'

'Have we conquered Memphis?'

'My faithful died while fighting for the true faith and have reached paradise. I shall make that woman Nephthys talk, find out how to enter the House of Life and ruin their hopes of resurrection. And then we shall leave Abydos.'

'There are guards everywhere, my lord. Your safety, your—'

'You reason like a woman. Take two bags of salt and meet me at the shrine where Shab is hiding.'

The Twisted One was on the alert for the slightest movement. Fortunately, neither soldiers nor guards disturbed the peace of this village of tombs, where living stones communicated with Osiris.

Shab parted the willow branches masking the entrance to the shrine and saw the tall figure of the Herald, accompanied by his handmaid.

He went out to meet them and bowed. 'I'm sorry, my lord, but the House of Life is still inaccessible. The guard is changed frequently, and at night and so many lamps are lit that there are no areas of shadow. Even a cautious approach, at a good distance, would be extremely risky.'

'We can never take too many risks when we have the great good fortune to serve the Herald!' snapped Bina.

Shab hated this jumpy, impulsive female. Sooner or later, her master would tire of her. Unless Bina betrayed him in one way or another, in which case the Twisted One's knife would stop her doing any harm.

'I know how to assess danger,' he retorted.

'Nephthys holds the key to the House of Life,' said the Herald. 'Here, before this shrine, she will become my wife and she will refuse me nothing. If she has the unfortunate idea of resisting me, you shall deal with her, my friend. The point of your weapon will soon loosen her tongue.'

'Lord,' begged Bina, 'why not simply torture her?'

The Herald stroked her cheek. 'You can no longer transform yourself into a lioness. I shall turn Nephthys into a new weapon against Abydos.'

'Marrying that Egyptian, that—'

'That's enough, Bina! Remember God's commandments: a

man has the right to take several wives.'

The Twisted One nodded. Nevertheless, Bina still worried him. Possessive and jealous as she was, might she try to take revenge on her master?

'Shab,' said the Herald, 'sprinkle this salt as far as the desert. It will mark out the path that will enable us to get past the barriers.'

'Where are we going, my lord?'

'To Memphis.'

'So we have won!'

'Not yet, my friend. Our enemies believe that their military superiority means they are now safe from disaster. They are badly mistaken.'

It was dawn on the twelfth day of Khoiak, and Isis must take a vital step forward. If she failed, she would be responsible for Iker's second death, which would be irreversible.

Was she wrong or right to confront destiny, to reject the inevitable and hold back the usual course of mummification in order to attempt the impossible? As an initiate of the Way of Fire, could she behave like an ordinary wife?

Doubt overwhelmed her. And yet love alone guided her thoughts and deeds: love of knowledge, love of the radiant life beyond death, love of the Mysteries that mapped out her path, love of the Divine Work, love of one exceptional man whom she wanted to free from unjust torment.

By unlocking the doorways of the heavens, by transforming the House of Life into the House of Gold, the pharaoh had linked the three Osirises' different forms of life. Now they must strengthen the presence of the cosmos's transforming forces by bringing forth the eternal aspect common to minerals and metals, plant life, animals and humans.

Isis lit a single lamp. In the half-light, she could make out the brightness emanating from the celestial cow, whose radiance touched both the plant-based Osiris and Iker's mummy.

Taking off her clothes and standing naked before the invisible powers, the Widow began the mysterious work of regenerating her husband and brother.

'I bring you the divine limbs, which I have reunited,' she told him, 'and I build the foundations for your resurrection.'

First, the work of the bee, symbol of the pharaoh's monarchy and producer of the plant-based gold that was to be transformed into metallic gold. Using the green gold of Punt, Isis fashioned a double mould, one cubit in length, for the front and back halves of Osiris's body. As she touched it, the soft metal grew rigid. In the mould she laid a piece of linen, an evocation of the solar ship, which permitted the reborn soul to travel the universe. Then, mixing sand and barley, she fashioned a mummy with the head of Iker wearing the White Crown.

Isis' heart missed a beat. Could her murdered husband's spirit bear the weight of royalty?

The mould did not shatter. Osiris, the perfect realization of gold, had agreed to act as a receptacle for Iker. East and West were united.

The Widow laid the mould in a bronze vat pierced by two holes. Four supports made of the miraculous stone from Wadi Hammamat formed the celestial pillars. Underneath was a basin made of pink granite. At the corners of the vat, vultures and uraei created an impenetrable magical barrier which nothing impure could harm.

The Widow took the stone of transmutation, that is to say, grains of barley. Safe within the husk, their germ and pulp celebrated the union of male and female principles. By the light of the flame, the nature of the grains changed. This caused a fusion between the masculine, fertilizing fire and the feminine, nurturing fire, the two complementary and inseparable aspects that presided at rebirth.

Now these fires must be regulated, in order to prevent fatal overheating. Their energy must be transferred into Iker's mummy very gradually, in small amounts.

Isis used the vases brought back from the Ibis province. The alabaster, covered in a thin layer of gold, gave off fine, pure rays of light. At regular intervals, she poured out a tiny quantity of *nun* water. Resistant to all forms of pollution, it could regenerate spontaneously.

As the night wore on, Osiris's lymphatic fluids flowed, containing all the vibrations of matter, visible and invisible. The plant-based Osiris turned black, proving that the linked transformations had been successful.

The Widow lifted the granite basin containing the fluid. As she was about to moisten the mummy, she hesitated. If the fluid were too corrosive, it would destroy the mummy. Too weak, and she feared that it would produce only a semblance of life and trigger the process of decomposition.

But it was impossible to go back now.

Like the annual flood, like the water of purifications that came forth from the sacred lake, the Osiran liquid washed Iker's mummy clean of death.

'May the sky-goddess bring you into the world,' whispered Isis, 'may the barley mixed with sand become your body, may the radiant spirit that travels the celestial vault be reborn.'

This volatile spirit must be stabilized in the mineral and plant-based Osirises, which were capable of absorbing the time of death and of being reborn after their own apparent death.

There were no burns, no stains, and no signs of damage. The Royal Son's mummy was intact, and had been nourished by the regenerative fluid.

Every night until the twenty-first day of Khoiak, the Widow would tirelessly continue this transfer of energy.

Thirteenth Day of Khoiak
Abydos

'I want to talk to you away from prying eyes and ears,' the Herald told Nephthys. 'We have serious decisions to make, have we not?' At last she had come back: beautiful, elegant and smiling. Using his charm and his seductive voice, he would make her his slave.

The couple walked along the processional road leading to the Stairway of the Great God.

'I am fond of this lonely, tranquil place,' confessed the Herald. 'There is no human presence here; only tombs, stelae, offering-tables and statues to the glory of Osiris. Here, time does not exist. There is no difference between the great and the humble, for they are all linked to the eternity of the murdered and reborn god. Can such a miracle take place again?'

'During the Mysteries of Khoiak,' said Nephthys, 'Osiris experiences both that tragedy and his rebirth.'

'We temporary priests are kept apart from the Great Secret. But you, being a permanent priestess, must know it.'

'The rule of silence seals my lips.'

'Would a wife keep secrets from her husband?'

'The rule permits no exceptions.'

'It should be changed,' said the Herald, without raising his voice. 'Nobody should allow a woman to suppose that she could be equal to a man, still less his superior.'

'Where does your certainty come from?'

'From God himself, for I am his sole interpreter.'

'So Osiris has passed on his message directly to you?'

The Herald smiled. 'Soon Osiris will die once and for all, and I shall apply the commandments of the true God. Once I command his armies, I shall impose the new faith upon the whole world. Its opponents do not deserve to survive.'

Although deeply afraid, Nephthys managed to appear calm. There was only one man who could speak like this, and that was the Herald!

'Let's sit down on this wall, my sweet one. This garden is charming, isn't it?'

Through the curtain of willow leaves, Shab watched his master and the Egyptian woman.

The Herald took Nephthys's hands tenderly. 'You will be saved, for you will forget the teachings of Osiris and serve me without question. Do you promise that you will?'

Alarmed, Nephthys lowered her eyes. 'It would turn my life upside down, but . . . I don't want to be separated from you.'

'Decide, and quickly.'

'It is just that everything is happening too fast.'

'Time marches on, my beautiful one.'

'If we leave Abydos, will other disciples come with us – Bega, for instance?'

'Why do you single him out?'

'The Shaven-headed One knows he employed you here.'

'Bega employed Asher; he does not know that I have replaced him. Bega is stupid and unbending; he will never change. He and any others of Osiris's followers who are incapable of converting will die here. On the other hand, the Servant of the *Ka* has long since turned away from the old ideas. He defiles rituals, weakens Abydos's links with the ancestors and waits impatiently for the moment when he can follow me and declare his faith openly. My courageous servant has enabled me to prepare for the defeat of Osiris at the heart of his own kingdom.'

Nephthys now knew the identity of the Herald's principal accomplice, a permanent priest whom everyone had thought beyond reproach! Bega was a mere decoy, used to attract unjustified suspicions and divert the investigators from the real enemy.

'Will Abydos be destroyed?'

'You, my senior wife, shall help me hasten its end.'

'How?'

'Why are there so many guards, day and night, around the House of Life?'

If she did not give him a satisfactory answer, he would kill her. Nephthys knew her life was in danger, but she did not regret it because it had enabled her to discover the truth. But if she was to pass it on, she must live. Then again, betraying the real secret was out of the question; it would be better to die. She must give the Herald plausible information, fitting in with what he probably knew already.

She said, 'A major ritual of the Great Mysteries of Khoiak is taking place there.'

'You are permitted to enter that building, I believe?'

'Yes, to assist my sister Isis.'

The Herald stroked her hair. 'My tender wife, have you looked upon the Mystery?'

'Glimpsed . . . only glimpsed.'

'Isis is leading the process of resurrection, isn't she?'

'Yes, together with the pharaoh.'

'What is the foundation for this process?'

'They're using the many states of spirit and matter.'

'Can you be more precise?' Suddenly, his voice had become imperious.

Nephthys hesitated for a long time. 'Iker . . . Iker is drifting between life and death. Assimilated into the mummy of Osiris, he will be subjected to the ordeals of transformation.'

'Has Isis triumphed over the initial ones?'

'The greatest difficulties are yet to come, and I am not hopeful of her success.'

'Give me more details, and describe what she is doing.'

'She often works alone and . . .'

'You must tell me everything, my sweet one, absolutely everything.'

Shab was preparing to leap out of hiding. He would explore this female's flesh with the point of his flint knife, and force her to confess.

Before resorting to extreme methods, the Herald decided to adopt a different strategy. Supremely confident of his charm, he took the beautiful Nephthys into his arms and kissed her, at first gently, then with the force of a man affirming his conquest.

A few paces away, hidden behind an offering-table and hanging on every word, crouched Bina. Try as she might, she could not remain passive. Her entire existence was crumbling. Never would she permit this slut to benefit from her master's favours.

In a frenzy, she snatched up a big stone and leapt out, screaming, 'I'll smash your skull!'

Believing the Herald was in danger, Shab seized the opportunity to be rid of this dangerous madwoman at last. His knife plunged into Bina's neck just as her arm swung down on Nephthys.

The Herald dragged Nephthys aside and gazed at his servant, whose face was contorted by hatred.

'I loved you,' she gasped. 'You had no right . . . no right to . . .'

She fell to the ground, dead.

Nephthys took advantage of the moment to run away.

'Catch her,' the Herald ordered Shab.

The Twisted One was only too pleased to oblige. Running at breakneck speed, he did not see Sekari leap out of a neighbouring shrine, spear in hand.

Shab felt a violent blow, and he stared in astonishment at the spear plunged deep into his chest, impaling him. 'You . . . I never spotted you. How is that possible?' The Twisted One vomited a tide of blood, swayed and fell dead, face down.

Knowing that Nephthys was safe, Sekari dashed off in pursuit of the Herald, who threw a handful of salt at the path traced out by Shab. Immediately, the ground caught fire. Tall flames leapt up and formed a protective wall, enabling him to reach the desert and leave the Great Land. The dumbfounded archers fired volleys of arrows, but in vain.

As soon as the flames died down a little, Sekari examined the path, which was strewn with smoking ashes. There was no sign of a corpse.

'I found out who the traitor is,' Nephthys told him. She was still trembling, but her voice was steady.

One question was already haunting Sekari: what was the Herald planning to do next?

Fourteenth Day of Khoiak
Abydos

At dawn Senusret entered the House of Gold, bearing the Osiran sarcophagus brought from Byblos.

'I bring you the provinces and the towns,' he told the threefold Osiris, 'each one inhabited by a divine power. They unite in order to recreate you.'

From the sarcophagus he took fourteen vases, corresponding to the parts of the Great God's body. The vases for the head, the spine, the heart, the fists and feet were silver; those for the eyes, neck, arms, fingers, legs and phallus were gold; and those vases for the ears, the chest and the thighs were black bronze.

The king poured water from each vase on to Iker's mummy; the regenerative liquid caused the rebirth of the organ of Osiris whose embryo it preserved. Then he mixed gold, silver, lapis-lazuli, turquoise, red jasper, garnet, cornelian, galenite, incense and aromatic herbs. After crushing and sieving them, he obtained a preparation designed to open up the energy channels that ran through Iker's mummy. Its lymph, water, blood, lungs, bronchi, the golden pouch of the stomach, belly, entrails, ribs and skin were provided by the provinces.

'The whole country is your *ka*,' chanted the pharaoh.

'Each part of your body is the secret representation of a province. Everything intertwines and relaxes, everything mingles and re-forms, everything mixes and is resolved, that which was far away is reintegrated. You are no longer experiencing the life of an individual, but are experiencing that of the earth and the sky.'

Senusret brought to life his son's fourteen *ka*s: speech, venerability, action, fulfilment, victory, illumination, the ability to govern, abundant food, the capacity to serve, magic, radiance, vigour, the light of the Pesedjet and precision.*
'Thanks to them,' he predicted, 'you will regain your sight, your hearing and your creative intuition.'†

A gentle brightness enveloped Iker. This phase of the transformation had succeeded.

'I reunite the parts of my brother's body,' declared Isis. 'He is united with the primordial ocean and is fed by its waters.'

The king gathered the Widow's tears in a gold vase.

As they left the House of Life, he told his daughter, 'I must go to Memphis. The Herald has fled. He cannot threaten Abydos directly, so he will try to wreak devastation using his principal weapon: destructive fire.'

'There were worrying disturbances in the cauldron of the Red Mountain,' Isis recalled.

'They were dispelled by the Souls of Nekheb and by your quest,' said the king. 'But there is another cauldron, near Memphis, and it is enormous. If the Herald succeeds in making its contents pour out, the city will be destroyed. Only I can confront him and stop him.'

'If you don't return by the thirtieth day of Khoiak, all our efforts will have been in vain and Osiris will not come back

Hu, shepes, iri, wadj, nakht, akh, was, djefa, shemes, heka, tjehen, user, pesedj, seped.
†*Maa, sedjem, sia.*

to life. Without you, it is impossible to continue the work to its conclusion.'

The king embraced his daughter. 'We have just taken a decisive step; think only of the next one. Doubts, anxieties and fear of failure will assail you, but you are the High Priestess of Abydos and you have walked the Way of Fire. Already a new life dwells within Iker. Make it grow and flourish. On the thirtieth day of Khoiak I shall be at your side.'

When the Shaven-headed One and Sekari interviewed him, Bega managed to maintain his composure and put on a show of surprise.

'Yes, I did employ Asher, along with many other temporary workers who were artisans recommended by their village headmen. He underwent the compulsory test, then worked for a trial period. His work was completely satisfactory, so he was permitted to return to Abydos at regular intervals.'

'And he never said or did anything that surprised you?' asked Sekari.

'I rarely saw him, and was not concerned in his work. The priests who supervised him said his behaviour was faultless.'

'What do you think of the Servant of the *Ka*?' asked the Shaven-headed One.

'He's a perfect permanent priest, irreproachable and conscientious – though I should add that, because of his disagreeable and misanthropic nature, we do not spend a lot of time together.'

'And you have noticed nothing unusual about him recently?' persisted Sekari.

Bega seemed astonished. 'From my point of view, absolutely nothing. Wild rumours are circulating. May I know what is going on?'

'The rebels who infiltrated Abydos have been wiped out,'

said the Shaven-headed One. 'Unfortunately, their leader managed to escape.'

'Their leader? You mean . . . ?'

'The Herald, who had assumed the identity of Asher.'

Bega cleverly simulated utter consternation. 'The Herald? Here? I cannot believe it!'

'The danger has been averted,' said the Shaven-headed One. 'The Mysteries of Khoiak will be celebrated normally.'

'I am stunned,' admitted Bega. 'Nevertheless, I shall carry out my duties to the very best of my ability.'

'The Herald, here . . .' he muttered as he left the room.

'Unbending and naive,' commented the Shaven-headed One. 'He did not notice evil attacking Abydos. He's so preoccupied with his tasks that he forgets the upheavals of the outside world.'

'All the same, I shall continue to watch what he does,' decided Sekari.

'You would do better to take an interest in the Servant of the *Ka*. How was he able to deceive us for so many years? Such duplicity horrifies me! Why should we not arrest him immediately?'

'For three reasons. First, we need definite proof, for he'll deny everything. Second, we need to find out what mission the Herald has entrusted him with – in other words, how he intends to attack the House of Life. Lastly, we must know if he has any accomplices.'

'The wait will be worrying,' said the Shaven-headed One. 'On no account lose sight of him.'

'My brother in the Golden Circle, you have my word on it.'

Fifteenth Day of Khoiak
Abydos

During the night, Isis had poured water from the *nun* on to Iker's mummy, to prevent any excess of the regenerative fire that enabled the new organs of the Osiran body to flourish.

Sensing the difficulties that the young sun was experiencing in emerging from the darkness, she gazed up at the sky. The Bull's Hoof* was sparkling abnormally. The anger of Set was trying to break apart the alchemical metals that made up the cosmos, and prevent the growth of the minerals and plants.

'Be silent, transgressor, drunkard, stormy one, creature of excess, sower of chaos, you who cause separation and dislocation!' Isis shouted. 'The sun of night repels your attacks, it calms your tumult! You shall not prevent the stars' alchemy from transforming light into life. The heavens and the stars obey Osiris and pass on his will. The eye of Horus, his son, will not submit to death.'

Black clouds hid the moon, thunder rumbled and crashed. Then the celestial vault shone with a thousand lights, peaceful and serene.

The moment had come to perfume Iker's mummy with the

*The Great Bear.

venerable unguent. It would enable him to live with the gods, to experience true purity, safe from all taint, and to repel death.

Isis crushed gold, silver, copper, lead, tin, iron, sapphire, haematite, emerald and topaz. To this mixture she added honey and olibanum, which she moistened with wine, oil and essence of lotus. After heating, the divine stone was born.

The Widow applied it for a long time to each part of the Osiran body, changing the virtual into the real.

At sunset, Nephthys helped her to lay Iker's mummy in the sarcophagus found in Byblos. Adorning the inside of the cover was Nut, Lady of the Beautiful West and gateway of the sun. The Royal Son's feet touched the sign of gold, and his head became a star.

'You rest in the heart of the stone,' chanted Isis. 'This sarcophagus is not a place of death and decomposition, but the body of light of Osiris, the provider of life, the alchemical crucible and the ship that makes the great voyage across worlds. With their wings, your two sisters will provide you with the life-giving breath for a good journey.'

Sixteenth Day of Khoiak

Abydos

The Shaven-headed One arrived bearing a statue of Nut, sky of the gods, with which the High Priestess of Abydos must assimilate herself in order to continue the Great Work.

'I have seen the Herald,' Nephthys told him.

'Did he say anything about Iker?'

'No, he wanted to marry me and turn me into one of his slaves. His magic is formidable, and he has terrifying powers. He won't give up. The House of Gold is still in danger.'

The Shrine of the Bed was three and a half cubits tall, two wide and three long, and was made of ebony covered with gold. Inside, the Shaven-headed One placed the mould of the god Sokar, into which he poured alchemical material from a silver vase, the result of the first fifteen days' toil. On the golden bed, the transformations of the Master of the Depths would take place, parallel to those of Osiris. Sokar would offer righteous souls the chance to know the pathways of the other world.

'The goddess Nut is the cosmos and the celestial road,' the Shaven-headed One intoned. 'Travel through the body of the Sky-Woman, Isis, pass through the twelve hours of the night and gather their teachings.'

Facing the statue, the High Priestess began the journey.

At the first hour, the goddess's hands magnetized her, and she heard the song of the tireless stars and the decans.

At the second hour, Nut swallowed the old, worn-out sun. Isis saw Sia examine Iker's body and pour water from the *nun* to defeat its inertia. Rising up from the depths, the royal falcon renewed the body's slumbering faculties.

At the third, silent hour, fires were lit. Among the tall flames, which gave off an intense heat, were those of the Herald, which assailed the House of Gold. A bolt of lightning repelled them, and a strong light enveloped Iker's mummy.

At the fourth hour, spirits armed with knives killed the enemies of Osiris. Isis gazed upon three trees, an aquatic region, and fish-headed creatures with their hands tied behind their backs. Confusion, uncertainty and instability reigned. As a sign of mourning, the young woman unbound her hair. Would the new sun be born?

At the fifth hour the supporters of Set launched a fierce attack. The Herald was not giving up. Decapitated and bound, they failed. Isis sat down on a plant which was a creator of *ka*, in the shade of the tree of Hathor. Iker's heart began to beat, breath filled his windpipe, and his stomach re-formed.

At the sixth hour, Isis stood over the mummy, giving him both her love and the ability to move in spirit. In a jar wherein a fire burnt vigorously, the Widow placed the remains of the supporters of Set, causing the old materials to separate and life to be born again. The residues of the past that could not be used lay at the bottom of the jar, no longer preventing the soul from taking flight. The fire eliminated harmful moulds, leaving behind the gentle warmth and humidity needed for growth. The seminal fluid developed.

At the seventh hour, the sun danced and opposites were reconciled. The liver received Ma'at, and the divine falcon-faced child appeared.

At the eighth hour, Horus, surrounded by the ancestors, gave new life to Osiris, whose gall bladder began to function again.

370

At the ninth hour, there was a wall and flames. The only one who could pass through was he whose heart was recognized as righteous and who was perpetually regenerated. The companions of Osiris helped him to swim, to vanquish the tide and to reach the land. Torches lit up the temple; the intestines preserved only energy.

At the tenth hour, the uraeus flamed and fear was controlled. From the vulva of Nut, the map of the universe was born. She placed her heart inside Iker's and gave him the ability to remember. He then recalled what he had forgotten.

At the eleventh hour, the Stone of Light burnt with all its brightness and the eye of Ra opened. Isis allowed herself to be absorbed by his flame, stepped aboard his ship and received his successive initiations.

At the twelfth hour, the final doorway of the nocturnal journey repelled the forces of destruction and allowed through the alchemical child, born of the *nun* and of the source of life.

Exhausted, the Widow gazed down at Iker. 'Your head is engaged with your bones, the sky-goddess assembles them and reunites your limbs for you; she brings you your heart. Your eyes become the ship of night and the ship of day. Traverse the firmament, and join with the radiance of the dawn.'

Seventeenth Day of Khoiak
Abydos

The Shaven-headed One led a procession round Senusret's Temple of a Million Years and round the Great Land's main burial-ground. The permanent priests and priestesses carried four miniature obelisks and divine signs, calling upon the forces of creation to bring to fruition the mysterious work of the House of Gold.

After being declared innocent, Bega had thought of leaving Abydos or of contenting himself with his offices, giving up his bitterness and ambition. But the reddening of the tiny head of Set and a painful burning sensation dissuaded him and reminded him of the Herald's orders. After the departure of his master and the deaths of Shab the Twisted and Bina, Bega was alone. The strain was harming his health: his legs were swollen and his complexion sallow. But the Herald's last follower in Abydos must see things through to the end and find a way to interrupt Isis' work.

Beside him stood the Servant of the *Ka*, as ill-tempered as ever. Completely self-contained, the priest spoke to nobody and concentrated on his role.

Sekari watched the two men. The Herald's accomplice showed neither anxiety nor edginess, as if he felt beyond the investigators' reach. As for Bega, he seemed as sour-tempered as his colleague. Were they in league?

A shadow. A narrow, long shadow which came from nowhere. Thinking this was an attack by the Herald, Isis sought the best angle of strike and plunged the Blade of Thoth into the spectre's belly. Pinned to the floor, it contracted and disappeared, absorbed by the floor of the House of Gold.

When she had got her breath back, the Widow explored every nook and cranny of the building. There was no trace of the shadow.

On board a boat heading for Memphis, the Herald suddenly bent double.

His neighbour, a seller of pots, was concerned. 'Are you ill?'

Slowly, the Herald stood up straight. 'No, it was just a moment's tiredness.'

'If I were you I'd consult a doctor. Memphis has some excellent ones.'

'That won't be necessary.'

In fact, he had been wounded in the belly. When his neighbour was not looking, the Herald swabbed away the blood with a linen kerchief. The High Priestess had destroyed a part of his being, the murderous shadow that could pass through walls. No matter. He would not need it to launch the final assault.

Eighteenth Day of Khoiak
Abydos

Isis lit acacia-wood torches painted red. Their gentle flame would prevent any harmful force from attacking the House of Gold.

Still linked together, the three Osirises were continuing along their path towards the Light, as was the statuette of Sokar in the Shrine of the Bed. The Widow continued to moisten Iker's mummy with water from the *nun*, gather the lymph and use it to nourish the body of resurrection.

Suddenly, a sky formed above him. From it was born a sun-disc, from which rays shone, illuminating the Royal Son. This greatly accelerated the growth of his organs.

Isis' voyage through the sky-goddess and her knowledge of the twelve hours of the night had brought about this success, which was proof that she had overcome another obstacle between death and life. The regulation of the alchemical fires had found an echo in the world beyond.

Tirelessly, the Widow resumed her work.

Bega had no way of getting inside the House of Life, so he would have to act on the twenty-fifth day of Khoiak. On that day, Isis and the Osiran mummy would have to emerge from the House of Gold and ritually confront the supporters of Set, who were intent upon preventing them reaching the tomb in the Wood of Peker, the place where the final phase of resurrection would take place.

He would kill Iker a second time, ruin Isis' work and proclaim the triumph of the Herald. Bega still hoped that, after achieving this brilliant success, he might take power by presenting himself as the only authority capable of maintaining order.

But there was a major problem: Sekari was still suspicious and gave him no room for manoeuvre. The only solution was to provide proof that the Servant of the *Ka* was guilty. Once convinced of that, Sekari would take no further interest in Bega.

Nineteenth Day of Khoiak
Memphis

Senusret knew that at the eighth hour of the day Isis had placed the statuette of Sokar on a gold plinth before burning incense and exposing it to the sun. Little by little, the Light was pushing back the darkness and breathing new energy into the Osiran mummy.

The king's return to Memphis did not go unnoticed. Now that the rebel network had been defeated, all fear had been lifted. Word of the king's arrival spread rapidly: lovers of feasting, dancing and music were going to have a fine time.

Accompanied by the queen, Senusret gathered together the King's House.

'This is no time for rejoicing,' he told them. 'The Herald had assumed the identity of a temporary priest to infiltrate Abydos, aided by several accomplices. Some of them are dead, but their leader has escaped.'

'How many allies does he have left?' asked Sehotep.

'At least one permanent priest in Abydos is still betraying his brotherhood, but Sekari will flush him out.'

'Is Isis' work being accomplished?' asked Senankh.

'Many stages have already been completed, and the Osiris Iker is beginning to live again. Has the whole of the rebel network been destroyed?'

'Yes,' replied Nesmontu. 'Half those rats died when we smoked out their underground lairs. The others were brought down by spears and arrows. To my mind, the city has been completely cleansed. Tjaty Sobek's plan was the right one.'

'The credit should go to Sekari,' said the Protector. He handed the king a detailed report and a list of the main criminals. 'The rebels were led by Medes, secretary of the King's House.'

Senusret thought of the sages' warning: 'He whom you have fed, and raised to the highest offices, will strike you in the back.'

'I agree with Nesmontu,' said the tjaty, 'and believe Memphis has been now fully cleansed.'

'This is the Herald's last trick,' said the king. 'He hopes to make us believe we have won. In Abydos, his last follower will try to interrupt the process of resurrection. And here in Memphis that demon will call down destructive fire.'

'How?' asked the queen.

'By opening up the cauldron of the Red Mountain, and pouring its contents over the city.'

The Herald drew in great lungfuls of the burning air of the Red Mountain, an enormous quartzite quarry to the south of Iunu. Here the blood-coloured firestone came into being. He was going to misuse its power to burn up the old sun and prevent the rebirth of its successor, which was revived during its journey through the body of Nut.

Every night all the temples in Egypt took part in this battle against the powers of darkness. Would those powers impose their rule or would a new dawn rise? Without the rituals, and unless the words of light were passed on, the world was condemned to decline.

According to pharaonic spirituality, the world must be saved not by a faith but by being governed and directed according to the righteousness of Ma'at. That was the main principle, and it must be destroyed, by imposing an absolute truth which no one could escape. Soon, Memphis would be nothing but ashes and lamentations. An immense flame would rise to the summit of the heavens, proclaiming the Herald's triumph.

Twentieth Day of Khoiak
Abydos

At the eighth hour of the day, Isis and Nephthys purified themselves, cleansed themselves of *isefet*, shaved their bodies, wrote their names upon their shoulders, and covered their heads with ritual wigs. They then wove a large piece of fabric destined to cover the Osiran body when it was transferred to its house of eternity.

Outside the House of Gold, the guards were as vigilant as ever. The Shaven-headed One was always present when the guard was changed, and he visited the Tree of Life several times a day. It was showing no signs of weakness.

Sekari was following the Servant of the *Ka*. The old priest strode along with a firm step, never turning round, and carried out his duties scrupulously. Going from shrine to shrine, he paid homage to the ancestors by speaking the words of the sages. His head held high and his gaze direct, he barely responded to the temporary priests' greetings. During his tour of the site, he met no possible accomplices, and then he returned to his official dwelling, where he was served a frugal lunch.

Sekari was puzzled. He should have gone away but his instinct told him not to move, and he witnessed a surprising scene. In a fit of rage, the Servant of the *Ka* stormed out of his house, broke a wooden tablet into pieces and smashed the remains with blows of his heel.

Sekari waited until the priest had gone, then collected the fragments and put the tablet back together. It bore a finely engraved sign, easy to identify: the head of the beast of Set, with its long snout and erect ears. The sign of the Herald's followers.

Twenty-first Day of Khoiak
Abydos

This decisive and dangerous day marked the entrance into the heavens of all the gods and the end of the germination of the plant-based Osiris.

Isis and Nephthys removed the stone masking an opening in the roof of the shrine where the mould lay, kept moist with water from the *nun* since the twelfth day of Khoiak.

The relationship between the three Osirises was enduring. Now a delicate operation must be carried out: the two-part golden mould must be removed from the vat of black bronze. If any cracks appeared, all hope would be lost.

Solemn-faced and with a firm, precise hand, Isis checked for flaws: there were none to be seen. After covering the two parts of the mould with incense, she bound them firmly together with four papyrus strings. Thus the throat, thorax and the White Crown worn by the mummy were no longer at risk of damage. The sun flooded the mould, the vat and the plant-based Osiris.

'Rest for a little while,' Nephthys urged Isis. 'You're exhausted.'

The Widow looked at Iker. 'When he has been delivered from death, I shall rest beside him.'

*

Devastated, the Shaven-headed One examined the reconstituted tablet. 'The Servant of the *Ka* an accomplice of the Herald . . . I still cannot believe it!'

'But here is proof,' said Sekari.

'Has he any accomplices?'

'I don't think so, but I'm keeping a constant watch on him.'

'Would it not be better to arrest him and make him talk?'

'He seems to have a tough shell – he'd keep silent. I'd prefer to let him prepare for his next crime and catch him red-handed.'

'That's very risky,' said the Shaven-headed One.

'Don't worry, he won't get away from me. Ask Bega to be specially alert. If he spots anything suspicious, however small, he must inform us immediately.'

Twenty-first Day of Khoiak
Memphis

Oblivous of the terrifying danger that menaced it, Memphis had resumed its normal life.

As soon as his soldiers returned, General Nesmontu went to see the king. 'My men found no trace of the Herald, Majesty. The quarry of the Red Mountain is closed and deserted. My lads were extremely careful and saw no sign of human presence. As you ordered, the area has been surrounded by the army. If the Herald's hiding there, he'll get no outside help.'

'He is indeed hiding there,' declared Senusret, 'and nobody will be able to detect him until he shows himself.'

'Is he waiting for the twenty-fifth day of Khoiak?'

'I believe so,' said the king. 'He knows from his accomplice priest at Abydos how the Mysteries progress. If Isis is successful, on the twenty-third day all the rocks in the country will be recharged with energy and the cauldron will regain strength and vigour. On the twenty-fourth day, Set will try to steal one of the elements of the ritual. And on the twenty-fifth day, he will send out his supporters to attack Osiris.'

'The Shaven-headed One and Sekari will defeat him.'

'I am not certain they will, because the Herald will unleash the destructive fire at dawn on that day. The fate of Abydos will depend upon the outcome of our duel.'

'Majesty, permit me to fight in your place,' begged the old general.

'Your courage would be in vain. None but Pharaoh can wield the power of the Double Crown, and even I cannot be certain of defeating such a formidable enemy. Take the members of the Golden Circle to Abydos, watch over the house of resurrection, and call upon the ancestors for help.'

'Majesty . . .'

'I know, Nesmontu. Even if I win, I will not have time to reach Abydos by the thirtieth day of Khoiak. In my absence, Iker will die. There is one hope, however: tomorrow, the construction of a new and exceptionally fast boat will be completed. Choose a crew of strong men who can sail day and night. The north wind and the river will be our allies.'

'You will be victorious, Majesty, and you will reach Abydos in time.'

Twenty-second Day of Khoiak

Abydos

Wearing a crown of greenery evoking the resurrection of Osiris, a priest guided three oxen, one white, one black and one spotted, as they drew a plough through the soft earth. They were followed by labourers wielding hoes, symbols of the divine love,* in order to perfect the furrow opened up by the animals. On this day of the god's burial, all those of just voice, alive and dead, were celebrating a festival of regeneration.

Taking seed from little bags made of plaited papyrus fibres, the permanent priests measured it out with the aid of a golden bushel, equivalent to the eye of Osiris, before using it to feed the furrow. A final ploughing would cover it.

These funeral ceremonies were joyous, for they announced the rebirth of the nourishing barley and wheat after the seed, in the god's image, had accomplished its transformations towards the Light. In carrying out this ritual, the Brotherhood of Abydos was ensuring the support of Geb, the earth-god.

Cleared of all suspicion, and no longer being watched, Bega had no interest in any of this. He was preparing for his

*The root, 'mer', means not only 'hoe' but 'love' and 'channel'. It is also a reference to the pyramid (mer), the Osiran body in which creative love circulates.

crime on the twenty-fifth day. As the Shaven-headed One had recommended, he stood next to the Servant of the *Ka*, who was attentively watching the ritual of the four calves: white, black, red and spotted.

Coming from the cardinal points, they sought out, found and protected the tomb of Osiris from his visible and invisible enemies. Liberating the sacred land from evil, they purified the ground by trampling it down and closed off access to the place of the Mystery.

In the absence of the king – an excellent sign in Bega's eyes – Isis held the four ropes that controlled the calves. Each rope-end was shaped into the *ankh*, the Key of Life. Clearly the Herald was forcing the king to fight on another front, and the battle was so fierce that Senusret was being forced to neglect Abydos.

This observation revived Bega's hatred and bitterness. Like his colleagues, he planted a feather of Ma'at in one of the four chests containing the fabrics destined for the *ka* of Horus, Osiris's successor. Thus Egypt, reunited in the image of the universe, was celebrating the rediscovered unity of the Osiran body.

Isis and Nephthys fashioned two circles of gold, the great and the little sun, and lit three hundred and sixty-five lamps in the full light of day, while priests and priestesses brought thirty-four miniature boats, which would be crewed by statues of the gods.

At nightfall, they travelled across the sacred lake. And the barley of the plant Osiris became gold.

Twenty-third Day of Khoiak
Abydos

Escorted by seven lights, Anubis, master of the underground chamber of the divine fluids, brought to the Osiran mummy the heart that would draw the thoughts of the immortals, a scarab made from obsidian. Then he surrounded the body with amulets and precious stones, so as to free the flesh from its perishable nature.

At the same moment, Isis removed the statuette of Sokar from its mould, placed it on a granite plinth covered with a reed mat, painted its hair in lapis-lazuli, its face in yellow ochre, and its jaws in turquoise, drew complete eyes and handed it the two Osiran sceptres before exposing it to the sun.

Iker's face took on an identical hue.

Anubis presented him with five grains of incense. 'Emerge from sleep; awaken. The House of Gold fashions you, like a stone re-created by a sculptor.'

Isis raised the two feathers of Ma'at that had been given to her by the Walker in Djedu. Waves of energy sprang from them, ensuring the unity of the universe.

'I open up your face,' said Anubis. 'Your eyes will guide you across the dark lands and you will see the Lord of Light when he traverses the firmament.'

Christian Jacq

He took the chisel made from celestial metal and called 'Great in Magic', and placed its tip on Iker's lips. Blood flowed through them once more.

The first part of the work had been accomplished.

Twenty-fourth Day of Khoiak
Abydos

The development of the plant-based Osiris and the first manifestation of life by the Osiris Iker proved that the growth of the mineral and metallic Osiris was taking place in a harmonious manner. Inside the celestial cow the divine body was being reconstituted, and its unity was affirmed more clearly each day. Applied to the multiple states of spirit and matter, the venerable stone was fulfilling its role of transmutation.

Iris would so have loved to embrace Iker and kiss him! But if she did she might snuff out the minuscule spark of hope that had just appeared. Now that it had emerged from inertia, the body of light must remain pure from all human contact and would not be endowed with the power of movement until other formidable ordeals had been undergone.

The stones in the quarries were being charged with energy, and the cauldron of the Red Mountain was filling with power. Soon the Herald would have a terrifying weapon at his disposal.

Isis thought of Senusret. Would he manage, once again, to achieve victory in an unequal fight? Faced with the Herald, would the pharaoh's intelligence, courage and magic be enough? Tomorrow the Widow might lose her father, and if he was not present in Abydos on the thirtieth day of Khoiak in order to finish the Great Work, Iker would not come back to life.

On this day when the symbol of resurrection was buried in the embalming workshop, Isis wrapped the statuette of Sokar in new bandages, shut it inside a sycamore-wood chest and laid it on branches from the same tree, the earthly abode of the sky-goddess. For seven days, each day counting as one month, the effigy would experience a gestation linking matter to the cosmos. Iker would benefit from this and would be reborn at the heart of his Great Mother.

As Nephthys was preparing to use a piece of red cloth, her sister tore it from her hands and threw it to the ground. The fabric burst into flame, endangering the mummy. Isis caught up a gold vase containing *nun* water and poured some on the flames, extinguishing them.

'Yet another attack by the Herald,' she said. 'Using the rage of Set, he tried to steal this cloth and interrupt our work.'

'Does he know everything that is happening here?' asked Nephthys in alarm.

'His accomplice informs him. But neither the traitor nor his master can pass through the walls of the House of Gold, because I destroyed the shadow-spectre.'

'Tomorrow we must leave here and confront the followers of Set,' Nephthys reminded her. 'The energy of their god is vital to the mummy. I fear the worst. If the Herald's creature succeeds in misappropriating it for his own benefit, Iker will be mortally wounded.'

'We have no choice.'

Bega was jubilant. The Shaven-headed One had accepted his suggestion that tomorrow, during the enactment of the struggle between Horus's supporters and Set's, the Servant of the *Ka* should be placed among the latter. Either he would try to act alone, or if he had accomplices they would be obliged to unmask themselves. Bega himself would – not without a certain heroism – stay with the suspect, prevent him from doing any harm, and alert the forces of order at the slightest threat to the Osiran mummy.

In fact, when the procession made its first stop, Bega intended to kill Isis, tear apart the mummy and accuse the Servant of the *Ka* of having committed these terrible crimes. In his role as a follower of Set, Bega would be armed with a club. It was no ordinary club, but the Staff of the Lake, made of tamarisk-wood and capable of striking down any enemy. Particularly since the Herald had charged it with destructive power.

Twenty-Fifth Day of Khoiak
Abydos

The Shaven-headed One, Isis and Nephthys removed the ship of Osiris from the House of Gold. In it Iker's mummy rested once more, covered with the fabric woven by the two priestesses. The work of the God of Light, the tongue of Ra, the ship was composed of pieces of acacia-wood equivalent to the parts of the reconstituted body of Osiris. Only one who was of just voice could board it and sail with the *Imakhu*, the Venerable Ones, vanquishers of the dark who were capable of rowing both day and night.

'We shall go to the Great God's house of eternity,' ordered the Shaven-headed One. 'May we become powerful and radiant* like him.'

The procession was led by two jackal-headed priests, the Way-openers. Then came Thoth, Onuris, who wielded the spear used to bring back the distant goddess and appease the terrifying lioness, the falcon Horus, the male and female Readers of the Rule and of the ritual, the bearer of the Cubit of Ma'at, the priestess carrying the libation vase, and the female musicians.

The attack by the followers of Set took place near the

User and *akh*.

sacred lake. But as soon as they raised their staves they came up against the ship's radiance, which rooted them to the spot.

'Set and the evil eye have been repelled,' declared the Shaven-headed One. 'Their names no longer exist. Ship of Osiris, you have seized them. Let us capture the rebels with the fishing-basket, bind them with ropes, run them through with knives and deliver them up to the execution-block of oblivion.'

The followers of Set collapsed. The Shaven-headed One performed the symbolic gestures: cutting off their heads and tearing out their hearts.

The first part of the ceremony over, the Servant of the *Ka* got to his feet, grumbling. He did not like playing an attacker of Osiris, but he was not in the habit of disputing his superior's orders. The other supporters of Set were delighted to be freed from this difficult duty and able to prepare for the Onion Festival.

Still carrying the Staff of the Lake, Bega slipped away. The members of the procession were momentarily scattered: it was the ideal moment to act. Neither Isis nor Nephthys could resist him. They would join Iker in oblivion.

His bitterness was at its peak, and he regretted nothing. By selling himself to the Herald, he had satisfied his thirst for vengeance and power.

'So,' said Sekari, 'it was you after all – the coward among cowards, the most vile piece of filth.'

Bega turned round, every nerve on edge. 'You were still spying on me!'

'I never believed the Servant of the *Ka* was guilty. A matter of instinct and experience . . . The Herald was trying to deceive us so that the way would be open for you. That way stops here.'

The priest tried to knock his opponent down. Sekari dodged aside, but was not quick enough to avoid the Staff of the Lake, which hit him hard on the shoulder. Stunned, he fell to the ground.

Isis and Nephthys stepped in front of the mummy.

'At last you and Iker are going to die!' roared Bega, raising his fearsome weapon.

Rearing up to his full height, North Wind brought his front hooves down with all his weight on the priest's back. The traitor dropped the Staff and screamed hoarsely as he fell, his spine snapped in two. He was in his death throes, his eyes filled with terror. Flesh-Eater trusted his friend and had thought it unnecessary to attack; he merely sniffed the wounded man and then backed away, sickened.

The members of the procession gathered around the dead man.

'This is the hour of the first judgment,' said the bearer of the Cubit of Ma'at. 'Is this permanent priest worthy to be mummified and called to the court of the gods? If any here has cause to criticize him, let him speak.'

'Bega violated his oath and served the cause of evil,' declared the Shaven-headed One. 'He strove to destroy the Tree of Life, sully the Mysteries of Osiris, and murder the High Priestess of Abydos and her sister Nephthys. The list of his crimes is enough to condemn him. He shall not be mummified. He shall be burnt together with a red wax figure of Set. Nothing shall remain of him.'

The Shaven-headed One washed Isis' feet in the silver bowl of Sokar, then placed a garland of onions round her neck. All the participants in the Mysteries would don similar collars, shaped like the Key of Life, before offering them at dawn to the souls of the just and thus giving them back the light.* The onion ensured that the face was purified, the heart in good health, and the serpent of night driven away.

At the end of the ritual, Iker's five senses were opened a little way. But making them effective required more transformations.

*The root, '*hedj*' means both 'light' and 'onion'.

The Great Secret

Now that Set had been mastered, evil driven away and the way made clear, the ship of Osiris returned to the House of Gold.

His wounded shoulder bandaged, Sekari took up his watch again.

Isis could not rejoice at their success, however remarkable it might be, for her heart was full of anguish. Would the pharaoh or the Herald emerge victorious from the battle of the Red Mountain?

Twenty-fifth day of Khoiak
Memphis

The pharaoh spoke each word of the dawn ritual as if he were celebrating it for the last time. In a few hours from now, the city of Memphis might have disappeared, engulfed by a torrent of fire, which would then be unleashed on Abydos.

Wearing the Double Crown and a kilt bearing the image of the phoenix, the king left the temple and set off for the Red Mountain. Some distance from it, he ordered his escort to stop and wait where they were.

Isis had succeeded in her work so far: Iker had attained the fringes of resurrection. But the last stages would be formidable.

The quarry was flaming; its stones had become the fuel for a fearsome fire of Set. It made the lava in this gigantic cauldron bubble; the lava was capable of annihilating the pharaohs' works of eternity, which had been carried out since the earliest dynasty.

Rid now of his band of incompetent followers, the Herald could feel his destructive power growing. In striking Egypt, he would strike the whole world and deprive it of Ma'at.

At the edge of the quarry, indifferent to the terrible heat and burning ground, stood Senusret.

'Here you are at last, Pharaoh,' said the Herald. 'I knew

you would not run away and that you think yourself capable of confronting me. What vanity! You shall be the first to die, before those madmen who refuse to accept the true faith.'

'Your allies have been defeated.'

'That is unimportant. They were fools who belonged to the past. I am preparing for the future.'

'A belief imposed by force, intangible and murderous dogmas . . . Do you call that a future?'

'My mouth expresses the commandments of God, and humans must obey them!'

The king stared deep into the Herald's red eyes, which flamed in anger, unable to bear the presence of this stubborn adversary.

'I possess the absolute, definitive truth,' declared the Herald, 'and no one can alter it. Why do you refuse to understand that, Senusret? Your reign is at its end; mine is beginning. Sooner or later, the people will bow down and acknowledge me.'

'Egypt is the kingdom of Ma'at, not of a fanatic.'

'Kneel and worship me!'

The White Crown was transformed into a ray of light so dazzling that it made the Herald draw back. Mad with rage, he seized a burning stone and threw it at Senusret. A ball of fire brushed the king's cheek. A second stone, thrown with greater accuracy, struck his forehead. From it sprang forth a uraeus; the cobra spat a flame which made the stone shatter into a thousand pieces.

The Herald could not see Senusret clearly, and could find in him no foundation for *isefet* which would enable the servant of Set to break down his defences.

Despite the furnace-heat, Senusret was advancing. The spiral adorning the Red Crown detached itself, flew across and wound itself round the Herald's neck. He managed to free himself, but it left a deep wound. Soaked with his own blood, he roared out his pain to the very bowels of the earth.

'Demons of hell, rise up from the depths, lay waste this land!'

The ground cracked open and flames and smoke poured up out of the cracks. Senusret took the golden vase and sprinkled its contents around. The tears of the Widow put out the fire.

The Herald tried in vain to unleash the flood of lava. Its burning river turned against him, transforming him into a human torch.

'I am passing away, Senusret,' he screamed, 'but I am not dying. In a hundred years, a thousand, two thousand, I shall return and I shall triumph!'

His body disintegrated, the heat died down and the quarry lapsed into silence once more.

Egypt had prevented the Herald from spreading his poison, and the victory of the Double Crown had proved the permanence and radiance of Ma'at. But the harmony of the Two Lands and their links with the invisible, priceless treasures, remained under constant threat. Once before, at the end of the golden age of the great pyramids, the country had almost disintegrated. Only the pharaonic institution had stood firm against an apparently inevitable decline. By restoring it, Senusret had strengthened the work of his predecessors.

One day the dams would burst, and the Herald would use the breach to unleash a massive assault. And there would no longer be a pharaoh there to stop him.

Senusret must go with all speed to Abydos, in order to bring Iker back to the light.

The fast new boat was moored at the main quay in Memphis, ready to leave. On board a crew of experienced and highly skilled sailors.

'We shall travel day and night,' the king told them. 'Our destination is Abydos. We shall reach it on the thirtieth day of Khoiak.'

The captain was stunned. 'That's impossible, Majesty! No wind, however strong, could—'

'The thirtieth day of Khoiak.'

'Very well, Majesty. But there is one more vital detail: what name is the boat to be given?'

'She shall be called *Swift One*.'

Twenty-sixth Day of Khoiak
Abydos

The priests harpooned the hippopotamus of Set, one of the favourite incarnations of the god of cosmic disturbances, and grilled the clay statue on a burning altar. On the threshold of decisive days for the resurrection of Osiris, it was vital to destroy any manifestations of disharmony which might interrupt the alchemical process.

Before the start of a new procession, Isis gazed upon Iker's mummy. He was not yet healed of death, but a latent life impregnated his body of resurrection. She feared the entrance into the land of Light, an extremely difficult transition. But neither Iker nor his wife had any choice.

She tried to enter into contact with her father, and saw an immense wall of flame and a human form being devoured by it. Then the flames calmed down, red gave way to blue, and the wind swelled the sails of a boat. Senusret was returning to Abydos!

Senusret – or the Herald? If victorious, the Herald was certainly capable of thought control. Aboard the boat there might be a fanatical mob, determined to lay waste the realm of Osiris.

The Shaven-headed One came up to Isis. 'We have a delicate problem. We must now sacrifice another incarnation

400

of Set, the wild donkey. One of the priests feels that North Wind's presence is unacceptable and is demanding his expulsion or worse . . .'

'What? Put to death Iker's companion, who saved our lives and punished Bega? That would offend the gods and draw down their fierce anger! Moreover, expelling him would deprive us of the power of Set, one of the vital alchemical fires.'

'Then what do you suggest?'

'Once his sin is expiated, Set carries Osiris on his back for ever and swims, keeping him on the surface of the ocean of energy. He becomes the indestructible ship, able to bring him to eternity. North Wind shall play that role.'

Pricking up his right ear as a sign of acceptance, the donkey calmly and solemnly received his precious burden. Flesh-Eater led the way as a procession of all the priests and priestesses circled the Temple of Osiris. The permanent priestesses played their flutes, while the priests sprinkled the ground with incense. The Shaven-headed One pulled a sledge, symbol of the god Atum, 'He Who Is and Is Not'. Beyond human understanding, this creative duality, made up of inseparable terms, contained one of the greatest secrets of the outpouring of life.

Sekari and Flesh-Eater remained on the alert. Bringing Iker outside like this exposed him to considerable danger. The Herald no longer had any accomplices in Abydos, but during his long stay he might have embedded curses here and there.

Possession was taken of the sacred space without incident. At the regular pace of the animal of Set, Iker's mummy became charged with the strength essential to pass through the next stage.

Inside the House of Life, Isis and Iker were alone before the *akhet*, the gateway to the land of light that the pharaoh opened

401

during the dawn ritual, in order to renew creation. To enter like Osiris and accede to resurrection meant becoming an *akh*, a being of light. In this form, the god united with his image, his symbols and his bodies of stone, while preserving the Mystery of his uncreated nature.

Communing with Osiris required the daily practice of Ma'at. Either Iker was in a state of righteousness, and the work would continue to be accomplished, or else the intense radiance of this gateway would destroy him. Other conditions were also necessary: successive initiations, the unity of the course of action, respect for oaths and silence, and the worship of the creative principle. Would Iker's earthly experience have equipped him to meet these demands?

It was the Widow's task to attempt the reunion of the *ba*, the soul-bird, and the *ka*, the energy of the world beyond. Upon this encounter depended the fulfilment of the *akh*. If the first two elements refused to be linked, the third would not appear.

Isis spoke the words of transformation, and called for the awakening of the *ka*, nourished with power, and the coming of the *ba*, gorged with sunlight. Enveloped by a dazzling brilliance, Iker's mummy passed through the gateway and immediately underwent a process of transmutation equivalent to the one experienced by the metallic Osiris. Once the *ba* and *ka* had been joined, the *akh*-bird, the ibis *comata*, could take flight.

'Ra gives you the gold that came forth from Osiris,' chanted Isis. 'Thoth marks you with the seal of the pure metal born of the Great God. Your mummy is unified and stable like the stone of transformations that comes from the Peak of the East. Gold lights up your face, enables you to breathe and gives movement to your hands. Thanks to Ma'at, the gold of the gods, you pass from perishable into imperishable. She remains with you and does not leave the body of resurrection.'

The full moon, the reconstituted eye, shone brilliantly, yet it did not prevent the star-sign of Sah being seen, as it rose out of the west.

Isis took a sceptre which ended in a five-pointed star and touched Iker's brow with it. Then, with difficulty, she lifted a huge cedar-wood harpoon decorated with two snakes, and placed its hook on the mummy's face.*

'Appear in gold,' she chanted, 'shine forth in mingled gold and silver, live for ever.'

---

*A ritual harpoon 2.60m long was found in a tomb at Saqqara.

Twenty-Seventh Day of Khoiak

Abydos

The Shaven-headed One went to the landing-stage to greet the Great Royal Wife and the other members of the Golden Circle.

'A dreadful journey,' grumbled Nesmontu. 'There was no wind, several sailors fell ill and the river tried to play bad tricks on us. Still, we're here at last.'

'If you hadn't taken the helm and heartened the crew,' said Sehotep, 'we'd still be far from here.'

'Will the pharaoh arrive in time?' asked the Shaven-headed One worriedly.

'We don't know the outcome of the battle,' said Senankh. 'If he was victorious, His Majesty will use a new and exceptionally fast boat.'

'Is the Great Work continuing?' asked the queen.

'Iker stands at the gateway to the land of light,' replied the Shaven-headed One.

Everyone was anxious. The Royal Son was young and inexperienced. Would he be sufficiently well-equipped spiritually?

'Isis' love will succeed in transferring the death,' said Nephthys.

'It is not necessary to have hope in order to set to work,'

the Shaven-headed One reminded them all. 'We must fulfil our ritual duty by preparing the bread of resurrection.'

They fashioned it in the shape of the primordial mound where the first glimmer of light had taken form.

Isis enabled Iker's spirit to scale the light and to move, using its rays. They entered every part of his body and renewed his flesh.

'At the heart of the sun your place is spacious and your thoughts are a fire, lining East to West.'

Beneath the nape of the mummy's neck a circle of light formed. It produced a gentle flame, which enveloped the Royal Son's face without burning it. Iker was experiencing a form of existence which belonged to gold. If it did not communicate with the outside world and did not show itself outside, it would feed only on its own substance and would eventually be exhausted.

The Widow must await the sign announcing the next stage.

The queen was impassive, the Shaven-headed One ill-tempered, Sehotep tense, Senankh inscrutable, Nesmontu impatient and Nephthys desperately anxious.

Sekari, North Wind and Flesh-Eater continued to keep watch on the area around the House of Life, even though it was perfectly well protected.

'Death is an enemy like others,' said the old general. 'If you find the weak point in its breastplate and attack at the right moment, you can overcome it.'

Sehotep did not share this optimism. After his close brush with the ultimate punishment, he foresaw the worst. Resurrection on the thirtieth day of Khoiak seemed to him very far off, if not impossible.

Senankh believed in Isis: she had overturned many obstacles which had been thought indestructible. However, the last three days of the month of Khoiak would be perilous, he knew, and if the king was not present the Widow's actions were doomed to failure.

'There it is!' exclaimed Nesmontu, looking up.

A grey heron was flying high in the sky. With incomparable grace, it descended towards the Great Land and landed on the bread of resurrection. A messenger from the creative principle at the world's origin, the soul of Osiris, it had the eyes of Iker.

Twenty-eighth Day of Khoiak

The strong, steady north wind was a remarkable phenomenon, and the captain used it to the full. Half the crew remained on duty while the other half rested. As for Senusret, he stood constantly at the prow and did not sleep.

'We still have a small chance of success, Majesty,' said the captain. 'I did not think even *Swift One* could sail so fast. Let us hope nothing happens to slow our progress.'

'May Hathor protect us. Do not forget to keep feeding the fire on her altar.'

Iker had crossed the threshold of the land of light; the flaming gateway had not rejected him. Gold was irrigating his veins; life remained in the mineral, metallic and plant-based state. On the thirtieth day of Khoiak, the king would try to bring it to its human expression.

Two-Stumps, one of the oarsmen, wanted to strike a decisive blow against Senusret.

His daughter, Little Flower, had sold Iker to the guards because he refused to marry her. Ever since then, Two-Stumps' life had been one long succession of bad luck. First he'd lost his farm, when the authorities found that he had falsified his tax declarations; then Little Flower, eaten up by remorse, had suddenly died; finally, he himself had suffered serious illness and the progressive loss of his teeth.

And who was responsible for all this? Iker and his adoptive father, Pharaoh Senusret. But how could Two-Stumps take revenge on such powerful individuals?

At the very bottom of the abyss, fate had smiled on him. One of Medes's men had recruited him as a messenger, entrusted with passing on information to rebels in other parts of the country, and given charge of a boat used by the royal message service. Two-Stumps had later been promoted to team-leader and had become an important member of Medes's network. But then fate had frowned again and brought about Medes's downfall.

Two-Stumps had only just managed to escape when the rebels in Memphis were wiped out. When he heard that a special boat had been built by royal command, and would soon be leaving on an important voyage, he had decided to gamble all or nothing. He had succeeded in being taken on as an oarsman and had informed Medes's last few supporters of an opportunity to loot a cargo vessel transporting fabulous riches.

They would regroup, and attack the *Swift One* shortly before she reached Abydos. Two-Stumps would kill the captain and set fire to the boat, which would have to make for land. The attackers would take on the king, who would succumb to the weight of numbers. The *Swift One* would never reach her destination.

Twenty-eighth day of Khoiak
Abydos

In order to bring forth the radiant spirit of Osiris, the members of the Golden Circle hauled a sledge carrying the primordial stone, symbolic of Ra. Its radiance impregnated the Great Earth and, inside the House of Life, produced the decisive transformation of the plant-based Osiris. Stems of barley emerged from the mummy's body, announcing the resurrection of the natural cycles, which were expressions of the supernatural. This plant-based gold was flowing through Iker's veins.

The transfer of death was continuing to take place, for the Widow had made no mistakes. But ultimate success depended on Pharaoh, for it demanded the passing on of the royal principle. Only the fire of Horus, son of Osiris, could accomplish the resurrection.

And a different fire, the fire of the Herald, might be approaching Abydos.

'I'm still uneasy,' Sekari confided to Nesmontu.

'Could there still be supporters of the Herald in Abydos?'

'It's unlikely.'

'If he left any traps set here, the Golden Circle will spring them.'

'But what if he's emptied the cauldron of the Red Mountain? The torrent of fire won't take long to reach us.'

'Senusret has won,' declared the old soldier. 'A king of his stature is a stranger to defeat.'

'Don't forget how long the journey is between Memphis and Abydos. And not all the rebels have been killed. The survivors might join together and attack the boat in one last attempt – which would be even more dangerous because it would be desperate.'

The general was not amused by this theory. This time, he shared Sekari's fears.

'Wouldn't you like to shave your head and read the Rule every day?' the Shaven-headed One asked Sekari.

The latter could not conceal his astonishment. 'I don't understand.'

'The weight of the years becomes too heavy, and one's office overwhelming. Abydos needs a new Shaven-headed One. You, my brother, have travelled the world a great deal and braved many dangers. Is it not time to lay down your mat and devote yourself to what really matters? My ignorance of the world has made me make many mistakes. Your natural suspicion will serve you well.'

'Are you really sure?'

'I shall put forward the name of my successor to the pharaoh.'

Isis had remained with Iker, and was reliving their moments of happiness. It was not a long-gone, nostalgic past, but the firm foundation upon which the eternity of their love was built.

Twenty-ninth day of Khoiak
Abydos

At dawn on the penultimate day of Khoiak, Isis adorned Iker's chest with a *usekh*, a broad collar with nine lotus petals. An emanation of Atum, the Creator, it protected and stabilized the *ka*. None of the elements of life reassembled during the alchemical process would be dispersed. Made up of four hundred and seventeen pieces of glazed porcelain and hard stones arranged in seven rows, the *usekh* embodied the Pesedjet, the brotherhood of creative powers that constantly begat the universe.

It was now time for a very dangerous procedure: to bring out the celestial cow, which had been entirely transformed into gold, and inside which the final phase of transmutation was taking place, shielded from human eyes.

The sun's radiance was vital to it, but would it be unified and strong enough to bear it? If the metal cracked, if the contact with the outside world damaged it, the failure would be irreversible. The plant-based Osiris would wither, and Iker would die for ever.

At the head of the procession, Isis and Nephthys carried the golden cow containing the mineral and metallic Osiris. In the gentle autumn sunshine, they had to walk seven times round the god's tomb. Sekari, Sehotep, Senankh and

Nesmontu pulled the four mysterious chests. The queen and the Shaven-headed One alternately spoke the words of protection.

None of them could suppress their anxiety. All were looking out for the smallest sign of damage, which would be synonymous with disaster. And yet the two priestesses did not speed up their pace. Sehotep's mouth was dry.

A fragment of the cow's back changed colour. The minuscule flaw did not get any bigger, but it flapped its wings.

'A golden butterfly,' whispered Senankh. 'Iker's soul is accompanying us.'

The ceremony continued without further incident.

There were about thirty of them, all good-for-nothings who had worked for Medes, a collection of criminals accustomed to causing trouble. Sooner or later they would fall into the hands of the guards, so they had nothing to lose. The message from their friend Two-Stumps delighted the leaders: a whole vessel stuffed with goods for them to loot. They were already discussing how the booty was to be shared out, and the rule of seniority was adopted: the longer you'd been a bandit, the more you'd get.

Chewing the tips of the reeds they were hiding in, they waited for the happy event.

'There's the boat!' shouted a lookout.

Its sails swollen by a strong northerly wind, the splendid vessel was travelling at incredible speed.

'That's no cargo boat,' said one of the leaders in annoyance.

'Look more closely,' said one of his comrades. 'There, at the prow. You'd swear it was—'

'Who cares? As soon as they reach land, we attack.'

Near the central cabin, flames rose skywards.

*

Darkness was falling. Silently, the Great Land of Abydos prepared to experience the penultimate night of Khoiak.

And the pharaoh had still not arrived. In his absence, the rites could not be celebrated at the due time and all Isis' work would go for nothing.

The queen withdrew to the palace, near Senusret's Temple of a Million Years. As if no danger threatened Abydos, the priestesses and priests carried out their usual duties.

Nesmontu stamped his foot impatiently. 'An ambush – I'm sure the Herald's last supporters have set an ambush for the king. At dawn, I'm going to sail down the Nile.'

'It would be pointless,' said Sehotep.

'But he may need us.'

'It's the other way round: we need him. Only he can vanquish the death to which the Herald has condemned Osiris and Iker.'

Senankh did not have the heart to put on a show of optimism.

'Despite the dangers,' said Sekari, 'Senusret will undoubtedly sail all through the night. We must not give up hope.'

Thirtieth Day of Khoiak

Abydos

Unable to sleep, General Nesmontu paced up and down the quay. As soon as day broke, he would sail north to find the king and help him. How could he have imagined, for one moment, that the Herald would win and unleash his hordes of killers?

Accompanied by an extremely strong north wind, the sun rose. In the distance the general saw a narrow but powerful boat. He ordered his archers to draw their bows.

In the prow of the boat stood a huge man. Senusret!

Nesmontu bowed before the king who was the first to disembark. Pharaoh thanked Hathor for granting him a good journey and then went straight to the temple.

'Any problems?' Nesmontu asked the captain.

'As regards sailing, none at all – *Swift One* well deserves her name. Unfortunately, I did lose an oarsman.'

'Was it an accident?'

'No, it was an extraordinary thing. Yesterday evening, just before night fell, Two-Stumps caught fire. He burst into such a mass of flame that there was nothing we could do to save him. And just then about thirty men leapt out of the reeds and massed beside a small landing-stage. But when His Majesty looked at them, they couldn't run away fast enough – a lot of them were trampled to death.'

Nesmontu joined the pharaoh, who was being welcomed by the queen and the other members of the Golden Circle. This was no time for congratulations, for the final phase of the Great Work would be perilous.

Senusret entered the House of Gold, ritually embraced Isis, and adorned the head of the Osiris Iker with the crown of those of just voice, a simple ribbon decorated with drawings of flowers.

'The firmament shines with a new light,' he chanted, 'the gods expel the storm, your enemies are vanquished. You become Horus, the heir to Osiris, recognized as worthy to reign, for your heart is filled with Ma'at and your actions are in accordance with her righteousness. Rise up to the heavens with the light, the incense smoke, the birds, the ships of day and of night, pass from existence into life. Spirit and matter are united, the primordial substance that came forth from the *nun* fashions you. It removes the barriers put up between the reigns of minerals, metals, animals, plants and humans. Travel across all worlds and experience the moment before the birth of death.'

The pharaoh opened the *khetemet* he had brought back from Madu. 'You, the Widow, feed the body of resurrection with Osiran fluid.'

Was the mummy going to dissolve, or would the work attain its completion?

Iker opened his eyes, but they gazed only upon the world beyond.

The king and queen went to the Temple of Osiris. Lying on the paved floor of the main shrine was the *djed*, the pillar of stability.* Holding the 'Power' sceptre, the queen stood behind Senusret and passed on to him the strength needed to raise it up with the aid of a rope.

'He who was lifeless lives again,' declared the pharaoh,

---

*'*Djed*' also meant 'speech' or 'formation'.

'and rises again outside death. The *djed*, constantly enduring, grows younger as the years pass. The spine of Osiris is once more filled with vital energy; the *ka* is at peace.'

The royal couple perfumed the pillar with incense.

Inside the celestial cow, the goddess Isis came towards her brother Osiris in the form of a female kite, rejoicing because of her love. Precise as the star Sothis, she landed upon the phallus of Osiris, which had been transmuted into gold, and the seed of the Great Work entered her. Horus the keen-eyed was born of his mother, and 'it was radiant for the Reborn One as a being of Light'.*

'While remaining a woman,' declared the queen, 'Isis has played the part of a man. She has taken on both polarities, knows the secrets of the heavens and the earth. A Venerable One who has come forth from the Light, she is the pupil of the creative eye. Horus is born of the union between a star and the alchemical fire.'

Isis and Nephthys put on gowns with large, many-coloured wings. With the king, they returned to Iker and moved them rhythmically, providing the awakening one with invigorating air.

'Your bones have been brought back to you,' Isis told Iker. 'The parts of your body have been reassembled. Your eyes have opened once more. Live life, die not of death. It is leaving you and going far away from you. You were indeed dead, but you live again more even than the Pesedjet, safe and sound, for the master of unity.'†

Isis wielded the sceptre brought back from the Thigh province of Lower Egypt. The three leather thongs, symbolizing the successive skins of the threefold birth, brought the Osiris Iker into the daylight.

'The Light gives you life,' decreed the king, touching the

*Pyramid Texts 632a.
†Sarcophagus Texts, chapters 510 and 515.

416

Royal Son's nose with the tip of the key of life, the sceptre of fulfilment and the *djed*.

A burning sun poured its rays upon the mummy.

'The doorways of the sarcophagus open,' said Isis. 'Geb, regent of the gods, gives back sight to your eyes. He stretches out your legs, which were bent. Anubis gives strength to your knees; you can stand up. The powerful Sekhmet draws you to your feet. You regain consciousness thanks to your heart; you regain the use of your arms and legs, you accomplish the will of your *ka**.'

The skies of Abydos became lapis-lazuli blue, and turquoise rays lit up the Great Land. The Tree of Life, the Acacia of Osiris, was so tall that it seemed to touch the sky. All at once it was covered with thousands of white flowers giving off a divinely sweet scent.

The Golden Circle reunited around the reborn Osiris. To the east were Pharaoh, the Great Royal Wife, Isis and Iker, who was thus at last part of this brotherhood he had so longed to join; to the west were the Shaven-headed One and Sekari; to the north were Nesmontu and Sehotep; to the south was Senankh.

The pharaoh celebrated the invisible yet real presence of Khnum-Hotep, Djehuty and General Sepi, and reminded all present of the Rule, unchanged since the earliest times. 'All that matters is the vital office entrusted to each member of this Circle. It consists not of preaching, converting, or imposing an absolute truth or dogmas, but of acting in righteousness.'

The brotherhood placed the *khetemet* and the transmuted Osiris in his house of eternity, whose entrance lay to the west. The Great Work was installed upon a basalt bed formed of the bodies of two lions symbolizing yesterday and tomorrow.

*Pyramid Texts, chapter 676; Sarcophagus Texts, chapter 225; *Book of Going Forth by Day*, chapter 26.

Two falcons guarded the head and the feet. The master of silence would remain here until Khoiak the next year. In celebrating the Mysteries, the initiates of Abydos would then try once again to bring it back to life.

With the exception of Senusret, Isis and Iker, all the members of the Golden Circle left the tomb.

The pharaoh gazed at the doorway to the world beyond. 'After his departure, Iker has returned. Only Osiris is reborn, a few others accede to transmutation. Now the Royal Son is able to come and go. What is your wish, Isis?'

'We wish to live together for ever, never to be separated again and to rest in peace, side by side, protected from evil. Hand in hand, we shall pass across the threshold of the land of eternity and we shall see the Light, at the perfect moment when it is reborn.'

'The Osiris Iker must pass through this door,' said Senusret. 'If you accompany him, you will pass through death. Despite your knowledge of the Way of Fire, you may perish. It is for you to decide.'

Crossing Over

Under the protection of the sparkling star Sothis, and nourished by the tears of Isis, the Nile's annual flood was ideal. The year promised to be a happy and prosperous one.

The tjaty was recovering slowly from his initiation into the Golden Circle of Abydos. Accustomed to struggling ferociously against the enemy, and never drawing back in the face of danger, Sobek had not expected such revelations or to be so overwhelmed.

He was deeply proud to serve a land capable of passing on the Great Secret. Through the Osiran experience, the Two Lands were built day after day from materials imbued with the light of the world beyond. Ensuring the people's earthly wellbeing was not enough. Also, and above all, the windows of the heavens must be opened.

General Nesmontu came to see him, bringing good news. 'Things are going very well. There's no trouble in Syria or Canaan, and we have a stable peace in Nubia.'

'Do you think we can now lift the last of the special security measures in Memphis?'

'The Herald's death took the heart out of his last few supporters. I don't think there's any more risk from them.'

Senankh arrived at that moment, laden with papyri. 'The king has just informed me of a large number of reforms that must be undertaken urgently,' he said. 'I shall need the tjaty's support. And I am to inform the commander of our armed forces that their management is to be improved.'

Nesmontu puffed out his chest. 'I don't know why I don't resign and join Sekari. As the new Shaven-headed One of Abydos, he doesn't spend all his time dealing with dull administration.'

'Don't deceive yourself,' disagreed Senankh.

Nose in the air, the old soldier went off to take Flesh-Eater and North Wind for a walk. They wouldn't regale him with nonsense.

'When it comes to Nesmontu,' sighed the tjaty, 'I give up.'

'You needn't worry. He keeps firm control over expenditure, and every one of his soldiers would die for him. Nobody could ensure our safety better.'

'I know, I know,' said Sobek. 'Has Sehotep returned from Abydos yet?'

'The restoration of the Temple of Osiris will keep him there a little longer.'

'Tell me honestly, Senankh, do you agree with the king's latest decision?'

'His eyes see further than ours can. He truly sees reality.'

Sobek agreed. Above them was this giant of a man who could correct his ministers' mistakes and detect the smallest gleam of light at the heart of the darkness. Calmer now, the tjaty felt able to fulfil his burdensome task.

'Has the head steward been informed of the visitors' arrival?' he asked.

'I took care of it myself. He will treat His Majesty's guests with the proper respect.'

All Memphis was in a state of high excitement, and buzzing with rumours. Was it true that Senusret was preparing to name a new Royal Son, whom he would prepare to succeed him? People placed wagers on one name or another, but few bet on the heirs to the capital's wealthy families, for the king took no heed of appearances and was concerned only with fundamental qualities.

The palace's head steward was anxious that there should not be even the smallest imperfection in the proceedings. He hurried out to meet the pharaoh's guests, avoided asking them too many questions about their journey and their health, and confined himself to guiding them to the king's office. The door was ajar.

'Here we are, this – this is it,' he stammered before making himself scarce.

Senusret's strong, deep voice greeted his visitors.

'Come in, Isis and Iker. I have been waiting for you.'